COMING IN DEAD LAST

THE AFTERLIFE TRILOGY

BOOK 3

ANNI SEZATE

Chicken Taco Publishing
Phoenix, AZ

ISBN: 979-8-9870656-7-9

Library of Congress Control Number: 2025919782

Any references to historical events, real people, or real places are used fictitiously. Names, characters, and places are products of the author's imagination.

Printed in the United States of America.

First printing edition 2025.

Chicken Taco Publishing

www.annisezate.com

Publisher's Cataloging-in-Publication Data
(Provided by Cassidy Cataloguing Services, Inc.)

Names: Sezate, Anni, author.
Title: Coming in dead last / Anni Sezate.
Description: First edition. | Phoenix, AZ : Chicken Taco Publishing, [2025] | Series: Afterlife trilogy ; book 3. | Audience: Young adult.
Identifiers: LCCN: 2025919782 | ISBN: 9798987065679 (paperback) | 9798987065693 (hardcover) | 9798987065686 (e-book)
Subjects: LCSH: Mediums--Fiction. | Demonology--Fiction. | Spiritual warfare--Fiction. | Angels--Fiction. | Good and evil--Fiction. | Faith--Fiction. | Belief and doubt--Fiction. | Young adult fiction. | LCGFT: Paranormal fiction. | Religious fiction. | Young adult fiction. | BISAC: YOUNG ADULT FICTION / Religious / General. | YOUNG ADULT FICTION / Paranormal, Occult & Supernatural. | YOUNG ADULT FICTION / Romance / Multicultural & Interracial.
Classification: LCC: PS3619.E998 C65 2025 | DDC: 813/.6--dc23

To you, for being you.
It's a very important job.

Also by Anni Sezate

THE AURELLA TRILOGY

Aurella the Witch

Aurella the Sorceress

Aurella the Demon

THE AFTERLIFE TRILOGY

I Fail at the Afterlife

Greetings from Rock Bottom

Coming in Dead Last

PART ONE

HIM

I didn't mean to kill her.

I didn't even mean to hurt her; I just lost control. I was triggered, and the monster took over. I don't know what I could have done to stop it.

By the time I came to, she was dead in my arms…

chapter 1
A DAY IN THE LIFE

"All right, that's class. Make sure you study for the test coming up." The wispy-haired, bespectacled Professor Tatum adjusted his glasses before glaring sternly at the audience. "And before anyone asks me when that is, you can look—"

There was a discordant chorus of: "On the syllabus!" or "Look at the syllabus!" or, from the weirdo behind me, "Your mother's butt."

"All right, get out of here," the professor said. He turned off his five-hundred-year-old projector and gathered his papers. College students stampeded down the steps of the auditorium.

I sighed and rubbed my eyes as people filed out around me. Mortality was still just as exhausting as ever. Once upon a time, I was an angel too stupid to realize that front desk duty was actually a dream. But of course, I had to go looking for trouble and become a demon hunter and get mixed up in all this demon crap. And then I somehow ended up mortal for saving someone's life? That still didn't make sense, and I had no idea what I was supposed to be doing here. My new ability to see dead people hadn't cleared up any of that.

Despite my lack of direction, I decided to go back to school because it was time to start moving forward with my life. I was only a couple of months into nursing school, and I was exhausted. Why nursing school? Maybe because I'd been in and out of hospitals a lot in the past year and saw how much nurses help people. Helping people was kind of my job as a guardian angel, so why not have some overlap between the two? For real, though, how do people go to school and work at the same time? I still had my glorious position as a Chuck E. Cheese "cast member," but I'd cut back on hours since my homework load was trying to kill me. Not only that, but I had demon hunter duties to add to the pile as well. Not that I was doing much to help. They could all fly and shoot stuff out of their hands, and I was just the mortal who sat in on meetings and "consulted." But at least I could see them now.

And then there was that one angel in particular who seemed to grasp everything so much more easily than everyone else. After constantly holding her hand when she was living—of necessity at first, then for comfort—I was still struggling with the fact that I couldn't touch her. Every time we had a demon hunter meeting, my hand would automatically reach for her, then we'd both remember, and our faces would fall. At first, her hand would reach for mine too, but she'd stopped doing that a while ago, more accepting of her situation than I was.

I blinked, noticing that the lecture hall was almost empty.

Sighing again, I shoved my laptop into my bag and pushed the dinky little desk arm down next to the chair.

"Why are you all sad and alone?"

I blinked and looked up at this random girl sitting next to me. She had black hair in two buns tied at the top of her head with different colored scrunchies. She wore a lime green sweater that was so bright it was almost reflective.

I vaguely remembered her from a group project last semester. We didn't talk much, but I remembered she was the one who demanded I let her make the PowerPoint "cute." I was the one who compiled our information into the PowerPoint, so I was a little offended, but she did, admittedly, make it look nicer.

"You need to cheer up, sir!" she said with a terrible British accent.

"Excuse me?"

"A smile!" she said, pounding on the desk and looking around herself. "He's capable of smiling, people!"

"Who are you, again?"

She folded her hands and sat up straight, trying to look very studious. "I am a student of…medical studies."

"Obviously," I said, grinning. "We've been in classes together. I was asking for your name. I'm sorry I forgot."

She stood up and raised an eyebrow. "The answer shall come in its own due time, oh forgetful one." With a gigantic smile, she threw her bag over her shoulder, curtsied, and left me blinking in confusion.

"What was that?"

Jake floated up next to me. He was on guard duty today,

making sure no demons attacked me during class. It's super fun when that happens. I love looking like I'm crazy in front of an audience while demons encircle me in a tornado of Darkness.

Jake considered and gave me a look. "She's kinda cute."

I gave him a sideways glance but didn't answer.

"And she's a weirdo," he said, "so you've got that in common. You should ask her out."

I put my phone to my ear, using Sandra's little trick for talking to dead people in public without looking crazy. "Dude, you sound like my grandma."

He held his hands up. "You don't have to date anyone if you don't want to, but don't hold yourself back because of Sandra. She's dead. She's moved on. You can too."

"Thanks for the permission," I grumbled. Even though I could see dead people now, his casual statement still felt like plunging a knife into my heart.

As I zipped up my backpack, I noticed a little piece of paper on my lap with the name Kiki Li and a phone number. *The answer shall come in its own due time…* I snorted. All right, weirdo.

A drawing of a fuzzy little creature with big eyes and oversized teeth smiled up at me from the corner of the page, looking way too pleased with itself.

Jake laughed and started cheering and dancing around me. "She's got the hots for you!"

I smiled and shook my head. "Shut up. And no one says, 'got the hots' anymore."

I threw it in my backpack and got up to leave.

"Thank you," I said to the professor as I passed his desk. He nodded distractedly as he packed up his briefcase. I hadn't checked the syllabus lately, so I wasn't sure when the next test was. I already had three papers due by Friday that I had barely started. I wouldn't have time to study tonight because I worked closing, so it would have to be tomorrow, sometime after my late class and before or after the demon hunter meeting at seven, and—

"Hello?" Jake shouted. "Are you hearing me?"

I blinked and looked around. Some guy shot past me on his skateboard. I was so caught up in my thoughts that I hadn't realized I was halfway to my car.

I put my phone to my ear again. "Sorry, what?"

"I said, I have to go. Hermes has a job for me. Your mum is scheduled to take over bodyguard duty tonight, but I'm not sure when she'll get here."

That was one downside to working with angels. They didn't use clocks or watches. Most things were scheduled "next week," or "later," or "right now." Being dead made it a little easier to just drop everything and appear wherever you were needed.

I tried to ignore my increasing heart rate at the thought of being left alone. It was stupid and childish, but whenever angels left me, demons attacked. And I could see them now. At least Sheila hadn't come after me again. As much as I should have been grateful for that, it worried me. Partially because I lived in constant fear that she would pop up out of nowhere. Partially because it meant that something might have happened to her, and since we had dated a while, I still had a stubborn sense of protectiveness for her.

"Yeah, okay," I told Jake. "See you later."

"You gonna be all right?" He looked at me with genuine concern. That look was new, and I was still getting used to it. Jake had always been there for me and sympathized with my lame little plights, but ever since going wandering in the Hurricane, he was a lot more empathetic. Having suffered as he had, and knowing I'd experienced something similar, had bonded us in a way.

I nodded. "I'll live."

He raised an eyebrow as if to say, "Will you, though?" His skepticism was warranted. I seemed to have a habit of almost dying.

"Go ahead. I know what happens when you don't listen to Hermes."

He rolled his eyes. "He's not going to turn me mortal for checking your car for demons. I'll go right after that, I promise."

I shrugged, secretly grateful.

Turns out there was someone in my car. We both saw the silhouette as we entered the parking garage, and I instantly tensed.

"One sec." Jake's face hardened into his serious defender look as he shot forward, ready to kick someone's butt. But after sticking his head in the window, he just turned around and gave me a thumbs-up. "Just your mum. I'll see you later. Don't die!"

He disappeared, and I peeked in the driver's side window. My mom was sitting in the passenger's seat, checking her reflection in the rear-view mirror. I smiled and got inside. "Whatcha doing?"

"I just realized that we don't have any mirrors in The Resting Place. Did you know that? I must say, I look a lot younger as a dead person! And look—my elevens are gone!"

She pointed to the place between her eyebrows where she used to have two wrinkles.

"I liked your elevens," I said. "They made your face look lived in."

She shrugged. "I can put them back if you want. It doesn't really matter to me."

I smiled. "It doesn't matter to me either."

The radio spasmed out, and my mom and I both frowned.

Then a demon dropped through the roof and screamed bloody murder in my face. I screamed and instinctively tried to punch it, slamming my fist into the horn. Mom shot it away with a ball of Light before I was finished screaming. Unable to contain myself, I got out of the car and paced back and forth, holding my hand to my chest and trying to breathe normally again. I gulped and bent over, resting my hands on my knees, trying to force my lungs to breathe in and out. Overreaction? Maybe. But I was a little traumatized, and jump scares were not great for my PTSD.

"That guy kind of looked like your great-uncle Waldo," Mom said next to me. "You know the one with the wart next to his eye who tooted during your grandma's funeral?"

I snorted and laughed. I stood up and leaned against the side of the car, giggling and trying to breathe. Eventually, the laugh subsided, and I sighed, still grinning. That was my mom's little tactic whenever I started hyperventilating. She made me laugh. It didn't make sense that it worked, seeing as laughter also makes it hard to breathe, but somehow it counteracted it.

"Thanks, Mom."

She smiled. "Any time, love."

chapter 2
I MAKE MY BOSS CRY

"I'm sorry, you want a pepperoni pizza with the pepperonis picked off?" I rubbed my forehead. "Do you mean a cheese pizza?"

The woman at the front of the line at Chuck E. Cheese looked up from her phone in irritation. "What?"

I forced a smile, glancing at the lengthening line behind her in which six boys were currently wreaking havoc, adding to the noise of arcade games and blaring Disney song covers. I winced at some toddler's shrill scream coming from the ball pit and tried to ignore my growing headache. "Would you be interested in a cheese pizza, ma'am? It's basically a pepperoni pizza without the pepperoni."

She rolled her eyes and blew hair out of her face. "I know what a cheese pizza is, and I don't appreciate your sarcasm, little boy. Cheese pizza is not the same. Cheese pizza has no pepperoni flavor. Pepperoni pizza with the pepperonis picked off has a pepperoni taste, but it's still vegetarian. And before you tell me to pick them off myself, it's against my vegetarian beliefs to touch meat."

Yes, because true vegetarians support the usage of meat for flavor as long as it isn't consumed. Kill the cows, just don't eat them! I blinked and tried not to smile like I was cracking my teeth. "All right. Pepperonis picked off. What else can I get for you?"

The rest of the order took about ten minutes because of all her special requests, like, for example, chocolate milk with the bottle on the side. She wanted it poured into a cup because her son doesn't like the ribbed edges at the top of bottles, but he still wanted the bottle to play with later. Also, wings, but only the drumsticks without fatty pieces, cheesy bread with the cheese on the side, and a salad without lettuce. I wasn't sure how Liam was gonna swing that, but I wrote it down anyway. Placating annoying people took less energy than arguing with them.

When I finished her stupid order, she ripped the receipt from my hand, dropped it on the floor, and walked away.

"Have a nice day!" I called.

The group with the insane boys was next in line. I say "in line," but they were actually running, giggling, and shoving in and out of the line while the lady in charge tried to shout her order over the tumult. The order itself went by just fine until the lady ordered five small drinks for the boys, and I asked her if she meant six.

The mother swore and turned back to count again. "Did I miscount? I sent out four invitations. Randy? Randy, where is . . . No, no, that's five."

I frowned and pointed at the kid standing a little apart from the group. He looked familiar. "Is he not with you?"

She looked back again, then turned to look at me like I was

crazy. "Who?"

It wasn't until then that I noticed that he was slightly translucent.

"Oh, uh, never mind," I said quickly. "I counted wrong." I kept glancing back at the boy throughout the transaction, not wanting him to disappear before I had a chance to figure out his problem. Not that I ever had much luck helping wanderers, but this was a child. I couldn't just let him—

I gasped as recognition hit me. "Asher!"

He was one of the wanderers who used to hang around Sandra's apartment when she was alive. I'd wondered what happened to all of them, but I couldn't bring myself to go back and check. I wondered if anyone would ever live there again, or if the hauntings would scare everyone off. Maybe they all dispersed when she left.

Asher had actually made some progress last time I'd seen him. He was the one who yelled, "What the fart?" when Sandra and I kissed. The memory made a smile creep across my face, but it quickly faded as I realized how much this kid had regressed. He was back to staring off into space again, barely aware of his surroundings.

I'd only whispered his name, but the mom froze and glared at me, her bottom lip suddenly trembling. "What did you say?"

"Uh," I pulled the receipt from the machine and handed it to her. "Nothing. I just remembered I need to pick up my nephew, Asher, after work. Sorry, I'm a little scatter-brained today. Your pizza should be ready in just a few minutes. Thank you!"

She looked like she wanted to say something, but she quickly took the receipt and herded the rowdy boys over to a table. The wanderer boy hesitated. I snapped and curled my finger toward myself. He looked like he was about to disappear, but I did my best to copy Elena's mom glare. He reluctantly floated over. Before the next couple in line was done arguing over what they wanted, I whispered, "Come see me after the party, okay?"

He looked uncertain, but I gave him another stern look. "Okay?"

He shrugged and followed the group he'd been hovering around.

"Dude…"

I blinked and spun around. My boss, Preston, was standing on the other side of the cash register with his hands in his pockets. It was incredible that he was still employed as a manager. Though he had changed a little since I'd gotten here. I had to give him credit for that.

"What?"

He looked at me like he was worried I had a contagious disease. "You're doing that thing again."

"What thing?"

He grimaced and said, "Joanna's gonna take over for you. I need to see you in my office."

I looked nervously over at Asher, hoping he wouldn't disappear before I came back. I bit my lip and looked behind me to where my mom was standing. (My dead mom, who was currently guarding me.) Not wanting to talk to her in front of Preston, I looked back and forth between her and Asher, hoping she'd get the hint that I wanted her to keep an eye on him while I was gone.

"I'm your bodyguard, I need to come with you," she protested.

Preston's mom appeared behind him. She was dead too. "I'll keep an eye on them, Gloria. We'll call if we need you."

Mom hesitated but eventually nodded. I reluctantly followed Preston as Joanna, with an uncomfortable smile, took my place.

"So, what's up?" I tried not to squirm in the uncomfortable metal chair in front of Preston's desk. I say "desk," but I really wasn't sure there was an actual desk under all the junk.

"A couple things actually . . ."

He sucked his lip and looked at the wall as though hoping words would appear there. No such luck, so he switched to staring at the ceiling, which also did not provide him with any answers.

"What's the deal, Preston?"

"So . . . It's been observed that you've been a little, uh, off . . . for a while." He switched from leaning forward on the desk to clutching his armrests. "Lots of staring off into space and talking to yourself. And flinching when nothing's there. Weird stuff like that."

I narrowed my eyes. "Observed by whom?"

"Just a few employees. Like, all of them, actually. They talk, you know."

"And they came to *you* about this instead of *me*?" I asked incredulously. "No offense, but—"

He held up his hands. "No, no, I'm with you. It's . . . weird to have people coming to me about things. They said they didn't want to offend you, but they were also worried about you and figured I wouldn't be afraid to say something because I apparently 'have no problem being blunt.'" He shrugged uncomfortably. It seemed like he was having a hard time being blunt.

"What are you implying?" I asked carefully.

He leaned forward on his desk, crushing a bag of Cheetos. "Just tell me you're not high, all right? I don't want to fire you, you're a great employee, but, as I learned my first week here, tripping out at work is kind of frowned upon."

I scowled and folded my arms. "I am not high!"

He sighed uncomfortably and pinched the bridge of his nose. "Shoot. I was kinda hoping you were."

"What are you talking about?"

He chewed his lip again and leaned back in his chair. I shoved a fast food bag aside so I could see him better. He might have gotten a little nicer, but he was still a slob.

He dropped the nervous, polite face, finally giving up on being tactful. "All right, is there some kind of antipsychotic you should be taking? Because you're acting like a schitzo, and it's freaking people out."

"Preston!"

That was not me. Norah, his mom, frequently scolded him for his lack of tact. He looked to his left where I'd just shared a rueful look with her.

"Okay, that's what I'm talking about!" he said, gesturing in his mom's direction. "You're making faces at nothing! Do you see stuff that isn't there?"

I sighed and looked up. How did Sandra handle this? What was I supposed to say? I couldn't tell him the truth, or he'd think I was nuts. But he already thought I was nuts. If I agreed that I was mentally ill, would he tell everyone? Would they all treat me differently? I'd found a nice little community here. Would it be better for them to think I was insane and aware of it, or insane and in denial?

Norah pursed her lips in thought. "I think you should tell him."

I clenched my jaw and glared at the ground, hoping she knew that glare was meant for her.

"Tell him, David. It would make him feel good to know he's someone's confidant. No one's ever trusted him before."

I sighed and looked at her, raising an eyebrow.

She smiled, guessing what I was thinking. "Yes, people have had reason not to trust him. But he's changing, can't you see that? He needs this."

"Fine," I said, looking at Preston. "I'll tell you the truth, but you're gonna think I'm crazy. Well… craz*ier*." I cleared my throat and then immediately chickened out. "Are you sure?" I asked his mom.

Preston held his hands up. "What the hell, man! Are the demons talking to you? Do you need an exorcist? Or a tracheotomy?"

"You mean a lobotomy?"

"Whatever! You're creeping me out, man, and I'm this close to letting you go. I can't have you scaring customers because you're tripping out on mushrooms or legit crazy in the head."

I frowned. "You're one to talk. You just admitted that you spent your first week getting high in your office." I leaned forward in my chair. "And even if I were schizophrenic, that wouldn't automatically mean I'm dangerous. There are plenty of nice people whose brains are a little confused."

His eyes widened. "So, you are crazy?"

I sighed. Once I told him the truth, there was no going back. He'd never see me the same way again, and if he spread rumors about me, no one else would either. I'd either be this weird spiritual dude they secretly came to ask about dead people, or I was the psycho off his meds, and everyone would be walking on eggshells around me, afraid my insanity was catching.

"Dude!" Preston demanded.

"I'm not crazy!" I blurted. I sighed again and rubbed my forehead. "I'm a medium, or mediator, whatever you want to call it." I couldn't believe *Preston* was the first person I was telling about my ability. I shook my head in annoyance and spat it all out. "I can see ghosts. Angels, demons, everything in between. I'm not insane, but my life is. My dead girlfriend shows up out of nowhere. And my mom. And my grandmas. And random ghosts all the time. There's one next to you right now. And to answer your earlier question, the demons don't talk to me, they attack me, so that's fun."

Preston stood up fearfully, inching behind his chair. "Oh hell, you really are going psycho. Are you having an episode? Are you gonna get violent? Or start a seance or something? Should I call the cops?" He started searching for his phone under all the junk on his desk. A stapler and a couple of thumb tacks fell to the floor. Part of me kind of hoped he'd step on one.

"Sit down, son, and listen!" Norah urged.

He didn't sit, but he paused, unsure of himself.

"Look, I know it's hard to believe, but it's true," I said. "I could prove it to you, but you'll probably get mad at me. Or start crying. I don't know, different people have different reactions when someone claims their dead relatives are nearby."

His face went blank. "What dead relatives?"

It was almost as if there had been background music on the whole time, and it suddenly turned off. The room was instantly filled with silent tension.

"Uh…" I cleared my throat. "Your mom?"

"Who told you about my mom?" he asked in a soft voice. He went unnaturally still. That was terrifying. Preston is loud and expressive. He is *never* still or quiet. It made me shiver. This dude was gonna kill me.

"Uh, well, actually, you told me about her. But she did too," I said as calmly as I could. "She's right next to you, by the way."

His face looked like he was having a seizure, trying to decide which feelings to express. The suspense was killing me.

"Her name is Norah. She died when you were ten." I said. "I'm sorry for your loss, Preston. That had to have been really rough."

I knew before I finished the sentence that that was the

wrong thing to say. There's nothing Preston hates more than pity. Except maybe me.

His eyes went wide and wild, his nostrils flared. He stormed around the desk and grabbed my shirt from the front, yanking it upward. "Who the hell do you think you are? Are you stalking me?"

I'd learned by now not to be reactive when people are overcome by powerful emotions, so I took a breath and tried to remain calm. I'd kept myself calm when facing Malum; I could certainly do it facing Preston.

"Tell him… bumblebee," his mom said.

"Uh, bumblebee?"

His mouth popped open, and he released me. I fell back into my chair, smoothing the creases in my shirt.

"What did you say?" he whispered.

"Bumblebee," I repeated. "What is that? Does that mean something?"

He slowly sat back on his desk, blinking in shock. He was silent again, and I didn't dare move. "Anything else?" he asked hoarsely.

I looked at his mom, who said, "Tell him that I loved the roses, but the tulips were my favorite. Especially the purple ones he brought on my birthday."

I repeated what she said, and his eyes bugged out even further. He put his hands to his hair and froze in shock. In a shaky voice, he said, "If you're screwing with me, I will kill you."

I held my hands up. "Not screwing with you. I would never joke about something like this. She's definitely here."

Norah concentrated, and the lights flickered off and on, off and on. I raised an eyebrow at her. We—I mean angels—aren't supposed to give signs. Not only do they defeat the purpose of faith, but they tend to frighten mortals more than they help them. She just shrugged.

Preston swore and ran from the room, wiping his eyes. I heard him yell, "Out of the way!" followed by a crash and a squeal. He cussed someone out in the hallway as his loud footsteps fled the building.

I gave Norah a deadpanned look. "That's your son."

With an exasperated sigh, she hurried after Preston. "Don't you walk away from me!"

I looked around at the empty room. "Well, that went well."

At least one thing worked out. Asher was right where I left him. Mom was sitting next to him as they watched the boys running around the arcade.

"Did you make Preston cry?" Mom asked. "He just ran out the door yelling at everyone."

I joined them on the bench and sighed. "He asked me what was wrong with me. He thought I was crazy or high, and his mom said I should tell him the truth, so I did. After I brought up his mom, he kinda freaked out."

"I see."

"I know it was stupid, but his mom told me to."

"Hmm." She made that face grown-ups make when they're judging you for being stupid but trying to hold back their comments. I decided to change the subject.

"Did he say anything?" I gestured at Asher, who had

floated closer to the arcade games.

She shook her head. "He's just been wandering. Staring off into space. Every now and then, he looks sadly at the boys, and then his eyes glaze over."

"There's gotta be some connection here. Do you think they're his family? I mean, not all of them, obviously, but maybe that's his mom and maybe one of the boys is a brother."

"Asher, honey," she called. "Is that right? Are they your family?"

His shoulders tensed, but he didn't turn around.

"Do you think you can convince him to come to the house after work so I can talk to him?" I felt this overpowering sense of responsibility for the kid. I was the only living person around who could see him, and I had to do what I could to help him.

"I'll try," Mom said. "Just a heads up, you're going to be on your own for a few hours. Jake has a meeting, and I go on messenger duty in a few minutes. But Hermes said he'd send help your way if you need it, all right?"

I nodded and smiled. "Messenger duty? When did you get that job?"

"Recently! I like it. Well, I have to go, honey. Have a great day!" She blew me a kiss and disappeared.

Just then, I realized that I'd been having this conversation with her in broad daylight in the middle of Chuck E. Cheese. I slowly turned around to see if anyone had noticed.

Yep . . . Tala and Liam were looking at me and whispering. Once they saw that I'd noticed, they looked away nervously.

Great.

I put my hand to my ear like I had an earbud in and held my phone in front of me. "Love you too, Dad!" I then put the fake earbud in my pocket and pretended to hang up. I tried to act nonchalant as I walked their way and sighed. "My dad won't stop calling me at work."

Tala and Liam pasted on smiles. Tala said, "He's probably just checking up on you. After . . . you know, all the stuff you went through after the accident. I'm sure he's just worried."

The accident where my girlfriend and I got run over, and she died in my arms? I loved it when people brought that up.

"Hey, what happened with Preston just now?" Liam asked, quickly changing the subject when he saw me tense. "He just ran away crying. Did you tell him off? I would have paid to see that!"

My face probably looked like a deer in the headlights. I'd given the gossip mill a LOT to talk about today.

"Oh… uh, no. It was a lens. I mean, a contact lens. It was his contact. It was crumpled up in his eye, and he couldn't get it out. I tried to help, but I made it worse."

Tala and Liam winced.

"That's the worst," Tala said just as a customer came up to the counter and the three of us realized no one was there to take their order. We each scrambled to our places and continued our grueling day of psychotic childhood fun.

HER

We met when I was fifteen. I was at a football game with my friends, and we couldn't stop laughing at the nerdy, messy-haired boy down on the track, cheering his head off for his brother, the star quarterback. I was bold enough to introduce myself after the game and was confused by how reserved he was in person. He clenched his hands and kept looking down as we spoke, though a nervous smile tugged at the edges of his lips. This cheering maniac was actually shy, which only made him all the more adorable. He was nothing like the guys I usually dated, but refreshingly honest and sweet. I gave him my number and smirked, pretending to have more confidence than I actually had.

I didn't know then that this was the man I would fall in love with.

He was also the man who would kill me.

chapter 3
SANDRA DOES IT BETTER

I about had a heart attack when I opened my bedroom door and saw Asher standing right in the threshold.

"Oh my gosh!" My hands flailed in front of me.

Asher didn't even flinch. He just stood there staring despondently at the floor.

I clutched my heart and took a deep breath, trying to chill out before I scared the boy off. It wasn't his fault wanderers are creepy. "How's it going, Asher?" I asked in an almost normal voice.

He continued to stare, and I blew air out my lips. He didn't move out of my way, so I tried to go around him without walking through him. He didn't even turn around to look at me. This kid was really regressing. Back when Sandra was alive, he actually spoke. He tracked things with his eyes. He was at least aware of what was around him. Now he was barely responding. I didn't think it was because he was trapped in that wandering nothingness, though. More like he was right at the cusp of lucidity and pretending that he wasn't.

I sat on the edge of my bed and decided to just wait until

he was ready to say what he needed to say.

Then, without prompting, he turned around and, still staring at the ground, said, "I need you to tell my mom something for me."

I blinked in surprise. I didn't expect him to just jump right to the point.

"Anything," I told him. "Was she the mom at the party?"

He nodded.

"What would you like me to tell her?"

His chin started to tremble, and he continued staring at the floor. "I want you to tell her that I'm sorry." His voice was thick, and tears started rolling down his cheeks. "She told me not to run off. She said to stay with her. But I wanted to get there first. So, I ran ahead, and I left the hiking trail to take a shortcut. But the shortcut was a dead end. I tried to climb up the side of the mountain to help me see my way back, but I fell and cracked my head. She found me there, and it was really bad." He hugged himself, slowly sinking to the floor to curl up with his knees to his chest. He rocked back and forth, whimpering and hiding his face in his knees.

I gaped at him, processing this poor kid's pain. Head injuries aren't always instant killers. This kid might have been suffering for a long time before he finally let go... And not only did he go through the trauma of dying, but he'd been carrying around this guilt since the moment he died, blaming himself for his mother's pain. I knew that feeling. Watching mom hurry to the bathroom at work to sob when the slightest thing reminded her of me. Elena driving to work in utter silence while tears silently fell down her face, not even alive enough to turn on some music. I had a thousand memories like that of my loved ones grieving, and now that I'd experienced grief myself, it hit harder. Sandra's death did a number on me, and if that's how my family felt when I died… that made it all the worse.

I knelt next to Asher and clenched my hands, wishing there was something I could do. I've witnessed plenty of people fall apart when I was a guardian angel, but then all I could do was talk to them and hope they got some feeling of what I was saying. Now I was in a situation where someone could actually hear me, but I didn't think words would suffice here. I mean, he was just a kid, and this kid needed to be held. My mom would have been great in this situation, but both she and Jake were busy. This had been happening a lot more recently. I didn't mind that they left me alone sometimes, but in this situation, it would have been great if one of them were here.

Hermes, is there an angel who can come help me with Asher? I think he needs a hug. And he might be willing to cross over. I've never seen him this lucid, and he might be on the verge of a breakthrough.

Before I'd finished my request, Sandra was there. She looked around in confusion, but once she saw Asher crying, she hurried over to him. She knelt next to me and said his name. Asher lifted his head suddenly and then cried harder, throwing his arms around her neck. "You came back!"

"Of course I came back," she said softly. "I'm sorry I left. I didn't mean to go, but I died. I crossed over and had to learn how to be an angel."

"Did you leave because I'm bad?" he sobbed.

"Of course not," she whispered, patting his back. "You're not bad. You made a mistake. All of us have. That doesn't make you bad."

I wondered how Sandra knew about his mistake. She hadn't been here when Asher told me what happened. She must have done her research. Otherwise, how would she have even known his name back when he was nonverbal? I wondered how many hours she'd spent gathering information on her wanderers to help them move on. I already knew she was incredible, but I was starting to realize that she did a lot more than I gave her credit for. I needed to step up my game if I was going to fill her shoes.

"I did something bad and then I died!" Asher wailed, and there was nothing either of us could do but let him cry himself out. I sat there, tensed and hurting for him while Sandra let him cry a river onto her shoulder. We shared a look of worry that, for a flash of a second, made me wonder if this was what it would be like to be parents—both of you worried and unsure if you're doing it right. Eventually, Asher ran out of tears and pulled away, wiping his face. He was momentarily distracted by the fact that his hands didn't come away wet. He gulped and took a deep, shaky breath.

"I'm really dead," he whispered.

Sandra nodded and forced herself to smile. "Yes, you are."

He looked up at her, surprised by her smile. "But dead is bad!" His lip quivered again.

Sandra put her arm around his shoulder. "No, it's not. It's just different. Everyone dies eventually, and then we move on and do something else. And guess what? The Resting Place is even better than here! You'll see."

He nervously looked at me, seeking my take.

I nodded. "I've been there, kid. It's so much better than this. I promise."

"Are there waterslides and roller coasters?" he asked hopefully.

Sandra and I chuckled and shared a look. "Why don't you come check it out yourself?" Sandra prompted. "You'll like it. I promise."

He looked down. "What about my family?"

"You can still see them whenever you want," I said. "You'll be their guardian angel, and you can help them whenever they need it."

Asher thought for a moment, then let out a long breath. His whole body visually relaxed like he'd been holding that breath since the moment he'd died. Something about him changed at that moment. I gasped as I realized that he was glowing slightly. It was faint but getting stronger by the second. He sat up a little straighter, and his eyes were clear and aware. I saw purpose in his demeanor. Asher looked like an angel.

He nodded to himself, moving more intentionally than I'd ever seen, and looked up at Sandra. "Okay, I'm ready."

"Do you want to come with me to talk to your mom?" I asked quietly.

He shook his head. "No, it would be too weird. Just tell her that I'm sorry and that I love her. Oh, and tell her that Randy can have all my toys except Batman. He's hiding it under his bed, but I want it back. Tell my mom to put it by my picture in the hallway, and then I'll know that she found it."

I smiled. "You got it."

Sandra stood and held out her hand with a smile. "You ready?"

Asher took her hand. "Thanks," he told me over his shoulder just as he and Sandra disappeared.

I sat there in stunned silence for I don't know how long. I'd just watched a wanderer cross over. It wouldn't have happened without Sandra and all the years she'd spent earning his trust, but I felt good for the small amount I'd helped. The message I promised to give to his mom lifted that burden of guilt from his shoulders. Suddenly, my gift of sight felt a lot more precious than it had before.

chapter 4
NO KID LUNCH

I was heading out after work when Preston came out of nowhere, grabbed my arm, and pulled me to the back hallway. I still didn't much like this hallway, but at least the scorch marks from the fire had been removed and painted over.

I pulled free from Preston's grip. "Dude, what—"

"Who else have you told?" he demanded. His face was hard and unreadable.

"About what I see? Literally no one but my dad and my sister. That's it."

"What about your friends?"

"I don't have friends."

He rolled his eyes. "Oh, shut up. You're annoyingly *nice,* and everyone likes you. Don't tell me you don't have friends."

"Yeah, well, all my friends are dead, so I didn't exactly need to tell them."

He made a face like I'd just said something nuts, then walked away shaking his head. I blew air out of my mouth and shared a look with Jake, who was hovering nearby. He shrugged. Preston had been avoiding me recently and acting really weird. I wasn't sure how I expected him to react, but at the moment I was walking on eggshells, not wanting to set him off further. I shook my head and left. This was a problem for another time.

I'd worked opening that morning, so I was out by one. Just in time for No Kid Lunch. I shot Elena a quick text.

Me: We still on for today?

Elena: yep. burgers and fries, or fish n' chips?

Me: You can eat fish? I thought it was bad for pregnant people?

Elena: some kinds of fish, but this kind is fine. I want fish and baby wants fish, so we're eating fish!

Me: Okay, fine! Be there in ten.

No Kid Lunch happened every Thursday for whoever was available to make it. If it's not self-explanatory, it was a lunch we had without any kids. Because sometimes grown-ups need a break from children in order to keep their sanity. It was always me and Elena, but sometimes Dad or Charlie came. Once, Sam came for a little bit, but he usually worked through his lunch break. Things were still a little awkward between us, but we were at least on speaking terms.

I met Elena at the old fish n' chips restaurant that was around back when we were kids. I was surprised it was still in business. The building looked its age, with the tan plaster chipping off the walls and the neon sign only partially lit up and flickering. The roof used to be red, but it had now faded to a dull pink. The dirt parking lot was just as full as ever. I was glad my family taught me to look past appearances as a kid, because you would never know that the food here was amazing based on its looks and location.

Elena, who was sort of starting to look pregnant, was sitting at a picnic table out front, wiping her section of the table with a baby wipe. Then she threw it at me. I caught it and threw it back in her face.

"Ew, David!"

"Let's get in line."

Elena picked up the wipe and tossed it into the trash can on the way inside.

"Jake, save our table, will ya?"

He raised an eyebrow like that was above his dignity, but then he shrugged and sat on the table, radiating Darkness. That usually did the trick. People can't see Darkness, but they can sense it, even if they don't realize it. They usually just call it "the creeps."

It was loud and stuffy inside, and the line wrapped around the aisles. Hungry people were crowded into booths with cracked red padding and napkins littering the floor. And yet we trudged onward. Because, yes, the food was worth it. Greasy, disgusting, delicious crap.

We finally got the goods and loaded it all up onto a red lunch tray with hot sauce, and Elena parted the way for me as I carried the precious cargo. Jake had succeeded in saving our table but was now joined by a friend. He was grinning and laughing, getting his charm on, which was weird to see with him radiating Darkness.

"Uh, Kelly?" I guessed.

The curly-haired blonde flashed her angelic smile at me. "Hey, David! Wanna play Barbies?"

I smiled and rolled my eyes as I set our tray down on the table. Back when I was a new demon hunter, Kelly helped me pick out an outfit for my first demon date with Sheila. This led to a bunch of angel ladies playing dress up with me like I was their Barbie doll. That was barely over a year ago, but it seemed like another life. I guess it kind of was.

Elena sat and looked around curiously. I'd been very open with her about this part of my life, so it didn't faze her to see me talking to people she couldn't see. She got mad when I didn't tell her who was around. It made her feel left out.

"Well, I should go," Kelly said to Jake. "Don't want to distract you from babysitting duty."

"Babysitting?" I grumbled.

Jake, who was radiating Light again, clenched his jaw and seemed to wilt slightly.

"You don't have to leave," I said quickly. "If anything, I'm extra protected with two defenders nearby."

Jake's face lit up, and Kelly shrugged. "I guess I could spare a couple of minutes."

Jake grinned, and they left the table to go flirt off to the side.

"Who was that?" Elena asked. She squirted hot sauce but missed the plate because she was looking around for the ghosts. I don't know why she did that when she knew she couldn't see them.

"Kelly," I said, glancing at the table they'd chosen to

occupy. I couldn't hear what they were talking about, so I doubted they could hear us. "Cute blonde girl from Tennessee that Jake's been crushing on forever. Hasn't asked her out, though, as far as I know. Dang it!" I'd jammed my straw too hard into the lid, and it now had a little hole in the side.

"Speaking of asking people out…" Elena bit a fry and looked at me curiously.

"What?" I asked flatly.

She set her hands on the table. "Okay, I'm gonna be frank."

"Can I be Betsy?"

She made an annoyed sound in the back of her throat and threw a fry at me. "Oh my gosh, you're so dumb. Focus. I was going to ask . . . Well, how long do you need to mourn? Because, as gross as it is to set up my brother, there's a girl I work with who's looking for a date to a work thing, and I think you might get along."

"Gross," I said around a bite of fish. "You're not setting me up."

"Why? Are you uninterested in dating in general? Is it the timing? Is it the person? The sexual orientation? What's the factor that's affecting your disinterest?"

"Sexual orientation? Are you asking me if I'm gay? I had a girlfriend!"

"That doesn't necessarily mean you're straight. Which is fine, no judgment here. I was just wondering."

"I like women. Exclusively. And if I were gonna go out with a girl, it would probably be this one."

I pulled out the paper Kiki left me. Kiki Li. I couldn't deny that her name had a cute ring to it. I'd been carrying her number around with me, waiting for a moment when I'd be brave enough to consider texting her. Part of me wanted to. She was cute and strange and weirdly intriguing. And I'd never had a girl just straight up give me her number, which was embarrassingly flattering. But a really big part of me was still getting over Sandra, and somehow this felt like a betrayal.

Elena yanked the paper from my hand, laughing. "What weirdo gave you her number? Did you ask for it?"

"Some girl in my microbiology class. And no, I didn't ask for it. She just gave it to me."

Elena leaned forward, completely forgetting about her food. "Have you asked her out yet?"

"I haven't decided if I want to."

Elena stole my phone from me and started dialing her number. I tried to wrench it from her hands, but before I could get it back, I heard a small "Hello?" from the other end. We both froze, and I glared daggers at my annoying, grinning sister. I sighed and slowly put the phone to my ear. "Hey, is this, uh, Kiki? Do you still deliver packages?"

Elena snorted, then busted up laughing. "You're so painful to watch!" I shoved her forehead away.

There was a sigh on the other end. "Never heard that one before. Yes, my parents are Studio Ghibli nerds. I'm named after a cartoon witch who delivers packages. Who are you named after? That kid with a sling?"

"Uh, yeah, actually." Was it just me making it weird, or was it her? I paused, not sure what to say next, and Elena gave me a "get on with it" gesture. "So, I was wondering if you would like to go out for coffee sometime?"

"Only if you pay for yourself. I can't afford to be your meal ticket."

"Uh…"

"I'm just joking! But for real, I'm very broke. I'm pretty smart, though, so if you need a tutor, I can help you with your average-sized brain."

"Um, okay. So, how about after class on Tuesday? Uh, next week. This coming week I'm a little busy."

"Hmm… I don't know. Why should I go out with you?"

I made a face. "You gave me your number!"

"Did I? Okay, fine."

And she hung up.

"That was weird." I shrugged and took a bite of fish.

"What? Did she reject you?" Elena didn't look sympathetic at all. She was grinning, the little turd.

"No, she said yes."

Elena wilted. "So does that mean you won't go out with my work friend?"

"Enough about my dating life!"

Jake and Kelly looked over at me, smirking, then leaned in conspiratorially. That's the thing about seeing the dead—you have an audience for literally everything. I mean, all mortals have an audience, but at least they aren't aware of it. I felt like my whole life was on stage. As much as I hated getting attacked by demons, I did sometimes enjoy the moments when both bodyguards were called away for important business. It gave me a second of privacy.

We ate the rest of our lunch without incident until the end, when Jake shot a bird with a ray of Darkness right as it flew overhead, and it dropped bird crap on my food.

Jake laughed hysterically. "I didn't think it would work! Sorry, mate."

I glared at him as I threw away our trash. My life was so normal.

HER

I saw it coming. It shouldn't have been a surprise. But I was young and naive, and all I could see was his crooked, nervous smile, and all I could think about was his arms around me. He loved me. I thought that would be enough, but it wasn't. There was evil inside. It would go dormant for a time, but then the slightest thing would send him into a rage, and my shy, nervous, fluffy-haired boyfriend was nowhere to be found.

We'd been dating for three weeks when I first witnessed it. We were playing Monopoly, of all things. I don't even know what triggered him—I think he lost a bunch of money?—but he upended the entire table. I screamed and backed away while he started throwing whatever he could get his hands on. His stepdad rushed into the room and restrained him from behind. He wrestled him out of the room while my boyfriend struggled in his grip, screaming profanities. His mom gently put a hand on my shoulder and kept me calm while she explained his condition—something called Intermittent Explosive Disorder. I wondered if there was some kind of medication he should be on for this, but I didn't feel like it was my place to ask.

A few minutes later his stepdad came into the room to let me know that he was calm again. Like, all of a sudden I was supposed to just move on from this, and everything was back to normal. I shook my head and walked out the front door. Yeah, no thanks. There was no way I was staying with some guy who turned psycho at the drop of a hat.

I'm not sure if I'd have gone back if I hadn't forgotten my keys. I'd left them in his bedroom earlier that day, so I had no choice but to face him. I sighed and walked back into the house, forcing myself to approach his door. I knocked tentatively. There was no answer.

"Hey, uh, I need my keys," I said.

I heard footsteps approaching the door. He opened it a crack and held out the keys to me. His hand was shaking. Some strange protective instinct made me want to comfort him. I impulsively pushed the door open wider, and he didn't even resist. That was how I knew he was himself again. His natural energy had always been calm and non-confrontational. He didn't want me to see him, but he didn't resist when I insisted.

His eyes were red, and his entire body drooped. He quickly looked away from me, and when I didn't say anything, he tentatively met my gaze again. His eyes were so sad. His chin quivered, and he took a step back.

"I'm sorry," he whispered. "I don't know why I'm like this."

I had no answers. I simply put my arms around him and hugged him. He was stiff at first, surprised I would touch him after witnessing his violence. Then he slowly curled into me, accepting the comfort I was offering.

Most people would say I was naive and reckless. I was. He was dangerous, but I just knew that wasn't really him. He was sick, but the kind, quiet boy I was falling in love with was still in there. The boy who found humor in little things and drew beautiful sketches of how the world could be and was always there for me with a smile and a hug and a bag of M&Ms whenever I was down.

So, like an idiot, I chose to stay with him, believing—like all teenagers—that love could conquer all.

chapter 5
STARSTRUCK ANGEL

Fifteen minutes before our scheduled demon hunter meeting, I heard a voice at my bedroom door say, "Knock, knock!"

"Yes?" I asked.

"It's Sandra. Can I come in?"

"Yep."

Sandra floated through the door and winced at the mess of books, highlighters, and flashcards covering me and my bed.

"Wow, you sort of knocked," I said. "Everyone else just pops up out of nowhere. It's like you guys are competing to see who can give me a heart attack first."

She shrugged. "Been there. Thought I'd offer you the courtesy I never got."

"Much obliged," I grinned. "You're early. Is everything okay?"

Suddenly, she seemed about to explode. "No, actually! I've got a bone to pick with you, Garcia!"

I recoiled. "What did I do?" Had she found out about Kiki? Was she angry? I hadn't planned on having this "let's date other people" conversation with Sandra and had no idea what to say.

"I know there are way more important things going on in the world right now, but I can't believe you didn't tell me about the choir!"

"The angel choir?" What did this have to do with anything?

"That's what I said!"

I shook my head, trying to switch gears in my brain. "It's not like I kept it a secret. You never asked me about it. Why should I have brought it up? It's not like I was in it. I mean, I went to a couple of practices when my grandma dragged me along, but—"

Her jaw dropped and hung open until she couldn't listen to me anymore. "Why should you have brought it up? Oh, I don't know, maybe because of the *choir director!*"

She fake slapped me upside the head, and I rubbed it like it hurt. I knew by now what she was so worked up about, but she was so entertainingly flustered I felt like razzing her some more. "Which choir? The Resting Place has a lot of different choirs and bands. Right before I... *alived*... some old Mexican guy started up a mariachi band and—"

She growled and clenched her hands into fists. "You know that I mean the *main* choir! The famous one that's so good that there are Christmas songs about them. The one that apparently just shows up and sings with mortal choirs sometimes and makes everyone cry without knowing why. The one that got a new director a few years back, and she's one of the most iconic singers in the damn universe!"

I grinned. "So, you met Whitney?"

She just about fainted in front of me. "Oh my gosh, I almost died again! How could you not tell me!"

I chuckled. "Sandra, there are *tons* of famous people in The Resting Place. You can't walk two steps without running into someone who makes you think, *what show are they from?* You get used to it after a couple of years. Fame isn't really a thing on the other side—that's more of a worldly thing."

"I don't care if I'm worldly! It's *Whitney*! I cried listening to her warming up!"

"Did you talk to her?"

She groaned and sat on my bed. "Nothing came out! I just stared at her, and she smiled and patted my shoulder and was like, 'You're new around here, aren't you?' And I just nodded and cried. It was humiliating!"

I couldn't help laughing, and she groaned again, flopping back on my bed.

"Hey, if it makes you feel better, I did the same thing when I met Robin a few years back. I was doing front desk duty, and when he came to the counter I just stared at him with my mouth open. He smiled and was like, 'Catching some flies?' And then I screamed, 'OH, CAPTAIN, MY CAPTAIN!' And I completely froze. It was like my brain broke. Grandma had to take over for me."

Sandra sat up and smiled. "What did he do?"

"Well, my grandma took his papers, and he just winked at me and said, 'Get over it, kid. We've all got pixie dust now.' And then he backflipped and flew away, crowing like a rooster."

Sandra's eyes sparkled. "Legend."

"Right?"

"And you gave me crap about Whitney."

I smiled, and both of us fell silent. This was the longest the two of us had hung out alone since she'd died. And right before a demon hunter meeting, I couldn't think of anything else to talk about that didn't involve death and demons. I was saved by the arrival of Daisy, closely followed by Ted and Bill, and then the rest of the team as they staggered in.

The meeting itself was a strange combination of boring and terrifying. Eventually, you get so used to bad news that it all starts to feel redundant. More angels captured, more dead people turning demon, more teenagers wearing Crocs. None of it would apply to me. They kept me on the team as a sort of consultant, but I never actually contributed. Someday they'd have me use my gift from Hermes to leave my body and join them in some epic fight, but that wasn't happening anytime soon. For now, my job was to just sit around and listen.

I sat slumped against my headboard and rolled an empty water bottle back and forth on my nightstand as Ying Yue had everyone review with the team what they'd learned while undercover. I only caught bits and pieces of what Ying Yue was saying. William was working with a demon that claimed to be high up in the ranks, Natalie and Ted had an undercover mission about something I wasn't paying attention to, Sandra and Jake were busy with rescuer and defender stuff, and Bill and Daisy were. . . something.

Sometime during Frederick's turn, I heard everyone gasp.

I blinked and looked up from the thread I'd been picking at, curious what everyone was freaking out about.

"What?" Jake asked incredulously.

"They have a judge down there?" Sandra whispered.

"Wait, where?" I asked. "What's going on?"

Ying Yue shot me a glare for my distracted interruption.

Frederick sighed and clasped his hands, nodding in confirmation. "Yes, I've had many recent discoveries. My assigned demon is a chief judge in the Red Zone. Contrary to popular belief, not all demons are sadists. There are some, especially among the older generation, who believe that their duty as demons is to bring justice to the wicked. They believe in obedience to the law and take it upon themselves to punish those who break it. They see themselves as executioners, rather than criminals. Malum, and many of the 'monsters' have strayed from fair and just punishment to pointless torture, and many of the—to use a modern phrase—'old school' demons, are not supportive of that abrupt shift in the purpose of demons."

The purpose of demons? I'd never seen them as serving an actual purpose. But I supposed that if people deserved punishment, who better to carry it out than demons? It still seemed pretty bleak, though. I hoped this judge lady rarely threw people into the Hurricane, and if so, that she eventually let them out. I also wondered what these demons thought was so "just" about tempting and tormenting mortals, innocent or not.

Raj blinked in awe. "Frederick, this is huge! You've discovered how to pull demons to our side! We appeal to their sense of justice and balance. And you've built a rapport with a powerful ally. Do you think she would openly support angels?"

Frederick shuffled uncomfortably. "Well . . . I am ashamed to admit that Honorable Judge Eurydice has already discovered my true identity, despite my efforts."

"Could happen to anyone," I muttered, thinking of my own blown cover.

Frederick smiled at me before he continued. "I don't know how I could have avoided it, as she apparently has the power to sense intentions. You see, Eurydice has been planning for some time, trying to find a way to contact the angels, hoping we would help her in her cause. When she discovered my identity, she said I was a 'gift from heaven'. Though I believe she was being facetious when she said so."

Everyone remained silent as they processed.

"Eurydice?" Natalie finally asked. "That's her name? Like the wife of that Orpheus dude?"

"The myths don't own all Greek-sounding names," Ted said.

Natalie shrugged.

"And you defo think you can trust this lady?" Jake asked, trying to hide his apprehension.

"Hermes himself told me she could be trusted," Frederick said confidently. "This demon has a code of ethics she has never strayed from. She's no angel, but she does not and will not hurt the innocent."

"Wow," I said, my eyebrows almost reaching my hairline. "If this lady is on our side, we might actually have a chance."

"We've always had a chance," Raj said. "But I agree that things feel a lot more achievable now. This gives us a major advantage. Way to go, Frederick!"

He took a gentlemanly bow, and we all clapped and cheered for him, smiles on all our faces. Well, most of our faces. I was mostly frowning, trying to figure out where the catch was. Things never went smoothly with us. There was always someone quitting or getting captured or turning mortal on our team. Something terrible was bound to happen soon.

"David?"

I flinched and sat up, my water bottle rolling off the nightstand and clattering to the floor. "What?"

Everyone looked at me.

"Any updates?" Ying Yue asked impatiently.

"Uh . . . you didn't exactly give me an assignment." Did she have to call on me right after Frederick? I didn't need any more help looking pathetic in front of the team.

Raj winced, and Ying Yue bit her lip guiltily. Yeah, they definitely didn't know what to do with me. "Well, that's going to be changing soon."

I raised an eyebrow skeptically, but she'd already moved on from me.

Raj stepped forward. "In fact, everyone's roles will be changing slightly. After meeting with the defenders, it's been decided that it's time to take a more offensive approach. Our main problem, other than Malum's evasion, is that our numbers are dwindling while the demons' numbers are growing. While we support Sandra and the rescuers in trying to convince certain demons to come to the Light, we've decided on a plan that will bring demons to our side of the war, without requiring them to become one of us."

The room went silent.

"How do you expect us to accomplish that?" Natalie asked.

"By subterfuge," said Ying Yue. "Convince your assignments that all the demons are doing it. Subtly, of course. Make comments about how all the demons are joining the angels, since Malum is such a harsh taskmaster. Spread word about a movement throughout the angel hunter ranks. Make your demon friends think that they are the outliers if they choose not to."

"So, gaslight them," Daisy said dryly.

"Essentially. Our job is to gather intel by the use of deception for the greater good. You knew what you signed up for."

That shut Daisy up. Only Ying Yue could do that.

They continued to talk strategy throughout the meeting, and I'm not going to lie, I zoned out again. Could I have contributed? Maybe, but some childish part of me didn't want to. If they had no use for me, why should I even be here? I had homework to do, and nothing they were talking about even applied to me. If anything, it just made me feel like they were only humoring me by including me, which was kind of embarrassing. So, I just sat there spinning my empty water bottle around on my nightstand until they wrapped it up and disappeared.

chapter 6
DON'T TOUCH BATMAN

I made good on my promise to Asher and looked up his address after class the next day. According to my maps app, his house was about twenty minutes from campus. After confirming my coffee date with Kiki, I hefted my books and made my way to my car.

Almost a half an hour later—the maps app lied—I was finally parked in front of a suburban house in a quaint little neighborhood. The ash trees were evenly spaced along the road, and there were legit picket fences separating the yards. It was late afternoon, so the sun had that special kind of stripey brightness where you're in shadow one second, but you take a step, and the sun is blinding your eyes. A woman was walking her dog on one side of the street, and two kids were riding their bikes on the other. I took a breath to psych myself up for this. This was one of those occasions when Jake had to leave before my mom showed up, so I was alone and very much felt it.

Eventually, I made myself get out and shut my car door a little too hard, startling the woman walking past with her dog.

I smiled awkwardly and made my way down the sidewalk to the house with the giant bougainvillea bushes. I closed my eyes and paused as I approached the door. When I opened my eyes, Asher was next to me, glowing in a stereotypical white robe.

I grinned smugly. "I knew you'd want to be here."

He stuck out his tongue.

"You want to do the honors?" I gestured to the doorbell.

Asher concentrated and glared at the doorbell until the little button pushed in, resulting in a faint chime from inside. That was one thing Asher had over the other newbie angels. While he didn't have much experience as an angel, he had a lot of experience interacting with the physical world as a dead person.

The door opened, and the woman I'd seen at Chuck E. Cheese smiled politely. "Hello?"

I smiled nervously. I'd rehearsed over and over in my head different ways to explain myself and my "seeing dead people" thing, but I ended up throwing it all out the window.

"Hi there. I have a message for you from Asher."

The woman's eyes watered, and she stepped back. "Asher? Wait, I recognize you from Chuck E. Cheese. You said Asher's name."

"Yeah," I said. This was going slightly better than I hoped. She wasn't cussing or crying like the last person I told about dead people. "Yeah, I saw him there at the party. I'm a mediator, so I can see the dead. Anyway, I talked with Asher, and he said there was something he wanted to tell you."

She took a nervous step back from me, mistrust warring

with hope.

A tall man walked up behind the woman. "Who's this?"

The lady looked back at him. "He says he's a medium and has a message from Asher."

The man's eyes widened, and he frowned, shoving the door in my face. I sighed. I knew they'd think I was crazy. Asher wasn't deterred.

"Do the secret knock," he said.

"What's the secret knock?" I asked.

"Me, my dad, and my brother had a secret knock to keep girls out of our tree house. One knock at the top of the door, two knocks at the bottom, and three in the middle."

I shrugged and followed his directions.

There was an awkward moment of silence, then slowly, the man opened the door. "What was that?" he whispered, his face paler than before.

"The secret knock?"

After a beat, he gestured me inside without a word. The woman still looked skeptical but didn't protest. I blinked in surprise and followed them inside. I hadn't expected the knock to work, but maybe, just maybe, they sensed that Asher was near.

Their house was one of those annoyingly perfect houses that don't seem like real people live in it. There was a minimalist farmhouse kind of vibe with chestnut wood flooring going down the hallway, and a smell of cinnamon in the air. The white walls were lined with family photos, calligraphy quotes, and Jesus pictures. The decor and furniture were minimal, but quaint. I didn't relate to this kind of perfection, having grown up with my family's special brand of chaos, but I couldn't deny that it felt homey in its own way.

I sat on the blue sofa they'd gestured toward while they sat in two matching armchairs across from me. There was a toy dump truck on the glass coffee table and some crayons scattered across the fuzzy white carpet. A small granola bar wrapper stuck out of a crack in the couch. So, there was some sign of life in their house after all. This made me more comfortable.

Before taking his seat, the man shook my hand. "My name's Dean, and this is my wife Bethany."

"I'm David," I said, clearing my suddenly dry throat. "Nice to meet you."

Had I already told them my name? I couldn't remember. Dean leaned against the arm of the chair his wife was in and took her hand. They looked at me expectantly, and I suddenly lost all power of speech. How did I speak to the parents of a deceased child? I had no experience with this. Well, I did watch my parents grieve for me when I died. And my death was also an unexpected accident. Maybe I had more in common with Asher than I thought.

As if on cue, my mom showed up. I looked at her with panicked eyes, and she smiled sadly. "You know what to say. We lost our child, but you also lost your parents. You can relate to this more than you think."

I remembered our first hug after she died, and my nose got that prickly feeling that comes when you're trying not to cry.

"You said you had a message from Asher?" Bethany

prompted nervously. "Is he . . . okay?"

I nodded, swallowing the lump in my throat. "I do have a message from Asher. And yes, he's okay. He wants you to know that he's so sorry about what happened. He never meant to cause any trouble when he ran off that day, and his guilt has haunted him ever since. But he's learning how to let it go and forgive himself. And he wants you to know that he's watching over you and he loves you so much."

His mom's chin trembled, and her hand went to her heart.

I cleared my throat. "Also, I just want you to know that even though Asher got to the other side before you, someday you'll all be together, and I promise you it's all going to be okay. You'll hug, and it will feel like everything is right with the world again. Until then, just remember you have an angel watching over you. Just look for the signs, and you'll see them."

Somewhere in the middle of me talking, Bethany hid her face in Dean's chest, and they'd been clutching each other so tightly, it seemed like they would never break apart. Only Dean's face was visible, and he was silently crying. I couldn't tell if it was grief or joy that contorted his face, or a mixture of both, but I had no idea what to do. There's something incredibly sobering in seeing a grown man cry, and I felt like I had to just let the moment breathe.

Asher, who'd been trying to hide the fact that he was crying too, joined in on the hug, and I swear they felt it. They seemed to sigh in relief as he relaxed into their embrace.

Eventually, Asher pulled away, wiping his tears out of habit, then frowning as they disappeared before he had the chance. "Okay, enough of the mushy stuff." He sniffed and glared at me. "I want you to tell them the rest of what I told you. And no more adding cheesy words in."

"What are you talking about?" I asked.

Bethany and Dean pulled apart and looked at me, bemused. "I'm sorry?" Dean asked.

"Sorry," I said. "I was talking to Asher."

They both startled, their eyes widening further. "Is he here right now?" Bethany asked.

I nodded and smiled. "He was hugging you just now."

Bethany clutched her cheeks as more tears streamed down her face.

Asher groaned. "*Mom!* Enough with the crying."

My mom put a hand on Asher's shoulder. "You can't tell a mother not to cry, honey. She's got to let it out."

Asher rolled his eyes.

I cleared my throat awkwardly. "Okay, um, he does have one more message for you."

Dean leaned forward earnestly. "What is it?"

I bit back a smile. "He wants me to tell you that Randy can have all his toys except for Batman, which Randy is currently hiding under his bed." Asher disappeared and rematerialized next to a side table with school pictures on it and gestured emphatically at his own. I pointed at his photo. "He wants you to put it right there, next to his picture, so he can see it and know that Randy doesn't have it."

Dean threw his head back and laughed at the ceiling. "He would say that." He promptly left the room and returned with a little boy, fiercely clutching Batman to his chest.

"But I want it!" the kid whined.

Dean knelt next to him. "Randy, that's Asher's favorite toy. You can have all the rest, but he wants that one back."

The kid stomped his foot. "He can't even play with it!"

Asher walked up to his brother, suddenly seeming older and sadder. I had to remember that he was older than he appeared. If he were alive, he'd likely be a teenager by now. I wondered how old he felt. Those five years as a wanderer seemed to have frozen him at ten, but maybe now that he was awake and aware, he felt those years catching up to him.

He sighed. "Look, if you really want it, whatever. But you have everything else, and I just wanted to feel like I was still part of things around here."

Randy blinked, then frowned at the ground like he was thinking.

"Hey!" Asher grinned at me, snapping back to his ten-year-old personality. "Did he just hear me?"

I smiled and shrugged. "Maybe. Kids are pretty good at hearing angel whispers."

Asher got up in Randy's face and burped. I had a feeling Asher was going to be messing with his brother a lot after this.

Randy frowned down at the Batman, then sighed, dropping his arms. "Oh, fine!" He stalked over to the side table and tossed the Batman onto the table. "I hope you're happy!" he grumbled as he stalked out. Then he reluctantly stuck his head around the corner and looked around. "I do hope you're happy, Asher. I love you." Then he shyly ran away.

Bethany, completely amazed by the one-sided conversation, looked at me. "Where is he?" I pointed to where Asher was standing. She knelt in front of him. "I love you, baby. And I forgive you. I miss you, but I hope you're happy where you are. We're going to be okay, and so are you. I'm so glad you're here with us."

Asher grimaced down at his insubstantial arms, then looked over at me. "Could you give her a hug for me?"

I nodded and knelt next to Bethany. I felt awkward about hugging a stranger. My mom wouldn't have. She'll hug anyone who's even remotely upset, with or without their permission. I cleared my throat. "This is from Asher."

Then I awkwardly put my arms around her. Before I had time to regret it, she threw her arms around me. My mom, standing behind her, smiled and whispered, "That's from me!" Well, crap. Now I was crying. I'd missed Mom hugs… I sank into Bethany's hug like I was her own son, and it was annoyingly emotional. Which wasn't helped by my mom having a moment with Asher in the background.

Eventually, we broke away, smiling and sniffling. I didn't realize how much I'd needed that.

I don't exactly remember what was said after that, or when exactly I left their house. They both thanked me profusely when I finally walked out the door, and I saw a lightness in them, as though a burden had been lifted from their shoulders. I wondered if they had sensed that, for a long time, Asher had not been okay. If that were the case, they knew now that he was safe and happy.

I walked to my car with an irrepressible smile on my face.

I felt amazing. I never realized what my gift could do for others. I was ashamed to realize that I'd mostly been focused on how it could serve me. But I finally started to realize that I could lift burdens. I could provide connection and closure at the same time. It was humbling to remember once again that this life wasn't just about me. Somehow, as a mortal, I was rediscovering what it meant to be an angel.

HIM

She should have left me once she found out. That's what I tell myself, but really, I should have left her or at least gotten help. I was an idiot, and I was afraid that I'd be locked up. I know I can't blame it all on my father, but he acted like my condition was a choice, and his solution was to beat it out of me. I won't describe the ways he hurt me, but most times when he lashed out, I was so injured that I couldn't get up anymore. When my mom suggested taking me to a doctor to get me checked out, she got the same beatings. Doctors were crooks out to get your money. Real men didn't need a lying shrink to solve their problems. If I couldn't get a handle on my issues, I deserved to be beaten.

My dad died when I was ten, and that's when my mom finally took me to a psychiatrist. I was diagnosed and medicated, and everything was supposed to be fine.

But my body never reacted the right way to the medication. One gave me horrible migraines, another gave me seizures, and another made me suicidal. By the fourth try, I simply lied about taking it. The side effects didn't seem worth the benefit. Especially when none of them really cured my condition. I still exploded no matter what medication I was on. The only psychotherapist in the area that we could afford "didn't work with kids." I guess when you work for a private practice, you can be pickier about your clientele. Eventually, we found someone, but he died of a heart attack about a week after our third session. It was like fate was deliberately working against me. Nothing helped, nothing worked, so I just gave up and learned to live with it.

I did eventually marry the girl I loved, and for a long time, we made it work. She learned to recognize signs that an episode was coming on and reacted immediately. She'd run away and lock herself in a room and wouldn't come out until I knocked and told her it was safe. She could tell by my voice if it was true. If I were banging on the door screaming, she knew better than to open it. Always, I'd come to surrounded by destruction with only a hazy memory of doing it. Shattered dishes, thrown chairs, broken windows, holes in walls . . . we knew better than to buy nice things.

But she always saved herself, and she was always there afterwards to help me pick up the pieces.

Until the day she wasn't.

HER

I got very good at noticing when an episode was coming on. His entire body would tense, he'd suck in a breath, then he'd scream in rage. From the time he tensed up, I usually had about three seconds before he started throwing and breaking things. I was quick, and I was always safe behind a locked door before he even noticed I was gone. There were some awkward false alarms. One time after scrambling to the bedroom and locking the door, I heard his knock far sooner than should have been possible. His rages were short bursts, but they usually lasted five to ten minutes at least.

"It's safe," he said sullenly from the other side. "It was just a sneeze."

His face when I opened the door was mortified. Usually, he was too caught up in his anger to watch me run away. This time, he saw my fear, from my first gasp to the terrified way I scrambled away from him.

There was nothing for either of us to say, so we just held each other, both hurting for the other's pain.

chapter 7
WORKPLACE HARASSMENT

I was distracted at work because of the whole Asher situation. I couldn't stop smiling, thinking about how he was going to be just fine. Sandra was taking care of him. He was the first wanderer I'd ever witnessed cross over. A heavy realization struck me as I realized I hadn't helped a single wanderer cross over in my ten years as an angel . . . Had I been a bad angel? Shouldn't I have been able to help even more wanderers as an angel than I could as a mortal?

Why was Sandra better at everything than I was? She was a better medium and a better angel. I wasn't necessarily jealous—okay, I was a little jealous—but I mostly just felt ashamed, to be honest. I had never been the perfect demon hunter, but I thought I was a decent angel. I tried my best, and I cared about helping others. But maybe I could have tried a little more. Cared a little more. I was retroactively realizing that maybe I wasn't nearly as angelic as I thought I was. And it was a little humiliating to have a newbie angel like Sandra teach me that.

I blinked, remembering I was at work, and tried to refocus

on the task at hand. I wiped the remnants of pepperoni and Parmesan onto the floor. After readjusting the condiments, I swept the floor, which had more food on it than the table had. No doubt a toddler had sat there.

As I moved on to the next table, I glanced at Jake, who was sitting on a table looking bored. After making sure no one was around to see me talk to myself, I asked, "So, what's going on with Kelly?"

Jake blinked out of his reverie. "Huh?"

I swiped my rag across the table he was sitting on. "Kelly. Do you like her?"

Jake shrugged. "What's not to like?"

I sighed as I readjusted the tipped-over napkin dispenser. I'd been talking to Elena too much. I was used to her throwing too much information at me. Jake shared the bare minimum unless he was gloating, which he didn't do as much as he once did. I was worried that the guy still wasn't quite his old self since returning from the Hurricane. I mean, he still grinned and made fun of everyone, but he was more pensive, like his mind was going back to that dark place. After seeing him as a wanderer, even watching him zone out made me fear he was slipping back into that hopeless state.

Shaking my head again, I moved on to the next table. "Do you like her enough to ask her out?"

He frowned at the floor. "Uh, maybe. Not sure."

I stopped what I was doing and looked at him.

"What?"

"What's the big deal? You like her. Just ask her out."

Jake rolled his eyes. "And do what? Take her out for a

cuppa? How do angels even date?" My mouth popped open, and Jake held his hands up defensively. "What?"

I pointed at him with my broom handle. "You, who apparently kissed every girl in his high school, are asking me how angels date? You gave me so much crap when I was freaking out about that. Have *you* not gone out with anyone since you died?"

He shrugged in embarrassment. "Well . . . no."

I glared at him, then moved on to my next table. "If I could throw something at you, I would. After all the crap you've given me about girls, and you—"

"All right, all right!" He held his hands up and grinned. "I know. I'm pathetic. I flirt with them, but once they start to show interest, I do the Harry."

"The what?"

"I run," he translated.

I plopped down on a bench, my mind blown. "Are you telling me your reputation with girls is a lie?"

He considered. "Not a lie, exactly."

"'Exactly' has three syllables." Throwback to an old inside joke.

"Oh, put a sock in it. I did pash a bunch of girls in high school." He grinned cheekily. He saw my confused expression and clarified. "You know, snog." Then he sighed. "But dying kinda put a damper on it all. And I've never actually 'dated' a girl. All the advice I gave you when you were freaking out about Sheila was from movies. And now, after going wanderer, I just don't think I'm in a good place for dating. My head's a dog's breakfast, mate."

I'd known Jake for almost twelve years, and this was the most transparent and honest conversation I'd ever had with him. I mean, I'd spilled my guts to him countless times, but when he went through stuff, he either pretended he was fine, got mad, or shut down. I knew I had more tables to clear, but I felt like this was important. He was sharing, and I wanted him to know that I was listening.

I frowned at him. "You know I get it, right? Like, I'm about to say a bunch of stuff that's gonna sound like a load of crap, but you have to remember I've been there."

He shrugged and nodded.

"I know the only person I dated as a dead person was Sheila, who ended up being a psycho wannabe murderer, but things really weren't so bad when we were dating." He snorted, and I cracked a smile. "Okay, I know how that sounds. But really, it's not that much different than dating people when you're alive. You just go somewhere you like, and you talk. And you don't have to kiss her. I mean, you can if you both want to, but you don't have to."

He made a face. "Is it even as good?"

I chuckled. "It's the same as kissing a living girl, as far as I can tell. You don't have a physical body, so it's not as, like, physically enjoyable . . . but you connect more on a spiritual level, which is kinda cool. Just don't *ever* kiss a demon. It's disgusting. I literally barfed Darkness when I got back to The Resting Place and—"

A sudden *whooshing* sound distracted me, and before I could react, a basketball hit me in the head, throwing me back onto the bench. I sat up slowly, rubbing my head, getting ready for Jake's laughter, but he was standing protectively in front of me, with legit Light machine guns in his arms like he was some kind of video game character. I followed his gaze and met the eyes of four demons across the room. The glare I shot at them was a horrible idea. I saw them mouth the word "medium" to each other and grin.

This is the reason I still had bodyguards.

Initially, it was because of Sheila, but she hadn't come after me since the Hurricane. I could think of only two reasons for that. One, she could be in the Hurricane herself. Malum really liked to punish her. Or two, Malum thought *I* was in the Hurricane, so he didn't need to sic Sheila on me anymore. A few months ago, I used my gift to leave my body and rescue my mom and Jake from the Hurricane. Sheila had miraculously helped me. But then Malum showed up, so I told her to push me into the Hurricane to make it look like she'd captured me as she was ordered to do. That way, he wouldn't punish her. I was okay with this because my out-of-body experience was temporary. I suspected Malum assumed I was still in there, which was why he stopped sending Sheila after me. Either that or he found out, and she was in there now.

But that didn't mean my life was free from demon attacks. Maybe I wasn't being targeted by Malum anymore, but just being a medium—or mediator? I still wasn't sure what the difference was—put a huge target over my head. Apparently, it's way more entertaining for demons to attack people who can actually see them. I wondered why Sandra never had this problem when she was alive. Maybe she had a better poker face. She couldn't tell the demons apart from the angels or wanderers, which probably made it easier for her not to react like I did.

Regardless of the reason, I was being attacked again.

Jake may have been standing protectively in front of me, but that couldn't stop the demons from moving things with their minds. Before I saw it coming, a napkin dispenser walloped me in the head.

"Ouch! *Really?* In broad daylight?"

Jake's face was grim and calm. He was no longer my "mate" but Captain Williams, defender of The Resting Place. He shot them down, moving his guns left and right, as chill as someone hosing down their lawn. He hit most of them, but one demon kept evading his bullets by disappearing and reappearing somewhere random. That one kept trying to hit me with things. Forks, Skee-Balls, a diaper. Why is there *always* a diaper?

"Get out of here!" Jake said over his shoulder.

I couldn't believe the demons were being so bold. Usually, they were subtle. If you make it too obvious that you're haunting a place, people don't come back, which defeats the purpose of haunting. But here they were openly attacking me in front of witnesses. I looked around to see if anyone had noticed random objects flying at me, but all my coworkers were looking down dejectedly. I noticed a fifth demon shooting Darkness at my friends. Darkness can't physically hurt mortals, but it can affect them emotionally. Each time the demon hit them, I saw their shoulders slump and their eyes cast downward. Some older angel was shooting balls of

Light at the demon, but he wasn't doing well. I was pretty sure that was Tala's grandpa. He had terrible aim.

A pizza tray smacked me in the face.

"GO!" Jake yelled.

I clutched my now-bleeding nose and booked it to the exit, which was blocked by a demon, so I pivoted to the hallway. Not a lot of hiding places. I could go in the bathroom, but I had images in my mind of shattered mirrors flying toward me. The Chuck E. closet was a no-go. *Never going in there again.* The only other option was Preston's office. I sighed and booked it to his door. Without knocking, I scrambled in and shut the door behind me.

"What?"

I turned to see Preston, looking tired in front of his computer.

I leaned against the door. "Uh, can I hide in here for a minute?"

He made a face. "Why?"

"Uh . . . reasons." I pursed my lips and looked away evasively.

He seemed to struggle with himself, then rummaged around on his desk until he found a box of tissues and tossed it at me. "Take one before you bleed on the carpet."

I quickly pulled out a few tissues and held them to my nose.

He narrowed his eyes. "Are you okay?"

"Yep," I muttered through the tissue.

"Does this have something to do with your weird little secret?"

"Mmm-hmm."

He frowned at me, deliberating whether or not to pry further.

His mom, hanging out by the window, turned to look at me. "Is there trouble out there? Do they need help?"

"Uh, well, Jake's out there, and I think Tala's grandpa, but I'm sure they wouldn't say no to an extra angel. There's like five demons out there."

She nodded and disappeared.

Preston, who'd been watching my one-sided conversation with skepticism, stood up, instantly alert. "Demons? Here? Do we need to evacuate? Did you seriously just run away? Why'd you just leave everyone out there to be attacked by demons? What's wrong with you?"

I almost smiled. "Well, look at you being all concerned for your employees' welfare."

He scowled and searched around his messy desk until he found a stapler and flung it open. He was halfway to the door before I grabbed his arm and pulled him back.

"What are you gonna do, collate and staple them?"

He paused and frowned at his weapon of choice.

"It's fine, there's like three angels out there taking care of it. And I'm not a coward. I ran because I was their target. I figured I should get out of there so people around me wouldn't get hurt."

He ripped his arm out of my grip and scowled at me. "What makes you so sure you were their target?"

"Uh, maybe the basketballs, forks, Skee-Balls, and napkin dispensers they were throwing at my head. They weren't doing that to anyone else."

He frowned. "Why would they target you, specifically?"

I sighed. "Because I can see them. It's more fun for them to attack when they have an audience that can witness their creepiness. And there's a particular demon that really wants to kill me, but that's a different story."

Preston leaned back against his desk, a look of concentration on his face. He suddenly looked at me. "The Chuck E. closet. That was a demon that locked you in when the place was on fire, wasn't it?"

I tapped my nose twice in a "right on the nose" gesture. Then I winced. Ouch.

"They almost killed you!"

I gave him a rueful smile. "Yep."

He scooted further away from me like I had a disease. I scowled at him, then winced, touching my temple. I could feel a bruise forming. I was sure it would be very attractive once it grew to all its goose-egg glory.

Two glowing angels floated in. Jake nodded and said, "All clear. That old bloke out there said he'd come get us if they came back."

Norah—Preston's mom—nodded and went back to hanging out by the window.

"Okay, well, they're gone now," I said to Preston. "Thanks for letting me hide out here." I left before he could say anything else.

chapter 8
WE PLAN ANOTHER JAILBREAK

After all the excitement at work, I forgot we had a demon hunter meeting planned. Ten angels were in my bedroom, and based on the lack of focus, they had been waiting for me for a while. Frederick, Sandra, and Bill were in a heated discussion in the corner. Daisy, Natalie, and Jake were doing target practice by hitting increasingly smaller targets around my room with demon killer bullets. Ted and William shared puzzled expressions as they huddled around some kind of report. Raj and Ying Yue, their backs to the task force, seemed to be speaking telepathically as they frowned at each other.

"All right, let's get started," Ying Yue said once she noticed I'd entered the room. I gently closed the door behind me and sat on my bed, leaning against the headboard.

Ying Yue whispered something to Raj, then turned back to the group. "We have serious business to attend to."

The demon hunters finished up their conversations and settled into place. Most just stood along the walls, but Natalie and Daisy shared the armchair in the corner, and Sandra sat on the other side of my bed, perched on the edge.

"Without beating around the bush," Raj said, "the next rescue mission will happen very soon, and they'd like our task force to lead it. Not only does David know how to get there, but according to him, we need archangels to cut through the Darkness down there, and we have four of them here on our team."

That sobered everyone immediately.

I still wasn't sure exactly what an archangel was, but apparently, I was one. It happened when I was in the Hurricane during my rescue mission with Sheila, and Light shone from my body bright enough to cut through the Darkness around me. I was told afterward that being an archangel meant we had more power. Frederick said there were other parts to it as well, but it was a conversation we were supposed to have with the Big Man. I hadn't yet had that conversation, but I assumed it would come once I died again. Regardless, the fact that I was an archangel now meant that I had to be one of the angels lowered down into the pit, and that shot a jolt of panic through me.

My heart started hammering, and my throat felt dry just thinking about going back to that place. I tried to push out the reverberating echoes in my head from that torture hole. The red mists, the tortured screams, that voice . . . I shook my head and tried to force myself not to get lost in the memories, but it felt like the Hurricane Darkness was pulling me back in.

I felt Sandra's eyes on me, but I ignored her, looking over at Jake instead. His face was hard, and he was staring off into space with a glazed-over look in his eyes. His memories were even worse than mine. Even thinking about the Hurricane got him looking like a wanderer again. There was no way I was letting Raj or Ying Yue make him go back there.

Raj cleared his throat, and I realized there was a whole conversation happening that I was missing out on.

"I still don't get why we want to avoid him anyway," Daisy said. "Isn't our job to track him down? Well, it looks like we tracked him down. We found the place where Malum hangs out and tortures people. Why don't we just ambush him there?"

"First of all," Ying Yue said, "We can't confront him in his territory. He'd be too powerful and could summon backup with the snap of his fingers. This mission is not to capture Malum, but to rescue our own."

"That sounds like a job for the defenders," Frederick said. "Why is this duty being placed upon demon hunters?"

"Defenders aren't great at subterfuge," Jake muttered, trying to remain a part of the conversation.

"We still have not addressed how we will ensure that Malum is absent when we arrive," William pointed out.

"That has been worked out already," Ying Yue said.

"And?" Daisy prompted.

She looked at Raj.

"It's confidential," Raj told us. "We've been instructed not to share that information because if one of you is captured between now and then, our plans will be compromised. And if you are captured, keeping the rescue plan intact would be in your best interest. Just know that Malum will be momentarily distracted, and we'll have an estimated thirty minutes for the rescue."

Thirty minutes? That wasn't much time.

"How do we make sure no demons find us down there?" Natalie asked. "You said Malum will be taken care of, but what about other demons? The Red Zone is their home court. And Malum isn't the only one who can throw people into the Hurricane."

Frederick held up a hand, then moved that same hand to his chin as he considered his words. "Eurydice might be of assistance in that area. I am sure she could momentarily ban demons from entering, and they dare not question her due to her station. She is not a supporter of Malum, you see, and, as the head of the Demonic Council, she has political power among the demons that predates Malum's new regime. As the chief judge, she is unhappy with the lack of justice brought on by Malum's schemes. I believe she would be happy to be a part of any plan to bring about his downfall."

"I would like to meet with her," Ying Yue said. "I doubt it would be as simple as just banning demons from the Hurricane, but I'm sure we can come up with something together. Let's find a place of contact after today's meeting."

The plans for the jailbreak continued. I paid as close attention as I could, but a part of me was dissociating. The thought of returning to the Hurricane was looming like the Grim Reaper. And something still nagged at me. As we were wrapping up, I hesitantly raised my hand. Raj nodded.

"Um, are we ever gonna discuss Sheila? I mean, she helped me pull a bunch of people out of the Hurricane, and then

Malum showed up. He had to have figured out what she did by now and thrown her in for helping us. If she's down there, shouldn't we rescue her too?"

"Serves her right," Jake muttered. "She threw me and your mum in there. She's a demon—she deserves that place. She probably likes it."

"Nobody deserves that place," I said quietly.

"What about murderers and pedophiles?" Natalie countered.

"Last I checked, Sheila wasn't either of those things."

"You don't know that," Daisy said darkly.

"She saved me twice!" I said, exasperated. "She's not just evil. There's good in her. She just makes bad decisions sometimes."

"Bad decisions?" Jake shot back. "That's what you call torture? She planned that, David! She's evil!"

I noticed Sandra had been quiet. "Sandra?"

"You know I'm not a fan," she said with a grimace. "She possessed me and you. And tried to kill you a ton of times. Don't you remember when she attacked you in the shower? Or when she set that crazy dog after you? Or when you almost burned to death in a closet?"

I shivered involuntarily. Sandra, not missing my reaction, pursed her lips and tilted her head, blinking at me in a way that said, *"See?"* Okay, so Sandra wasn't going to be my ally on this.

"I agree with David," Ted said quietly. Everyone looked at him. "People can change. I have a feeling she isn't really a fan of Malum. No true demon would save someone, especially if they got nothing but grief for it, and that's exactly what she did."

Bill nodded. "Everyone deserves a second chance."

"Not evil demons who torture people!" Jake said.

Raj sighed. "Our problem is obvious. We're imperfect beings trying to judge another imperfect being."

Ying Yue got a speculative look. "What if we turned this to our advantage?"

"How so?" William asked.

"We rescue as many demons as we can if they agree to be imprisoned in The Resting Place. I'm sure many of them would make that choice. We don't torture demons like they do in the Hurricane. And it would be good for us to have more demons imprisoned where we can see them. We could question them and get more information. And that would be fewer demons for Malum to use in his army."

"We don't have enough prison cells for that," Jake said. "That's why defenders just fight off demons instead of capturing them. We only imprison those we're specifically ordered to."

Natalie shook her head. "You're right. There aren't enough cells. I work in the prisons, and there isn't enough room to make a real difference."

I perked up. "Hang on, since when do you work in the prisons? Oh my gosh, were you there when—"

"Cool it, *chuvak*," she said. "I wasn't there when Malum was released. I was off duty."

"What if we save demons that don't want to be there if they agree to become angels?" Sandra asked. "After being treated so poorly as demons, they'd have to be open to something better. Maybe they'd emerge from the Hurricane hating Malum so much they'd do anything to take him down."

"They wouldn't do that," Natalie said. "They hate angels. And it wouldn't work, anyway. To stay in The Resting Place, you have to want to be there for the right reasons, and if they're only there for vengeance, they wouldn't be angels."

"There are plenty of cells in The Waiting Room," Ted said quietly.

There was a pause, and everyone looked over at him.

"What the heck is The Waiting Room?" I asked.

"I've heard the name before," William said, "though I've never known what it was."

That caught everyone's attention. William and Frederick had been around longer than anyone I knew. It didn't seem possible that there was something they didn't know about.

Ted shrugged. "Well, you wouldn't know about it unless you're an usher like me and Daisy. Or if you've gone through it yourself."

"We're all ushers to an extent," Ying Yue said. "I've ushered several family members over. I've never heard of The Waiting Room."

Daisy rolled her eyes like she'd had several people try to point out how pointless her job is. "First of all, not everyone has family to usher them over. Second of all, have you ever tried to usher someone who wasn't ready to come to The Resting Place but wasn't far gone enough to be a wanderer or a demon?"

"I have," Raj said slowly. "An usher came and took them . . . somewhere."

Daisy raised her eyebrows and held out her hand.

"So, what is it?" Sandra asked.

Ted gestured for Daisy to explain.

"Not everyone's ready to meet the Big Man right away. They just can't face him. But they also don't want to become a demon or a wanderer. The Waiting Room is a safe place to wait until you're ready to meet the Big Man."

"Where is it?" Jake asked. "How long has it been there? What do they do, just sit there? What's the point? What if we put demons in there and they broke out?"

Daisy pursed her lips and blinked. "Want to ask fifty more questions?" When Jake didn't answer, she sighed and continued. "It's in the back," she said vaguely. "And no, they don't just chill—it's not like a hospital waiting room. It's sort of like a holding cell. They go to their own dark little rooms, and the only way out is for them to accept the Big Man and leave with him. But while they're waiting, they're sitting there torturing themselves. They're alone with nothing but their thoughts and memories of all they've done with their lives and all that's been done to them. It's a hellish place, but one with light at the end of the tunnel. They can leave whenever they feel ready to accept him."

"If we held demons there," Frederick said, "their only choices would be to stay there forevermore, or leave with The Big Man, essentially becoming angels themselves?"

Daisy nodded. "And they'd know those are the only two options. You can't get in unless you accept that."

"I think I'd rather take demons there than leave them in The Hurricane," I said. "They're being tortured either way, but at least in The Waiting Room, there's hope."

"It's not a bad plan," Raj said slowly. "This way, they're still contained so they can't hurt anyone, but it's not quite as inhumane as The Hurricane."

"What if they don't choose to go to The Waiting Room?" Bill asked.

Frederick cleared his throat. "For those that are still coherent, we could provide three options: remain in the Hurricane, go to The Waiting Room, or be held captive in prison in The Resting Place. Then, when the prison cells fill up, as they are likely to do, we narrow the choices down to the Hurricane or The Waiting Room."

"We wouldn't want to just free all that we can in the name of mercy?" Ted asked. "I mean, they're being tortured. If you came across someone being tortured, even a bad person, wouldn't you want to stop it?"

"Sheila and I just released anyone who wanted out," I said quietly. "No ultimatum."

"This is war," Ying Yue said soberly. "We cannot afford to be merciful to demons when the fates of the innocent are at stake."

"What if some of them are too far gone to choose?" Jake asked quietly, frowning down at his crossed arms. "And how could you even know demons from angels if their Light's gone out?"

Everyone got quiet, realizing the need to be sensitive with this topic.

"Then we choose for them," I said firmly. "We err on the side of mercy and take them to The Waiting Room, because those souls are in greatest need of The Big Man. If they end up not wanting to be there, we'll let The Big Man sort it out."

"What if they say they want to go to The Waiting Room, but break away before they get there?" Daisy asked.

"War is nothing if not a series of calculated risks," William said. "I believe this plan is worth the risk."

"Are we all agreed?" Raj asked.

Everyone nodded, and we commenced planning the nitty-gritty details of our jailbreak. I was grateful to overhear Raj quietly telling Jake after the meeting that he wouldn't be coming with us. It had been decided that no angel who'd been previously captured would ever return, as a mercy and also because they could be a liability if they froze. I guess I didn't count because I hadn't technically been captured. I wasn't so sure about not being a liability, though. Regardless, I was relieved for Jake. The poor guy couldn't help letting his relief show. He ran his hands through his hair as he looked up and sighed. I knew he thought he was weak for his fear, but honestly, he was the bravest of all of us. After being tortured to nothingness, he was still here, fighting. I hoped one day I could be as brave as him.

HER

We never planned on having kids, but it just sort of happened. We discussed adoption and abortion when I got pregnant, but I'd secretly always wanted to be a mother. It was the biggest fight we'd ever had. He said he'd leave me if I kept the babies, worried he'd hurt them. But when I went into labor, I needed him. And then when the twins were born, I needed him even more. I never knew my father, and my mom had died by then. He was the only one I could rely on. So, he stuck around, and the two of us made thorough plans to keep the kids safe from him. I think I knew deep down that it couldn't last, but I just . . . wanted to keep my family together as long as possible.

He was a good father. Any chance he got, he held our girls close, closed his eyes, and smiled like he was the luckiest man in the world. He spent as much time as possible with them, which probably wasn't safe, but I couldn't find it in me to take them away from him. I never left them alone with him, but there were times my caution seemed unnecessary. The girls loved him. He fed them applesauce, sang silly songs, and danced goofy dances. I can still hear his quiet laughter harmonizing with the girls' screeching giggles. "Daddy funny!" they would say.

Even his episodes didn't happen as frequently, which was a blessing for all of us. It wasn't difficult for me to run away in time, but gathering two babies was a challenge. I suppose he really did love us. When his rage came over him, some tiny sane piece of him ran away from us, so I had time to grab my babies and run. They still heard him, though. "Daddy scary," they would say, holding me tightly.

It was always the twins' room that we would run to, so they'd have books and toys to distract them until their dad cooled down. Then he would knock on the door and quietly say, "It's safe." We would wait a few minutes just in case, and then we'd go about the rest of the day as usual. Well, we pretended to, anyway. You can't exactly ignore scissors sticking out of the wall.

chapter 9

TEENAGE DAD

There were still a few angels lingering in my room from our meeting when the shouting started.

"WHAT? You expect me to…"

I sat up quickly, knocking my water bottle off the nightstand. Dad was yelling from the other room. Actually yelling. I strained to hear the rest of what he was saying, but it was too muffled. I frowned down at the floor, trying to catch bits and pieces.

"WHY CAN'T YOU DO IT? You can't just dump him on me after . . . Then you do it! . . . No, I don't . . ."

I hadn't realized everyone in my room had stopped talking, frowning in the direction of my dad.

I slid off my bed and scurried to the door. "Uh, I'm just gonna go see what's up."

No one objected, so I ran down the stairs to find my dad basically breathing fire as he angrily shoved a cookie in his mouth. He listened to whoever he was talking to on the phone, then groaned, cookie crumbs spraying out of his mouth. Gross.

Mom appeared, as chipper as ever, until she saw Dad's face. "Whoa, what happened to him?"

"Uh, Dad?" I said quietly.

His eyes darted to me, then away. "Fine. *FINE.*" He hung up and threw his phone onto the couch.

He started pacing the walkway between the kitchen and living room, looking down and clenching his fists. I'd never seen him this way.

I leaned against the back of the couch and folded my arms nervously. "Uh, what's up?"

"Your grandfather's coming to stay," he said gruffly. His face looked like he'd just taken a bite of a particularly sour lemon. He sighed and leaned against a barstool, his shoulders so tense they were practically touching his ears.

I blinked. "What's wrong with that? You love Tata Ramon."

"Wrong grandfather, son."

"Whoa, Grandpa Todd? I didn't know you guys, like, spoke."

"We don't," he snapped.

Mom, hovering nearby, said something under her breath that sounded like "oh boy . . ."

I pulled myself up to sit on the back of the couch. "Uh, so why is he coming to stay? And why don't you want him to? And how come I've only met him once? Did you guys have a fight or something?"

I probably should have had these answers by now. I could have asked Grandma Gertie all those hundreds of times we had front desk duty together. I could have visited Grandpa

Todd as an angel. But I never did. I never felt a connection to him, and if he was bad enough for my open-minded and forgiving dad to hate him, I wasn't interested in getting to know him. I was just now starting to realize that was probably not the best way for an angel to think and behave.

Dad closed his eyes and sighed. "Your grandfather and I never saw eye to eye. I was never what he wanted in a son, and your Aunt Sara wasn't who they wanted as a daughter. Instead of sports, I did art and theater, while your aunt Sara took auto shop and weightlifting. We just . . . didn't fit their idea of who we should be. Grandpa wanted me to stay on the farm and take over for him one day. I hated that stupid town and wanted to get out. He didn't like that. Sara wasn't my greatest fan either because she *did* want to take over for Dad, and he always overlooked her because she was a girl. She resented me and thought I was ungrateful because I didn't even care about the thing she wanted the most. Well, she finally got what she wanted when I left town and never came back." He paused for a breath, then muttered, "And then there was the stuff with your mother . . ."

I leaned forward. "What stuff with Mom?"

I felt bad for eating up all this gossip that Dad was upset about, but I'd never heard my dad talk about his past, and I was thoroughly intrigued. He'd always skirted around the topic of Grandpa, hating to speak ill of anyone, but suddenly it was like the floodgates had opened and he couldn't hold it back any longer.

Dad turned toward me, glaring at the floor. "Your grandparents are old. A little bit of racism comes with the territory because of the world they grew up in, but they refused to even try to step outside their bubble. They never respected your mother or her family. They thought she was a bad influence on me. They were always making these assumptions that Mexicans are all dangerous, illegal gangsters who were stealing all our jobs. At one point, Dad, trying to look philanthropic around his buddies, offered your mom a job as a cleaning lady. Your mother has never cleaned another person's house a day in her life, nor was she even looking for a job, but he just thought, 'Well, she's brown, so she probably cleans houses.' And he always spoke louder around her with huge gestures as if she didn't speak English. It just . . . the way he treated her wasn't okay, and your grandma wasn't much better."

He sighed and leaned against the counter. "I did cave to their pressure eventually and got engaged to this girl they'd been shoving at me since I was fourteen, but I couldn't go through with it. I left her at the altar and ran back to your mother. That was the last straw, and your grandparents and I never spoke again. Except that one time they came to town for a funeral and thought they'd stop by to judge my way of life. They came for the funeral of a man they'd met three times but didn't come to my wedding or the births of their grandchildren . . . and I know your mom invited them. She always did, even though I told her not to." He pinched the bridge of his nose and shook his head.

I had no idea what to say. I'd never seen my dad as having such a depth of emotion. He always seemed happy, like nothing bothered him. I mean, I knew my mom's death hurt him deeply, but that was a tragedy. Not an estrangement from unloving parents. I'd always just assumed it was a casual thing, like they'd just grown apart over the years because they lived in different states. I guess that was a childish assumption—people don't grow apart like that for no reason. And there was obviously a lot more to it than my dad could sum up in one sitting. His whole life, he'd felt this way.

And then there was the fact that the Grandma Gertie I knew wasn't like that at all. Well, okay, she was really pushy, but she was still kind and forgiving. I cleared my throat and quietly said, "I don't know if it helps to know, but Grandma isn't like that anymore. She's like best friends with Nana Maria. Maybe Grandpa has changed too?"

Dad glared at me.

"So why is he staying with us if you guys don't get along?"

Don't get along? I shook my head at that euphemism.

Dad growled and started pacing again. "Because he's stubborn! Sara says he refuses to slow down, and he keeps getting injured trying to take care of the farm the way he used to. He broke his hip today, and she said that was the last straw. She's packing up all his things, and once his surgery is over and he's clear to go, she's driving here to dump him on me. She wants me to babysit him so she can take care of the farm in peace."

"Like . . . from now on? Or just while he recovers?"

"I don't know!"

It was so weird hearing my dad talk like this. I could see the teenager he once was in the set of his mouth and his rolling eyes. I'd only ever known my dad as a dad. But that wasn't all he was, was it? He'd had this whole other side in him all along. He was fed up and rebellious. He had a dream and followed it, despite the expectations placed on him. Dad had a story, and I didn't know all of it. Suddenly, I felt foolish for never realizing that his story began long before I was born.

A small piece of information fell into place. *I* was here, and I was supposed to be dead. "Uh, you said he's coming *here?*"

Dad stopped pacing again and rubbed his face. "Yes. They'll be here in about a week, probably. I'm sorry, son. You might need to stay with one of your siblings for a while. He's old and not very healthy. Seeing you might give him a heart attack or something. If I had a choice, I'd keep you here over him, but he's coming whether I like it or not." He kicked one of the barstools like an angry child.

Mom sat on the counter watching him with concern. "This might be a good opportunity for you to repair your relationship." I couldn't tell if Dad could feel her angel whispers. He continued to pace. Mom turned to me and said, "Tell him what I said."

"Uh, I don't think he wants to hear that right now," I said under my breath. Mom and Dad both glared at me, and I gulped. "Uh, Mom says this might be a good opportunity to repair your relationship."

Dad rolled his eyes and threw his hands up. He looked up as though Mom was in the ceiling. "Gloria, I heard you the first fifty times you told me to call him. Enough about it! I'm not listening anymore!"

Mom and I widened our eyes. Jake, whom I just noticed

had followed me down, was leaning against the wall, looking back and forth between us, fully intrigued by the show. He tried to look like the stoic bodyguard with his arms crossed, but the twitch of his mouth gave away his entertainment.

Mom was the kind of offended that ladies get when they're too affronted to even speak. She looked about ready to slap him. I scooted off my perch on the couch and scowled at my dad. "Hey, don't talk to her like that. She's your wife and a freaking angel, and she's trying to help you. Don't shut her out. Do you have any idea what it's like to be constantly ignored? I mean, most mortals have more of an excuse because they don't always know to listen, but you know better!"

Dad threw his hands up and stormed out. "I can't do this right now! You have six days to pack up."

There was a long, awkward silence as the three of us stared after him in shock. Then Mom stormed after him, yelling in Spanish, and I was left with Jake.

"Well, that was intense," he said.

I shrugged and shook my head. Not gonna lie, I was a little offended my dad was just kicking me out like Elena had not that long ago. I mean, I was his son. I knew Grandpa had greater need than I did, but it still stung a little.

I trudged up to my room and flopped onto the bed face down. I didn't look to see which angels were still lingering there in my room, but I could feel them staring at me. They continued their conversations like I wasn't even there. Sounded about right.

Where was I supposed to go? Elena didn't want me around

with demons attacking me all the time. I wasn't comfortable going to Sam's house, not while things were still awkward between us. For a second, I thought, *Well, the only logical place to go is Sandra's. I hate being a burden to her, but she wouldn't turn me down.* And then I wilted as I remembered once again that she was dead. Maybe I could start looking for my own place . . . but could I even afford that on a part-time Chuck E. Cheese salary? Not likely. Where the heck did Dad expect me to go? I groaned into my arm, completely overwhelmed by my situation and resentful of my grandpa for ruining everything.

chapter 10

UGLY BABY

I sat in my squeaky auditorium chair, drumming my fingers on the little desk while Professor Gibbons droned on about microbiology. I forced myself to take out my laptop and start typing notes, but my mind was so full of demons and panic and fear of dating and grandpas that I found myself typing gibberish as I absentmindedly drummed my fingers against the keyboard.

My phone buzzed, and I got a text from Kiki that was a picture of the back of my head and my laptop screen of psychotic nonsense. I looked behind me to see Kiki only two rows back. I turned around and sank into my chair. Kiki sent me a text.

Kiki: ARE YOU BROKEN

Me: Yes

Kiki: does your robot kind malfunction near technology

Me: Pretty much

Kiki: do you need a psychologist or a robot doctor

Me: Pretty sure a robot doctor would just be a

mechanic.

Me: Stop looking at my notes.

Kiki: im not copying your drunken cyborg nonsense

I stopped texting to type on my laptop: THE SECRET OF THE UNIVERSE IS…

Kiki: nicolas cage … no, poptarts

Me: I thought you weren't looking at my notes?

"This will be on the test!" Professor Gibbons said loudly right before he changed the slide. *Shoot, I missed it!*

Me: How could either of those things be the secret of the universe?

Kiki: he told me

Me: Nicolas Cage? Or a specific pop tart?

She didn't answer, so I looked back at her. She was studiously staring at the professor's PowerPoint presentation, so I turned back around. Then my phone buzzed. I opened Kiki's message and snorted. It was a picture of a Pop-Tart with Nicolas Cage's face on it. How did she make that so fast?

We didn't text for the rest of class, but I may as well have been on the other side of the country for how much I got out of the presentation. My mind had switched from fixating on *Demons, Hurricane, Malum, Grandpa, Hurricane, Darkness, Hurricane, we're all gonna die!!!* to *Kiki, Sandra, Kiki, Sandra, Nick*

Cage, Kiki, Sandra, Pop-Tarts, Kiki, Nicky, Nicky, who's Nicky? Then I was distracted trying to imagine what a child of Kiki and Nicolas Cage would look like. It's always a fun time in my brain.

When class finally ended, I met Kiki at the door.

"You okay with the crappy coffee cart on campus?" I asked. "I'm kinda broke."

"*Vamonos!*" She linked her arm and pulled me behind her.

I don't remember most of what we talked about during our lame little date. It was mostly nonsense. I told her about wondering what hers and Nicolas Cage's baby would look like, and we eventually did one of those AI generators that predict the appearance of a couple's future child. I spat out my coffee and couldn't stop laughing. It was probably the ugliest baby either of us had ever seen.

Kiki was gagging at the picture, and I was still wiping my dripping chin. Raj appeared out of nowhere, standing in the middle of our table. The look on his face instantly sobered me. I looked up at him, my thumping heart already knowing what he was going to say.

"It's time," he said. "Meet us at your house. Defenders are waiting in your room to protect your body while you're gone."

Then he disappeared along with Kiki's giggles.

"Uh, are you okay? What was that about? Are you malfunctioning again? Do you need some motor oil or something?" She half-smiled like she was trying to force herself not to look scared and concerned.

My stomach dropped, and I blinked. Somehow, it was just

now sinking in that I was expected to go *back* to the Hurricane. For a moment, all I could hear was that evil voice telling me how I'd never escape. Mom, fading. Jake already gone. Screams and wicked laughter along the howling wind, like the breath of evil incarnate.

"Uh, David?" Kiki asked.

I jumped about a foot in the air, remembering where I was, but the fear remained. Shaking, I wiped my chin on the back of my hand and stood up. "Uh, I'm so sorry, I have to go. Family emergency." Kiki looked hurt, like she suspected I'd just made up an excuse, so I tried to smile. "I'll text you later, okay?"

"Okay," she said with a disappointed half-smile. "Good luck. I hope everything's all right."

Then I threw on my backpack and booked it to my car. The momentum of running was the only way I could force my feet forward.

HER

There came a day when that little piece of sanity failed him.

The girls were playing with the TV remote, pushing buttons at random. The TV seemed to be having a seizure— soap opera, music video, kids cartoon, sitcom, over, and over, and over. At the time, I had gone to the kitchen to grab something; I don't even remember what it was. It was an unforgivable mistake to leave them alone with him for even a second. I'd never done it before, not once. I even locked them in the bathroom with me anytime I used the toilet or the shower.

Some intuition had me sprinting to the family room before his rage even began. I reached them just as he stood and screamed, "ENOUGH!" lunging for the girls, or the remote. I wasn't sure which, but I wasn't taking any chances. Before he could reach them, I jumped between them and shoved him away with all my strength. "You will NOT touch them!" I'd never done that before. I'd never confronted him. I knew right then that I was going to die. That look in his eyes was pure evil and hatred. I looked back at the girls and yelled, "Go to your room!" They were only three, but they didn't need to be told twice.

While my head was still turned, he slapped my exposed cheek hard enough that I stumbled and fell. Then he gripped me painfully by the shoulders and threw me up against the wall. Other than that first time at his parents' house, I'd never been around while he lost control like this, and I'd never been the one he turned his wrath on. My eyes were wide with tears. My bottom lip and chin quivered, but these things meant nothing to him. I always thought that if this situation ever happened, he'd love me enough to control himself. I thought our history would be enough to overcome this psychotic impulse. I was the only one in his life who had stood by him through everything. His brother was ashamed of him, his mom and stepdad were afraid of him, his friends had turned their backs on him. I was the only one who knew who he really was and loved him through it all. None of that meant anything to him.

I don't know how long it lasted—likely only a few minutes, but it felt like hours. And then he screamed, "GO TO HELL!" I don't really remember what he did to me, but for five agonizing seconds, my head felt like it was going to explode. And then I died.

My mom was there. One moment, I was seeing my reflection in the cold, evil eyes of the man I loved. The next moment, my body fell to the floor, and I didn't go with it. Looking down at my wide, glazed-over eyes, I knew that the body that had once been mine was dead. He knew it too, and it was then that he snapped out of it. All the blood drained from his face.

"No . . ." he whispered. He fell to his knees, sobbing. He held my body to his chest, keening and whispering my name. The part of me that knew him better than anyone else in the world knew that this was his greatest fear.

A hand touched my arm, and I flinched. It was my mom. She died when I was eighteen. I couldn't believe that the man who had held me and cried with me when my mother died was the man who had just killed me.

"Come with me, love," Mom said softly. "Come away from all that."

"Mom?" I whispered, my lip quivering.

She gently pulled me close and wrapped me in her arms.

"It's time for you to go," she said gently. "Come with me."

"The kids!" I cried.

"They'll be taken care of, baby. They'll be safe."

I looked back. His phone was to his ear, and in a nearly unintelligible voice, he sobbed, "I just killed my wife! Someone needs to take my children away from me!"

The old me might have felt for him, but this man had just taken everything from me. My plans and dreams, my babies, my entire life! Our children would grow up without a mother because of him! We were supposed to be a family, and he destroyed everything! He destroyed me!

That part of me that loved him died when I did. He could rot for all I cared. My hands curled into fists, and my face hardened into a snarl.

Mom quickly spun me away from the man I hated and feared more than anyone or anything since. I would never, ever forget that look in his eyes when he turned his anger on me. Not only did he beat and kill me, but he would have done that to our babies! I wanted to strangle him!

"Come," Mom repeated urgently. "It's over. Let it go."

I went with her. But I did not let it go.

chapter 11

JAILBREAK

I swore when I saw my dad's car in the garage. Not that he had anywhere else to be. I just didn't want to deal with him. Did I lie or tell him the truth? How could I keep him out of my room? I didn't want him to find my unresponsive body and worry I'd gone into a coma.

Shaking my head, I went inside and faked a few sneezes.

"Bless you!" Dad called from the family room.

I grabbed a few tissues as I walked down the hall and blew my nose loudly.

"Want some food?" Dad asked, barely looking up.

"Nah, I'm just gonna go to bed," I said, slumping my shoulders and dragging my feet.

Dad blinked and looked away from the screen. "Are you sick? Do you need something?"

I blew my nose again. "Nope. I'm just gonna go to bed. I just want to sleep."

He frowned with concern but nodded. "All right. Text me if you need anything."

My bedroom was packed with my whole team, plus a few additional angels that I didn't know. I tried not to drink in the faces of my friends as though this was the last time I'd see them. If we didn't all make it out of this, I didn't know what I'd do.

"Everyone, form up into your teams," Ying Yue said.

Raj, Bill, and an angel I didn't know gathered near my nightstand. Raj's eyes darted around the room, worry for each team member apparent in his tight expression. The unknown angel had the look of a defender, but she kept clearing her throat and shuffling from foot to foot, not making eye contact with anyone. Bill's eyes were wide as he looked around at everyone's terrified faces, wondering what he'd gotten himself into.

Frederick, Sandra, and another unknown angel stood near my window on the opposite side of the room. Frederick scowled and clenched his jaw, failing to hide his apprehension. Even he'd frozen in the face of Malum. The unknown angel bowed his head as though praying. Sandra closed her eyes and forced herself to take a deep breath. She'd faced Malum too, in the form of a possessed high schooler with a gun. I remembered that moment when I'd touched her hand and felt all of her fears along with her. That felt like ages ago.

The rest of my team sorted themselves into groups as instructed by Ying Yue. William, Natalie, and Daisy found each other and stood near my bed. William put his arm around a shaking Natalie and whispered something about being strong. Daisy, with a determined scowl, grasped

Natalie's hand in a grip of iron. I couldn't tell if it was more for her own comfort or for Natalie's.

That left me, Ying Yue, and Ted. We gathered in front of my dresser. Ying Yue was the only one who wasn't visibly panicking. Her hardened face was like an angel of vengeance, a determined warrior who couldn't afford to focus on anything but her goal. Ted, on the other hand, seemed like he was about to pass out. He looked pleadingly at Raj across the room, seeming to be speaking into his mind, but Raj just shook his head.

My panic was growing more by the second. Watching all my teammates struggle with their own fear only added to my own. They didn't even know. They had no idea how terrifying this place really was, and yet each one of them was petrified. I tried to follow Sandra's example and take a deep breath, but it didn't help. Each breath I took only brought my panic closer to the surface.

"Defenders?" Raj said.

Jake and some other defenders I didn't know stood at the foot of my bed. They were there to guard my body once I left it. I couldn't bring myself to look at Jake. I don't know why. Maybe because he *did* know what the Hurricane was like, and I couldn't handle his fear on top of my own.

"Let's review the plan," Ying Yue said in a surprisingly even voice.

Frederick cleared his throat. "Euridice, the High Judge of the Red Zone, has a distraction planned to keep Malum and other demons away. We were not given the details in case one of us was captured and tortured for information before the jailbreak."

"Where are my seekers?" Raj asked. Frederick, William, and I raised our hands shakily. We, along with Raj, would be lowered into the pit where we would *shine* to attract angels and find any demons interested in leaving. Did I have the power to shine like I had before? What if I lost myself? What if I failed?

"Extractors?" Ying Yue said.

Sandra and Natalie forced themselves to raise their hands, and Bill cleared his throat in acknowledgement. Ying Yue would be the fourth extractor. Their job was to keep hold of us seekers while we were lowered down into the Hurricane. They would help pull the prisoners from the pit and hand them off to the ushers.

"Ushers?" Raj prompted.

Ted, Daisy, and the two other angels raised their hands. Their job was to cuff the prisoners—all of them because it would be hard to immediately distinguish angel from demon without their glow—then take the prisoners to a predetermined neutral territory where they could sort them out and figure out where they were going. Defenders would be waiting at that location to hand the prisoners off to so that the ushers could return to the Hurricane as quickly as possible for more prisoners.

"Does everyone understand their duty?" Ying Yue demanded.

We nodded, all too overcome to speak.

"We resort to Operation Backstab if attacked," Raj said. "All of you will radiate Darkness and fight me and Ying Yue as convincingly as possible. It's the best way you will avoid capture."

What if something goes wrong? I wanted to ask. *What if I fail? What if we're captured? What if we lose?*

By the time the meeting ended, I was a mess. There was no room to pace, so I just shuffled back and forth in my two-by-two-foot square of open space, clenching and unclenching my hands. My mind kept flashing back to the last time I went to the Hurricane. The red mists. The screaming souls. The evil, cackling voices. That being that attacked my mind and heart. I kept hearing the voice. *"You'll never return! You failed! You've lost! You doomed everyone!"* I squeezed my eyes shut and did my best to ignore it. It was fine, I was with friends this time. Friends who could get hurt or captured if I failed. I couldn't fail. I couldn't think. I just had to do it. But I *really* didn't want to. What if I couldn't? What if I froze? This whole thing started with me freezing!

I missed the last part of what Ying Yue had said, but suddenly everyone was looking at me. Oh, right, it was time to go. They couldn't get there without me because I was the only one who knew how to get to the Hurricane. This all depended on me. But I couldn't make myself move. I was *freaking out.*

I didn't know how many people were staring at me, but I definitely caught Raj's eye. Before he could make his way toward me, Jake did. He tried to put his hands on my shoulders but obviously failed.

"Mate, this conversation will be easier if you leave your body now."

"What?" I gasped.

"Lie down. You don't have to go yet, just leave your body so we can have a little chat, angel to angel."

Leaving my body actually sounded like a great idea. Maybe my anxiety and panic would be muted without a beating heart that was hammering faster and faster in my chest.

I nodded and walked through all the angels to flop on my bed. I closed my eyes, hearing my heart beating in my ears.

Hermes. Do it now, please.

And suddenly, it was like everything holding me together just vanished, and my body slipped off. My eyes widened, and the gravity of the situation sank in. This was it. I couldn't just put myself back into my body. I had a mission to do, and I'd just committed to doing it.

"David, are you ready?" Ying Yue asked. Everyone was staring at me.

I completely froze. I wanted to sink into the floor or fly away. What was wrong with me? I'd done stuff like this before! Why did I choose now to completely lose it?

"Give us a minute," Jake said. Then he took hold of my arm and yanked me into the hallway. "Look at me, mate."

How could I still hyperventilate? I wasn't even in a mortal body!

Jake put his hands on my shoulders, grounding me. I took a deep breath and looked at him. I'd never seen this much concern on his face. That was how pathetic I was acting.

"Hey!" He shook my shoulders.

I tried to focus on his face. "W-what?"

His eyebrows furrowed, and he pursed his lips. "You can

do this, David. I know you can."

"I don't know about that," I whispered.

"I do. You didn't even know what you were doing last time, and you still saved me. You were a hero then, and you're going to be a hero again. It's not going to be as bad as last time. It's going to be different."

I gulped. "How can you know that?"

"Because this time you have a plan. You have friends and backup. And you know how to fight the Darkness."

"I do?"

"Could the demons touch you when you did your flashy shine-like-the-sun thing?"

I shook my head. "No, they scattered. And I couldn't hear that v-voice anymore."

"Well, this time you'll go in already shining, so no one will be able to touch you. Not once. No one will torture you or hurt you or put horrible things in your mind. You'll have a protective bubble around you from the start. And you'll have three other angels near you doing the exact same thing."

"We won't be near each other," I said, still shaking. "We're spreading out to cover more of the pit. I'll be alone."

Jake shook me again. "No, you won't. You're never alone. Remember whose Light you're shining."

I took a deep breath and nodded at him. He was right. It wouldn't be like last time. I wouldn't be tortured this time. Maybe I could do this. And the fact that Jake cared about me enough to remind me of that was really comforting.

I threw my arms around him. "Thanks, man."

He patted my back, then pulled away, one hand still on my

shoulder. "You ready?"

I nodded, then shook my head. "Not really."

He raised an eyebrow.

"I mean, yes?" I tried.

He shook my shoulders. "ARE YOU READY?"

I took a deep breath and nodded. "Yes!"

"ARE YOU ALONE?" he shouted.

"No!"

"WHAT ARE YOU GONNA DO?"

"I'M GONNA KICK SOME DEMON BUTT!"

Jake chuckled and pulled me back into the room.

Before we left, I looked around at everyone, so worried about all these people I'd grown to love. Oddly enough, after I chatted with Jake, their terror made me braver. It helped me focus my energies on protecting them rather than worrying about myself.

I gave my creepy, empty body on the bed a glance, then turned my back on it.

"Okay, everyone," I said. "Circle up."

We stood in a circle and took hands so they would be pulled along when I apparated over to the Hurricane. I nodded my thanks to Jake for the confidence boost. Then I took a breath, closed my eyes, and did it.

I'd been having nightmares about the actual pit, but I'd forgotten how terrifying it was just being near it. You could *feel* the evil. And even from the outside, you could hear the screams. Right away, we spread out in groups of three: one seeker, one extractor, and one usher per group. I was with Ying Yue and Ted. As much as I trusted and respected Ying Yue, I wished it were Sandra lowering me down. As stupid as it was, I wanted the excuse to hold her hand again like we used to. But this was my assignment, and I had to focus.

All the extractors and ushers made sure to radiate Darkness so they wouldn't catch immediate attention. Raj, Frederick, William, and I took our places along the pit and exploded with Light. Then our extractors took our arms and lowered us in.

It was terrible, but not nearly as bad as it had been the first time. Jake was right. I wasn't alone this time. I mean, I'd had Sheila the first time, but I hadn't been sure she wouldn't just drop me. Ying Yue's grip was solid—if we were both alive, she'd be cutting off my circulation. And my Light *was* like a force field. The demons near me immediately shrieked and scattered, leaving behind the miserable wretches they'd been torturing. Some of them shrank away, while others were too gone to even respond. Some of them had scratch marks on their faces and clumps of hair missing. They were bony and emaciated like starved prisoners. This shook me. Spirits shouldn't show physical damage like that, but our outsides tend to match our insides regardless. What torment did they feel to project such broken exteriors? Jake had looked just as bad. I really didn't give that guy enough credit for bouncing back the way he had.

I took a deep breath and forced myself to think. How did I get them to come to me? When my mom was here, I called her name, but I didn't know these people.

One of them, still glowing slightly, looked at me and blinked, shielding his eyes. "Who are you?" It was hard to hear him over the wind and screams. I shivered at a particularly agonized shriek.

"I'm an angel," I shouted, hoping he could hear me. "I'm here to get you out."

He hesitated.

I forced myself to remain calm. "Look, man, even if it was a trap, things can't get much worse for you, can they?"

Slowly, he approached me, but before he took my hand, I said, "Can you help me out by grabbing a few more people?"

The evil wind continued to roar while the guy blinked and processed what I'd said. He shook his head and slowly dragged a woman along with him, handing her off to me. I let go of Ying Yue with one of my hands and lifted the other woman's hand until Ying Yue caught hold. By the time she lifted the woman out, the guy had come back with a man who had gone full wanderer. I sent him up as well. Then my helper staggered, and his Light flickered like a flashlight that was almost out.

"I can't save them all," he whimpered. His arms covered his head, then he shook and covered his ears. "Stop it, stop it! I didn't mean to! I didn't mean it! Stop hurting me! Please... *Let me out! Get me out of here!*"

I gulped and shivered at his agony. I immediately sent him up to Ying Yue. What a brave man to stay behind when he, himself, was suffering and fading. I felt horribly guilty for asking him to stay even a second longer than necessary.

I was sad to lose his help, though. No one else approached

me or even seemed to notice I was there. I wanted to cover my ears. It seemed like the screaming was getting louder.

"Come with me if you want to escape!" My voice echoed, and I thought I heard that other voice echo back. *No escape!*

Don't panic, I told myself. *Don't panic.*

But suddenly, inhuman demons were swarming me, screaming in pain at my Light but determined to bring me down. They surrounded me, screaming and wailing like someone was forcing them after me. What was I supposed to do? Last time, the Light itself was enough to make them scatter. They still couldn't touch me, but they created a barrier between the other prisoners and me. I'd have to pass them to get to the prisoners, but I couldn't let go of Ying Yue, or I would become lost as well. The Darkness was getting harder and harder to fight.

With a grunt, I forced a beam of Light from my hand and swung it back and forth, blasting them in the face. Some of them screamed and disappeared, but a few remained. Fingers snapped next to my ear. I looked over at Ying Yue's free hand and blinked in surprise at what looked like a Light grenade. I grabbed it, pulled the pin out with my teeth, and threw it at the demons. Light blasted most of them away. Then I pulled a gun from my pocket that I'd saved as a last resort. It was full of demon killer bullets. I shot the three remaining resisting demons, and they dropped like puppets with cut strings.

I didn't offer to save them. We were only there to save those who wanted to be saved. Or wanderers who likely would want to be saved if they were in their right minds. But trying to drag me down was a pretty clear indication that these demons weren't looking for salvation.

Unfortunately, another wave of demons came toward me.

"Hurry!" I shouted at the dead-eyed spirits around me. "I can get you out! Come on!" Wind whipped around me faster and faster, like another barrier between me and the ones I could save.

"David?" a voice croaked.

I turned my head slowly, terrified to see who I thought it was.

Pale, exhausted, and flickering Darkness, Sheila approached, staggering through the miniature cyclone surrounding me. I'd seen corpses that looked better than her. It was like one of my zombie dreams. I wondered why my Light didn't hurt her. Or maybe it did, and she was just past feeling.

"Sheila…"

Ying Yue started snapping S.O.S. in my ear in Morse code. It was time to go.

"I'm sorry," Sheila cried, tears running down her cheeks. Her eyes were bloodshot and sunken into her face. "I'm sorry for everything. I'm sorry for hurting you and for throwing your friends in here. No one deserves this. I'm sorry! Please forgive me! Please save me!"

I was brought back to a pivotal moment right after I'd been made alive again, only to take a bullet to the chest. I was dying, and no angels were around to take me home. I pleaded with Sheila to save me and heal me, and instead of dragging me down with her, she did it. She saved me.

I didn't see a demon before me, but a traumatized and broken woman. Without a second thought, I reached out and took her hand. Ying Yue yanked her up, then frantically snapped S.O.S. again. It was time to go. Despairing in all the souls I was leaving behind, I reached up with my other hand, and Ying Yue pulled me out.

Finally, I could breathe again. Looking around, I saw that my group and Frederick's group were the only ones left. One of the demon hunters I didn't know took their last prisoner away, leaving Fred and Sandra behind. But I only observed that for a split second because Sheila was shrieking like she was on fire.

Ying Yue was struggling to cuff her while Ted froze unhelpfully.

Sheila screamed and clutched my arm, digging into my arm with her nails. "HOW COULD YOU?"

Frederick and Sandra hurried over, trying to help restrain Sheila, who was absolutely losing her mind.

"Get out of here, Sandra!" I yelled.

She hesitated but did as she was told. Sheila hated her, and I assumed that's why she was freaking out.

"HOW COULD YOU BRING *HIM*?" Sheila shrieked. "I WAS ALREADY BEING TORTURED! WHY ARE YOU DOING THIS TO ME?"

"Whoa, calm down!" I yelled, trying to pull her off me. "What are you talking about?"

Ying Yue yanked Sheila's hands behind her back while Frederick cuffed her, but she continued to resist, trying to shoot us with beams of Darkness from her eyes.

"Come on, Sheila! You have to let us save you our way, or I have to throw you back in the Hurricane." It hurt me to say it, and I worried I wouldn't be able to actually do it.

"Then take me away! Lock me up! Anything to get away from *HIM*!" she screamed.

Frederick yanked her firmly to his side. "I'll take her." He began to disappear, but before he and Sheila were gone, she screamed and kicked Ted, who still stood there frozen. It wasn't a frantic flailing kick. It was calculated and aimed. She kicked him straight in the stomach. Right down into the Hurricane. Ted mouthed her name as he fell.

"NO! David, take my hand!" Out of nowhere, Ying Yue jumped in after Ted, arm outstretched toward me.

But at that moment I was jerked sideways and dumped back into my body.

chapter 12
AFTERMATH

I screamed, sitting up so fast I saw spots. I slid off my bed and wobbled, holding the wall for support.

Jake dropped his guns and tried to steady me, but I was mortal again, and he couldn't touch me. "What's the matter? What happened?"

"I need to see Frederick and his captive now!"

"What?"

"NOW!" I screamed.

Jake nodded and disappeared without question. I sank down to the floor while the other defender stood guard, guns up and ready. "Is there a threat?" he demanded.

"There might be," I said. "Stay alert."

Other members of my team were in the room as well, but I wasn't paying attention to them. My head fell into my hands. A member of my team was just thrown into the Hurricane by a girl whom both Ted and I had defended. We believed in her when no one else did, and she kicked him in! Then my mentor jumped in after him, and because of my stupid mortal time limit, I couldn't catch her!

Frederick arrived within a couple of minutes. He hadn't taken Sheila to The Waiting Room or the prisons yet. Either because she was still struggling or hadn't decided which one she wanted. Jake trailed behind him, followed by Raj and Sandra. I looked around to count the other angels that had returned safely. To my relief, all were back. All except for Ted and Ying Yue…

Frederick frowned at me expectantly. "I was told to bring the demon here first. I assume you have a reason." He obviously hadn't seen what had happened. They were in the process of disappearing when Sheila did it.

"What happened?" Raj asked.

I marched up to Sheila, wanting to throttle her. "WHAT IS *WRONG* WITH YOU? WE SAVED YOU AND GAVE YOU A SECOND CHANCE, AND THIS IS HOW YOU REPAY US?"

Everyone around us flinched away at my volume and looked at me with wide eyes. They'd never heard me yell like that. I don't think *I'd* ever heard myself yell like that. I stood there panting as Sheila struggled, and I impatiently gestured for Frederick to remove her gag.

"*HE's* what's wrong with me!" she shrieked. "*HE* deserves the Hurricane!"

"Who the hell is *he*? Or *him*? You're constantly obsessing over this unnamed male pronoun! And what does this have to do with . . ." The world tilted sideways. "Wait, you mean *Ted?*"

"DON'T SAY HIS NAME!"

My head reared back in shock and confusion. "Ted is your

mysterious *him* that you're so terrified of? Are we even talking about the same person?"

"I SAID, DON'T SAY HIS NAME!"

"What, you've got something against *Ted*? Is that why you kicked him into the Hurricane?"

"You *what*?" Raj's jaw dropped as his eyes filled with horrified tears.

"Yeah!" I exploded. "And Ying Yue went after him! I was supposed to hold onto her so she could come back out, but I was sucked back into my body! They both fell in because of Sheila!"

Raj froze in shock, and Jake swore.

I turned back to Sheila. "What did Te—*he* do to you?" I couldn't imagine Ted hurting a fly.

"You think he's a perfect little angel," she spat. "He's not! He deserves the Hurricane. The number of times I stood by him and defended him, and how did he repay me? He beat me and killed me! Our children are orphans because of him!"

My brain felt like it was short-circuiting with all this new information. Sheila and Ted had *kids*? *Together*? And he *killed* her? How could this be possible?

I shook my head. "I think you're either lying or confused, Sheila."

"She's not," Raj said quietly, covering his eyes with the heels of his palms.

We all looked at him.

He shoved his hands back away from his eyes. "I know his history. Ted told me. He almost quit in the early days when we first started the demon hunters because he was worried the Darkness would trigger an episode. But—"

I rounded on Raj. "Wait, she's telling the truth? Ted *killed* Sheila, and he got into The Resting Place? *How?* And somehow Sheila's the demon? What's going on here?"

Jake stood there with his mouth open. "Wait, Ted killed someone? *Our* Ted? The accountant nerd?"

Frederick was furious. "We've had a murderer on our task force from the beginning?"

"It wasn't his fault," Raj said, rubbing his temples. "He had a mental condition. He didn't mean to, and he did his time in The Waiting Room after he died." He narrowed his eyes at Sheila, and I saw a look on his face I'd never seen before. It was . . . *vengeful.* All of a sudden, he looked like a demon on the warpath. And yet his eyes were still full of tears. "If anyone deserves the Hurricane, it's her. After what she did. Not just what happened today. She's the one who caused all of this! I'm sorry for what you suffered, but you doomed the world for your vengeance. I didn't want you to be saved, but I trusted David's instincts. That was a mistake."

I was stunned. Raj, my compassionate mentor/therapist, was shouting and pointing fingers, ready to doom someone to hell.

"What are you talking about? What did Sheila do?" Then it dawned on me. She'd all but confessed to me before, and I was just too dumb to understand exactly what that meant. I turned slowly to Sheila. "You released Malum. From within The Resting Place. That's how you got on his good side. You weren't always a demon, were you? You were an angel, and you released the most dangerous demon in existence."

"She didn't just break her contract; she shattered it into a million pieces," Raj growled.

"I did what I had to," she screamed. "*He* killed me, and he would have killed my children had I not stepped in front of them. And the Big Man just let him in! Like what happened to me didn't mean anything! Like he didn't care! I was angry, and I . . ."

Tears were streaming down her face, and there we came to the root of it. Beneath all her anger was hurt, and I couldn't blame Sheila for feeling the way she did. I also couldn't blame Raj. What Sheila did was unthinkable. Ted, however . . . I couldn't believe he could do something like that. He took her life. She was traumatized, and I'd witnessed that in how she couldn't even say his name. *Him*. He was her *him*.

"Hang on a sec," I said, rounding on Raj. "You knew about this? You knew her connection to Ted and how she was the one who released Malum? Didn't you think that would have been important information to share? I was dating her, for crying out loud!"

"I knew what happened, but I didn't know his wife was Sheila. It wasn't until right before the jailbreak that he pulled me and Ying Yue aside and explained it all. He was worried that his being there would be a problem. We should have listened." He pinched the bridge of his nose.

"Let's just go back and swap them," Daisy said. "Grab Ted and leave Sheila."

"You wish to save the murderer?" Frederick growled.

Daisy raised his voice. "And how many deaths has Sheila caused by releasing Malum?"

"Ted was on our team, and he lied to us," Natalie muttered.

Bill, in a surprising display of anger, shouted, "He had a right to his secrets! How would you like all your past mistakes thrown out into the open?"

"Mistakes?" Jake yelled. "You call domestic violence and murder a *mistake?*"

"The true mistake was trusting *her*," Raj spat. "I wish Ted had said something when he found out David was dating his psychotic wife."

"So, it *is* Ted's fault!" Jake shot back.

This was just too much. Everyone was shouting at one another, throwing blame left and right, and it all just blurred into a confused buzzing in my ears. It was too much.

Eventually, I'd had enough.

"Everyone shut up," I yelled. "It's pointless to sit here pointing fingers when we have an actual problem on our hands!"

"We need to send her back to the Hurricane," Raj whispered dangerously, pointing at Sheila. He looked unhinged. And he was radiating Darkness. "She can't change—she's proved that. And someone must be held accountable."

There was more shouting until I stood on my bed and shouted, "HEY!"

Dad knocked and peeked his head in. "Is everything all right?"

I didn't have time to reassure him that his son, standing on his bed and screaming at nothing, wasn't crazy. "Not now,

Dad!"

His face darkened. "Now listen here—"

I sighed and hopped off the bed, rushing to the door. "I'm sorry for shouting, but we have an emergency we're dealing with, and everyone's freaking out. I'll explain it to you in a minute. Please, just give me some time."

He frowned. "All right . . ."

Once the door was closed, I turned back to the tense angels, all glaring at one another. "Right. Everyone needs to chill out. There are a billion little decisions by a ton of different people that have led to this. We could blame Sheila for releasing Malum. We could blame Ted for murdering her and kindling her anger. We could blame Ted's mental condition, whatever it was. Or the prison guards for not catching Malum. Or me, for freezing and doing nothing. Or Hermes for not getting there in time. It doesn't matter! There is only one enemy we're up against. We can't waste time fighting and blaming each other while Malum's out there causing mass panic and suffering."

Raj, in a weird combination of sorrow and fury, yelled, "David, you're letting your feelings cloud your judgment. Sheila is the one who let Malum out. We wouldn't be in this mess if it weren't for her. She caused all of this, and consigned Ted, Jake, and *your mother* to the Hurricane. She deserves to suffer for—"

"THAT'S ENOUGH!"

I don't know if his face was more shocked or furious. I should have shut my mouth. At the very least, I should have been embarrassed for shouting at my task force leader, but I was done.

"You know what, Raj? I respect the heck out of you, and I've always trusted you completely. But even though you're this wise archangel, you aren't perfect, and I think I'm just now seeing that. Right now, you are *wrong*. Yeah, Sheila has done some evil things, and maybe your anger is completely justified. She probably deserves to be punished for what she did. But you have no right to consign *anyone* to the Hurricane. You were down there surrounded by your Light, but you have no idea what it's like to be down there without that power. You're helpless and at the mercy of a Darkness so all-consuming you either have to exist in constant agony or give up your humanity just so you don't have to feel. Do you remember what that place did to Jake? What it did to me? It's torture like you can't even imagine, and *no one deserves that!* If they do, it's not up to us. And weren't you just criticizing Sheila for throwing people in there? You think doing the same thing is going to make any of this right?"

"But Ying Yue and Ted are innocent and—"

"I'm not done!" I said, cutting off Raj. "The fact of the matter is, while you're over there blaming Sheila, and I'm over here blaming Ted, at the end of the day, there is only one person who has any right to judge any of us. As far as I know, the Big Man hasn't condemned any of us. He let Ted in, he let Sheila in, and he let you in. He gave all of us the chance to come back, even though we've all screwed up in so many ways."

I looked around at everyone's shocked expressions. "I'm not saying people shouldn't be held accountable for doing evil. Maybe some people really do deserve the Hurricane. What I'm saying is that it's not up to *us*. We are angels. We save; we don't *torture*. Got it?"

They all nodded their heads, some—including Raj—looking down at their feet in shame.

I slumped back on my bed, suddenly drained. I had to clench my knees to keep my hands from shaking. I'd never spoken up like that before, and after we'd all been through that day, my courage was completely spent.

Raj stiffened suddenly, and his Darkness bled back to Light. "I need to report to Hermes. We'll meet again soon. In the meantime, don't go anywhere alone." He scowled at the ground rather than look at me as he added, "That includes you, David." And then he disappeared, leaving us all feeling lost, frightened, and in mourning for our captured friends.

HIM

I got three years in prison for voluntary manslaughter. It would have been ten—which is still too few—but they attributed my actions to extreme mental illness. Three years for killing my wife. She was the sun, the moon, and the stars to me. My fiery angel with her enchanting smirk. I still see that smirk when I close my eyes. The way she'd look at me as though smug that she got to keep me all to herself. She did love me, I know that more than I know anything. She loved me as much as I loved her. And for killing my love, I was sentenced to three years in prison. Three years for ending another person's life. I deserved death. I deserved hell.

I spent most of my prison time in solitary for getting into fights. Prison wasn't great for my condition. Unfortunately, I'd never been very big or strong, so halfway through my episodes I'd come to and realize I was getting my ass kicked. After a fight that almost killed me, they put me in protective custody. I wished they hadn't. I wanted to die.

I tried to do it myself after getting released. Several times. This landed me in a mental institution where I spent the next ten years of monotonous self-loathing. I never saw my kids again. My family disowned me. I was alone.

As much as I deserved my suffering, I couldn't live with myself anymore. That's why I was glad when I got sick and the doctors told me I was dying. As I lay there growing weaker and weaker, all I wanted was my mom. I cried for her at night but begged the pitying nurses not to contact her. I couldn't face her hatred or shame or fear or whatever it was that had kept her away for thirteen years.

She came anyway. I wasn't sure if she was really there; I'd been hallucinating, and I couldn't see very well. But I felt her hold my hand, and I heard her crying. I felt her touch my face and wipe my tears. "I'm sorry I never visited, baby. Please forgive me. Your stepfather wouldn't let me. He thought you'd hurt me like you hurt her. And I was afraid. You were alone for so long, and you probably needed your mommy, but I was afraid of who you might have become. I was afraid you weren't you. I'm so sorry. You never deserved any of this. Oh, my son . . . I wish you were a little boy again, before any of this happened. I'd hold you in my arms and we'd run away somewhere safe, and I'd never let you go."

There was a steady stream of tears down my face from that moment until I died. Because, as much as I deserved to, I didn't die alone.

PART TWO

chapter 13

SOAP OPERA AT WORK

"Hey, you okay?"

I blinked and realized I'd just been standing at the ticket counter, staring at nothing. Chuck E. Cheese was pretty dead this time of day. Two kids were fighting over a Skee-Ball, and their grandma was sitting on a bench, snoring. It was silent except for random sounds from arcade games as they tried to entice nonexistent children to waste their worthless tokens. Even the lighting was melancholy with the overcast sky outside.

But I hadn't been paying attention to any of that. I'd been worrying about how I'd spoken to Raj and disrespected him in front of our whole team. And I couldn't stop replaying the scene of Sheila kicking Ted into the Hurricane. His look of pure shock at seeing her, as frozen as I had been when I first met Malum. And then Ying Yue jumping after him, her arm outstretched toward me as I disappeared . . . She had trusted me to pull her to safety after rescuing Ted, and I let them both fall. Or had Hermes let them fall? He was the one who chose when to put me back into my body. Did he know what a critical moment that was, or was my time simply up?

I still wasn't sure what I thought about Ted. It was hard to get over the fact that he killed someone and still made it into The Resting Place. It made me wonder how many other angels I had interacted with who had secrets as black as murder. But I knew Ted, and that just wasn't who he was. He was quiet, calm, and kind. He defended Sheila when I suggested we rescue her too, which, knowing their history, made a lot more sense now. She was his wife. Why hadn't he said anything when he realized I was dating his *wife*? Did he still consider them married? I mean, The Resting Place does treat marriage a little differently, since marriage is often seen as "till death do you part," but most still choose to stay married. They just have another ceremony, like a vow renewal.

And what were we going to do with Sheila? She was a victim and a criminal. What was with her screaming at us to take her to prison in The Resting Place? Maybe she was safe from Malum while she was in our custody. They'd probably interrogate her soon, and I had a sudden fear that they'd hurt her. I mean, it was against our guardian angel contracts to cause harm, but so were a lot of the things we did as demon hunters. Maybe I could insist that I do the interrogating. They'd probably let me since I had more of a rapport with her. They would probably see it as a tactic to throw her off since she had such mixed and confusing feelings about me.

We hadn't even begun plans for the next jailbreak. There were too many factors we couldn't account for yet. We had to debrief people in The Resting Place, and there would probably be some big meeting, like when I shared my idea to ambush Malum back when I was dead. On the one hand, I felt like we needed time to create a solid plan, but on the other hand, my friend and mentor were being tortured every moment we waited. Jake confided in me afterward that he hoped they'd go wanderer quickly. It was an awful state to be in and even worse to come out of. Eventually, they'd have to confront all the horror when they came to, but at least if they shut off their emotions, they wouldn't be continuously tortured the entire time they were in the Hurricane.

Was I selfish for not dropping everything to try to save them the way I'd saved my mom and Jake? Or was I using common sense by waiting for orders from my superiors, rather than going rogue and possibly getting myself captured with them? Would I have acted differently if it had been Sandra? Was it wrong if the answer was yes?

"Earth to David!" Preston said, snapping in my face.

I blinked, dragging my focus back to the present. "Huh?"

"I asked if you were okay."

"Oh. Uh, yeah. I'm fine." I rubbed my eyes. How was I expected to deal with all these mundane human problems when angels and demons were literally at war?

He raised an eyebrow. "You sure? Don't get mad, but you don't look fine. And I don't know if I'm just bad at reading people or if you're just really confusing. You're nice to everyone most of the time, but then sometimes you get all mopey and don't want to talk to anyone."

I sighed and leaned against the ticket counter. "There's a

lot on my mind that I can't talk about. And then if I try to, *some people* yell and run away."

Preston rolled his eyes and sighed. Then he pulled up a stool and leaned against the ticket counter. "I'm listening."

"Why?" I asked suspiciously.

"Why do you think?" he snapped. "Geez, I start trying to act like a decent person, and you're over there looking at me like I'm the spawn of Satan. Did it ever occur to you that maybe I just want to be your friend?"

I blinked in surprise. Preston wanted to be my *friend?*

The front doors slammed open, and we broke eye contact to watch three men barge in, laughing and swaying and very clearly intoxicated. Their raucous laughter was a weird shock after the near silence of an empty arcade. Even the grandma and her kids had gone.

Typically, Preston would take care of a situation like this, but he'd just sworn and fallen off his stool.

I hurried around the counter to help him up. "You okay?"

He shook his head, staring at the three men like a deer in the headlights. The only other time I'd seen him like this was when the building was on fire. "We need to get them out of here. They can't be here."

"Who are they?" I asked.

"My dad and brothers," he said with gritted teeth. "They can't be here."

I couldn't tell if he meant they weren't allowed or if he was in denial that they were there.

Before I could do anything, Liam hurried up to the three men.

"I'm sorry, gentlemen, but there is no alcohol allowed on the premises." He nodded to a beer bottle that one of them was still holding.

"Isn't this a party place?" the youngest one asked. He was dressed like a frat boy but had platinum-blond buzzed hair and a large diamond earring.

The guy next to Earring Boy sneered. "Yeah, Dad just picked up me and Ivan so we could celebrate with the birthday boy!" He was sloppier, but still bougie in a name-brand hoodie and sweats. He was probably about six foot four, and surprisingly thin for someone with a voice that sounded like Andre the Giant.

The shortest one was clearly the oldest by a few decades, with salt and pepper hair and a gray five-o'clock shadow. He wore a button-up shirt with the sleeves partially rolled up, tucked into tan pants, and shiny brown shoes. He had a navy-colored sweater loosely tied around his shoulders. His Rolex alone probably cost more than the entire contents of my bank account several times over.

He smirked at Preston and held out his arms in a self-congratulatory way, as though we were all so lucky for his condescension. "Happy Birthday, son! Let's go celebrate!"

Preston, red in the face, sneered at them. "Get back in your limo and leave me alone. My birthday was three months ago, idiots."

The man's smirk melted away. He sidestepped Liam and stormed up to Preston. Preston gripped the stool like he was going to push the guy back with it, but the man knocked it from his hands and grabbed him by the shirt. He lowered his voice to a dangerous growl. "What did you call me, boy?"

Preston's face reminded me of Sheila being confronted with Ted, and I winced. "Get your hands off me," he said in quiet fury, trying to hide the quaver in his voice.

The man lifted his hand suddenly, and Preston flinched. The man smirked and lowered his hand. Then he slapped him anyway. I hopped over the fallen stool, and Jorge dropped his mop to join me.

"Let him go," I said, trying to sound unafraid.

"What do you want, Dad?" Preston growled.

The man leaned in. "Janessa and I are getting married, and she wants to meet *all* my boys. So, you're coming with me, Ivan, and Harrison, and we're going to be one big happy family. Got it?"

Preston laughed humorlessly and shoved the man away. The man stumbled and momentarily lost his balance while Preston's hands clenched into fists. "One big happy family? With boys from three different mothers, and sisters you didn't even tell us about? How many families do you have, Dad? Are you going to invite them all?"

The tall dude, the one they called Harrison, joined us. "He just wants to have dinner, loser."

Ivan, the blond brother, joined in. "Yeah, what's your problem, ass face?" He shoved Preston, who stumbled back a step.

Preston shoved Ivan, who knocked into their dad. The three drunk guys rushed at Preston, but I pushed him behind me just as Jorge held Harrison back by his arms, and Liam held back Ivan. The dad was the only one left alone, and he smirked, trying to step around me to get to Preston. The man reeked of cologne and beer. I stood my ground and held my arms out behind me, but I'm not gonna lie, I was questioning what the heck I was doing there. If this got physical, I would be no help except to become a punching bag. I wasn't keen on adding "get beat up" to the list of ways I'd almost died.

The man chuckled darkly and looked past me at Preston. "You live under my roof, you follow my rules, boy. Or I'll beat your ass so hard you won't remember what hit you."

I couldn't believe what I was hearing. I'd never heard anyone speak like this in real life. And why did his brothers look like trust fund snobs while Preston was here working overtime at Chuck E. Cheese? There was something really weird going on here.

Preson's mom appeared in a burst of light. "Don't take the bait, Preston!" She glared at the dad so harshly that I almost expected him to start melting.

"I have the police on the line!" Piper called from behind the food counter. Her voice shook as she tried to bravely meet the man's eyes.

The dad sneered. "You'll see what comes from disrespecting your father tonight, you ungrateful little bastard!"

"No, he won't," I blurted, hardly knowing what I was saying.

The man looked at me and laughed. "What are you, his little chihuahua bodyguard? You can bark all you want, but you can't bite!" The brothers laughed with him.

"He won't be coming home because he's staying with me

now—indefinitely," I said, trying to hide a quick swallow. My mouth felt as dry as the desert. "And I suggest you get out of here before you're arrested for assault and trespassing."

The man slowly stepped up and glared down at me, trying to intimidate me. It was weird how, logically, after facing Malum and descending to the Hurricane twice, I knew this stupid little man was not scary. Not in the grand scheme of things. But at that moment, I had to clench my hands to hide that they were shaking.

"You best hope I don't see you again," he said to me.

I thought of all I'd been through and tried to put this situation into perspective. This man was a mere mortal, and if we were both dead, I could kick his demon butt. Summoning my courage, I smiled at him, and something in my face caused him to pause. Then his face hardened, and his body tensed, squaring up to punch the smile off my face. I closed my eyes and cringed backward just as the light right above the man shattered, showering him with bits of glass. I looked over to Norah and smiled wider. This man had better get out of here, or this mama bear was gonna break all the rules and haunt him all the way home. The man shook the glass off him, looking around in confusion. Then he backed away and gestured for his sons to join him. They pulled out of Liam's and Jorge's grips and followed, tossing a few curses back at Preston as they left. Once the door shut behind them, I turned around to look at Preston. His face and neck were flushed with anger and humiliation, and his left cheek was swollen.

"Go to your office to cool down before you say something

you don't mean," I told him. "We can take care of things out here."

He stormed past me with his mother trailing behind.

"Thank goodness they left," Piper squealed. "I forgot to dial nine first to call an outside line, and I never got through to the cops."

I chuckled nervously. "You were great, Pipes." I took a deep breath and found my hands were still shaking. The adrenaline was wearing off now, and as confident as I had been at the moment, I couldn't stop thinking about how bold and stupid I'd been. The dude could have pulverized me. Shaking my head, I pulled out my phone and called my dad, who picked up after two rings.

"Hey, kid, what's up?"

"Can a friend of mine stay at the house for a little while?"

chapter 14
WE SAVE OUR BOSS

I knocked on Preston's office door after everyone got settled back into work. "Hey, can I come in?"

"NO!"

His mom stuck her head through the door and nodded, gesturing me inside.

"Just for a sec?" I tried.

"I said no!"

Norah nodded encouragingly. "He's just testing to see if you care enough to keep trying."

I turned the doorknob. "I'm coming in."

"I said—"

But I'd already come inside, shutting the door behind me.

"Get the hell out of here!" His eyes were red rimmed from crying.

"No. You said you wanted to be my friend. This is what friends do."

He dropped his head into his hands. "What do you want from me?"

I sat in the chair in front of his disastrous desk. "How old are you?"

Preston frowned up at me. "Why do you care?"

I just waited for him to answer.

"Twenty-three. Why?"

Even though I'd never actually been twenty-three, somehow that sounded like a baby to me. In the body I was in now, I could be close to a decade older than him. "Why are you still living with that guy when you're old enough to have your own place?"

He sighed and dropped his hands. "I can't get an apartment. I spent all my money on school, and I'm in so much debt that my credit score is probably lower than your crappy minimum wage paycheck. And I have a criminal record, which doesn't help because they always do a background check." At my raised eyebrow, he rolled his eyes and said, "My brothers used me as a getaway driver for a lot of stupid crap they used to do. They also liked to hide drugs in my car and not tell me about it."

I frowned. "Okay, there is so much to unpack there, but back to the apartment and money thing. Why didn't Mr. Country Club pay for your school?"

"Well, as you may have noticed," he said through gritted teeth, "he doesn't particularly like me."

"Why? Why does he treat you differently from your brothers?"

Preston sighed and leaned back in his chair. "My mom was his maid. When she died, I was supposed to go live with my uncle, but he had a nervous breakdown and couldn't handle me, so he sent me to go live with my dad. Dad didn't know me and didn't want to deal with some random kid he had with the *help*, but he let me stay at the house, *out of the kindness of his heart*. He mostly ignored me at first. But then he discovered I was easy to put down and had a lot of fun laughing at me and pushing me around. My brothers joined in because they liked that he was taking his crap out on me instead of them."

I frowned. "And you thought if you acted like them, they'd accept you?" I was making an assumption here, and I hoped he wouldn't be offended.

He sighed again. "They weren't as hard on me when I talked and acted like them. Eventually, I got tired of fighting them and just let them drag me down with them. I started to humiliate and hurt people to draw their attention away from me, and most of the time it worked. If I joined in on their fun, they mostly left me alone. And then it was just kind of part of who I was. But ever since I realized what a jerk I've become, I've been trying to be better. Which means they've gone back to treating me like garbage."

He scowled and looked down. "But I don't care. I decided it would be worse to turn out like them."

Suddenly, a lot of things about him made a lot more sense. I also realized that when I demanded him to be better, the stakes were a lot higher for him than I knew. It didn't excuse the way he'd acted, but it explained it.

"And how did you end up working here?" I asked. "Your brothers don't look like they've worked a day in their lives."

"I'm the only one who pays rent because I don't count as part of the family. I was a product of a fling he had with a housekeeper, not one of his snobby girlfriends. When I went broke, Dad called in some favors to get me this job. Likes to act like he's a real philanthropist because of it. I think he just likes having something to hold over my head. *I gave you everything you have, you ungrateful little bastard!*"

I knew he was only giving me the bare minimum. The situation was obviously worse than he made it out to be. What a screwed-up life. And here I thought I'd suffered. No matter what I'd gone through, my family had always loved me. The only one who'd ever loved Preston was his dead mom.

I slapped my thighs. "Right. Well, you're not going back there again."

He scowled at me. "What makes you think I want your pity?"

"Do you want to get out of there or not? The guy abuses you. I don't care what you've done; you don't deserve that. Nobody does."

"I can't just leave."

"Yes, you can. Come on."

Preston sat up in panic. "I don't have any of my stuff with me. I can't go back there now and pack up all my things. You challenged him and made him feel like an idiot, and he's gonna take it out on me. He won't let me leave!"

I thought for a moment. "Aren't they all going out to dinner right now with his girlfriend?"

Preston nodded.

"Let's go get your stuff while they're gone."

"No!" He was genuinely panicking now, clutching his chair's armrests. "We can't. He'll find out. He has security cameras and everything."

I'd never seen him this panicked before. Not even last year, when the building was on fire. I could see the frightened and abused child in his face.

"He's not going to leave his fancy dinner just because he sees you coming into the house," I assured him.

"Yeah, he would! He wants me under his thumb where I belong!"

I breathed out through my nose, thinking.

"I'll disable his phone so he can't view the security footage," Norah said suddenly. "And I'll be your lookout. I'll let you know when he's on his way home."

I smiled. "Yeah, that could work. Let's go."

He stood up suddenly. "What? What's happening?"

"Your mom's gonna disable his phone so he won't be notified by the security system."

He gripped my arm. "How the hell is she gonna do that? She's a freaking ghost!"

"Angels can mess with electronics and stuff. You know how that freaky light exploded when your dad was about to hit me? That was her."

He glared at me skeptically. "No offense, but why would she do that for you *before* he hit you and not when he *actually* hit me?"

"She hadn't shown up yet," I said quickly. "Dude, you know she would have done that for you if she'd been there sooner."

He shook his head dejectedly. "I doubt it. She's never intervened before. The guy's been kicking me around since I was a kid."

Norah sighed. "Tell him I have helped in every way I was allowed; he just didn't notice."

I passed along the message, and Preston rolled his eyes. I glanced nervously at my watch, and Preston sighed, pinching the bridge of his nose. "Fine, whatever. Let's go before I change my mind." He started marching toward the door, then paused. "Wait, how do we make sure we're out of the house before my dad shows up?"

"Your mom said she'd be our lookout. She'll let us know when your dad's leaving, so we know when to book it out of there. But we should go now. I bet we could even bring Jorge and Liam with us if that makes you feel better."

"No," he said, his face turning red.

I leaned in closer and lowered my voice. "Look, I know it feels embarrassing to admit, but it's okay to need help. Can I ask them to come with us? Please?"

He cupped his forehead in his hand and groaned, but after a sigh, he nodded.

I gently pushed him out of his office before he changed his mind. Jorge was still mopping the tile in the entrance, and Liam was at the cash register with Piper. Joanna had taken my place at the ticket counter, but she and Piper kept shooting each other looks and whispering.

"Jorge, Liam, we need your help," I said.

They both stopped what they were doing and hurried over to me and Preston, who kept glancing nervously out the door.

"We need help packing up some stuff and would feel better if we had some extra people there."

The boys looked sympathetically at Preston and nodded

with determination.

Suddenly, Piper was next to us. "I'm good at packing! And I still have boxes in my car from helping my sister move last week! Can I come too?"

"We can use my truck," Joanna offered.

Preston stared. "What?" I couldn't blame his incredulity. He'd been awful to all of us, but the girls took the worst of it. And here they were volunteering to help him, despite the risk.

"Let's just all go," Liam said. "We don't have any parties scheduled tonight. We can just put a sign on the door that says we're closed for maintenance.

Preston's mouth fell further, and he looked around at us like we were nuts. "What? No. This doesn't make sense. You can't drop everything to help me. What have I ever done to help any of you? Like ever?"

"Nothing," Joanna said bluntly. "You're an asshole. But even assholes need help sometimes."

"Also, your dad's an even bigger . . . butthole than you are," Piper added, "and I don't think anyone deserves to live with that."

"Um, we should probably go now," Liam said, checking his watch. "We're wasting time, and I really don't want to run into that guy again."

"Good point," I said. "*Vamonos*, people! Let's lock up and get out of here."

Preston was still sputtering when we finished turning everything off and locking up. I couldn't blame him. An outpouring of support like this would be hard to comprehend when he was surrounded by people who treated him like trash.

We all piled into Piper's Corolla and Joanna's Tacoma. As we drove off, I felt like I was on another rescue mission with the demon hunters, and felt an out-of-place grin lift the corners of my mouth.

Preston's dad's place was a wannabe White House, complete with Greek columns, a perfectly manicured lawn, and a garage full of cars that probably cost more than my entire life. The inside was even more ridiculous. As we followed Preston down the marble-tiled halls and up the curved staircase, Liam swore in appreciation, and Piper gaped long enough that I had to go back for her and drag her along.

Preston's bedroom was bigger than my dad's family room, which gave me a little relief. I was afraid this was a Harry Potter situation, and he was being kept in a closet or something. But the room was covered in crap, so it was very clearly Preston's. Clothes were strewn across every surface along with random junk. Clearly, their housekeeper didn't even bother going in there.

"Uh, where do we start?" Joanna asked, looking at the overwhelming bedroom of filth.

"Doesn't matter," Preston said, clearing his throat. "Just throw stuff in boxes. I'll sort it out later. We have to hurry."

Most of us took what he said to heart and threw important-looking things in boxes as quickly as possible. Joanna put bags over her hands so she wouldn't have to touch his clothes, unsure if they were dirty or not. Piper, however, couldn't handle the disorganization and quickly folded and sorted things, labeling boxes as we went. Preston hurried in from his attached bathroom with a bunch of toiletries he'd thrown into a backpack.

"How are we doing on time?" he asked me quietly.

I turned away so no one could hear us. "Your mom hasn't shown up yet, so we're good. She said she'd let us know when he leaves."

Preston nodded and went back to throwing things in boxes. "We don't have to take everything."

"Yeah, we're not going to have enough boxes for that," Piper said nervously, looking around at his gargantuan room.

"It's fine," Preston said. "I don't need much. Let's just use up the boxes and leave whatever can't fit."

We were done in less than an hour and were already loading things into Joanna's truck when Norah appeared to tell us that Jerk Dad was on his way home. We didn't take into account that the guy drove like a maniac and arrived sooner than anticipated. We saw his BMW careening down the road toward us as we pulled out of the driveway. Piper, Liam, and Jorge had already left in Piper's car, so at least they were safe, but the guy definitely saw us.

Preston swore. "That's him! Go, go, go!"

Joanna's face took on a look of calm concentration as she narrowed her eyes and sped down the road, clipping a garbage can in the process. I looked out the back window to see if he was following us.

"Uh, guys! He's tailing us!" I said.

"Siri, call 9-1-1," Joanna said as she took a sharp right turn onto a main road.

As her car rang on speaker phone, Preston's dad slammed on the horn. He'd been cut off by a row of cars behind us.

"9-1-1, what is your emergency?"

The man made it onto the main road and was honking and swerving through cars to get to us.

I leaned forward to talk to them so Joanna could focus on driving. "Uh, we're driving, and a crazy, drunk guy is chasing us down Carrington Street. We're heading, uh . . ."

"North," Preston said, nervously looking over his shoulder. "Just passed Corvel Boulevard."

Joanna continued swerving in and out of cars, but we were cutting it close. We were going to get into an accident; I just knew it. A truck she'd just cut off honked at us as Joanna swerved in front of them. I clutched the seat in front of me, my heart trying to beat out of my chest.

"Can you describe the vehicle?"

"Blue sedan," I said, biting my lip and looking behind us. "Don't know the license plate."

"Uh…" Preston hit his head with his palm, trying to jog his memory. "I think it's THEKING? Wait, no, that's the Audi! This one's the BMW, right? Yeah, pretty sure this one says URLOSS."

I raised an eyebrow, and Preston shrugged and held up his hands.

"Can you describe the driver? Do you know why he is chasing you?"

"Middle-aged white male, light brown hair, 47 years old, somewhere around 200 pounds," Preston said. "His name is Charles Weiss, and he's my dad. He, uh, doesn't like that I'm moving out, even though I'm legally an adult."

Several people honked behind us, and I looked back to make sure the guy hadn't caused an accident.

"Do you suspect he has any weapons in the car?"

"No idea," Preston said quietly, as though the thought had just barely occurred to him.

"How many people are in the car with you?"

"Three of us," I said. "We—"

There was a crash, and Preston and I spun around. The BMW had just driven over the sidewalk and down a ravine. We could hear him honking and swearing from half a mile away. Joanna looked back too and had to quickly swerve to avoid a car.

"Watch out!" Preston yelled.

"Sorry!" she squealed, the calm facade finally fading.

Sirens screamed in the distance, and we watched as they quickly caught up to the downed BMW.

"The police have arrived. Please drive to safety. You may hang up now."

We all seemed to let out a breath at the same time. No one spoke until I realized Joanna had no idea where we were going, and I directed her to my dad's house. The tension followed us all the way home.

My dad was waiting outside when we got to his house, and he demanded all the details. His jaw was clenched as he helped us unload Preston's things, and I was too tense to assure Preston at the moment that my dad's anger wasn't directed at him, but at his father. He'd already cleared most of the junk out of Elena's old bedroom, which had been used for storage for years. With everyone's help, we had all of Preston's stuff in Elena's room in about ten minutes. He awkwardly thanked everyone as they left.

After everyone was gone, I pulled my dad aside and gave him the lowdown on the entire situation, and he sighed, immediately calling his attorney to help Preston get a restraining order. He'd never be able to go back home, but I didn't think it had ever been much of a home to him anyway.

HIM

My guardian angel was a no-show when I died. Somehow that didn't surprise me. What did surprise me was that there were no demons there to drag me away. Instead, there was an old woman who somehow looked soft and stern at the same time. An usher, sent by Hermes. She held out her hand and said, "Come with me."

When she told me where we were going and who I was going to see, I panicked. I couldn't go there. I couldn't face him. I put up such a fight that she sighed and said, "All right, son. We won't go straight to him. We'll go to The Waiting Room, where you can wait until you're ready."

Not all angels know about The Waiting Room. Only ushers and those who have gone through that way know of it. The angel—Vivian was her name—led me through a dark hallway with doors as far as you can see. After stopping in front of one of the doors, she said, "This is The Waiting Room. You are here by choice, and you can leave at any time, but there is only one way out. While you are here, you will suffer for what you've done wrong in your life. No one will harm you; the torture will be in your own mind. Each day, the

Big Man will come to your door and ask if you're ready to come with him. He can and will take away your suffering when you are ready to accept him. Now you must decide: do you choose to enter in, or will you wander on your own?" After my frightened nod, she opened the door. 'Enter into your suffering, and emerge when you are ready to accept his help.'"

So, I sat in that dark room alone with my thoughts. I replayed the screams of the twins. My family disowning me. My attempted suicide. The poundings I got in prison. My father beating me over and over. The look of fear and disgust on my teachers when security had to restrain me at school. The many times I'd been fired. The friends who abandoned me. The seizures, headaches, and suicidal thoughts from all the failed medications. The feeling of having a broken mind and a body that did evil things. And over and over I thought of the woman I loved who was murdered by my own hands.

Each day, there came a knock at the door, and a voice asked, "Are you ready to let me in?" Each day, I ignored him. I didn't deserve to leave this place. I deserved Hell.

chapter 15
NEW ASSIGNMENT

I did not think through the implications of Preston staying at my dad's house before he moved in. Like the fact that you could often hear me talking to myself in my room as I met with dead people trying to capture a demon. Or the fact that I was getting kicked out in a few days because my grandpa was moving in, and I was supposed to be dead. I figured I should probably let him know that I would be leaving soon.

I knocked on his door at around nine that first night, about fifteen minutes before our next demon hunter meeting. He opened the door, and I saw that he'd already given the room the Preston treatment. Everything was everywhere, all over the floor.

"I'm just organizing," he said. "It looks worse than it is."

"You do you," I said. "I, uh, need to talk to you real quick."

He glanced at me wearily as he folded a shirt. "I don't want to talk about it."

"No, not about you, it's about me."

He paused in the act of putting a shirt into the bright blue dresser drawer. I was momentarily distracted by the Sharpie scribbles of stars and smiley faces Elena left on it. One of them said "I <3 Nick." Who was Nick? I looked around and smiled as memories flooded back. I'd forgotten Elena was obsessed with the Jonas Brothers. There was still a poster on the wall. And her bedspread was a very ugly purple quilt with nail polish stains. The pink nightstand drawers were open, revealing various beauty products, magazines, and books.

"What?" Preston asked.

"So, I'm gonna be talking to some dead people next door for a little bit for . . . reasons. If it bothers you, just put on headphones."

He just shrugged.

I sat down on his bed. "Also, I forgot to tell you that I'm moving out soon. Will that be weird for you since you don't know my family?"

Preston raised an eyebrow. "It's a little late to say yes to that. I already made a scene and packed up all my crap behind my dad's back. If I go back there, he's gonna kill me."

"Yeah, well, sorry I didn't tell you before. It's just my grandpa's moving in, and he can't see me because . . . things are weird."

Preston stiffened. "Does he hurt you?"

"No! No, he just . . . doesn't like me?" I tried.

He raised his eyebrows, deadpanned.

I sighed. "There's just stuff I can't get into."

Preston rolled his eyes and got back to folding his clothes. "Whatever. Don't tell me then. Just know you're being a total hypocrite."

"Maybe one day I'll tell you about it, but I don't think today's the day. Anyway, good luck unpacking. My dad says you can stay as long as you want."

I hurried from the room before his glare bored a hole in my head.

The demon hunter meeting was the most uncomfortable and depressing meeting we'd had. No one was talking, joking, or debating as I walked into my room. It was dead silent. (No pun intended.) Everyone was on time, and they were all just standing there waiting for me. The effort it took Raj to lift his head and smile looked equal to the effort it took me to do a pull-up. Hint: a lot. I hadn't seen or talked to him since I screamed at him the other day, and I was genuinely too cowardly to face him today, especially when he seemed so depressed. I just silently made my way to my usual spot on my bed, avoiding eye contact.

I expected the meeting to begin right away, but the silence continued. Slowly, I looked up and glanced around at everyone. Not only were they depressed, but there was a sense of paranoia as well. I was wrong. We weren't all there. Someone was missing.

"Fred, have you seen Will lately?" Raj asked finally.

Frederick frowned and shook his head. "The last we spoke was the day of the jailbreak."

A wave of nervousness swept through the demon hunters. Sandra's eyes welled up, Natalie bit her lip, Daisy scowled even harder, and my hands went to my head. Three. We were missing three members. William had never been late to a meeting before, and I had a bad feeling in the pit of my stomach. Poor Raj made a great effort to pull himself together while in front of us.

"I'll investigate William's absence after the meeting," he said in a low voice. "Let's review updates since the last time we met."

No one said anything. Raj frowned and looked around at everyone.

Bill cleared his throat. "We weren't given new assignments after our last meeting."

Raj sighed and shook his head, remembering that he'd spent the entirety of that meeting yelling and pointing fingers. "I understand. I don't expect all of you to have gone on any new assignments, but does anyone have any general updates since we last met? Any discoveries or information to share with the group?"

It was too quiet. I hadn't needed to warn Preston about the noise after all. I hadn't spoken and didn't plan to.

"Unfortunately," Frederick started, "Eurydice, the Supreme Judge of the Red Zone, has pulled out of our agreement."

Raj narrowed his eyes but didn't speak.

"I apologize that I don't have better news," Frederick said.

My heart sank. Was literally everything going to fall apart?

Raj frowned and blinked thoughtfully at the floor. He seemed to make up his mind about something and stood up suddenly. "All right. Enough with updates. I have new assignments for each of you. Jake and Sandra, I want you to scope out the demons you've been befriending, but meet up with them as angels." Their mouths popped open, but before they could protest, he continued. "Don't blow your cover, just see if they're open to talking to angels. You used disguises when you were undercover, right?"

They nodded.

"Good. Make sure they don't recognize you. I want you to see if any of our efforts to sway demons have shifted at all. See if they're at least willing to talk to you about becoming allies. Daisy, you go with them. I don't want them outnumbered."

She nodded, and Raj turned to Natalie. "Natalie, you and Bill will work on recruiting demon hunters. I know it's not as exciting as undercover work, but we're desperately short-handed. Use your creativity. Flyers, public speeches, sign-ups, whatever you can think of. This assignment is just as important as any you've ever had."

Natalie and Bill nodded.

"Frederick, I'm going to partner with you for an assignment I'll share with you after our meeting."

"Yes, sir," Frederick said, tipping his imaginary hat.

"David, you're going to train new recruits."

I flinched and sat up. Had I heard him right? "I'm sorry, what?"

Everyone looked at me.

"Your assignment is to train recruits," he repeated.

"Wait, what? Me?"

I couldn't remember the last time I'd been given an actual assignment, let alone something as nonsensical as this one.

Raj looked at me, almost stone-faced, but I could see a hint of desperation behind his mask. "We need more demon hunters, but with all of our duties and so few angels, we're stretched too thin to train them all. We can't stop our current duties right now, and we need new demon hunters to be prepared to be sent on missions immediately.

"You're the most logical member of our team to train them. All the rest have assignments and other duties. This is something you can do as a mortal. You don't have to be able to create Light and Darkness to teach others how to do it, and you don't need to be an angel to pass on your knowledge of how to go undercover as a demon hunter."

"Wait, I'd be teaching angels how to create Light too?" I asked. "Don't all angels know how to do that already? We—I mean you guys—learn that as soon as you get to The Resting Place."

Raj pursed his lips and looked down. "Well, that's part of the challenge. Some of the recruits will be brand-new angels. We're now recruiting any and all angels who are willing, experienced or not. Most of our new recruits are just off their interview and tour. They don't know anything yet. And I'm sure Natalie and Bill will find a lot more for you to train."

"Wow, you guys must be desperate," I said under my breath.

"You have no idea," Natalie muttered darkly.

"Can you accept this assignment?" he not quite pleaded. "Immediately?"

"Okay," I said with a nervous gulp. "Wait, did you say immediately? For how long? How many people am I teaching?"

"People are dying a lot, so there's a lot of newbies," Jake said in a low voice. "How long did it take to train us?"

"A few months at least," Daisy said.

I slid off the bed to my feet in a panic. I'd turned off my school and work stress during the meeting, but it all flooded back and piled onto this new duty. My voice went up an octave. "Okay, I'm sorry, but I don't have endless free time to take a few months off! I'm not trying to complain or be selfish, but I have school and work and homework and my own family to watch over. Do I need to quit all of that? I mean, I'll drop out of school if I have to, but—"

"Don't drop out of school!" Sandra said, glaring daggers at Raj. I'd been avoiding her gaze, but now I couldn't look away from her. She seemed to glow brighter than the rest. "Like us, David has a very busy schedule, but unlike us, he has to make time to eat and sleep and just live his life." She turned her glare on me. "He's already not getting enough sleep, and he needs to take better care of himself."

Why did my stomach fill with stupid little butterflies to know that she noticed me and was concerned about me? I couldn't help a small smile.

Raj cleared his throat, and I tore my gaze away from Sandra. "She's right. You're alive and have different needs than us. How about an hour each weekday? I know that's a lot, but this is pretty urgent, kid. We're dropping like flies. You could really help us out. Is an hour each weekday doable? Your schedule's a little more rigid than ours, so you can pick the time."

I exhaled and sat down in relief. "Yes. That's doable." Maybe, if I didn't die from the stress. "Can I at least have a week or two to plan before I begin?"

Raj nodded. "One week."

We wrapped up the most uncomfortable meeting of my life, and one by one, they all disappeared. Well, all except Jake, who was on bodyguard duty. I was very grateful for this. I worried how long it would take Malum to discover we had Sheila, his most ardent supporter, in our custody. Would he also find out that I wasn't in the Hurricane, the way we'd tricked him into thinking?

I left my room to find Dad conked out in his recliner, watching the news. All but the kitchen lights were off, and flickers from the TV flashed across his sleeping form. I didn't want to wake him for this, so of course, when I backed up, I ran into the hallway credenza with all the framed family photos. I quickly caught one of the many pictures of Baby Gloria before it hit the outdated pinkish-tan tile.

Dad snorted awake and sat up. "Oh, hey. Did you get some food?"

I sighed as I set the picture down carefully. "Yeah. I'm good."

He rubbed his face and yawned. Approaching warily, I sat on the arm of the couch, wondering how to bring this up.

"Something on your mind?" He muted the TV and gave me his attention.

"I was wondering if I could use the living room on

weeknights for . . . angel stuff? It will probably be really late, so you won't be disturbed. I just need a bigger space than my bedroom." We could use the backyard, but I wanted some privacy from the neighbors who might hear me and think I was crazy.

Dad frowned. "Angel stuff? When are they going to leave you alone and let you live your life?"

I paused and tried to put it delicately. "That's not the point, Dad. I'm not here as like a second chance to live my life however I want. I'm here to fulfill my duties as an angel, I'm just alive while I do it."

He scratched his five o'clock shadow. "What are you going to use the living room for? Meetings?"

"Sort of. I'll be training new recruits. Brand new angels."

"People that just died."

"Pretty much."

He shook his head and frowned. "I'm sorry, son, I don't think it's going to work. You're grandpa's moving in soon, and—"

"Oh crap, I forgot!"

I had a moment of deliberating whether or not I wanted to react maturely, but I was so tired. I groaned and fell back onto the couch with my arm over my head. What was I going to do? I couldn't have demon hunter training meetings at Elena's or Sam's houses. It would be too risky, let alone strange. And it wasn't like I could just rent a study room out in the library or break into a high school gym at night.

Dad stood up and nudged my shoulder with his leg. "Go to bed, son. It can wait 'til morning."

I sighed and rolled off the couch. Dad patted my shoulder and pushed me toward the stairs. I had planned to grab some food and stay up late studying, but my dad's grip was unyielding, and I went up to bed like a good little boy. I was too tired to deal with anymore.

chapter 16
UNCLE RICHARD

Grandpa's impending arrival couldn't be ignored anymore, so I called Elena and begged her to let me stay at her house for a little while. I assured her that I had bodyguards who would fight off all the demons, and one of them was Mom. This mollified her, and she agreed without too much begging on my part. It really was pathetic that, as her older brother, I was begging her for a place to stay. I needed to get my own place. I'd finally started looking for apartments, but I couldn't afford any of them on a part-time Chuck E. Cheese salary. *Freaking impossible rent* . . . Maybe if Preston and I got a place together, we could afford the rent between us. I shuddered at the thought. One thing at a time.

The week passed by way too quickly, and I still hadn't figured out where I'd be training demon hunters. I hoped Grandpa would be leaving after he recovered because Dad's house would be ideal for my situation. The house was big enough to host a huge group of angels, and both he and Preston already knew I saw dead people. I didn't envy Preston the awkward situation of being in the middle of a very unhappy reunion between father and son. Not that he'd be around either of them much. Since he'd moved in, he had spent all of his time in his room.

Grandpa was expected within the hour, so Dad and I said quick goodbyes as he helped me load my bags into the car.

"I'm sorry for dumping Preston on you with all the grandpa stuff going on."

Dad patted my back. "I don't mind housing someone in need. He isn't a problem, and I'm glad you stood up for him."

"Maybe you can come visit Elena's house sometime?" I asked. "I don't want to never see you again just because Grandpa lives with you."

"We'll get together, son. Good luck."

Then he hurried inside, hiding whatever complicated emotions he was feeling.

That night, I was dragged all across Elena's house by the kids trying to show me every toy and play every game they could think of for three seconds before moving on to the next one. Eventually, Elena took pity on me and announced bedtime. The kids agreed to go to bed only if I read them their bedtime story. My heart swelled at the honor. We all squeezed into Ginger's bed, and I read them *Rainbow Fish*, *Chicka Chicka Boom Boom*, and a few silly poems from *Where the Sidewalk Ends*. Rocco eventually conked out, and I carried him to his bed and tucked him in.

It was oddly comforting snuggling into the crappy air mattress in the workout room, hearing Elena and Charlie in the kitchen as they quietly argued and laughed and yawned while locking up the house. A strange pang of loneliness struck me as I lay there listening, and I couldn't figure out why. I was surrounded by loved ones, but somehow I felt alone.

I bolted upright at a loud knock at the door.

"Uncle David! Open up!"

I covered my face and lay back down.

"I'll be out in a minute!" I said through my hands.

The knocking continued.

Elena's voice carried down the hall. "Ginny! Leave him alone! Come eat your toast so we can get you to school! Dad already left to take Rocco to daycare, and the bus left fifteen minutes ago!"

I stared at the slow-moving ceiling fan. I was sleeping on a deflated air mattress in my little sister's house. Embarrassment washed over me. I was in my late twenties. I was almost thirty! Probably. It was frustrating in the extreme that normal people my age were done with school and had actual careers, while I was still a broke college student working at Chuck E. Cheese and living in my sister's workout room.

"I wanna play with David!" Ginger screamed, still outside my door.

Elena groaned, her heeled shoes clopping closer. "He'll be here when we get back!"

"No, he won't!"

I sighed and sat up. I tried to rub the sleep from my eyes as I stumbled to my feet and opened the door. "It's okay, Gin, I'll come ride with you on the way to school."

"No, you won't," Elena said, pulling Ginny's arms through the backpack that looked just about as big as her. "I'm heading to work after."

Ginny whined and stomped her foot. "But I want him to come."

"How about I drive you to school?" I offered.

Elena paused and raised an eyebrow. "You'd do that?"

"Sure. Do you need anything while I'm out? I don't have work until eleven, and I don't feel like doing homework."

Elena ran to the fridge and threw a magnetic notepad at me. "Grab some groceries, will you? I'll Venmo you." She kissed Ginny's forehead and rushed out the garage door.

I knelt down in front of Ginny and smiled. "I'll give you one piece of chocolate from your mom's secret stash if you promise to eat some real breakfast before we go."

She flashed a gap-toothed grin. "Okay!"

I sighed as I pushed the shopping cart down the grocery store aisles and checked Elena's list.

It was weird how, even though physically I was in my late twenties (or early thirties, I wasn't sure), I still felt like an impostor shopping at the grocery store. Like, I wasn't supposed to be old enough to do this alone. This was a task for grown-ups, and part of me didn't feel old enough to be a grown-up. I'd heard that this wasn't an uncommon feeling for adults—they're always surprised at how old they are—but I'm sure a lot of it had to do with me not actually being alive since I was seventeen.

My phone buzzed in my pocket as I came down the pasta aisle. I pulled it out and smiled.

Kiki: ugly baby wants to know when he gets to meet you

I sent her a GIF of Taylor Swift shaking her finger with the caption "NEVER EVER EVER EVER."

Kiki: rude

I tried to decipher Elena's overly loopy handwriting, but I couldn't stop thinking of the fact that Kiki was asking me out again. Or, asking me to ask her out? Either way, she was interested.

Me: If you leave the spawn of Chucky at home I'll take you out to dinner next Thursday.
Kiki: . . .
Kiki: ¯_(ツ)_/¯
Me: Um, what does that mean
Kiki: figure it out

I stopped rolling the cart and sighed, scratching the side of my chin as I considered how to even process this strange woman.

Me: I'm taking you out Thursday.

Kiki: dammit

Kiki: fine

Kiki: xoxo from baby voldemort

I smiled cheesily. She'd made a Harry Potter reference. I shook my head again and put my phone back in my pocket. Then I consulted Elena's list again. I finally deciphered the word "pasta," which was a win, except she'd left no explanation. Did she want spaghetti? Rigatoni? Bowties? Angel hair? As I was deliberating between spaghetti and angel hair, weighing both boxes in my hands as though that would make a difference, someone called my name.

I looked up and froze. The man staring at me gaped in astonishment. His beard was grayer than I remembered, and his face was more wrinkled, like cracked leather left out in the sun. He still looked impressively strong and capable, as he always had. The Rodriguezes had a certain walk—like they knew hardship and weren't about to let anything stand in their way—and my mom and her brother both had it. He wore the same clothes as he always had: cargo shorts, a denim button-up shirt with his name stitched to the front, and chunky yellowish-tan work shoes with socks that went halfway up his calf.

It was Uncle Richard. The man who'd watched me fall to my death. We continued to stare at each other, each of us frozen. I didn't even know he'd moved back to town. He'd paused halfway down the aisle, looking at me like . . . well, like I'd returned from the dead. I had no idea what I was supposed to do in this situation.

Eventually, he shook his head and said, "I'm sorry . . . You look like someone I used to know." His voice brought back memories, but it was too quiet. I'd worked with him outside, so I was used to him shouting. His shout was the last thing I heard before I died.

Lunch break's over, mijo! Get down from that platform.
DAVID!

Don't move! I'm coming, David!

I froze, warring between letting him go and running after him. I didn't want to go through the whole explanation about why I was here, but I also didn't feel like I should pass up the chance to talk to the man who felt responsible for my death. He cried the most at my funeral.

I left my cart by the pasta and ran after him. "Wait!"

He turned around warily. "Can I help you?"

"No," I said, "but I can help you. You thought I was your nephew who died eleven years ago in a construction accident while on your watch. Dorky seventeen-year-old with glasses and self-esteem issues. You called him Baby Blues."

His eyes widened. "How do you—"

"I can see the dead, and they speak to me sometimes. David is here, and he's telling me he has a message for you."

He was too shocked to respond.

"He says . . . It's not your fault. I was supposed to die that day, and if I hadn't died falling from the platform, I would have just died some other way. It was my time to go, and it had nothing to do with you. I never once blamed you. I want you to know that I'm happy where I'm at, and I want you to be happy too. Let go of the guilt you've been carrying and enjoy your life. Me, my mom, and your mom are all watching over you."

Tears sprang from Uncle Richard's eyes. He floundered for something to say, but nothing came out.

I hesitated. "Can I hug you on David's behalf?"

He pulled me in, and we hugged in the middle of the aisle for a good long while. Several people made a U-turn when they reached us, unwilling to get involved in this awkward show of emotion next to the tomato sauce.

Eventually, Uncle Richard pulled away and wiped his eyes. "Is he still here?"

"Yeah."

He looked around and said, "I love you, *mijo*."

"I love you too, *tio*," I whispered.

And then, without another word, he grabbed his cart and moved on, smiling and wiping his face on his sleeve as he hurried away.

I walked back to retrieve my cart and froze again, caught off guard by another surprising and uncomfortable encounter. Raj was waiting for me. He was smiling in his proud mentor/therapist kind of way, like he'd just watched me make a breakthrough.

"Sorry to interrupt, kid. I didn't mean to intrude on your family reunion."

"Uh, it's fine," I said, not meeting his eyes. I hadn't seen him one-on-one since the jailbreak. I still couldn't believe I'd shouted at him and scolded him in front of our whole team. I don't know what came over me.

"Do you want to talk about it?" he asked, gesturing in the direction my uncle had gone.

"How about we save it for a session?" I said awkwardly. "Was there something you needed?"

"We're having a meeting. Are you free?"

I nodded at my feet.

"Good. Finish your shopping and we'll see you soon."

I still hadn't looked up at him.

"David. Look at me."

I could hear he'd come closer. I nervously looked up. He didn't seem angry at all. He seemed like the usual, kind and understanding Rajesh I'd come to know. And his eyes sparkled like they used to. He must have visited the Big Man since I'd last seen him. When I met his gaze, he gave me a sad smile, and I wasn't sure what it meant.

"Raj, I'm so sorry for how I spoke to you. I was so out of line. I don't know what came over me—"

Raj held up his hand, and his face sagged with remorse. "No one was ever in more need of a reprimand than I was at that moment. I let my fear, anger, and remorse take over, and I let the team down. I'm sorry, kid. You were right. Thank you for being brave enough to take a stand."

I shuffled my feet and looked up at him nervously. How did I feel even more uncomfortable than I had before? And also pity, because I could see that doing his job was so much harder without Ying Yue. He was always the support we needed, but she was the driving force. I got the weird sense that Raj never aspired to lead. He was smart and powerful and knew his stuff, but, like me, he was more comfortable following orders than giving them. And then I felt another wave of guilt for feeling uncomfortable with seeing my superior as human. I mean, watching your leader lose it would be uncomfortable for anyone. But why should it? Were they less entitled to their feelings than the rest of us? Shame on me for never once asking Raj how he was doing…

I tried to smile through my guilt. "It happens to the best of us. I reacted the same way when my mom was captured. Is there . . . uh, anything I can do for you, Raj? I can't imagine having to do all of this by yourself."

Raj smiled sadly. "I'm not alone. I know that. But thank you. Imagine I'm patting you on the back in a fatherly way."

I chuckled, and he grinned.

"I'll see you soon," he said. "Jake told me about your living situation, so we'll meet you at your sister's house. It's empty right now." Then he disappeared.

I blew air out through my lips. I had not anticipated such an emotional trip to the grocery store.

HIM

Alone in the Waiting Room, I suffered, punishing myself with my own memories. I ignored the Big Man each day he came to my door, but one day, I was too weak to say no.

Through the door, he asked me if I was ready to come home.

"I don't know where home is," I whispered.

"Will you let me in so I can show you?"

I can't remember anything more difficult than forcing myself to walk to that door and open it. But I couldn't stand this suffering anymore. Somehow, I got the door open, and the first thing he did was put his arms around me. Me. A killer. He held my head to his chest. I told him every awful thing I'd ever done and begged him to punish me.

Rather than cast me out, he pulled away from me and said, "You've been punished enough." I cried harder because the way he looked at me . . . he knew. And he cared. No one else cared for my pain; they all thought I deserved more. But he held me when I cried and said, "I'm not here to punish you. I'm here to make you whole."

After I pulled myself together enough to sit up, he explained why I had been the way that I was. Apparently, there was an incident when I was very young when my father injured me enough to give me brain damage. That, along with the psychological damage from his abuse, created my disorder. The Big Man explained that he knew I never wanted to hurt anyone and that the monster inside me was not the true me, but a manifestation of my ailment. Then he looked at me sternly and said, "But did you do all that you could to find treatment for your condition?"

Ashamed, I admitted that I hadn't. I didn't continue searching for a better option when the medication didn't work. I didn't continue searching for a therapist who would take me after facing a few setbacks. I allowed my father's views to color my actions, even though deep down I knew he was wrong.

"I was wrong," I whispered at the end. We were sitting on the floor, and I pulled my legs close and hid my face. "I'm sorry, I'm so sorry."

"Look at me."

It was so hard to force myself to look at him, but I was done running. When I finally lifted my eyes he said, "I have already forgiven you. It is you who must forgive yourself. I don't expect this today—it will take time—but you do not have to spend that time in here. Are you ready to move on?"

I nodded slowly.

He smiled. "Good. Now it's time for someone else's confession. Come with me."

He took me to his office and had me wait on the bench. Then, minutes after our arrival, there was a knock on the door.

"Come in," he said.

In walked a woman I hadn't seen since I was five. It was my grandma. Apparently, a contributing factor to my struggles in life was that my guardian angel—Grandma Kate—hated me, and never actually did her job, so I was constantly surrounded by demons. Typically, the job of guardian angel would have gone to my father once he died, but he hadn't gone to The Resting Place . . . After watching the kind of person I had become, Grandma Kate gave up on me and didn't even show up to usher me to The Resting Place. She was now on probation. She wasn't kicked out or anything—nothing so drastic as what happened to David— but most of her duties were stripped away. Part of her plan toward earning them back was apologizing to me. It was very awkward for everyone involved, and from her look of disgust, I didn't think she actually meant it.

When she left, as I sat there thinking about how no one loved me, the Big Man turned my head and looked me straight in the eyes. "Enough with those thoughts. I love you. Let that be enough."

I broke down again.

How? How could he love a monster?

The meeting was short. Most of the team wasn't available, so it was just Raj, Sandra, and Bill. The three of us sat around Elena's scuffed-up coffee table. I bounced up the second I sat down, quickly sweeping Ginny's Legos off the couch, then settling in more carefully to avoid being impaled by more toys.

Sandra started off the meeting by sharing that she and Jake still hadn't met up with their assignment yet, and Bill shared how he had been busy passing around a sign-up for demon hunter recruits.

"You could just leave the sign up at the front desk," I told him. "Everyone goes there eventually to turn in their reports. Your sign-up sheet would get a lot more visibility there."

Bill nodded thoughtfully. "Why didn't I think of that?"

Sandra smiled at him. "Maybe because you've never had to turn in guardian angel reports."

I blinked. "What? How do you get out of that one?"

Bill grinned. "My entire family is dead."

Normally, that's not something someone says with a smile,

but Bill, himself, was dead, so it made sense. I wondered who his family was and if I'd ever met any of them. Had Sandra? Surely they would have visited Bill when he was a wanderer. Maybe that was how Sandra knew so much about her wanderers: dead family members who came visiting as angels.

"I don't have anyone to check in on, so I've been doing extra time as an usher and demon hunter," Bill explained.

I wanted to ask Bill about his family, but I didn't feel like this was the moment.

Raj turned to me next. "Have you found a place to teach yet?"

I sighed and shook my head.

"Don't worry," he assured me. "We'll figure it out. Something will open up soon. Moving on to general updates . . . another jailbreak has been attempted."

"What? When?" Sandra demanded. "Why weren't we a part of this?"

Raj sighed. "Moustafa sent another team a couple of days ago. She felt we were missing too many members. William still hasn't turned up."

"How did they get there?" Bill asked. "Don't they need someone who's been to the Hurricane to show the way?"

"Frederick went with them," Raj said somberly.

My heart sank. "And?"

He sighed. "Frederick is fine, but their team was even less successful than we were. They saved two, but lost one, and then quickly abandoned the mission when demons from outside of the Hurricane attacked."

"Do you think they were tipped off?" Sandra asked.

Raj's face hardened, and he nodded. He didn't offer any more information.

Sandra and I shared a worried look.

Raj cleared his throat and looked at each one of us. "Be careful with whom you trust. And if you have updates, make sure they come to me before anyone else. And remember that anyone could disguise themself to look like me, so make sure it actually is me before you say anything."

"How do we know if it's you?" Sandra asked worriedly.

"Well," Raj said, "an impostor would likely be radiating Darkness, for one. But as an extra precaution, ask them something only I would know. I'd give you a passcode, but that's not secure enough. A passcode could leak . . . You'll just have to be creative."

"Why did I tell you I wanted to be a demon hunter?" I asked quietly, suddenly worried about everyone's identity.

Raj smiled. "That you just wanted to do something with your life. But be more creative with your question next time. There were a lot of people that heard you yell that out."

"What was the first thing I asked you when we had a one-on-one check-in?" Sandra asked.

He chuckled. "You asked if you could have an afro as part of your Evil Sandra disguise."

I grinned and tried to imagine it.

"What was my band's name in college?" Bill asked.

"Rabbit in Space," Raj said, then cut us off before we had a chance to laugh. "You guys are doing this wrong. Now everyone here knows the answer to your secret question. Come up with a new one for next time and make sure no one else is around to hear. Anyway, the point is to be overly cautious with what you share with people, even when we meet as a team. Understood? I'll be checking in more with our team members individually as often as possible."

We nodded, and Raj dismissed us.

It was a short meeting that left us a lot to think about. What did he mean by "be careful with whom you trust?" Did he suspect the person who had tipped off the demons about the jailbreak? Was it someone on our side? How was that even possible?

I let out a puff of air and looked down, distracting myself by pulling on a loose thread on the couch. It was definitely possible. We all knew of an angel who turned against everyone. She was currently in prison and still wasn't talking.

It wasn't until 10 PM, as I was digging through my backpack, that I realized I'd forgotten one of my textbooks at Dad's house, and I had a test in that class the next day. All my highlights and notes were in that specific book. I clenched my fists and pursed my lips in frustration, cursing myself for not just going digital like all the kids did these days. I could picture exactly where it was—under a bag of sour cream and onion Lays on the side table next to the couch. I paced back and forth with my hands in my hair in the workout/guest room, thinking of how I was going to bomb this test without another study session tonight. I texted Preston to see if he could bring it to me, but he had his notifications turned off. And Dad would be sleeping by now. The only solution would be to sneak back into the house and grab it, hoping Grandpa wouldn't see me. He was old and probably in bed, right? I let out a long breath and snatched up my keys.

I met Charlie in the hallway as he locked up for the night.

"I left something at my dad's. Just gonna go grab it real quick."

He nodded and yawned. "Go out the garage and shut it behind you. You remember the code?"

"Yep."

I did what he said and hurried across the wet lawn to my car. It was silent but for the sounds of crickets and a couple of cars out on the main road. The flickering streetlight took me back to that night Sandra and I went for a walk, and only one of us returned.

I shook myself from the flashback and hurried to my car. I felt like a thief in the night. Every little sound had my head whipping around in panic. Once I closed the car door behind me, I sighed and leaned my head back on the headrest. "What is wrong with me?"

"There are several possible answers to that question."

I screamed and whipped my head around so fast my neck popped.

"Sorry, sorry!" Sandra said.

I clutched my heart, leaned my head back against the headrest, and tried to remember how to breathe. Then I groaned and leaned my head against the steering wheel. This was getting old.

"I am so sorry! Are you okay?"

After another few breaths, I sat back against my seat again, my heart still trying to pump out of my chest. "What are you doing in my car?"

"I saw you sneaking out, and I was curious. Where are your bodyguards?"

I shrugged. "They're busy. I think Mom's on messenger duty and Jake's being all captain-y and leading his troops on a raid or something. They can't be with me 24/7."

"And what are *you* doing in your car?" she challenged. "Isn't it a little late for a drive?"

I smiled a secret smile to myself. She couldn't have known I'd be in my car right now, which meant she'd tracked me. She'd wanted to see me. Not that that meant anything. Nor did it mean anything that when she tracked me, she ended up RIGHT next to me. The closer an angel is to a person emotionally, the closer they end up physically when they track them down. Again, not that that mattered.

I put the keys in the ignition and started the car. "I left a textbook in my dad's living room, and I have a test tomorrow, so I'm gonna sneak in and grab it."

She was quiet, so I looked over at her at the next stoplight. "What?"

She raised an eyebrow. "You're not very sneaky. You're kind of a clumsy mortal."

"True. But I'm banking on him being asleep because he's old."

She shrugged and raised her eyebrows. "Probably." She turned toward me fully and pulled her feet up next to her. "On a totally unrelated note, do you have any tips on how to crack your little friend? We need information from her. I've tried every tactic I know, but she either just stares at me or starts leaking Darkness, so I have to hop away before it gets on me. She's been resistant to everyone who tries to talk to her. Nothing phases her."

I sighed. "Somehow that doesn't surprise me. Maybe I could talk to her."

Sandra was silent, so I looked over to see her raise an eyebrow.

"What? She likes me."

Sandra rolled her eyes. "Yes, because stalking, attempted murder, and manipulation are signs of affection."

I shrugged. "She had essentially sold her soul to the devil. I don't think she had much choice in the stuff she did to me. And everyone conveniently forgets that she rescued me twice. I really don't think she'd hurt me even if she wasn't under constant guard."

"I think being under constant guard protects her from Malum," Sandra said thoughtfully. "She seems oddly calm. Regardless, how do you think you'd question her while she's in prison? You can't get into The Resting Place."

I tried not to wince at that. "Maybe some of you could bring her to me. You should run it by Raj if you see him."

Sandra just frowned and didn't answer. She *really* didn't like Sheila.

I turned onto my dad's street and parked along the curb. After a pause, I asked, "Do you wanna come in?"

She shrugged. "Someone's gotta watch your back. Can't have you dying while you still have a mission to accomplish."

"What mission? Training demon hunters? I could do that

as a dead person a lot easier."

"No, I mean the bigger picture. You're clearly still needed alive."

I didn't respond. I was doubting that more and more these days . . .

"Hey." She waited for me to look at her before she continued. "I think you need to stop looking for a specific reason why you're here. People are so much more than tools to accomplish one specific task and then be thrown away. There isn't just one reason we exist. It's like you're wanting to know the entire point of being David."

"But I don't know what the point of being David is," I said quietly.

"To be David!" she said with exasperation. "To be you! Everything that you are! You're wonderful, David! You're amazing! You don't have to save the world to have a point. You *are* the point."

I blinked in surprise. It was like she'd just shot me with a ball of Light. I smiled at her. "Thanks, I guess?"

She returned my smile while maintaining her intensity. "Just remember that it's gonna be all right. Somehow, someday, all of this will make sense."

It was hard not to believe her with her deep brown eyes looking at me so earnestly. I blinked and forced myself to look away as I got out of the car. "You can come with me if you want. Just be quiet, all right? I don't want to wake anyone up."

She laughed.

"What did I just say about being quiet?" I demanded.

"Oh, you weren't making a joke? I'm dead, smart one. You're the only one that can hear me."

"Right . . ."

I skulked up the sidewalk leading to the front door. From the shuttered windows on either side, it seemed dark inside. Before I could pull out my key, Sandra flapped her hands at me.

"Wait! Lemme try. I've been practicing this."

She stared intently at the door until the silence was broken by a metallic click, and the door slowly creaked open.

I raised an eyebrow at her. "Creepy."

She just smiled.

I did feel a lot less panicked about this whole situation with Sandra here. What seemed like an impossible covert operation twenty minutes ago now seemed like a simple task. Like someone screaming that they're drowning before realizing the water's only knee-high.

"Where'd you leave it?" Sandra asked in a normal voice.

I pointed right ahead of me at the table next to the armchair. Before grabbing it, I ostentatiously snatched the open bag of chips next to it and popped one in my mouth while glaring at Sandra. It didn't seem that long ago she was eating chips in front of me that I couldn't eat because I was dead.

She rolled her eyes. "I hope they're stale."

I shrugged. They kind of were. With a sense of relief, I hugged my textbook to my chest and—

"Well, look who finally decided to show up!"

I dropped my book and froze, my eyes as wide as saucers.

It was so quiet I could hear my heart beating in my chest. That quiet, rough voice of an old man had not been Sandra's. Nor was it my dad's.

"Yes, I'm talking to you," the voice repeated. "Turn around, son."

I slowly turned around. Grandpa Todd was looking right at me. At least, I was pretty sure this white-haired, stooped old man in plaid pajama pants and a white undershirt was my grandpa. I'd only met him once. I swore under my breath and looked over at Sandra. She cringed.

"Uh . . ."

Before I could stumble through an explanation, Dad threw open his bedroom door and ran down the hallway. He looked back and forth between me and Grandpa. "Okay, I can explain."

"No need to explain," Grandpa said. "I know everything. Your mother's kept me in the loop."

Preston's door opened, and he stuck his head over the second-floor railing, his hair a curly mess. No one else seemed to notice him.

"What?" Dad demanded.

"Your mother," Grandpa said. "She told me David was around. Don't worry, I know the whole story. He was dead, but now he's alive, and he can see dead people. All of it."

Dad's mouth popped open. "My mother? What the heck are you talking about?"

I narrowed my eyes at Grandpa. "Wait . . . Do you see dead people *too*?"

"*What?*" Dad demanded.

Grandpa nodded and looked at Dad. "That's another secret I've kept. It wasn't personal. I didn't tell anyone. Your mother didn't even know until she died."

Dad just stared at him open-mouthed, and I waited for him to blow up at Grandpa. But he just threw his hands up and stormed off, grumbling, "Why can everyone see them but me?"

Sandra, Grandpa, and I looked at each other. Upstairs, Preston shook his head and yawned. There was a thump and a groan, and his door shut behind him.

Grandpa nodded and hobbled away with his cane. "I'm making pancakes."

I blinked and frowned. "Sure. Pancakes. That fixes everything."

chapter 18
PRESTON OVERREACTS AGAIN

It seemed I had a place to teach angels now, at least. I could come back to Dad's and use the living room for lessons. I'd have to explain it to everyone first, though, which I was not looking forward to. I suspected Grandpa would understand, but Preston didn't really grasp all this "other side" business.

Then there was the actual teaching. I couldn't decide if I was more terrified or excited to start training new recruits. I'd never taught anything more important than arts and crafts as a camp counselor, but I did sort of have a plan. I had a short and awkward meeting with Commander Moustafa about best training methods. She wanted to constantly throw new angels at me to train as soon as they died, but I pointed out that it would be hard to train brand-new angels alongside those who had experience. I'd have to back up and teach them the basics, while the slightly more experienced ones wouldn't get as much attention. I could have used them to help me teach the new ones stuff they'd already learned, but it still wouldn't be the best use of their time. So, I came up with a system.

My class would have four levels: Learning Light, Learning

Darkness, Undercover Work, and Combat Practice. I'd meet with each level for two weeks before moving them on to the next level if they were ready. This was WAY too accelerated than was probably possible, but desperate times called for desperate measures. I would meet with each group for thirty minutes each day, adding up to two hours of teaching total. This would happen from ten o'clock to midnight each night. It was late, but it was the only consistent time I was free every day, and I was usually up that late doing homework anyway. I wasn't sure when I would get my homework done, but I'd cross that bridge when I came to it. This schedule was going to kill me, but it was the best I could offer.

Moustafa had pursed her lips in disapproval, unhappy with the fact that brand-new angels might have to wait two weeks if they missed the cut-off for the start of Level One. She also seemed to think that eight weeks total was too long to wait for me to turn fresh recruits into demon hunters. There was, however, a reluctant appreciation for my clearly laid out system with organized units and lesson plans that even Sandra would approve of. This was only possible because I begged Raj for at least a week to prepare myself, and she seemed to think it had paid off.

"I've got to say," Moustafa said when I shared my binder of plans with her. "This is much more organized than I was expecting. Do you mind if I make a copy of your plans?"

Blinking in surprise, I nodded. I wondered how she would do that, since my binder was physical and she wasn't, but she pulled out an angel tablet she'd been holding under her arm and started snapping pictures of each page. How do angels have their own technology? I honestly don't know. How do planes fly? How does electricity work? How does my dad still like the Bee Gees? Some things I will never understand. Regardless, I'd impressed her, which made me feel good about myself for once.

I put off telling Preston about the meetings I was going to have until the night of my first training session. I'd already talked to Dad about using the living room for meetings before Grandpa came, so he was fine with it, and when I told Grandpa about it, he just nodded and said it sounded interesting. Honestly, I was having a hard time understanding Dad's problem with him. He seemed nice. And he made us dinner almost every night. Preston, however . . . I had no idea how this was going to go.

I knocked on his door at 9:30—half an hour before the impending first lesson.

"Come in," Preston said.

I found him lounging on the bed, staring at his phone. The room was still a disaster, covered in clothes and junk, but that was no surprise.

"What?" Preston asked, not looking up from his phone.

"I need to talk to you."

He sighed and set his phone down, then raised his eyebrows at me. I resisted rolling my eyes. His mannerisms were regressing into rudeness. He'd been trying so hard to be nice for so long, and I think the recent drama had sapped him of his energy to put in effort.

Steeling myself, I sat down on the edge of his bed. "You know how I have a weird situation?"

"What, you mean the fact that you claim to commune with the dead?" He flicked at a piece of lint off his sweatpants.

"Yeah . . . There's more to it than that, and I thought I should explain a little more, so you don't think I'm a psycho."

He chuckled and leaned back against the headboard. "That ship has sailed, but okay."

"So, you know how I told you I sometimes have meetings? With angels?"

Preston stopped fiddling with his phone case and looked at me. "And why is it again you have meetings with dead people?"

"Uh, we don't have to get into it right now. It's weird. But I just wanted to warn you, it's going to happen more often. Like on a daily basis, in the living room from ten to twelve each night. Just put on headphones or something so you don't have to hear us. I mean, me. You won't hear them. Just me."

He set his phone down and looked at me like I had just claimed that I was the reincarnation of Elvis Presley. "What could a living person need to meet so often with dead people for?"

I grimaced. "I don't know if I could really explain it all, and I doubt you want to hear it. I was just giving you a heads up."

I got up and headed for the door, but he stood quickly and grabbed my arm. "What are you hiding, man?"

I pulled out of his grip and shrank back at his intense glare.

"I'm not hiding anything. I'm just not sharing everything. You wouldn't believe me anyway."

"Give me a little credit. I am the only person at work who knows about your little secret. And I believe you now. You can tell me."

I was taken aback by how earnest he was. I remembered back to what he'd said before his dad showed up at work. He just wanted to be my friend.

"Tell him your story."

I jumped and turned around. Norah was behind me, standing next to Jake, whom I hadn't seen follow me in.

"Don't do it, mate," Jake said. "It's too weird. Plus, mortals aren't supposed to know about the other side."

"But friends share," Norah argued.

"Ugh, everyone, be quiet!" I said.

Preston sighed. "What am I missing?"

"Your mom says I should tell you my story. My buddy Jake says I shouldn't."

Preston held out his arm. "Well, obviously, do what Mom said. She's a mom. Look, I want to know. And I kind of spilled my life story to you already. Maybe it's your turn." He folded his arms, daring me to be a hypocrite.

He had a point.

I sighed and checked my phone. "Honestly, I only have like twenty minutes until my meeting starts, so how about this: I'll answer three of your questions and we can talk more about it another time?"

Preston shrugged and sat on his bed. "Fine. First question: What could you possibly meet with dead people about when you're not dead?"

I leaned against the dresser. "They're a group of demon hunters. We're trying to track down a demon who escaped his prison, and since I can see dead people, I'm sort of an honorary member. They put me in charge of training new recruits. That's what we'll be doing from ten to twelve each night. Demon hunter lessons."

Preston frowned. "And why would you know anything about how to track down demons?"

Ugh. I did not want to get into this right now. Why did talking about this with Preston make me want to squirm out of my skin?

"He told you some uncomfortable things about his life," Norah reminded me.

"I used to be an angel," I said quietly, looking down at the floor.

Preston laughed. "I get you're nice and all, but I wouldn't call you an *angel*."

"No, I'm not talking about my personality. I was literally an angel."

Preston stared at me, stone-faced. "Are you kidding me?"

I shook my head.

He scowled and tilted his head. "Okay, because it sounds like you're claiming to have been dead . . ."

I bit my lip and nodded. I thought he'd already heard me say this. He was at the top of the stairs when Grandpa was talking about how I was alive again after having died, but maybe we were too quiet for Preston to hear. Or maybe he'd been half asleep and didn't really know what was happening.

Either way, this was obviously the first he'd consciously heard of this.

Preston rolled his eyes and threw his hands up. "What the hell, David? I was preparing for something weird, but this is just . . . stupid! You're clearly alive. How could you have died? Unless it was like one of those miracles where someone's dead for like seven minutes and the doctors revive them. Is it like that? How long were you dead? Allegedly."

I cleared my throat and looked away. "Ten years."

He swatted the air like my idea was a fly. "No. I'm sorry, but you are an absolute lunatic. A nice lunatic, but still, you need help."

"I don't blame you for not believing me," I said quickly. "But I do have proof that I died. One sec."

I ran back to my room and dug out that box of stuff Dad left in my room after I died.

"Told you it was a bad idea," Jake said, following behind me.

"Shut up."

There was a program from my funeral service in it. *Sheesh, they chose the worst possible picture for it. Why did they pick one of me laughing like a dork?* I also took out the yearbook the school sent to my house senior year, when I was already dead. They dedicated a whole page to me because I'd died the summer before senior year, which I guess was worth noting in the yearbook? I wasn't sure why, not that many people knew me, but I guess it's freaky learning that someone your age was gone forever. They had my picture from Junior year and a few other pictures of me with some old friends that I had honestly forgotten about. *Wow, I wonder what Jason's up to?*

I ran back to Preston's room and shoved the yearbook and funeral program in his hands. While he was still frowning at them, I pulled up my old Facebook account that I'd made inactive once I *alived* so none of my coworkers could look me up and see all the sad "RIP, I miss you!" posts from friends and family over the years. I always wondered why people did that. Believe it or not, angels don't have Facebook. But it must be cathartic for the people posting, like a way to process their grief.

"See," I said, showing the Facebook account to Preston.

"Dude, enough!"

He dropped the yearbook and program and knocked my phone out of my hand. Then he stormed out of the room and slammed the door.

"Yeah, that checks out," I muttered.

chapter 19
I PRETEND I'M A TEACHER

I tried to put Preston's reaction out of my mind as I headed downstairs. He'd driven off without explanation, and there was nothing I could do about it now, so I did my best to refocus my brain. Halfway down the staircase, I saw that my living room was already swarming with dead people. My heart was racing just looking at all of the fresh recruits. I felt like I should mingle and get to know them, but I felt too awkward to just go up to them and introduce myself. What if I forgot they were dead and tried to shake their hands? And what had Raj told them about me? They had to be confused by the fact that a mortal was teaching them how to angel. I took a swig from an old water bottle I'd left on the side table next to Dad's chair, trying to clear my dry throat.

I saw a familiar face in the crowd and did a double-take. His glowing, angelic aura split my face into a huge grin.

"Asher! It's good to see you! Uh, are you training to be a demon hunter?" I glanced worriedly over at Raj, who just shrugged. The demon hunters didn't have any age restrictions. If you completed training, you were fully qualified.

"I'm gonna kick their freaking butts," Asher said enthusiastically. "Then I'm gonna get Oliver to cross over and we'll be partners, and we'll kick their butts all the way back to H-E-double-hockey-sticks!" He kicked and punched the air with added sound effects.

"You sure you don't want to be a defender?" I said with a chuckle. "They do more butt kicking."

"I asked, but you have to be an angel for at least a year before they even train you! And then training lasts forever! Whatever. Demon hunters are still pretty cool. At least I won't have some boring job like working at the front desk or something."

I raised an eyebrow and smiled with half my mouth. "Yeah, we wouldn't want that."

Asher giggled. "I think I'd leave if they gave me that job."

I gave him a dry smile and turned back to Raj. He checked his clipboard and counted the angels again. "I think they're all here. Do you want me to stay a little while, or do you want to get started on your own?"

I thought about it. It would be nice to have Raj nearby, but the thought of him observing me with my first class made me nervous. Also, I felt like this was something I had to do on my own. It was my only contribution to the demon hunters, and I knew he had other things he needed to get to.

"I think I've got it. Plus, my mom's here, so I've got at least one experienced angel to help demonstrate." Mom and Jake had switched places right before people started gathering.

Raj smiled at me and pretended to put a hand on my shoulder. "You'll do great, kid. They're learning from one of the best we have." Then he disappeared.

I took a deep breath and looked out at the floating dead people in my living room. Unlike my demon-hunting team, which typically sat on or leaned against things, these angels just floated through everything, completely ignoring the laws of physics. None of them even pretended to touch the ground. That was pretty typical for new angels. There were thirty-five of them, and I couldn't decide if that was more or less than I was expecting. I doubted I was the only demon hunter trainer in The Resting Place, or I assumed the numbers would be higher. Plus, there would be others who would be joining my level two class who had already learned Light.

"All right, let's get started," I said. Unlike one of Sandra's classes, everyone went silent immediately and stared at me. It was weird and awkward. I took another quick drink from my water bottle. "So, you guys have volunteered to be demon hunters. What that means is, it's your job to help us track down Malum by going undercover and gathering information. Your job isn't to capture him, just to find out what you can. You're our intelligence force. That being said, it will be dangerous. If you want to pull out, you can at any time. I would, however, at least stick around until you finish learning how to create Light, since that's training you'll need as an angel, no matter what your job is."

An older lady in the back raised her hand.

"Yeah?" I asked.

"I mean no disrespect, but who are you? Why are we being taught by a mortal? I thought we weren't supposed to reveal ourselves to mortals."

I frowned, considering what to tell them. They didn't need to know all the gritty details, but they did deserve something. Also, I realized they needed reassurance that I actually knew what I was talking about. For all they knew, they were dumped into the class taught by the weird mortal because they were the dumb ones. While I had little confidence in myself, I had to acknowledge, at least compared to them, that I did know quite a bit about demon hunting. I mean, I was one of the first demon hunters that passed the initial tryouts. Also, I'd actually faced Malum on more than one occasion. I wasn't the best, but I wasn't the worst choice as a demon hunter trainer.

I sat against the arm of the couch. "Yeah, I should probably introduce myself. My name is David Garcia, and I'm a mortal medium, or mediator, whatever you want to call it. That means I can see you whether you reveal yourselves to me or not. I'm also a demon hunter. I know all about the other side and how to create Light and Darkness and all the demon-hunting skills I'm going to teach you."

"How?" someone asked. I looked around and finally spotted a tall guy with dreadlocks. "Can you make Light as a mortal? How could you know how to do it if you've never done it yourself?"

I sighed. "That's a valid question. I have a really strange history. We don't have the time to get into it, but believe it or not, I was an angel for about ten years. I'm just on a mission right now that requires me to have a body. And no, that doesn't *ever* happen, so don't think that might happen to you. I'm a . . . special case." Hopefully, that was the right amount of truth. It sounded completely insane to my own ears, but I always think I sound like an idiot, so I'm not the best gauge. There was a lot of murmuring and looks at me like I was nuts.

"The point is, I know what I'm talking about," I said. "When I was an angel, I was a trained demon hunter with real experience out in the field. Back when I joined, you had to do an interview and try out, and I passed both. You can pull out at any time, but I promise I'll help to train you up so that you'll be ready by the time I'm done with you."

I hoped, anyway. I knew that if anything happened to any of them, it would be my fault for not preparing them. Gosh, was that how Raj and Ying Yue felt every time I screwed up? Did they blame themselves?

There was total silence. I looked around at all the frightened eyes of the various newly dead people. They all seemed so . . . overwhelmed. Some of their eyes were shining like they were trying not to cry. These poor people had just gone through the trauma of dying and were suddenly thrust into this strange world of angels and demons. I sighed. This wasn't right. How could we just throw them into this terrifying job when they're still adjusting to the idea that they were dead? I could see them trying to look brave, trying to hide their pain and fear, and I saw myself in them.

I remembered that feeling of struggling to adjust but feeling like I couldn't say anything. Nobody in The Resting Place talks about the adjustment. Everyone just smiles and pushes you along, and eventually you come to realize that The Resting Place isn't so bad. It's actually amazing. But it's a hard transition. And the sad thing is, most angels are too ashamed to admit it.

I sat in my dad's armchair and leaned forward on my knees. "Okay, what's the best and worst part of being dead?"

The newbie angels frowned and looked at each other. This wasn't what they were expecting.

"Go on. Anyone. I bet no one has asked you how you're feeling about all of this, have they? Well, here's your chance. The best and worst part of being dead. Just shout it out."

It was quiet for a minute, but then a few tentative voices called out.

"Flying."

"Watching my mom cry."

"Not being sick anymore."

"Not getting to marry my fiancé."

"I don't have to pee anymore."

We all looked at the small lady in the front. She just shrugged. "It was a waste of time."

"What about you?" asked a man in the front. He looked like he was in his fifties, with a balding head and dark brown eyes.

"Me?" I asked.

"Yeah. You said you were dead once. What was the best and worst part for you?"

I hesitated, then nodded. I felt like they needed honesty, even if it brought out similar feelings in them. "The worst part was feeling like I ruined my family's lives. It took a long time until they seemed to be happy again, and I hated the feeling that I had caused that."

They all looked down quietly, knowing the feeling.

Sensing they needed a little hope, I added, "But the best part was being able to help them in a way that only angels can. I was able to be with them anytime they needed me. Even when they were too upset for company, I could be with them and comfort them. I was even more a part of their lives than when I was living because I knew everything that was going on. I was the ultimate stalker, but in a good way. Also, I'm realizing now, as a mortal, that I was way less clumsy when I was dead. Stubbed toes are the worst!"

Several of them chuckled, realizing they would never stub their toes again.

I stood up. "Okay, I think it's time we get started. I only get you guys for twenty more minutes before my Level Two class. I need you guys to focus up and try your best, all right? This is a super accelerated program, and I need you on your game." There were more than a few determined nods. I started directing them into rows and columns and had them float at different levels to mimic stadium seating so they could all see me. It was pretty creepy to see them all floating like that, staring at me.

"We're going to start by making Light. Don't worry if you can't do it at first. It might take a while to learn, but you'll all get it eventually. I once even saw a wanderer make Light." This surprised some of them, but I saw a few mouth, "Wanderer?" in confusion. They were so new that some of them didn't even know what wanderers were. Good grief.

"Oh, Mom! Stand in the front so you can demonstrate for me." I'd almost forgotten she was there. Mom smiled and stood next to me. "You guys can watch Gloria, okay? She's been doing this for a while." Mom calmly obliged and created a ball of light in each hand. There were murmurs of appreciation and surprise from the crowd.

I smiled at them. "You'll be doing that too in no time. So, listen carefully: hold your hand out in front of you—no, it doesn't matter which hand. Now close your eyes. I know it feels silly, but it helps." I waited until their eyes were closed and started speaking more slowly. "I want you to think about what gives you hope. Light is hope. Now think about your interview with the Big Man when you came to The Resting Place. He is where your Light comes from. He is more than happy to share his Light with you. Remember that. He wants you to spread his Light around."

Some hands were already glowing slightly! Holy crap, we were doing it!

I forced myself to remain calm. "Keep your eyes closed. It's easier if you aren't staring at your empty palm. Now I want you to will all those feelings of hope into your hand."

To my delight, about a third of the class already had a flickering little ball of Light in their hands.

"Open your eyes."

There were excited gasps as people showed those around them the little balls of Light they were holding like precious baby chicks. The rest of them frowned at their palms, looking dejected and frustrated. "Don't worry," I said. "I couldn't make it at first either." We went through the exercise again, and a lot of them were still unsuccessful. We didn't have the time for me to go around to each individual struggling student and coach them through, so I decided to try something different.

"Okay, those of you who have some Light, I want you to give it to someone who doesn't have any. Let them feel what it feels like. Now, those of you who have just been given someone else's Light, focus on the feeling, and try to make it bigger."

Several of them gasped in delight as their borrowed Light grew brighter. *Wow, that actually worked!*

"Nice work! Okay, I'm gonna call one row at a time to come join me at the front so I can see how you're doing. We'll switch rows until I've seen all of you. Mom, do you mind going around and helping people out? And uh, you there. What's your name? You seem like you've got the concept."

A little mousy girl with buck teeth pointed at herself. "Me?"

"Yeah."

"I'm Sarah," she said happily.

"Let's see what you got."

Both her hands lit up with balls of Light, and she smiled.

"Okay, wow! Yeah, you got it! You go around and help others too."

"Sure thing!"

I won't say it was the longest thirty minutes of my life, but it was definitely up there. I felt self-conscious and inadequate, but I hope I hid it well. They listened to me at least. And by the end of class, about two-thirds of them had succeeded in making some form of Light, even if it did flicker and go out eventually. Honestly, that was better than I'd hoped for after only twenty minutes of practice.

At 10:28, I cleared my throat to get everyone's attention. "Okay, we're going to wrap up now. You guys did great! We'll meet back here at the same time tomorrow, but I want you to keep practicing between now and then, all right? If you need help, you can ask literally anyone in The Resting Place. I promise that you will all get it. Okay, that's it. You're free to go."

One by one, they disappeared. Asher, by way of farewell, threw a ball of Light right at my face and grinned. "Take that, demons!" He spun around, kicked the air, and then disappeared. The kid was pretty impressive. Who knew he had all that inside him when he was wandering around, staring at nothing? It made me think about all the other wanderers who were still trapped in their minds. They were all so much more than they appeared.

The Level Two class was smaller, only about ten angels, and honestly, I don't remember most of it. I was so tired at that point that everything was a blur. I did appreciate that I didn't have to spend as long explaining myself at the beginning. The Level Two class wasn't newbie angels, and they'd already heard of me and my history. I wasn't sure if that was a good thing or a bad thing. For all I knew, I was a cautionary tale that angels told the newbies about why we should *always* listen to Hermes, or bad things will happen.

I didn't teach them Darkness yet. Memories of how my task force and I were affected by jumping right in made me cautious. I kept seeing Jake telling me I was useless and refusing to back me up. I kept remembering how hopeless and lost I felt and how I almost lost my ability to create Light. Despite the pressure to train them quickly, I wasn't going to make the mistake of turning all these angels into depressed and hopeless creatures. This had to be done carefully. So, I spent the entire time explaining the concept of Darkness and answering questions. It was kind of more of a Q&A session than an actual class, but I was okay with that. The more information they had, the better.

Preston stormed in halfway through my explanation of the effects Darkness can have on a person. I froze and eyed him warily.

"Uh, hey," I said awkwardly.

"Am I to believe there's a bunch of dead people in here and you're teaching them angel crap?"

"Yep."

Preston rolled his eyes and walked away. "Psycho."

A lot of the angels paused to watch the interaction, and one very strong-willed teenage boy frowned at Preston. "I don't like the way he's talking to you." He followed Preston as he walked toward the stairs, causing every light Preston passed to flicker and the frames on the walls to shake.

"Hey, no haunting, Leo!" I scolded.

Preston looked nervously around and ran up the stairs. "Get away from me," he yelled as he slammed his door.

I raised an eyebrow at Leo when he turned around. "Dude,

not cool."

Leo shrugged. "What, he can dish it, but he can't take it?"

I raised both eyebrows, and he rolled his eyes, returning to the barstool he'd been sitting on, and got back to spinning around in boredom.

For the first day, I think it went all right. I survived and at least got some of the newbies to make Light. But the second the last person disappeared, I flopped on the couch, thinking as I fell asleep that I'd give anything for a boring front desk job now.

HIM

I know our relationship wasn't perfect. Even without my dangerous condition, we struggled as a couple. She'd argue, and I'd make passive-aggressive comments. Sometimes she'd mimic me in a way that was so infuriating, I wanted to break things. The real me, not the monster me, and that's saying something. And sometimes I was so mopey, she would leave the house because she couldn't stand being near me. We weren't perfect, and I know that. But we held on. We kept trying through all the joy and all the pain. We fought for us, and we almost made it.

When I saw her the first time after I died, I wasn't thinking about the struggles. I was so ridiculously happy. Foolishly happy. I'd missed her so much. I missed her arms around me. I missed her laugh. I missed the way she'd scoop up our girls in her arms and fall onto the couch with them, laughing and giggling as they rolled onto the floor. The way she would dance as she cooked. Even the annoying way she'd throw wadded-up paper towels at my head when I wasn't looking. I missed her fierce compassion. The way she would stick up for anyone mistreated. The way she would say and do whatever had to be done. And despite her ferocity, she was kind. She knew when to tell me to get over it and when to snuggle up to me on the couch and just sit with me in my pain.

I'd spent so many years mourning her that the first time I saw her, my spirit lifted. For just a second, I forgot that I was the reason she was here. I wanted to run to her and spin her around in my arms and kiss her.

But the moment I saw her face, I knew it would never be like that again. I'd hurt her in the worst way possible, and it was very clear that she hadn't forgiven me. Her shaking hands clenched into fists. She looked like she wanted to murder me. I was afraid of her. It was like she was a completely different person.

Oh, the irony. Was this how she'd felt every time I had an episode? Seeing the person she loved turn into something dark and evil? It was horrifying. I had no idea why she stayed with me for as long as she did.

chapter 20
DEMON THERAPY

After a grueling day of school and work, as well as stress over the huge task of teaching demon hunters, I was relieved that I had another therapy session today with Dr. Asan (aka Raj). Well, I sort of looked forward to it. Therapy wasn't necessarily comfortable, but it was comforting, if that makes any sense. I had a safe space, and it felt good that I was getting myself together.

Throughout the session, Raj kept asking me questions about Sheila and digging into our relationship, which wasn't his typical style. Usually, we just talked about whatever was bothering me.

"And how did she gain Malum's trust?" he asked, leaning forward. "She must have told you."

I frowned and blinked. Something was off. Raj and I never discussed demon hunting business during sessions unless it was something that directly related to how I felt. A creepy prickling inside made me pause before answering.

I opened my mouth and hesitated. Then, cautiously, I said, "Raj, remind me what we talked about last time we met."

He frowned and looked down at his notes. "Well, we discussed the things that were bringing you down. Would you like to talk more about that?"

I frowned. "Who was it that I said I was so concerned about? Do you remember?"

He considered for longer than was necessary. "You were concerned about your angel friends and the stress they are under, as well as your family."

I bit my lip and tried to keep my heart rate from spiking. "Yeah, but who specifically did we talk the most about? You know how insecure I am; I just like reassurance you were listening."

His face hardened for a moment before he pasted on a compassionate smile. "We talked about the young man who lives with you now. Preston. And how your life has changed since he moved in."

WRONG. We'd talked about Kiki and how I felt guilty for liking her because a part of me was still hung up on Sandra.

I tried to force myself to breathe normally. Raj never forgets what we talk about. Never. But before I jumped to conclusions, I thought I should make absolutely sure.

"Right, we talked about how Preston living with me made things weird at work. What did you tell me about asking him for a promotion while he's living at my house? Did we decide that was unethical?"

He smiled. "As you remember, I told you to do what feels right."

That was something Raj would say. But I'd never even considered asking Preston for a promotion, let alone discussed it in therapy. And if this was the real Raj, he would have known that.

Calm down, calm down, calm down.

I could not freak out right now. The only way for me to salvage this situation would be if I were to get some information from whoever this impostor was. But the fact that he could impersonate Raj so well and radiate Light scared the crap out of me. Because if someone was trying to get information out of me through subterfuge, it wasn't an angel. This was a demon that had found a way to radiate Light. But that was impossible! If even I had a hard time making Light as an angel surrounded in Darkness, there was no way a demon could do it. You have to have good intentions! It's the Big Man's power! He doesn't share it with anyone who wouldn't use it for good. Maybe there could be a good demon that was able to make Light? But if they were good, why would they be secretly getting information out of me? Even more concerning, who else would know about the fact that I meet with Raj for therapy than someone close to me?

I wiped my sweaty palms on my thighs. *Calm down, calm down, calm down . . . don't tip them off you're on to them . . .*

How could I get information out of them without them knowing? I had to make good use of this time! After some quick thought, I decided to act scared about something and milk it. The impostor would know that Raj would try to comfort me by giving me answers, and the answers would have to be as correct as possible, because Raj knew quite a bit. They'd know I would see the crack in their facade if they couldn't answer something Raj would know.

"I'm kinda freaking out about what's going on," I said as evenly as possible. I let some of my nerves through on purpose, though. The real me wasn't made of stone. "Can we talk about it?"

He frowned in sympathy. "Of course. What's concerning you?"

"Well . . . to be honest, I think there's a mole in The Resting Place."

He froze.

"I know it can't be anyone on our team!" I said quickly. "But if there was a mole, how would they be able to get into The Resting Place?"

"They couldn't," he said slowly. "It's impossible to enter The Resting Place unless you have good intentions."

"What does that even mean?" I asked. "There were times I had bad intentions as an angel. I've been angry and rude before. How could I still get in?"

He shook his head. "Occasional rudeness, or selfishness, or simply making mistakes are just part of being human. Those aren't acts of evil. A person would have to consciously and continuously try to cause harm to others and refuse to change to be refused entry."

"Except for me . . ." I said slowly.

"You are a special case. The only thing keeping you from The Resting Place is the fact that you're alive. Were you to die, I have no doubt you'd return there immediately."

I nodded slowly. "And if an angel committed an act of evil, and wasn't sorry about it, would that person still be considered an angel?"

"Technically, no. Their act of evil would violate their contract, and their unwillingness to change would impede their ability to return to The Resting Place. I don't say it would be impossible for them to return, but they would have to truly repent of their ways. Besides, anyone who did something heinous enough to be exiled from The Resting Place wouldn't want to be an angel anymore. Take Sheila, for example."

I nodded. This demon was good at acting repulsed by the idea of working against the angels. If I didn't know Raj so well, this impostor might have fooled me. But even if they hadn't slipped earlier, I'd be able to tell by now that this wasn't Raj just by how he was speaking. He hadn't called me "kid" once.

I had to keep grilling them, because they knew Raj would do his best to explain something I was concerned about. Taking a deep breath, I leaned forward, carefully phrasing my words so they wouldn't be tipped off that I knew they were an impostor. "And how do I know if someone is an angel or a demon?"

"Their aura, of course. If someone is radiating Light, you can have complete confidence they are on your side."

I bit my lip, allowing myself to look nervous and scared. I hoped this quick lie wouldn't give me away. "But yesterday, when Jake was guarding me, an angel appeared. At least, we thought she was an angel—she was radiating Light. But then she attacked me. And when Jake threw Light at her, she screamed as if it hurt her, and the Light melted away. It turned out she was a demon after all. So, explain that. How could a demon like that radiate Light? And don't claim that she must have been an undercover demon hunter. When Jake tied her up in ropes of Light, it hurt her. Angels aren't hurt by Light. Just to be sure, Jake took her to the border of The Resting Place and told her to go through herself, and she couldn't."

I bit my lip. Would he believe this story I'd made up on the spot? It was the only way I could think of to get this possible demon to admit how they could make Light.

Raj gulped and licked his lips. "That is concerning."

"So, how was that possible? How could a demon radiate Light?"

"It wasn't Light," he whispered. "She must have disguised her Darkness to look like Light."

Inside, I was reeling, but I forced myself to scoff. "That's ridiculous." I hoped arguing with him would make him react like any other person, which is to prove your point to those who doubt you.

"It may seem ridiculous, but it's very possible. This is Light I'm radiating, correct?"

No, I thought, but I nodded.

Slowly, his Light started to change colors. It went from yellowish white to bluish white to bright cerulean blue to dark neon blue that was hard to focus on. My eyes bugged out of my head. Raj was radiating blue Light! What the crap! His blue Light slowly turned black, and then he reversed the color change progression until he was radiating Light again.

Okay, this was freaking terrifying. Demons could change the color of their Darkness, which meant they could make their Darkness look like Light. I could think of only one way to be sure if someone was a *real* angel. I was hesitant to use it on this impostor, though. Should I tip him off or let him think I was fooled so I could ask him more questions next time?

Hermes? What should I do? I don't want to blow this if it's possible that I could get more information out of him.

PROTECT YOURSELF. TRY YOUR TEST. YOUR SESSION IS ALMOST THROUGH, AND THIS DEMON IS UNLIKELY TO TRY THIS TACTIC AGAIN. ADDITIONALLY, IF YOU REVEAL THAT YOU HAVE CAUGHT HIM IN HIS LIES, HE WILL BE WARY OF YOU AND BE LESS LIKELY TO TRY TO FOOL YOU AGAIN.

Can you tell me who it is?

NO.

And why not?

I DON'T KNOW WHO THEY ARE. I CAN ONLY SENSE BEINGS OF LIGHT. I AM SORRY.

Fine. But where is Raj? Is he okay? Can you send him over here?

HE WILL BE ALL RIGHT. I WILL SEND HIM TO YOU AS SOON AS HE IS AVAILABLE. CONTINUE WITH YOUR INTERROGATION. YOU ARE DOING WELL.

I tried not to beam from the unexpected praise. I forced my nerves away and sat up straight, allowing my face to harden as I looked at Fake Raj. "Throw a ball of Light at me."

He startled and blinked. "I'm sorry?"

"Throw a ball of Light at me. If you're an angel, you can make Light, right? Well, mortals can feel Light too, even if it isn't physical for us. Prove to me you're the man you say you are. Throw some Light at me. I'll be able to tell if it's real or not."

He frowned down at his hand and formed a ball of pure

white Light. Was it just me, or was it . . . smoking? It was subtle, but there was a faint gray steam coming off it like it was burning. Was that the Darkness coming through? He took a deep breath, looked me in the eye, and threw it right at my face. The second before it hit me, while it was still sailing through the air, it changed color. A ball of Darkness hit me in the face and filled me with fear. By the time I looked back to where Fake Raj was sitting, he'd disappeared.

chapter 21
TOO MANY PEOPLE IN MY ROOM

I groaned loudly and fell back on my bed with my arm over my head. Why was everything so messed up? I couldn't even have a freaking therapy session without it getting hijacked by a demon! Why couldn't I—

A knock at my door startled me, and I sat up quickly. "What?"

"Uh, it's me! You begged me earlier to help you with your average-sized brain?"

I jumped to my feet with a squeak. Kiki. I'd completely forgotten that during class today I'd invited her over to study together. Dad must have let her up. I was so caught up in my conversation with Fake Raj, I hadn't even heard the doorbell. I hurried over to the door and threw it open. There she stood with her hair in pigtails and a striped crop top, looking like a tween from an early 2000s magazine.

"Whoa," she said. "You look crazy. Did you eat one of those brownies Val was passing around after class? I didn't think you were that stupid. Unless you knew what was in it. In that case, go for it!"

I shook my head quickly. "No, I just, you startled me. I was . . . uh . . . napping."

She raised her eyebrows. "You forgot, didn't you?"

I sighed and rubbed the back of my neck. "Uh . . . yeah, I did. But I do still want to study!"

I hurried back into my room and tried to straighten up as quickly as possible, throwing my shoes and a couple of shirts in the closet and straightening the comforter on my bed. She came in and plopped right in the middle of the bed, clutching her backpack to her chest.

"Okay, let's just clarify something really quick. When you said you wanted to study, did you mean study, or *study*? I mean, I'm good either way, but if you meant *study*, I might need a mint first because I'm not gonna lie, I just ate some onion rings and—"

My eyes widened, and I hurried to shut the door, not wanting to give any of the guys in the house something to talk about. "I meant, like, study what we're learning in class? Sorry, I'm not sure I'm ready to go *there* yet." Crap, I hadn't thought this through. Did everyone assume that studying meant making out? Or . . . more?

She sighed in obvious relief. "Good, because I spent way too long on these super cute flashcards, and I would have cursed you with a thousand paper cuts if you didn't give me the chance to show them off. I mean, look at them!" She dug a Ziploc bag out of her backpack and shoved it in my face.

I smiled and unzipped it, pulling out multicolored flashcards with loopy handwriting, hand-drawn diagrams, and weird little doodles decorating the edges. One had a little monster eating the corner of the page.

"Nice," I said with a smile.

She rolled her eyes. "Obviously." Randomly switching to a Cockney accent, she said, "All right, then. Sit down, you! We've got lots to cover."

Still smiling, I pulled my notes and textbooks from my nightstand and laid them in front of us on the bed. "So, I was thinking—"

"Oh, uh, I'm sorry. Didn't mean to interrupt."

I jumped and dropped my stack of notes. Raj was looking worried in front of my door. I went from annoyed to relieved to frightened to self-conscious in the span of thirty seconds. I bit my lip and looked from Kiki to Raj. I knew I should figure out where Raj had been and tell him about the impostor, assuming this was the real Raj, but the last time I'd hung out with Kiki, I ditched her, and I didn't want to do that to her again. Kiki narrowed her eyes at me.

I quickly grabbed my phone to pretend I had just gotten a call when none other than Mom showed up, right next to my bed.

"Ooh, do you have a date?" She clapped. "Good for you! Way to get back out there! But I do think you should keep the door open."

I jumped again, and by the time she'd finished talking, I involuntarily sighed loudly up at the ceiling. This could not be happening!

"Do you have a screw loose?" Kiki asked. "Do you need me to call your robot doctor?"

"No, I just—"

"I'm sorry, kid," Raj interrupted, "but I really think we should talk."

"It's not a great time at the moment," I muttered. "If you had been here earlier when you were supposed to—"

"I was a little busy, kid. If you step into the hall with me, I'll explain."

"What do you mean it's not a great time?" Kiki demanded. "This is the time you said, weirdo!"

"No, not you!" I said quickly. "I mean—Ugh, I don't know what I mean. Can you give me a second?"

I snatched up my phone and slid off the bed to my feet.

She got to her feet on the other side of the bed. "Are you gonna leave again? Dude, if you don't want to see me, maybe you should stop asking me out."

"Oh, dear . . ." Mom said. "You should fix this before she walks out."

"David," Raj said with forced patience. "I'm sorry, but we really need to talk."

Tracking my eyes, Kiki looked in the directions of Raj and Mom and bit her lip nervously. "Okay, weirdo, are you . . . talking to people?"

I repressed a groan as I fell back against my armchair. This was it. She was going to realize that I was totally crazy and run away, and there went my first chance to have a normal relationship with a normal girl.

In a last-ditch effort to salvage the situation, I picked up my phone again. "Kiki . . . I can't explain right now, but I need to answer this call right and—"

"Shut up. No one's calling you. I can see your home

screen, stupid."

"There's no need for name-calling," Mom chided.

I wilted. "I—"

"A man and a woman, right?" She had blurted it out and now bit her lip nervously.

I blinked, startled. "What?"

"There's a man and a woman. The man was the same one who interrupted us last time. I think."

My eyes bugged out of my face.

"Just say it straight, or I'm leaving now, and my earlier threat of a thousand papercuts from my freaking cute flashcards is back in effect!"

"Can you see the dead?" I asked quietly.

"Um . . ." Now Kiki was the one I wanted to demand to say it straight. "Not exactly? I don't know! I just sometimes sort of sense things? But I don't know if it's real, and I just thought that you might also sense something because you were looking in the direction of the two auras I was sort of getting a vibe from and—"

I giggled. "Oh my gosh, you're crazy too!"

Mom gasped. "There's a twist!" She raised an eyebrow and put her hands on her hips. "Son, I think you might have a type."

I rolled my eyes at Mom. "Can you not, right now?"

Kiki scowled at me. "Excuse me?"

"No, no, I wasn't talking to you! And you're not crazy, you're right. There's a man and a woman in here, and the man is the same one who interrupted us last time. That is so cool that you can sense people! What kinda vibe are you getting from them?"

She folded her arms nervously. "Well . . . If I'm not totally bonkers and making all this up, the dude is like exploding from all kinds of emotions. He's frustrated and worried and ashamed and also a little intrigued and seems to be assessing *me* now like he might want to use me for something—"

"No!" I said so loudly that everyone jumped. "You leave her out of this, Raj!" My heart was pounding thinking about what happened to the last girl I liked that got all caught up in this stuff.

Raj held his hands up in a placating gesture.

"And the lady is, like, super obsessed with you," Kiki continued as though I hadn't spoken. She frowned, tilted her head, and blinked. Then her face softened. "Is she your mom?"

Mine wasn't the only mouth that popped open. Maybe she couldn't see the dead, but she could sense their emotions and intentions! I didn't know anyone who could do that, including other angels.

Self-consciously, she clutched her arms. "Or maybe I'm really off and you were totally joking, and I've just made a fool of myself."

I shook my head and sat back down on the bed. "Kiki, that was incredible. Seriously, you were spot on."

She beamed and sat next to me on the bed, crushing my notes underneath her.

Raj cleared his throat.

I sighed. "Right. One sec." I forced myself to look away from Kiki and over at Raj. "Okay, well, now that the cat's out of the bag, what's up?"

"You want to talk in front of her?" he said with raised eyebrows.

I shrugged. "She already knows I'm crazy."

Raj frowned. "This is confidential stuff, David. Remember what I said. We need to be careful with what information we share with people."

He had a point. I doubted Kiki would or could betray us, but I still barely knew her. I nodded and slid to my feet.

"I promise I will come back this time," I told Kiki, "But I need to have a quick, private conversation with Raj."

She shrugged. "Fine. The dude's, like, super paranoid, so I wouldn't expect him to trust some rando lady freak."

I grinned, "You're not a rando lady freak, but I promise, I'll be right back!"

I hurried out the door and took Raj into Sam's old room, which was full of storage boxes.

Before I'd shut the door, he was saying, "I'm so sorry I missed our session, kid."

"Lemme guess," I said. "You were attacked by demons."

He frowned. "How did you know that?"

All my earlier feelings of freaking out rushed back at me.

"Because *someone* didn't want you to show up today and had some friends attack you to keep you occupied. Are you all right? A fight that lasted that long must have been brutal."

He sighed. "I won't lie; it was pretty brutal. They managed to wrestle me down to the edge of the Hurricane, but their grip slipped for a second, and I teleported out before they had the chance to throw me in."

"Oh my gosh, Raj! Are you sure you're okay?"

"I'm completely unscathed," he reassured me.

I sat down on a box. How could I have handled it if Raj had been captured too? I frowned suddenly, my heart skipping a beat. What if he *was* captured, and this was another impostor? Could Raj be wasting away in the Hurricane with Ying Yue, Ted, and William? How many more of my friends would they take?

"Throw a ball of Light at me," I said suddenly.

"What?"

"Just do it, please!"

A look of compassion came across his face. "You know the happiness is only temporary, kid. Once it wears off, your true feelings will just come right back—"

"This isn't about my feelings! I'm being serious! Just trust me and do it!"

He blinked in surprise but quickly threw a ball the size of a ping pong at my chest and filled me with hope. I was so relieved that I leaned back on the stack of boxes behind me and let out a loud breath. Then I grunted and sat up again. The corners of the boxes were not comfortable.

Raj looked at me like he thought I was off my rocker. "What's this about, David?"

I sat up. "Well, Raj, I didn't actually know you'd missed our session until about halfway through it."

He gave me a bemused scowl, which slowly melted into a look of horror. "An impostor?"

No one could deny that Raj was always quick on the uptake. I nodded, and he quickly sat down on a box next to me. "Are you okay? Did they hurt you?"

I leaned back on my hands. "I'm fine. I actually think I got more out of them than they got out of me, to be honest."

Raj flashed a quick grin. "Of course you did. Tell me everything."

I proceeded to tell him about our interaction and the things the impostor said and did that tipped me off.

By the time I got to the part of him showing me that Darkness can be disguised as Light, Raj's face had turned pale. "That is very concerning."

"That is an understatement," I said, mimicking his tone. He ignored that, instead creating a ball of Light and Darkness in either hand. He closed his eyes in fierce concentration, and slowly, each ball morphed from its original color to the opposite. The ball of Light turned Dark, and the ball of Darkness turned Light.

"Did you just do that on your first try?" I asked incredulously. I leaned in closely and could see slight hints that they weren't what they seemed. The fake Light gave off that subtle smoke, like Darkness trying to come through, and the fake Darkness had a faint white halo. Both tells were subtle enough that you wouldn't notice unless you were up close. I stuck my finger into the fake Darkness in his right hand and felt myself filled up with hope. The opposite happened when I stuck my finger in the ball of fake Light. It wasn't like the process of making a demon killer bullet, where we coated Light with a layer of Darkness. It was just disguising what was already there.

Raj dismissed both balls to put his hands to his head in

badly contained distress. "This is terrible. This must be why the number of captured angels has increased so much lately. It seems demons are tricking angels into thinking that they're their friends." He let his hands fall from his face. "We'll need to come up with some kind of protocol . . . A code word? No . . . Maybe a handshake? They'd feel the Darkness if they were touching them. No, then they'd have their hands on them and could drag them away. Honestly, I think just demanding them to throw a ball of Light at you is the safest and quickest way to reveal fake angels. That was genius of you to think of that on the spot."

"Another thing, too," I said, "is that you should keep an eye on which angels you haven't seen around The Resting Place. It might help us narrow down who the mole could be. He even admitted that there's no way they could enter The Resting Place unless they were an angel with true intentions."

The corners of his mouth were twitched into a grimace he failed to hide.

"You know who it is, don't you?" I asked quietly.

"I started having meetings with other angels only in The Resting Place for that very reason . . . I suspected the mole was on our team, and I knew that if they were working against us, they would always find some excuse to not meet with me in The Resting Place."

"Who?"

He frowned. "I don't know for sure yet, and I want to confirm my suspicions before I start throwing accusations around. False information can be dangerous. I have an idea for one more test to narrow down the possibilities. Just keep your guard up, all right? I'll let you know as soon as I know. If you're unsure about anyone's identity, do the Light test. You know what, do it even if you are sure. Never hurts to double check."

Another thing dawned on me. "Wait, does this mean we never had to learn how to make Darkness in the first place? If we could just mimic it by disguising our Light, we could have avoided being dragged down and depressed by the Darkness."

Raj shook his head. "To truly fool demons, the Darkness would have to be real. Take your impostor—he or she blew their cover after thirty minutes because you asked them to make Light and they couldn't. The fact that demon hunters can create both Light and Darkness gives us an edge over demons. But disguising your Light as Darkness isn't a bad skill to know. It would do in a pinch. You could teach your Level Two students how to do it as a step before making Darkness. But I'd dissuade them from depending on it."

"Yeah, that sounds like a good idea."

After a beat, he said, "Well, I'll let you get back to your friend."

I grimaced. "Is this a bad idea, Raj?"

He gave me a compassionate frowny smile.

"Please don't give me some vague therapist-y answer," I said quickly. "I'm asking Raj, not Dr. Asan. I just want some honest advice."

He nodded and smiled slightly again. "No one can decide this for you, David. You have to evaluate how you feel and what you want. But personally, I think if you feel good and want to be around her, you owe it to yourself to see where this goes."

"But I still love Sandra," I whispered, looking down.

"And you probably always will," he said gently. "You've given her a place in your heart, and that part will always belong to her, but over time, it might not take up as much space as it once did, and feelings can change over time. The fact that Sandra has a place in your heart doesn't mean you can't open yourself up to caring about someone else. Believe it or not, it is possible to love more than one person. God didn't make our hearts to be finite. They continuously expand as we make room for all the people we come to love."

After a beat of letting that sink in, I shook my head and chuckled. "You should write for Hallmark, man. That was beautiful."

Raj smiled in a way that crinkled his eyes. "Go have fun, kid. I'll see you soon."

chapter 22
DARKNESS

After three days of teaching my Level One class, all of the angels could create a solid ball of Light. There were a few stragglers whose Light still flickered and petered out after a few seconds. One of them was this old guy named Pietro who thought I was full of crap. He did not like or trust me, and he hated that he was being pushed off on the mortal teacher, as though that was some kind of slight to him. But at least everyone had made some form of Light. That Sarah girl was incredible and was a real help.

At the end of class, we had a little fun and I had them play catch with balls of Light. Maybe next week they'd be good enough to make Light bats, and we could play baseball. We could play in the living room and not even have to worry about breaking anything. The thought made me smile.

"All right, everyone, great job!" I said. "We're gonna end class with one last challenge. Let's see how good your aim is. Your ticket out the door is to throw a ball of Light at me. Fill me up with warm fuzzies!"

Some of them looked at each other and giggled. A few looked concerned that the Light would hurt me. Before I could reassure them that it was okay, Asher chucked a ball of Light right at my face with a *WHOOSH* sound effect. I flinched, but not fast enough to avoid it. Suddenly, I felt like the world was a ball of sunshine. "Nice shot, kid!" He karate chopped at me, then disappeared.

Soon, there was a meteor shower of Light balls coming at me, and it was kind of amazing. I couldn't believe the progress they made! They were so amazing! And I was amazing! And we could do this! This world was so beautiful and wonderful, and why should anyone ever be sad!

Okay, I was a little drunk on Light, but it was nice while it lasted.

My Level Two class appeared one by one, confused by why everyone from Level One was so happy. They weren't going to leave class so happy. It was like watching someone taking an AP calculus class observing kindergarteners enjoying finger painting. The wistful longing for days gone by made their faces sag. We hadn't even made Darkness yet, but they knew it was some really, you know . . . dark stuff.

After everyone was settled and sitting or leaning against something, I sat on the arm of my dad's worn leather armchair and welcomed them in with a Light drunk grin. You might be wondering why angels don't just throw Light at anyone who looks sad. It's because the effects are temporary—you can't live off borrowed light—and then you end up even sadder when the effects wear off. The hangover was coming, and then I'd be depressed for the rest of the night. But I wasn't ready to acknowledge that yet. I schooled my features and made sure I had everyone's attention.

We spent the first ten minutes reviewing safety precautions. How you could lose your ability to make Light if you aren't careful, and how you always need to keep the Light burning within you, even if you're radiating Darkness. It was a tough crowd today. It seemed like everyone's eyes were glazing over, and several in the back started having whispered conversations, totally ignoring me. Or worse, talking about me. I felt stupid that it hurt my feelings. I mean, I was the authority here—I shouldn't care what they think. I should be above that. But it also made me frustrated, because what I was saying was genuinely important to their angelic wellbeing and success as demon hunters. They had no idea exactly how dangerous this power was and what it could do to them. I took a breath and paused, wondering if I was failing all these people. It seemed my Light-induced high had worn off.

"Are we going to make Darkness today?" this girl named Chiku asked in an accent I couldn't place. She had these fierce elvish eyes that looked both whimsical and threatening at the same time. I could tell she was masking nervousness behind her bravado.

I sighed. "Yes, that's the goal, but you have to be prepared. Please listen because this is important. I know what it's like to lose your ability to make Light." Their impatient faces looked slightly more worried at that declaration. "I was overcome by the Darkness, and it ate away at my resolve and my faith. I started to fear the Darkness, and that only made the problem worse. It became extremely painful to even attempt to make Light. With some help, I was able to overcome that but just know that this is a very real thing that could happen to you if you're not careful. I wasn't the only one who was affected this way and—"

"Maybe you just weren't strong enough," Leo muttered.

I blinked in surprise.

"Hey!" I jumped and spun around. I hadn't known Jake was here. "You interrupt one more time, and I'll show you the kind of person I turned into when overcome with Darkness." He flared with Darkness, and the kid involuntarily stepped back. Smiling slightly in appreciation, I said, "That's enough, Jake. But thanks." He nodded and faded back into the background

"Honestly, the best way to keep control of the Darkness is to not be afraid of it. It's scary to realize that we have Darkness within ourselves, and even scarier to confront it. But once we confront it, it's easier to handle. Don't think of it as evil; think of it as a tool that is dangerous but can be used for good or bad. Just like any other kind of weapon. But as angels, we choose to use it for good."

I took a deep breath, trying to stop being so nervous and timid. I was in charge. My job was literally to tell them what to do. These people depended on me. What I was teaching them was by far more important than my feelings. I imagined creating a Light shield around myself to bounce off all the negative thoughts I kept having, and I stood a little taller. I was in charge. I could do this.

"All right. I'm going to explain how to make Darkness, but wait until my explanation is over before you try it. Actually, I want all of you holding a ball of Light in your hands throughout my entire explanation."

"Why?" someone shouted.

"I have my reasons." I waited until I saw most of them follow my directions, then gave a pointed look to the three in the back who ignored me. They sighed and did as I asked, and I finally began my directions. "So, making Darkness is obviously going to be the opposite of making Light. When we make Light, we think about hope, particularly our hope in the Big Man, since that's where our Light comes from. But Darkness comes from ourselves. It's any feeling or memory that brings us down and makes us feel alone. It's anything that makes us want to give up hope. Anything that can be used against us to weaken our resolve."

"I thought Darkness came from the Evil One," someone said in the back.

I quit my pacing, just realizing that I had been, and spotted the girl who'd spoken, partially hidden behind the couch. I smiled ruefully. "Oh no, the Evil One just enhances the Darkness. You all have Darkness. It's part of being human. As angels, we should focus on the Light, but Darkness is there, and it does serve a purpose. So, we confront it and use it, rather than run from it."

They looked a little skeptical, but I plowed on. "So anyway . . . What you do is you think of the Darkness inside of you, and you push it out into your hands. Pretty simple concept, but hard to do if you're not used to it. Uh, don't do it yet. We're gonna try something . . ."

I deliberated for a moment whether my idea was too challenging. Honestly, I was more concerned with their ability to make Light than their ability to make Darkness. If the

Darkness overcame them and they couldn't make Light anymore, they'd be no good to anyone. That was pretty much what happened to my task force. We were a mess. I don't blame Ying Yue and Raj for how they taught us. There's never only one right way to do things. I just knew that I wanted to do something different. If it ended up being too difficult, we'd simplify. Also, I felt like it was healthier to be able to hold on to both the Light and the Darkness at the same time, rather than swinging from one extreme to the other.

I faced the crowd. "All right, so all of you keep one ball of Light burning in one hand but extinguish the other." I waited until they complied. "It's really difficult to hold both Light and Darkness at the same time, but that ability is vital to being a demon hunter, so we're going to practice it from the beginning. Throughout today, always keep a Light burning. If it goes out, reignite it before trying Darkness again. Uh, Jake, wanna demonstrate?"

He shrugged, came up next to me, and simultaneously created a ball of Light and Darkness in either hand. Even I blinked in appreciation. When I was an angel, I got to the point that I could create one right after the other, and I was pretty proud of myself for that. But to do it at the same time? That was skill! Everyone's eyes popped open even wider when Jake smirked and shot a beam of Light and a beam of Darkness up into the ceiling without batting an eye.

"Show off," I muttered with a small smile. "I don't expect you guys to be able to do that yet. Just see what you can do, and I'll walk around to assist." I turned back to Jake. "Can you walk around and help, too?" He shrugged again, and we meandered through the crowd, observing angels staring at their hands, looking constipated. I knew what I was asking them to do was advanced for people who'd never made Darkness, but this class only lasted two weeks, so we needed an accelerated program. And I really felt it was necessary to hold on to their Light. Most of the suggestions and notes I gave had to do with keeping their Light burning, regardless of whether they accomplished Darkness.

Before I had time to wrap up class, Grandpa stormed into the room, looking ready to yell at me for all the talking, then paused when he saw the horde of angels. I don't know why he was surprised. I told him I had meetings at night. He raised his eyebrows in curiosity, then continued to the fridge and got himself a glass of milk.

I continued walking around, giving pointers to frustrated students. What I'd asked them to do was probably too hard. Maybe I should have let them start Darkness without Light.

No, THIS WAY IS BETTER. CONTINUE AS PLANNED.

I smiled upward. *Thanks, Hermes.*

Only three of them managed to create Darkness by the end of class. Leo tried to fool me by just disguising his Light, but one raised eyebrow from me, and he knew he was busted.

"They'll get it," Jake said.

I nodded and finally dismissed everyone.

chapter 23
SPYING ON GRAMPS

I was falling asleep on my homework about an hour before my next demon training session. We'd hit the one-week mark, which meant there was only one more week before they needed to be promoted to the next level. They deserved my full attention, so I rolled off my bed to steal one of Preston's energy drinks from the fridge. He'd eaten my entire bag of Cheetos, so I figured he owed me this.

As I headed down the stairs, I noticed the kitchen lights were still on. I heard Grandpa talking to a woman and froze in my tracks. There were no women in this house. Curiously, I crept down the hallway outside the kitchen and recognized Grandma's voice.

"You have to tell him," she said.

"And say what?" he grumbled.

I was going to walk in and say hello, but Grandpa's tone made me feel like I was interrupting something.

"Tell Sam the truth about why you stayed away. It's not fair for him to live with the perception that you never cared about him. Because that's what he thinks, Todd, he thinks you never loved him."

Yikes. I should not be listening to this.

"Of course I don't want him to think that. But the kid hates me, and he's entitled to that hate. I was a terrible father."

It was weird hearing Grandpa call my dad "kid." I seriously had never considered my dad as a kid. But he was one once, and that childhood was still a part of him.

"Todd, fix this while you still have time. Tell him the truth."

"I won't. It's not important now. It's in the past."

"Honey, think of Sam. What does he deserve? A heartbreaking lie, or a hard truth that allows him to make amends with the one living parent he has left."

Okay, it was time to go before I overheard more of this private conversation. Biting my lip, I forced myself to tiptoe backward toward the stairs. I smacked my elbow on the stair railing somehow and bit back a groan, hugging my elbow to my chest.

"Hello?" Grandpa called.

I didn't say anything, so Grandma zoomed through the wall and grinned. "Hey, pumpkin! I thought only angels spied on family members."

I grimaced. "Old habits die hard. Sorry. I was just getting a snack, but I heard voices and I . . . listened in."

"Come on in, David," Grandpa called. "Have some pancakes."

What was Grandpa's obsession with late-night pancakes?

I awkwardly smiled as I came into the kitchen. Grandpa

was sitting at the table behind a plate covered in maple syrup and crumbs. "Sorry to interrupt."

"My fault, I suppose," he said, taking his plate to the sink. "If I wanted a private conversation, I could have had it in my room."

I nodded and stood there awkwardly.

Grandpa pointed with a spatula at the plate of extra pancakes on the counter. "Have some."

"Okay." I filled my plate up and sat at the table while Grandpa filled up a glass with milk.

"Are we going to ignore what you overheard?" he asked, patting the milk from his sparse mustache.

I shrugged. "If you want to. It's not really my business."

"I guess not."

"So!" Grandma grinned and sat across from me as I took my seat. "I hear you're dating someone!"

I shook my head and chuckled. "Every time."

"It's tradition." She winked.

"We're still getting to know each other," I said. "But she's pretty cute. And smart. And weird. In a good way. I think. And she can sense dead people, so I don't have to hide that from her like I thought I would."

"Well, good for you! I've got to get back to the front desk, but it was good to see you, sweetie!" She blew Grandpa a kiss, which he caught with a smile, before putting it to his heart. Then she disappeared.

For a second, I wished Sandra were here to have seen that. She loved cute old couples.

Grandpa got up and started rinsing his plate off in the sink.

"So," I said around a bite of pancake, "Have you always been able to do that?"

"Dishes?"

"Talk to dead people."

He frowned and nodded. "Have you?" he asked with a raised eyebrow.

"No. It's a more recent development."

"Ever since you revived?"

"No, actually. Even more recent than that."

Grandpa set his plate on a drying rack and joined me at the table. He leaned forward with his elbows on the table. "Don't ignore them if they need help, but don't let them take advantage of you. Angels try, but they don't always do the right thing. Do ignore demons, but if you must acknowledge one, be very casual and unimpressed. I like to ask them their favorite color. Always throws them off. And wanderers respond really well to music. Used to bring out the old guitar every now and then, and some of them would start talking."

My phone fell out of my hand as I hurried to type this all down in my notes app.

"Don't tell everyone what you see; they can't all handle it, and it's not their business," he continued, "but don't hide it from people you care about. That was a mistake I made. Well, I've made a lot of mistakes. Pretty much everything I've told you was learned from doing the opposite . . . But I get the sense you're a lot smarter than me, so I think you'll be all right."

I looked up at him once I finished typing up the rest of what he said. My overcrowded brain would forget all of this if I didn't. "Thanks for the advice. It's so nice to talk to someone who knows how to do this." I set my phone down and leaned forward. "Have you met others like us?"

He nodded. "Five in my lifetime. All very different abilities. One of them could only see those who had recently died. Became a PI and solved a lot of homicides. Used to joke that there was a TV show made after him. I also met one on a bus once that could touch them."

My mouth fell open, and a piece of pancake fell out. "They could touch spirits?"

Grandpa shrugged. "Sort of. He felt their Light and Darkness physically, and since dead people radiate either aura, he could physically feel them. I don't think they could feel him, though."

"Whoa . . ."

"I, uh, have a strange ability, myself. I can sort of call them to me."

My eyes widened. "What?"

"I think about them and concentrate on my location. It helps if I have a picture. They get this tingling feeling, and if they follow the feeling, they appear wherever I am."

I snorted. "That's not real."

"Show me a picture of your friend. That girl who was with you that first night."

I still had a lot of pictures of Sandra on my phone. Was I supposed to delete them now? Was that part of moving on? Or was it okay to remember her the way she used to be? When she was kind of, sort of, almost mine?

I showed Grandpa a picture of a selfie I took of the two

of us while I kissed her on the cheek. She looked so happy, which always blew me away. That she could be happy with me. Grandpa took the phone and closed his eyes after I told him her name. He sat there in silence for ten long seconds, and I looked around, imagining crickets chirping. I had serious doubts this was going to work, but Grandpa was so insistent I figured I'd humor him. Then, suddenly, Sandra popped into existence right next to him in some undercover demon outfit, radiating Darkness and looking very confused.

"What the heck was that?"

My jaw dropped. "Oh my gosh, you're a witch!"

Sandra narrowed her eyes. "Excuse me?"

"Grandpa called you here! He's magical!"

"It's not magic," Grandpa grumbled. "I'm just highly in tune with the spiritual realm."

"Dude, you just did a seance. You asked for a picture and everything."

Sandra raised an eyebrow. "He what now? You know that voodoo stuff comes from the devil, right?"

Grandpa rolled his eyes and shook his head. "You sound like Gertrude. Her explanation for everything she didn't understand was 'the Devil.' I called you here with my God-given gift. No 'evil voodoo' here."

"What did you feel?" I asked Sandra.

She shrugged. "I don't know, it was just a sort of tugging feeling. I could have ignored it, but I was curious, so I followed the feeling and ended up here."

I nodded at Grandpa. "Wizard."

"Medium," he corrected. He stood up and stretched his

back. "I was just trying to show you that you're not alone, David. There's a lot of us out there, and we all have our little quirks. I'm here if you ever want to talk about it."

Then he left me alone with Sandra, and we just looked at each other.

"Okay, I actually do need to talk to you," Sandra said, "but I was kind of in the middle of something, so I'll make it quick. Are you still open to talking to Sheila? Because she weirdly wants to talk to you now. She's been kind of insistent, actually."

"Oh, uh, sure. When?"

"You've got a class coming up, so how about tomorrow night?

"Yeah, okay." I wondered what I should even say to her. Good thing I'd have a little bit of time to think about it. "So, is this your Evil Sandra disguise?"

"Yeah, why?"

I appraised her outfit, which was almost the same outfit she wore when we went clubbing that one time. Except now she had this amazing fro.

"What?" she said.

"You look good," I said with a grin.

She smirked and raised an eyebrow. "I know." Then she disappeared.

Crap, I thought, *maybe I shouldn't be thinking about how nice other girls look when I'm dating Kiki.*

HER

I was content in The Resting Place. I was safe and loved and fulfilled. The hardest part was watching over my babies from afar while they were raised by their grandparents. *His* mom and stepdad. I didn't hate them the way I hated *him*. It wasn't their fault their child was a monster. They loved their granddaughters and gave them a safe and loving home. I watched over and visited them every spare moment I had. All the other moments, I was an angel in every sense of the word, taking on any duty that was given to me. I was at peace, and I was free for thirteen years.

And then the unthinkable happened. I saw *him*. Walking out of headquarters in The Resting Place, looking like a happy little angel. My murderer, here, in The Resting Place.

I froze completely. He froze as well. Neither of us could say or do anything. I felt myself trembling as his face split into a stupid grin. A grin that squeezed my broken heart. Then his face fell, and he ducked his head in shame. The injustice of it all filled me with rage. I'd loved him and I stood by him, even when everyone else left. I loved him, despite his horrifying condition, because I thought I saw him for who he truly was. That messy-haired boy who could laugh with his whole soul.

That quiet teenager who just wanted to be loved. That scarred man who would never be free. I loved him because I knew the real him. I thought our love could overcome everything.

I was a fool.

He never loved me. If he truly loved me, he would have fought it. He would have stopped himself. But he didn't.

I wanted to rip his eyes out, but fear held me prisoner, trembling and weak. I shook my head in denial. This couldn't be happening. He couldn't be in The Resting Place! I was supposed to be safe here! Safe from him!

There was only one thing to be done. I disappeared, leaving him there in his cowardly silence, and reappeared before the Big Man's door. I barged in unannounced and demanded to know how the Big Man had let him in. I don't even remember what he said, I was too filled with rage. Then that rage gave way to fear. I couldn't stay in the same place as *him*. I just couldn't! How could the Big Man expect me to spend my afterlife rubbing shoulders with my killer?

Eventually, I realized that nothing I said would make a difference. I thought he was fair and just, but where was the justice in letting a murderer walk free? I deserved retribution for what was done to me, and instead, he showed kindness to my enemy. My anger at my killer transferred to anger at the Big Man. He knew it. I saw it in his eyes, and I hated that the main expression I saw on his face was one of sorrow. For me. Even though he knew that I was about to lash out in a way that was unforgivable.

chapter 24
INTERROGATION

Raj showed up at work the next day as I was washing the mirrors in the bathroom. I sprayed him with glass cleaner in panic, and he held up his hands.

"What was my first disguise when I tried out for the demon hunters?" I demanded.

"Mortal college kid," Raj said calmly.

"Throw some Light at me."

He complied, and I felt a brief surge of hope, confirming it was actual Light. I sighed and set the squirt bottle down.

"Just wanted to check in on you," Raj said. "How's it going?"

"Fine, I guess?" I shrugged as I leaned against a sink. "It's almost graduation day for my students. Most of my Level Two students have learned Darkness and will be moving on to Level Three, where I'll be teaching them about going undercover and stuff. The Level One students will move on to Level Two, and I'll be ready for a fresh batch of angels soon. So, I guess you can start gathering those for me if you can."

"That's great news, David. From the classes I've popped in on, it looks like you're doing a great job."

"What's new with you?"

He folded his arms. "Something strange happened this morning. There was some kind of unauthorized jailbreak. Three angels were set free by an unknown rescuer."

"What do you mean by 'unknown'? Couldn't they see their face? Were any of ours saved?"

Raj shook his head. "The rescuer hid their face, so we don't know their identity, but they were radiating Darkness. That doesn't necessarily mean it was a demon; it was likely an angel in disguise. The question is, why would they hide their identity? And no, we're still missing our three. I don't know why they weren't saved."

I slumped and prayed our friends would make it out soon. I couldn't stand the thought of them suffering like that. "Maybe it was a demon hunter in disguise, and they hid their face because the jailbreak was unauthorized, and they didn't want to get in trouble."

He looked at me sharply. "It wasn't you, was it?"

I laughed. "No, Raj, it wasn't me. I'm not about to play vigilante again anytime soon."

"On a different subject, Sandra says you have an appointment tonight with Sheila?"

I rubbed my forehead. I'd forgotten about that. "Yeah, that's tonight. Any particular information you want me to try and get out of her?"

"I think I'll just sit in with you and ask my own questions."

I frowned.

"What?" he asked.

"I don't think she's your biggest fan. You did kind of imply that you wanted her to be dragged down to the Hurricane last time you saw her. Somehow, I don't see her opening up to you."

"Ah." Raj blinked and pursed his lips. "You may have a point there."

"Probably best if I do this alone. She kind of likes me for some reason."

"You have a very guileless face, and you're easy to trust."

"I feel like you're just calling me gullible, but thanks?"

"To answer your question, any information you can get out of her about Malum, his plans, and especially his weaknesses would be helpful. I can give you more targeted goals after you've met with her the first time, based on the information you get." Raj stood. "I've got to go, but take care of yourself, kid. We'll regroup after you've interrogated Sheila."

I heard the door open and quickly pulled my phone to my ear. "Yeah, sounds good. Talk to you later."

Liam rounded the corner and paused when he saw my cleaning cart.

"You can use the bathroom," I said, "I was just finishing up in here."

I rolled the cart out of the bathroom, thinking about which questions I should be asking Sheila and how best to approach her.

• • •

Not long after dinner, I heard a knock on the door and smiled. My stupid little invention worked. "Yes?" I called.

"It's Sandra, can I come in?"

I walked over to open the door and let her in, even though she could have just floated through it.

"Um, that's genius," she said, gesturing toward the ball on a string I'd taped to the door. There was a sign under it that said, "Deceased individuals, please knock! Thank you!" It wouldn't do much good if they just appeared in my bedroom, but I was hoping that with time, I could train my friends to start outside my door and use the ball to knock before entering. I deserved some privacy.

"Thanks," I said. I didn't mention I came up with the idea after Raj and my mom popped in on me and Kiki having a moment.

"So, they should be by soon," Sandra said. "They're bringing four guards, and she's tied up at the wrists. They have another chain around her neck, which, personally, I think is overkill, but they said it's protocol, so whatever. Do you want me to stay, or . . ."

"Probably best if I do this alone," I said. "She's not your greatest fan."

"I'm not her greatest fan," Sandra mumbled.

"Anything I should know beforehand?" I asked.

"She seems nervous about something, but hesitant to talk, so approach her carefully. Her dignity has been compromised, so I think she's compensating by trying to act like she doesn't care."

Five dead people appeared in front of me, and I jumped.

"For future reference, please start outside the door and knock," I said, pointing at my invention.

The four angel guards glanced at my ball on a string, and a few nodded in appreciation. And then there was Sheila, right in the middle, stone-faced and trapped in chains of Light. She didn't look great. She was pale, and there were bags under her eyes. Her hair wasn't as shiny as it usually was. Dead people tend to look the way they feel, and clearly, prison hadn't been a great experience.

I looked over to ask Sandra something, but she had already gone.

"Hi," I said to no one in particular.

No one responded. I shrugged and sat on the edge of my bed, gesturing at my armchair. The guards shoved Sheila into it and stood guard around her. They were rougher with her than I liked. I wasn't used to feeling like angels were mistreating someone, but that was an issue for another time. I made each of the guards throw a ball of Light at me to confirm that they were, indeed, angels. The only demon here was Sheila.

"So, what do you want?" I asked Sheila.

She scowled at me. "Wow. Warm welcome. I can see why you have so many friends."

"I'm sorry, did you want a hug?"

She rolled her eyes.

"Why did you agree to talk to me?" I asked.

"I was bored."

I raised an eyebrow. *Sure.* There had to be some kind of bargain involved. Sandra was the one who convinced her, so what did she say to her? What did she know about Sheila that she could hold over her head?

Oh. Right.

"They agreed to let you see your daughters if you agreed to talk to me," I guessed. Her daughters with *Ted* of all people. I still couldn't wrap my mind around it.

She pursed her lips and didn't say anything.

"You know, I think you're going to have to actually talk for this to work."

She threw her hands up. "You haven't even asked me anything! You want me to tell you what I know? Fine: You're gonna lose, so you should just give up now."

"Great pep talk."

I let her stew in her annoyance a little longer because I was just as annoyed with her as she was with me.

"What?" she finally demanded.

I sighed. "All right, so the first, most obvious question: what exactly is Malum hoping to accomplish, and why?"

She looked down, raising her eyebrows. "I don't speak for him. But . . . I know that he hates Light. Any trace of it. And he wants to eradicate it."

"That's why he's capturing angels?"

She nodded.

"And all the mass killings?"

"I'm sure you already know this. I don't know why you're asking me." I didn't respond, and she rolled her eyes. "You know that The Resting Place is transient. Angels come and go. Malum is working to reduce the population of angels by making sure fewer people become angels when they die. The best way he knows to do that is with horrific, deadly atrocities that result in massive populations of people being so traumatized that they become wanderers instead of moving on. He'd rather have more demons, but wanderers are still better than angels in his book. And he can get more demons by capturing angels, throwing them into the Hurricane, and making a deal with them that he'll release them if they join him. It's really not that complicated."

I shook my head in contemplation. It wasn't complicated to understand, but how to prevent it? And what could I do to help?

"Hey, answer me this: what's Malum's problem with me? I'm just a random guy. I mean, I've met him a few times, but I'm not a threat to him. I haven't even slowed him down."

That wasn't what I intended to ask her, but I had always wondered.

She rolled her eyes. "You're not just a random guy; you're a guy that's scared the crap out of him."

I started laughing, and, insultingly, one of the guards started laughing too. At a pointed look from his colleague, he cleared his throat and shut his mouth.

"Sheila, that was hilarious, but you're wasting my time. If you want to be useful—"

She leaned forward. "I am being serious, idiot. Do you know how many people have shaken his hand and *not* turned into a puddle of fear? From that moment on, he's been obsessed with you."

I rolled my eyes. "He's seen through me and knows all my fears. He knows I'm pathetic. I'm not even good at lying. I mean, I can tell lies, but as you might have noticed, I'm not great at lying about who I am. He has to know that I'm nothing to be afraid of."

"You don't understand. Malum's language *is* deception. It's the only language he knows. I'm not sure he even understands what truth is. He believes everything a person says has some kind of double-meaning, and all people are just trying to manipulate each other for their own gain. It doesn't matter if you're an innocent, pathetic little angel baby. The fact that you've resisted him, rescued people from the Hurricane with the help of his greatest supporter and are somehow *alive* again after having died has him convinced that you're a mastermind to rival even him. He thinks all the times you've shown weakness were acts to throw him off. That's why he sent me and others after you instead of coming after you himself. He's *afraid* of you, as stupid as that is."

I could still remember the visions he sent me. The Darkness and fear . . . watching terrible things happening to my family and taking all the blame. It was laughable that Malum, the Prince of Darkness, who'd caused so much pain, fear, and destruction, could be afraid of me. But Sheila had no reason to lie to me, and she said it in such a matter-of-fact way. Maybe if Malum assumed I was more dangerous than I appeared, it could give me the upper hand somehow.

I sat back on my hands. "You sure have insight into his brain."

"Yeah, well, between you and me—and I guess these stupid prison guards—his little fear paralysis tactic goes both ways."

I tilted my head. "Meaning . . ."

"While he's reading your fears, he's vulnerable to you reading his. That is, if you have the presence of mind to pay attention when that's happening. It's how I learned how to do what he does."

I paused. "You are truly terrifying."

She grinned.

"But I'm still not afraid of you. Isn't that weird? After all you've done?"

"There's something wrong with you." She folded her arms and leaned back.

"Why are you sharing all of this? Is it so they reduce your sentence?"

She sat up suddenly. "I'm only helping because, like any sane person, I hate Malum and want to help you take him down. I'm not asking for a reduced sentence. I don't want that. Lock me up as long as you want."

"You just called yourself his greatest supporter," I pointed out.

"I was his best supporter. Doesn't mean I'm a fan. I was just the best minion he could manipulate to do his bidding."

I paused. "And why don't you want to reduce your sentence?"

She didn't answer.

"Sheila."

She remained silent.

"Does being in prison somehow protect you from him? Does it have to do with the chains of Light? Or Light itself? When you're surrounded by Light, are you protected from him?"

Her eyebrows went up involuntarily, and she muttered, "You're a lot smarter than you look."

"So, I'm right?"

She sighed and nodded.

"Care to elaborate?"

She rolled her eyes again. "Last thing you're getting out of me today, all right? Malum is like a bloodhound. Once he gets a whiff of your scent, in his case, your fear, he can find you wherever you are, and he can call you to him, forcing you to appear before him whenever and wherever he wants. But he can only scent Darkness. He can't smell Light, so to speak. Unfortunately for him, Light overpowers the scent of Darkness. So, anyone in contact with Light, even the smallest bit of it, is hidden from him. I mean, he can still find you if he knows where you are, but he can't sense you or call you to him. Unless you call him to you."

I blinked and thought of how screwed up it was that prison was the safest place for Sheila. But it made sense. It sheltered her from his influence. I'd want to be locked up too.

Another thing had me frowning. "So, he knew from the beginning that I was an angel in disguise? At that ambush, when I pretended to capture Natalie and called him to me, he knew I wasn't a demon because he couldn't sense me like he does other demons?"

"Yeah, I thought that was obvious."

It wasn't. I thought I'd fooled him at first. When I looked back on any of my brilliant ideas, literally none of them had worked. Well, except demon killer bullets. That was a pretty useful invention. But I couldn't take credit for saving anyone from the Hurricane because they wouldn't have even been captured in the first place if it weren't for me. At one point, I thought I was a pretty solid demon hunter, but looking back, I hadn't accomplished anything.

Someone knocked on the door and we both started.

"Yes?" I asked.

"Can I come in? I have a message for you, and I think it might be urgent." That was Grandpa's voice.

"What the . . ." I muttered. "Uh, yeah, sure, come in."

Grandpa barged in and then paused, taking in Sheila and her four angel guards. "What, did I interrupt an interrogation, or something?"

"Yes, actually," I said.

Grandpa shrugged. "A deceased individual asked if I would deliver a message for you."

I frowned. "Who was it?"

"A blonde, older woman, larger build. Didn't give me her name."

"Was it an angel or a demon?"

Grandpa paused and seemed to be chewing on his mustache as he thought. "All right, this is going to sound crazy, but I don't know what she was. It looked like she was radiating blue light? Maybe I need my eyes checked."

My eyes widened. Maybe this was the mole!

I turned to Sheila and the guards. "That's enough for today. Let's do this again next week. Same day, same time."

They disappeared without a word.

"Grandpa, there's nothing wrong with your eyes. Angels

and demons have learned how to change the color of their aura. My guess is this person didn't want you to know who they were or even what side they're on. What did she say?"

Grandpa looked down at a torn piece of notebook paper. "She said, 'Brace yourself. He knows.' Any idea what that means?"

I scowled and shook my head. I had no clue, but it didn't sound good.

chapter 25
YAY, MORE DEMONS

Okay, I am a nerd who obsesses over grades. I freak out if I don't get straight A's. But since dating Kiki, I'd been getting a lot of D's, and my grades getting sadder and sadder. I blamed it on our "study sessions." Every time we planned to study together, we didn't do much studying, and by the time we got around to it, it was time for my demon hunter classes. I wasn't going to stop hanging out with Kiki; the crappy grades were worth her company, but I couldn't stop stewing over it on my way to work.

Speaking of demon hunter classes, we had a run-in with a few demons during my Level One class the night after Sheila's interrogation. Jake was there, so he was able to fight the three of them off with surprising ease, but it was a close one. Jake tried to get General Wolff to provide a constant guard of one or two defenders for my class each night, but there weren't enough defenders to go around. As much as I hated seeing my students in danger, I was kind of grateful for the incident. They worked a lot harder after seeing the evil they would be up against. By the end of our last full lesson, all my students could create balls of Light and shields, and they were each finding their own preferred defensive weapon. So far, I wasn't a failure as a teacher.

The Level Two class was doing almost as well. I knew I'd made their lives harder by forcing them to hold a ball of Light while making their Darkness, but I felt it would keep them from getting dragged down by the Darkness like I'd been. And it was working. They didn't look like my task force had after we'd been using Darkness too long, all despondent and depressed and snapping at each other. On a real mission, they wouldn't be able to keep a ball of Light out, but some had gotten creative and hid their hand in a pocket. One dude kept his hand glowing but covered it with a glove of Darkness. Eventually, they'd have to learn to do what Raj taught me to "keep a Light burning in your heart," and do away with their ball of Light. I still wasn't sure how to teach that abstract and cheesy concept.

Those who hadn't yet grasped Darkness could at least change the color of their Light. I followed Raj's suggestion to spend a class explaining that it was possible to change the color of their Light to look like Darkness. It was an experimental class since I'd never actually done it before, but no one seemed to mind the lack of structure. There was a lot of laughter as people started randomly glowing magenta and green. I had ten out of fifteen by the end of the first class who had succeeded in disguising their Light as Darkness. After a few classes, they could all do it, even those who couldn't grasp actual Darkness. They all gave off that dark anti-light, similar to Darkness, but with a faint white glow around them. It would fool a demon from a distance, but I felt that Raj was right. To truly go undercover, they'd still need to depend on real Darkness.

I blinked as my phone's ring broke my train of thought. It was Elena. I answered her on CarPlay.

"Hello?"

"David? What are you doing?"

"I'm driving to work. Why?"

"I think there might be a ghost in the shed outside! Or a cat, I don't know!"

"The little shed or the big shed?"

"The big shed, obviously! Can you come check it out? Please? Charlie's out with his buddies, and the kids are sleeping over at his parents' house, and I'm all alone, and it's creeping me out!"

I sighed. "Yeah, sure. Let me just call in and see if I can come in late."

"Thank you!"

"It's fine. Be there in a sec."

She hung up, and I called Preston.

"Yep?" he said.

"Hey, uh, I'm on my way to work, but my sister thinks there's a ghost in her shed. I'm gonna go check it out."

"How late do you think you'll be?"

"No idea. But her place is only ten minutes from Chuck E. Cheese."

He sighed. "What duty are you on?"

"Cashier. Just pull Jorge from cleaning duty until I come back. I'll stay late to do cleaning duty to make up for it."

"Fine. Don't get eaten by demons."

"Demons don't—"

He'd hung up already.

Elena clung to my arm as we approached the shed in the backyard. So far, I hadn't heard anything suspicious, but her fear was spreading to me. Which was silly. I wasn't afraid of ghosts. I mean, demons weren't great, but—

A loud bang made us both jump.

"It's probably a cat," I said quietly.

I reached out for the handle, and Elena backed away. After a pause, I threw the door open, hurried inside, and closed the door behind me. I realized that was stupid, but I didn't want the demon to see Elena out there and go after her.

I found the light switch, and once I'd turned it on, a decaying zombie face was right in front of me. I screamed and jumped backward.

"David?" Elena yelled. "Are you okay?"

I took a deep breath, trying to force my thumping heart to slow down. "Fine! Just a second!"

The zombie face had transformed into a black mass that was slowly growing in the corner of the room. I took another deep breath but failed to keep my voice steady. "Hey, Mr. Black Mass. Can you not? I've got to get to work."

The demon paused, then swirled more quickly and started making evil laughing sounds. It sent a shiver down my spine, but it also reminded me for a second of when Sheila and I were in a haunted house trying to scare mortals. I tried to remind myself that this demon was just someone trying to put on a show. It was *trying* to scare me. Like bad actors, people *trying* to look scary or tough automatically did not succeed. If you try too hard, the audience won't buy it.

Well, unless you do something super dangerous, then it's believable. I had to stop this demon before it hurt me or Elena. What had Grandpa told me? Act casual around demons? I could do that, right? Demons were just people. Stupid people trying to scare you.

"Dude," I said. "Can you form into a person for a second? I need to ask you a question."

The black mass paused, likely confused by my refusal to cower in fear.

"So, you did hear me. Can you form into a person, please? I'm not going to have a conversation with a black mass. It's weird."

The darkness paused, then pulled into itself, forming into a demonic zombie with half of its face gone. The half of the face that was flesh had a red eye that dripped blood and gray wrinkled skin. The other side was just a skull. It had only patches of blood-soaked hair on its head. Its body was also part flesh-part skeleton, and it was completely naked, which was awkward. From the parts of its body that still had flesh, I realized this was a woman.

I made a face, "Lady, put some clothes on. Come on. Nakedness isn't scary, it's just weird. Who taught you how to haunt, anyway?"

"What do you want?" she screeched in my face. Her voice was rough and garbled and would have been quite scary if I couldn't tell how hard she was trying.

I held my hands up. "Um, you're the one in my sister's shed causing a ruckus. What do *you* want?"

Causing a ruckus? I was turning into Grandpa.

"I want to destroy you! I want to—"

"What's your name?" I asked.

She paused, then switched tactics. "I don't need to destroy you; you will destroy yourself! You don't know what you're doing. You're a burden to your family. You are ruining their lives! You'll never find love again! Your dead girl will move on without you, and you will—"

"Yeah, yeah. I'm the worst, and I'm gonna die alone. Clearly, you did your homework on me. Weird plan to come after me by hiding in my sister's shed, but whatever. You can go back to scaring me and destroying my life in a sec. I just have a quick question. What's your name?"

She paused, clearly taken aback.

"What's your name?" I repeated, snapping my fingers in her face. "Yo, just answer! It's not that hard of a question."

She folded her arms and sighed. The human mannerism looked odd on a creepy zombie demon. Then, in a normal voice, she said, "The name's Clarissa." Her voice was on the lower side and as dry as a bored teenager.

"Hi, Clarissa. I'm David. What's your favorite color?"

"Red," she said automatically, then blinked, surprised at herself.

"Mine's blue. Do you prefer words or numbers?"

"Words. I hate math."

"Pineapple on pizza?"

"Hell, no! What's wrong with you?"

I shrugged. "It makes things interesting. Hey Clarissa?"

"What?" she snapped.

"Can you put some clothes on?"

She blinked and looked down, suddenly uncomfortable having a conversation with someone while naked and zombified. In an instant, she was a human-looking woman in her 30s with brown hair in a braid, a flannel plaid shirt, holey jeans, and hiking boots. She looked like someone who lived in a cabin in the woods. I had this image in my head of her canoeing down the lake with her hair wisps blowing in the wind.

"Much better," I said. "And Clarissa?"

"What!" she repeated, increasingly annoyed.

"We can chat all you want but haunting me is a waste of time because I already know you're not scary. You try way too hard. Just saying."

Her nostrils flared, and her face flushed in embarrassed anger. Then she growled and poofed away in a black cloud.

I nodded in satisfaction, then left the shed.

"It was a cat," I said as I walked back into the house.

Elena waddled after me. "You expect me to believe you were having a conversation in there with a cat named Clarissa?"

I spun around and raised my eyebrows.

She rolled her eyes. "Yes, I listened in! Come on, what did you expect?"

"All right, fine. It wasn't a cat, but I annoyed the scary lady away, and she isn't coming back."

Elena hugged me, and it felt super weird with her belly in the way.

I smiled and pulled away after a second. "I gotta go now. You okay by yourself?"

She shoved past me and plopped down on the couch. She closed her eyes and whispered, "Do you hear that?"

I tensed, on my guard again. "What?"

"Silence," she whispered with a contented sigh. She pulled her feet up and buried her face in a pillow. "No more talking; this house will never be this quiet ever again. Leave me alone. Wait! Throw me that bag of donuts first."

I rolled my eyes, threw the donuts at her, and left.

Work was pretty somber, and I wasn't sure why until I talked to Raj. He was waiting for me outside my car after I clocked out. After I got in and squirted my hands with a glob of hand sanitizer—my workplace is overrun by gross children—Raj joined me in the passenger's seat and threw a ball of Light at me.

"You don't know what a platypus is," he said, by way of proving he was who he said he was. This was in reference to a conversation we had at the end of my first therapy session.

"I know what a platypus is!" I said indignantly. "I just got confused."

He raised an eyebrow. "After that session, when Elena texted you a GIF of a platypus, you said you thought they had wings. And then I taught you that those are called ducks and they go quack."

I rolled my eyes as I backed out of my parking spot. "Whatever. What's up?"

"Did you hear the news?"

"What news?"

"You've gotta pay attention to what's going on in the world, kid. Things are getting bad." He concentrated on my radio, and it snapped to a news station in the middle of a reporter's sentence.

"—still unknown who this mysterious terrorist organization is or who they are affiliated with. Their motives are also unknown at this time. Not a single terrorist involved in the bombing was left alive for questioning, and their bodies are still being identified as we speak. We will return later with more information on the tens of thousands of casualties in Manila, Philippines. It is speculated that this organization may be connected to the attacks on—"

Raj switched off the radio and I stared at it open-mouthed. Tens of thousands dead. Families ripped apart. And here I was worrying about my stupid grades. People were dying in the thousands. My heart felt like it weighed a hundred pounds. All that horror and terror caused by one evil demon. How? How can any being be so cruel? I literally couldn't understand. How does a person completely lose their humanity?

"So, this was definitely Malum, right?" I asked quietly.

He nodded. "Unknown terrorist organization, not affiliated with any particular nation? What do you know about Manila?"

I thought for a moment. "Nothing, really. I think it's a pretty populated area, though, right?"

Raj nodded. "One of the most densely populated cities in the world. If you want to take out a lot of people with little effort, that would be one of the first places to attack."

"You think he's controlling this terrorist organization?"

He nodded. "They have no demands, they just want people to die, and they don't care who it is. If I'm right, they're also tied to a bombing that happened last week in Dhaka, Bangladesh, another one of the most densely populated cities in the world. If this continues, it won't be long before someone starts speculating that a particular nation is causing these attacks and declaring war on them, leading to even more death."

I sat back in my seat and blew air out through my lips. "I talked to Sheila. What she said supports your theories. She says Malum wants to kill as many people as possible in the most horrifying ways to increase the percentage of people that become wanderers rather than angels. He hopes he'll get more demons, but he'll take wanderers over angels because they don't have Light."

Raj nodded. "I've been discussing this with other task force leaders. We're going to need to change our tactics because what we're doing isn't enough." He blinked and shook his head. "Oh, also, I have an interesting update I want to run by you."

I frowned, thinking back on all the times in the recent past that Raj had run something by me. "I appreciate being kept in the loop, but I'm curious about why you're specifically talking to me about all of this. You keep updating me without anyone else around." He seemed to be doing this more and more.

He shrugged. "You're good to bounce ideas off of."

I smiled. "Am I like your unofficial partner now?"

He smiled back sheepishly. "Do you mind? Since Ying Yue was captured, I've been humbled enough to realize I need some help."

Warm fuzzies blossomed inside me. Raj needed me and specifically wanted my help. After so many months of feeling totally useless to my team, it felt so good to be needed and trusted.

I smiled. "I'm honored to help in any way, Raj. What's your update?"

"I was visited by an angel I've never met, and he revealed to me that it's possible to escape the Hurricane without someone on the outside pulling you out. I'm suspicious of the information, however, since, after checking our records, it turns out the name they gave me was a fake—no angel in our records exists with that name."

I quickly slammed on the brakes. I'd almost run the red because I was preoccupied with our conversation. Once I'd stopped, I looked over at Raj. "Why would an angel lie about their identity?"

Raj shook his head. "I have no idea. That's why I'm suspicious. And it wasn't a demon disguised as an angel. They were radiating true Light; I even had them prove it."

"Well, they couldn't have made Light if they had bad intentions. Right? Were you in The Resting Place at the time?"

"No, but we were near it."

"So, what did they say? How do you leave the Hurricane?"

He shook his head. "It's so simple, I almost don't believe him. He said you just leave. Just like you disappear and reappear anywhere else. He said most prisoners there are so distracted by their torture they don't even try to leave; they just accept that they belong there."

I thought about it and shivered as I remembered being down there. "It makes sense. When I was down there, I was so lost and tormented, I didn't even think about leaving. I mean, I wanted the torture to end, but I just assumed I was stuck. How crazy is that? I didn't even try! I wasn't actually trapped; I just gave up."

Raj nodded. "He said you just have to remember who you are and then leave. You don't need anyone else to pull you out if you just trust in the Big Man. But he did say it's a lot easier to do that if you find another trapped soul to leave with you. Two people relying on each other's strength can be more powerful than one person alone. But the point is, it *is* possible to leave. You just have to remember who you are."

We were silent as we both contemplated this information, and the car behind me honked. I'd been driving too slowly as I pondered.

"You've got to tell everyone," I said. "This can save people and lessen the risk of capture if you don't have to send other angels down there to save them."

Raj nodded. "I agree. I've already shared this information with Hermes, Maustafa, and Wolff. I'm supposed to share the info at our next task force meeting. But . . ."

"We've been avoiding meetings because of the mole." Too

bad I couldn't go to The Resting Place. It had an automatic barrier to those with ill intent, so we could have meetings there without fear of a mole. I just couldn't come.

"Why don't you just have the next meeting in The Resting Place without me?" I asked.

Raj frowned. "We could, but that way we'd never actually catch the mole, only avoid them."

"If only we had a way to read them and sense their intentions . . . Oh!" A person came to mind who could solve all our problems. "No, that's not . . . Maybe? I don't know, it's too risky."

"What conversation are you having with yourself?" Raj prompted.

I bit my lip as I considered. "Well, I think I might have a way to catch the mole."

HER

Hermes, sensing a toughness in me that I didn't know I had, assigned me guard duty when I died. I was to help guard the demon prisoners in The Resting Place. There were weeks of training for something that seemed as simple as just standing there doing nothing, but guarding demons isn't so simple. Whether on Earth or The Resting Place, demons are demons, and they know how to get under your skin. They can't hurt angels, especially while imprisoned, but they can put thoughts in their heads. I was generally good at ignoring their taunts while on duty. I would distract myself by thinking of my daughters; sometimes I'd even hum to myself. But on the day he arrived in The Resting Place, my guard was completely down, and I had been assigned to Cell 1. Every guard knew that particular cell held the most hellish demon in memory. Usually, there are at least two people on guard there at all times, and if the task becomes too wearing on someone, Hermes immediately sends a replacement.

That day, as I stood there fuming, the demon crept into my mind.

You're angry . . . furious . . . and afraid . . . Oh, your fear is delicious!

I tried to ignore him, but in the state I was in, I wasn't

strong enough. And a part of me didn't want to fight it.

You want revenge. You want everyone to feel your pain. Especially the Big Man for showing mercy to your murderer, for letting that devil reside with angels!

He replayed my death in my mind over and over. I squeezed my eyes shut, but of course that didn't help.

"Are you all right?" Victor asked.

I nodded to my fellow guard.

You want revenge? Release me! I am the king of vengeance! I can help you! We will make your enemy suffer! We will make him writhe!

I gasped at the thought. I couldn't do that! Revenge was for demons, not angels.

Memories flashed before my eyes. HIM beating me, screaming at me, killing me. Our babies crying in fear, seconds from being hurt by their own father. And the Big Man forgiving him. As though all he'd done to me meant nothing. As though my pain and suffering didn't matter to him!

The Big Man doesn't care. He loves that monster more than you.

I felt my heart harden within me.

If HE was in The Resting Place, I didn't want it.

If HE was an angel, I didn't want that either.

I'd have my revenge, and Malum, The Prince of Darkness, would help me to bring my enemy down.

chapter 26
NEW BODYGUARD

I almost got into a car accident immediately after Raj left.

A demon appeared out of nowhere and screamed in my ear. I gritted my teeth and tried to ignore the screaming, and when they realized that tactic wasn't working, they floated in front of me as a dark cloud to impede my vision of the road. I tried to acknowledge them casually as I had Clarissa, but I was too frightened to speak. Car accidents were a huge fear of mine..

Someone help me! I pleaded.

I felt like I should pull over, but I couldn't see out any of my windows. In the Darkness, I found the button to my emergency lights and prayed cars would stay away from me. I heard honking and the sound of cars zooming past, way too close. I screamed at a small crunch sound to the right and was sure my mirror had just been scraped off by a speeding car.

Pull Over to the Right. The coast is clear.

I took a sharp right, blindly parked on the side of the road, and practically dove out of the car.

A motorcycle missed me by about three inches, and I screamed without air as I fell back and crawled away in that stupid, frustrating way people do in horror movies instead of just getting up and running. Turns out panic makes you stupid.

The demon then swirled around me in a tornado, and all I could do was curl up in a pathetic ball and pray it would end. I didn't notice at first when it was blasted away from me. When I finally lifted my head, I saw Jake pulling the demon to him with a whip he'd wound around the demon's neck.

"Leave him alone," he said in a dark voice.

The demon, whom I could now see was a very small man, quivered at the dangerous look on Jake's face. Jake released him, and the demon disappeared.

Jake sighed and looked over at me, pathetically curled up against my car. He raised an eyebrow. "You look like a roly-poly."

I let my legs slide out in front of me. "Can we pretend I didn't just curl up in a ball and wait for death?" I said in a shaky voice.

Jake gave me a half smile. "I won't tell anyone."

I shivered and got to my feet. "Any chance you can stick around for my lesson tonight?"

"I got ya back, mate."

Jake was beating himself up like crazy by the time we got to my house, and it didn't matter how many times I assured him it wasn't his fault that I almost got into a car accident. He kept trying to convince me that I needed a constant guard, despite my pointing out that the angels were stretched too thin and I wasn't important enough to take away from their duties. But the attacks did seem to be increasing and getting closer together all of a sudden. There was that group last night, the one in Elena's shed, and this one in my car. Something had changed. These demons weren't just having fun with some mortal medium; they wanted to hurt me specifically.

"I bet Sheila's behind it," Jake said darkly as we came in through the garage. "This was the kind of stuff she used to do."

I shook my head. "She's incarcerated. How could she be communicating with demons?"

"I don't know, but I'm sure she's behind it."

"I thought after all the Ted stuff came out that you were on Sheila's side."

Jake sighed in exasperation. "Obviously domestic violence and murder are wrong, but it doesn't justify dooming the entire world to Malum's wrath."

I hung my keys on the peg by the door and leaned against the wall as I thought. "If Sheila is behind it, maybe we could get it out of her. If she's not behind it, she might have insight into why I'm being attacked so much—"

I jumped as a demon appeared right in front of me, screaming like a banshee. Before it could do anything, Jake gripped its neck from behind and tossed it back the way it came. It didn't reappear.

I sighed loudly as I leaned against the wall. "This is getting old."

"We're doing this interrogation together," he demanded. "I'll have Hermes send her here with some guards, and she won't leave until we get some answers."

I didn't think Jake would be much help with this interrogation. He'd get too emotional. He had a personal score to settle with Sheila, as she was the one that sucked all the hope out of him and threw him into the Hurricane. All that trauma and the effects it had on his mind were because of her. (I'm sure there was also a certain amount of hurt pride that she beat him so easily.) But I didn't want him to leave me alone after I'd been attacked four times in less than 24 hours.

Surprisingly, Jake's mental request to Hermes was granted, and only five minutes after coming home, Sheila was in my room again, surrounded by guards. She looked worse than ever. Were they hurting her? Or was that just the effect of a demon being imprisoned in Light?

"Are you okay?" I asked without thinking.

Jake and Sheila looked at me like I was an idiot. Which… fair.

"We have some questions for you," Jake said darkly.

Sheila raised an eyebrow. "The angel I bested and his mortal sidekick want to ask me questions. How terrifying."

Jake clenched his jaw, and I took advantage of his wordless fury.

"This is important," I said.

"Lie to us and you will never see your kids again," Jake warned her. He knew what kept her in line.

"I'm aware of the arrangement!" she snapped.

"Are you in contact with demons?" Jake asked flatly.

"No! How many times are you stupid angels going to ask me that? I've been imprisoned this entire time! Ask my stupid guards!"

I looked at them, and the tall woman on the left nodded. "She hasn't had any contact with demons. She's under constant watch by at least two angels while incarcerated and four when outside the prison. Only one is switched out at a time, and these transfers happen while she's in her prison cell, so no risks are taken. It stretches our numbers, since so many guards are getting captured or quitting, but she is a priority prisoner."

"So why are a bunch of demons suddenly trying to kill him now?" Jake demanded.

I felt silly for making a big deal out of this. Millions of people in the world were dying, and Jake was mad about these tiny incidents that happened to me that weren't even fatal.

"I doubt the shed incident counts as trying to kill me," I muttered.

Jake shot me a look. "A shed? With dangerous tools? You're lucky you annoyed her away. She could have killed you!"

"You went into a tool shed with a demon?" Sheila shook her head. "You deserve to die if you're dumb enough to do that."

"It was at my sister's house, and she was home alone," I said defensively. "And she's pregnant. I wasn't going to leave her to fend for herself."

"You should have asked for help," Jake said angrily.

I held my hands up. "Whose side are you on? We're not having this meeting so you both can gang up on me."

"Whatever," Sheila said. "Like I said, I had nothing to do with the attacks."

"Any idea why they're attacking him?" Jake asked. "Before, they were just screwing around and scaring him. But in the last day and a half, he's had four life-threatening demon encounters."

Sheila folded her arms and leaned back against the chair. "My guess is Malum found out David's not in the Hurricane. Either he's sending random demons after you to kill you, or these demons are all opportunists hoping that if they kill you, they'll become Malum's new pet. It's no secret among demons that he's after you."

"So, what do we do?" Jake demanded.

Sheila rolled her eyes. "Obviously you guys need to be guarding him better than you are. What, do you need me to do your job for you? You guys are pathetic." She shook her head and blew a lock of hair out of her face.

A ridiculously stupid idea popped into my head. "Do you think you could do better?"

Jake shot me a look, and Sheila raised her eyebrows. "Better than your pathetic angel guards that are never even there? Yes, I could do better."

"Care to prove it?" I asked.

Jake, who'd been standing behind me, came in front of me, blocking Sheila. "What are you doing, you flamin' galah?"

"Angels are stretched thin," I whispered. "Even Moustafa

couldn't find a qualified angel to protect my classes for a couple of hours a day. Sheila's time, however, is totally open, and she'll do anything to see her daughters. Maybe we could put her on probation or something and have her guard me?"

"You dipstick!" Jake whispered furiously. "She's the original demon that tried to kill you! She'll just do it again! You'd be putting yourself right into her hands!"

I leaned forward. "She was only attacking me because Malum made her, and she's no longer in his good graces. And I think part of her feels bad about all the destruction she's caused by letting him out. I think she'd be willing to work against him."

"Oh yeah, and how do we keep her from going rogue and joining Malum again?"

"No sane person joins Malum," Sheila interrupted. We turned around sheepishly. We hadn't been whispering quietly enough. "Trust me, after the things he's done to me, I want nothing to do with him. But, to be frank, if you were to trust me to guard David, that would be a really idiotic move. You'd have no way to make me stick around or prevent me from hurting him again."

That was weirdly honest. Or was she trying to lull me into trusting her by appearing honest?

I looked at the guards. "How do you keep her from fighting you when she's in your custody?"

The tall woman shrugged. "She's never fought us. But the Light manacles reduce her power, and the chains connect her to us so she can't escape. I can see no way to keep her contained without us here, and since the whole point in your plan is to free up more angels to do their duties, it defeats the purpose."

I considered for a moment while Jake scowled at me. "Sheila, how did Malum have you under his power?"

"I've already explained this," she said through gritted teeth.

"Explain again."

She sighed in exasperation. "He could sense me and pull me to him whenever he wanted. He could also read all my fears, so he automatically knew if I was doing anything contrary to his commands. The only things keeping him from dragging me down to the Red Zone right now are the Light manacles that confuse his senses. He can't sense me when I'm touching Light."

"So, we leave the manacles on to hide you from Malum, and then if you do anything to hurt me or any other mortal or angel, we can just . . ." I turned to Jake. "Can Hermes call angels to him? Not just tell them to come but make them come."

Jake shrugged. "He never would. He's all about choices, not forcing people to do things."

"But he can take my spirit out of my body and put it back," I said thoughtfully. "So, I bet he has the power to call angels to him, he just doesn't because of the whole free will thing. I wonder if he could call Sheila to him by the manacles around her wrists, since his connection is with Light. The opposite of Malum. And if Sheila ever did anything to hurt me or anyone other than those attacking me, I could just ask Hermes to remove her, the way he would remove my spirit from my body."

Hermes, could you do that? Can you call Sheila to you by the Light on her wrists?

Without warning, Sheila disappeared, along with the angels who held the chains to her manacles. The next second, they all reappeared. Sheila's chains jangled as she shook her arms and legs like a cockroach had just crawled over her. "Ugh! I hate that guy! Don't do that!"

Jake's mouth popped open.

I grinned. "I think we have our solution."

chapter 27
HUMAN LIE DETECTOR

"Really? C? Come on, I don't study nursing, but it's obvious that the answer is A."

I sighed and pulled up a Word document so I could type at her. *It's a red herring. It looks like the right answer, but it's wrong. And don't talk to me while I'm testing.*

Then I went back to my pop quiz. Sheila shrugged and settled back into the empty chair next to me. She itched at her manacles and sighed. It was a weird arrangement.

My phone buzzed. Kiki sent me a picture of my computer screen.

Kiki: who are you talking to?

Me: A dead woman

Kiki: does she have the answer to number 3?

Me: It's D

Kiki: ask the dead lady

Me: She doesn't know anything. She thought the answer to 10 was A.

Kiki: it is A!

I surreptitiously switched my answer, hoping Sheila didn't see. Our ancient professor thought he was high tech by having us take a computerized quiz, but he didn't even mix up the questions. Kiki and I had been texting each other this whole time, and he had no idea.

Sheila sighed again.

"I'm sorry this isn't as interesting as you imagined," I muttered.

I'd been attacked a couple of times since she started bodyguarding me, but even with the manacles that reduced her power, she dispatched the demons before there was even a fight. The rest of the time, she just followed me around, sighing and groaning about how bored she was. I mean, this had to be more interesting than prison, right?

I pulled out my phone again.

Me: Are you sure about tonight? It's gonna be dangerous.

Kiki: well my baby daddy's a little worried but I told him to suck it

Me: Suck it Nick Cage!

Me: Please don't come if you don't feel safe

Kiki: if my boyfriend is going to act like an idiot it's my duty to point and laugh

Me: Um, did you just call me your boyfriend?

Kiki: are you going to be a five year old about this?

Me: Five-year-olds don't have boyfriends

Kiki: i had four

Me: What kind of a kindergarten did you go to?

I jumped when Sheila cleared her throat. The professor was just reminding us we had ten more minutes, and I was only on question ten of thirty. I dropped my phone in my lap and got back to work. Well, I tried to, but then Kiki texted me again.

Kiki: are you trying to kick me out of your evil plan?
Me: No, I'm just worried. Something bad might happen. It's a really bad plan.
Kiki: so was your face, but that worked out in the end
Me: Um… thanks?

"Dude, do you need me to take your quiz for you?" Sheila hissed.

I scowled at her, and she just rolled her eyes.

We set up our trap in my dad's living room and told Preston and Dad to take a hike. The fewer people we had to risk with this plan, the better, and I was already risking Grandpa and Kiki. Grandpa, Raj, and I sat around the kitchen table while Sheila hid around the corner and out of sight. The plan was to have Grandpa call the suspects to us one by one, and Kiki would read their energy and intentions. Speaking of Kiki . . .

I leaned back into my chair to see what she was doing in the living room. "Hey, Kiki! Let's get started."

She dug some things out of her bag and hurried over to

dump them on the table.

"What's this?" Raj asked.

Kiki must have sensed Raj's curiosity.

"Just setting the mood!" she said brightly. She set some incense on a dish and lit it with a lighter. I coughed, and Grandpa leaned back and wafted the smoke away from him. Then Kiki took some sage and started going around the table, shaking it around each of our heads.

"Um, what are you doing?" I asked.

"Isn't sage supposed to ward off evil or something?" She wafted the sage into the air.

Grandpa scratched his stubble. "If it did, wouldn't that defeat the purpose of what we're doing?"

Raj rubbed his chin, hiding a smile.

Kiki rummaged through her bag again and dumped a box of Pop-Tarts on a fancy dish like an offering.

I snorted. "What is this, Día de los Muertos?"

"I was thinking of The Hungry Ghost Festival, actually."

I laughed. "Did you just make that up?"

"No, stupid; it's Chinese. Not everyone's a Mexican, you racist."

"Whoa, how is that—"

"Can we get started?" Raj requested patiently.

Kiki shrugged and brightly plopped down next to me. I tried not to grin stupidly at her, but she was just so endearingly weird. Raj cleared his throat.

"Right," I said. "Okay, so let's review the plan. Grandpa will call each member of our team here, and Kiki will read their energy."

Kiki, who had taken out a pad of paper and a pen, raised her hand.

"Uh, yes?" I asked.

"Won't we know right away if they're lying if they show up with the wrong face?"

"Demon hunters are often in disguise, so that doesn't automatically mean they're evil."

She scribbled that down, then raised her hand again.

I raised my eyebrows. "Yes?"

"What if they don't come when Gampy calls them?"

"They don't have to come, it's true," Grandpa said. "I can't control people. But most people do come when they feel me tugging at them. It's apparently a very strange feeling, and they more often than not follow the feeling to investigate."

"Make sure not to reveal we know they're lying right away, or they'll get spooked," Raj said. "We need time to question them. When we find the mole, David's . . . bodyguard and I will take them to prison." He still wasn't a fan of Sheila; that much was clear. But at least he was being civil.

Kiki frowned and looked up at the ceiling as she concentrated on what Raj was conveying. "Okay, I didn't get all of that. Just a warning of some sort?"

"Don't say out loud if you sense deception," I said. "Just write it on your little pad of paper or something."

"Got it!"

"Ready?" I asked everyone.

They all nodded, then Raj said, "Let's start with Bill."

Grandpa needed a picture to call dead people to him, and

since we didn't have any of those, we were hoping that Raj transforming himself to look like that person would suffice. Raj transformed himself to look like Bill, and my grandpa frowned in concentration. He closed his eyes, and within three seconds, Bill appeared to his right, looking flustered and confused.

"What was—" He spotted Raj with his face, and his eyes widened. "What the . . ."

Raj transformed back into himself. "Hey Bill, we needed to talk to you. Thanks for coming."

They both automatically threw Light at each other. It looked kind of funny, but I was glad these angels were on guard enough that they were doing the Light test with each other immediately, without prompting.

"Do you have a minute for us to ask you a few questions?" Raj asked.

Bill looked around at each of us. "Is this an interrogation? Am I in trouble?"

"We just have a few questions," Raj reassured him.

"Okay."

Raj leaned forward. "Do you know who the mole is?"

Bill blinked at his bluntness. "No, I don't. Do you? Daisy and I have been talking, and we think it might be Natalie, but we aren't sure. She's just been really secretive lately."

What did that mean? I hated being so out of the loop with my team. I had no idea what was going on with any of them.

Kiki shoved her pad of paper at me and pointed at the word "clear" she'd written in the corner.

I gave her a look.

She started writing again. *"No Darkness or deception detected. Whatever they're saying, they're telling the truth."*

I relaxed muscles I didn't know were tense. If Bill had turned out to be the mole, after Ted had turned out to be a murderer, I think my brain would have finally snapped.

Kiki scribbled down some notes, and Bill raised his eyebrows, noticing her for the first time and zeroing in on how my hand had unconsciously been resting on her thigh. He raised an eyebrow, pointing at Kiki. I just smiled and shrugged. He frowned a little, for some reason, but covered it up with a smile and a thumbs-up.

We thanked Bill and sent him back, then moved on to Natalie. She, too, was clear and didn't know who the mole was, but suspected Jake. We continued with Jake and Daisy, and neither of them knew who the mole was. Sandra, who was next, suggested that the mole was possibly Ted. Malum offered to let people out of the Hurricane if they joined him, and Ted would have reason to want revenge on Sheila for kicking him in. It seemed far-fetched to me, but not impossible, so I had Kiki write it down as a theory.

Frederick was next, but he didn't appear at first. After trying a couple more times, a small man with freckles appeared.

"Frederick?" Raj asked. "Interesting disguise. Throw some Light at me."

The man blinked in confusion, then threw Light at Raj, confirming he was an angel.

Raj raised an eyebrow. "You can remove the disguise, Frederick. We know it's you."

He sighed and became himself again. "Please, do not tell a soul that I have escaped. I have been working covertly in the background, and there is much at stake. I cannot rejoin you at this time. It would risk too much."

"Escaped?" I asked. "From where?"

"What do you mean, rejoin us?" Raj asked tensely.

Frederick gave him a dark look.

"You were *captured?*" I asked incredulously. "Since when? For how long? I just saw you a couple of days ago."

Frederick's nostrils flared. "That was not me. I suspect it was the betrayer." His face turned murderous.

"Could you be a little less vague?" I asked.

"I cannot," he snapped. "They will know it was I who told you, and I am trying to remain hidden. By delaying my return to The Resting Place, I have been able to work even more covertly than before, if in significantly darker ways. Please do not inform anyone of my escape. It could be detrimental to all I have worked for."

"You're asking me to turn the other way while you do things that might go against an angel's contract?" Raj said quietly.

Frederick nodded. "In the name of good, some of us must sink to their level to learn their ways. I am sorry, but I would rather taint my own soul than risk any of you."

Raj looked about to protest, then sighed. "What else can you tell us?"

"I dare not risk revealing any more than what I have said." He thought for a moment. "How did you bring me here?"

Grandpa raised his hand. "That would be me."

Frederick blinked. "A medium with the ability to . . . You realize this is the same power that Malum has over his slaves?"

"Luckily, I'm not a power-hungry monster," Grandpa said.

"You'll keep this to yourself, right?" I said nervously to Frederick.

"Of course. I suppose I can say one more thing before I go, but I must be vague. If you discover these things the same day I was mysteriously pulled away, they will be suspicious, so I will give you hints that will hopefully take you time to decode. Three other members of our team have gone rogue. One has remained faithful, another has turned to the Darkness, and the other is lost. I've done what I can to help them, but I am just one man. I worry I am failing." He rubbed his forehead in exhaustion.

It hurt my heart to hear him say these things. I didn't judge him for breaking his contract; I admired the way he was willing to sacrifice himself to protect others, but it made me sad that he was separate from us. Our team was falling apart one angel at a time. Frederick had to feel so alone. One angel among demons, without any friends or support.

"Are you okay?" I asked stupidly.

Frederick's face cracked into a smile, and suddenly, he looked like our Frederick again. The one who would tip his hat to you and make you feel important just by the polite, undivided attention he gave to you. "I will be fine, lad. Do not worry about me. You must keep yourself safe. Understood?"

I nodded, and he started to disappear.

Before he was gone, he hesitated. Then he transformed himself into a man I didn't recognize with tanned skin and brown dreadlocks.

Raj started. "The angel that told me how to escape the Hurricane."

Frederick nodded and put a finger to his lips. Then he disappeared.

Raj and I looked at each other. That was a lot to take in.

Kiki cleared her throat. "In case anyone was wondering, I sensed worry and anger, but no deception. Whatever the angel said, he was telling the truth. And I'm almost positive it was an angel. I didn't sense any Darkness." When we didn't respond, she asked, "What did he say?"

"Frederick was captured a long time ago, but escaped the Hurricane," I said. "He's now deep undercover with demons to the point that he is apparently doing things against an angel's contract in order to learn more about them. Uh, maybe don't write that down!"

Kiki quickly scratched out what she'd written.

Grandpa shook his head. "What in the world have you all gotten yourselves into?" He leaned back and let out a breath.

"This is just the tip of the iceberg, my friend," Raj said darkly.

"Hang on," I said. "If Frederick was captured a long time ago, that was probably done by the mole, who then started using Frederick's face. So, who could that be? It would have to be someone who disappeared a while ago."

Raj locked eyes with me as he had the same thought.

"William. Frederick was there when we did our last jailbreak. It must have been William, disguised as Frederick, who sold us out. It makes sense."

I shook my head. "We don't know that for sure, though. William could have actually been captured. And it's very possible it was Ted that turned." I looked around to see if Sheila had come out, then leaned in and lowered my voice. "We all know now that he has a dark past. I don't want to believe it's him, but Malum would probably love the irony of having Sheila's bad guy as his new right-hand man."

"We don't have proof that it was Ted either," Raj said. "And even if Ted were spotted doing evil, it could just be the mole using his face."

"There is one other possible mole we haven't discussed." I looked at Raj, but both of us refused to even suggest Ying Yue would betray us.

Raj ignored that. "He said that of the three others that have gone rogue, one is on our side, one has turned, and another is lost," Raj muttered. "I'm assuming that means in the Hurricane? But he said he tried to help them but failed. What would prevent someone from being saved from the Hurricane?"

"The person could literally be lost," I said. "Or hidden. It's hard to find people down there. Or maybe he pulled them out, but they're a wanderer now."

"The question is, should we continue with our experiment, knowing one of them has turned and would likely attack us?" Raj asked. "Also knowing that it would endanger Frederick and possibly destroy his plans if we learned the mole's identity too soon?"

I leaned my chin in my hand. "I mean, wasn't that the whole point of this, though? We wanted to catch them and hopefully take them into custody."

Raj closed his eyes and concentrated, then he opened them. "Hermes says we should wait."

I leaned back with a sigh. "Well, this was a waste."

"Not completely," Grandpa said. "You know who to trust now. You can have meetings together again."

"Unless the mole uses the face of someone we trust," I said.

Raj shook his head. "No, we'd know because they wouldn't be able to create Light, and there would be two people with the same face. Unless they used Frederick's face again, but we already know anyone claiming to be Frederick is a liar since he's gone rogue too. I say we go back to having meetings together. We'll just do a Light check each time, and that should be enough. I feel better knowing who we can trust, even if we haven't figured out exactly who the mole is."

Sheila appeared behind me. "Are you guys done? I'm tired of hiding in that stupid closet."

I sighed and leaned back in my chair. "Yeah, we're done for now."

"What did you discover?" she asked darkly. I knew who she suspected the mole to be.

I made eye contact with Raj, who shook his head. Sheila may have been my bodyguard, but she hadn't earned all our secrets.

I turned toward her. "That's classified, unfortunately."

HIM

Our positions were wrong. It was unjust. How could she be down there with demons and devils while I resided with saints and angels? I tried to appeal to the Big Man, but he insisted that there was nothing he could do. Our positions were our choices. And while she deserved The Resting Place, she refused to reside in the same place as her killer. I was her personal demon. She had believed in me over and over and over, and I repaid her with a killing blow to the head.

Not only did I kill her, but just by being in The Resting Place, I doomed her to Hell.

chapter 28
ENOUGH WITH THE DEMONS

"Hey, uh, David?"

I was startled awake. I'd dozed off while Kiki had gone to the bathroom. We were studying. Right? I checked the clock. It was 10:05, and I was late for my class.

I rolled off the bed and looked around me. Kiki was calmly sitting on the other side of my bed, reading a book, and a couple of my angel students were floating awkwardly in my doorway. I swore. This was our last class before they graduated to the next level, and here I was snoozing away.

"I'll be right down, guys!" I told the angels. I waited until they left, snickering at me, then turned to Kiki. "Sorry, I uh, have to go. I have a meeting with some angels. Why didn't you wake me up earlier?"

She shrugged. "You looked tired."

I rubbed my face. "I'm so sorry. I'm all over the place right now. But I have a bunch of angels down there waiting for me, so it's probably best if you go now."

"You kicking me out?" She shook her head in judgment.

I thought she was joking, but I still felt awful for falling asleep on her. She started gathering her things into her bag and then stood in front of me with her hands behind her back.

"I will receive my compensation now."

I raised an eyebrow.

"For falling asleep," she clarified. "Three kisses in three different places."

"Um, okay?" I chuckled awkwardly and then took her head in my hands and kissed her head like I was her grandpa or something. Then I kissed her eyebrow because I don't know. Then I kissed her lips. She pulled me closer by the shirt for a few seconds, then pushed me away.

"All right, off with you!" She hit me in the butt with her bag as she herded me out the door.

"You're really off-putting, you know that?" I said, looking back at her.

"Shoo!"

She pushed me forward, and I grabbed her hand to stop her from hitting me as we went down the stairs. There was a Light fight going on. Younger angels were giggling, while the more adult newbies stood on the sidelines, rolling their eyes. Grandpa had left his room to investigate the noise. Lovely.

"Could you all keep it down?" Grandpa groused. "Some of us have to sleep, you know."

I hurried down the stairs, pulling Kiki behind me.

"Sorry, Grandpa. I'll get them under control. Here, I got you these earplugs so we wouldn't bug you." I fished the earplugs I'd bought for him from my pocket, and he nodded in appreciation.

"Before you get to your class, I have another message for you from that mystery dead person. The one that was glowing blue. They said, 'Stop trying to identify the mole.'"

I blinked. That sobered me immediately. How did they know we were trying to identify the mole? Did they know who it was? Why didn't they want us to find out?

"Was it a threat?" I asked.

Grandpa shrugged. "Honestly, it sounded more like a warning. Anyway, don't stay up too late." He took the earplugs from my hand, frowned at the chaos behind me, then grumbled off to bed.

I wanted to try and puzzle out that warning further, but there were a bunch of angels that needed guiding.

I walked Kiki out to her car and kissed her before she drove off.

"Not bad, teach." I spun around. Leo was leaning against the outside of the door with a smirk.

"Get back inside, kid. Also, thank you for volunteering to demonstrate a full-body Light shield. You're a real sport."

He grimaced. "You sound like an old man."

"Don't sass me, boy."

I followed him inside and looked around for Sheila. She'd had zero desire to hang out in my room with me and my girlfriend, so she said she'd wait downstairs. I figured that was good enough, since Kiki could sense demons, and we could yell for Sheila if we needed her. I finally spotted her leaning against the counter with her arms folded. I didn't recognize her at first because she looked like she was radiating Light. It only took a moment of scrutiny to recognize the faint smoky outline characteristic of fake Light. I nodded in appreciation. There was no need to frighten my newbie angels with a demon in their midst.

I whistled quietly to call everyone to order. You might wonder how one whistles quietly. Well, first you just have to suck at whistling. Then you whistle. That's pretty much it.

"Hey, everyone, you know I can't yell since people are sleeping. So, listen up. During the last class, we worked on Light shields. Leo kindly offered to come to the front and demonstrate . . ."

I trailed off, feeling like something was wrong. I looked around me. Nothing was out of place. No one was here who shouldn't be. And yet, there was a feeling of panic welling up inside me.

"No one move," I whispered.

Leo scoffed. "Nice try, but—"

Darkness filled the room until it was almost pitch black. What could be seen through the weak light shining through the mists were demonic zombies crawling out of the floor with eyes coming out of their sockets and black blood covering their skeletal bodies. Angels screamed, and I saw some of them disappear immediately, while others froze in place.

"Everyone, leave! Now! Get back to The Resting Place!" I screamed.

To my right, a demon threw a net of Darkness over a girl named Veronica, while another slowly put his hands around Mrs. Tempest's neck. One of the demons made her way toward me, wearing Sandra's face. Panic set in, and I forgot for a second that I was in charge of these people. I scrambled backward and fell into a chair. Someone screamed, and I blinked, remembering that I was the one in the least amount of danger here. While alive, they couldn't drag me down to the Hurricane.

Just as a demon swooped toward me, it was blasted away by an angel. Wait, no, it was Sheila still radiating her fake Light. She stood in front of me, throwing Darkness bombs that blasted the demons away from me with apparent ease. Many of the demons recognized her and disappeared immediately, but my brief moment of relief was short-lived. Braver demons took their place, and soon she was outnumbered at least five-to-one. It wasn't long before I completely lost sight of her.

"Crap, crap, crap, crap, crap!"

After another second of panic, I scrambled behind the chair and yelled, "ANGELS, USE YOUR LIGHT SHIELDS!"

Hermes, please send help! We're being attacked!

I saw a few flickers of Light in the Darkness and prayed they'd keep it up until more help came. Taking a deep breath, I dodged around a demon coming after me, climbed up on the coffee table, and yelled, "Don't panic! Light is stronger than Darkness. You can do this. Think of where Light comes from and shoot them with your Light."

I felt like such a pathetic coward, yelling at all of them to fight while I did absolutely nothing, but what else could I do? I had no power, and the Darkness was everywhere.

A few balls of Light flew through the Darkness, briefly illuminating devilish demons and the terrified angels. I was so proud of whoever managed that, but I knew their efforts wouldn't be enough. If none of them had been dragged off yet, it was only because the demons were having too much fun playing with their food. That wouldn't last forever.

"Those of you who can, follow my voice!" I figured if we all banded together, they'd have more of a fighting chance. Pietro, Leo, Mrs. Tempest, and a man named Howard crowded around me. So few? Were the others captured? What happened to Sheila? I thought I heard her scream.

Asher flew at me and tried to hug my legs.

"Get back to The Resting Place, kid! The rest of you form full-body shields in one hand! Use the other hand to throw balls of Light over the top. Don't worry about aiming yet, we just need some Light!"

Five balls of Light sailed through the mists, briefly illuminating angels trapped in the grips of cackling demons. Fortunately, or unfortunately, that caught the attention of the demons who zeroed in on me and grinned. I swore. These angels around me would be taken down because I was the one they wanted. I looked around for Sheila and couldn't find a trace of her. How had they overpowered her so easily? Previous experience taught me that typical demons were no match for her.

I could barely breathe from the panic. There was no way my two-week-old angels could fight them off. My Level Two class might have been able to handle this, which was probably why the demons attacked now. One of them had been spying on us and knew exactly when the rookies would be congregated. Now I had to worry about a mole in my class.

Hermes! What's going on?

HELP IS ON ITS WAY, BUT IT WILL BE A FEW MINUTES.

It takes one second for someone to poof over here!

THE ANGELS ARE BUSY. YOURS ISN'T THE ONLY DIRE SITUATION HAPPENING IN THE WORLD RIGHT NOW.

Can I leave my body to help?

THIS IS YOUR LAST CHANCE. IT IS YOUR CHOICE IF THIS IS HOW YOU'D LIKE TO USE IT.

A demon had just thrown a whip around Mrs. Tempest and was yanking her away, kicking and screaming. My heart plummeted. "DO IT NOW!"

My body fell off. I paused to wince as I watched my head smack against the fireplace mantle when I fell from the coffee table. I couldn't feel it at the moment, but I knew it wouldn't feel good once I woke up.

There was no time to relish the freeing sensation or explain to the few angels around me that witnessed me apparently collapse and die. Faster than I'd ever done, my hands burst with Light and Darkness, which I used to create several demon killer bullets that I shoved in my pockets. I created a Light gun and loaded it in record time. Mrs. Tempest was almost out the back door when I shot her demon right in the head.

The demon dropped her and fell to the ground. Demon killers couldn't kill, obviously, but a shot to the brain could incapacitate a demon with pain and confusion.

Two other demons flew at me and my little group. I shot

one of them in the chest but missed the second one. She'd thrown a whip around Pietro and was giggling as she pulled him in. I flew at them and formed my gun into a sword, cutting through the whip. Then I whipped around and sliced through her neck, kicked her friend away as he started to get back up, then stabbed him through the heart. They both clutched the place I'd wounded them and disappeared, leaving their comrades behind them.

A new demon flew at me, but before I could react, he was hit in the head with a ball of Light.

"Nice hit!" I grinned, looking to see who'd thrown it.

Two demons tackled me from behind. I struggled and panicked for a minute, watching balls of Light glance off them. Other than the fact that these angels didn't know how to fight yet, our biggest problem was the Darkness. We couldn't see who was coming up behind us. We needed more Light.

I gasped, remembering what I had done back in the Hurricane so long ago. I closed my eyes, took a steadying breath, and thought of where Light comes from. I believed with all my heart that I could access this Light. It was part of me. It was part of all of us. Forcing the Light from every pore of my body, I shone like the sun at noon. The demons who'd been holding me screamed and immediately released me, backing away in terror. My Light pierced the Darkness, and I could see everything around me. All the demons in my vicinity panicked and disappeared. There were three on the outskirts of the room with students in their clutches. I formed another gun and picked off as many as I could, but everything was happening too fast. So many of my students were either screaming in a demon's clutches, or dazed and flickering, as though their Light was about to go out. They couldn't handle this, and I wasn't enough to fight all the demons at once.

Before my despair could overwhelm me, several angels appeared in the middle of the fight. I didn't know any of them, but they must have been defenders, because they fought like a well-oiled machine. Demon hunters learn combat mainly for self-defense, and we only fight one or two enemies at a time. Defenders are the exact opposite: trained to attack hordes of demons as one. In thirty seconds, the remaining demons were in chains.

Before I had a moment to celebrate, a scream cut through the air. I spun around and saw a demon we'd missed dragging Asher away. They were starting to disappear.

"NO!"

I flew over as fast as I could and took hold of Asher's free hand before we were transported right to the edge of the Hurricane. The moaning wind whipped my hair back from my face, filling me with fear I did my best to ignore.

"You will not take any more of my friends!" I yelled as I yanked Asher toward me. The demon had too strong a grip, and when I looked up at the demon's face, I was so shocked, I let go.

He was radiating Darkness that exuded from him like an overpowering stench. His mask of hatred almost made his face unrecognizable. Almost. I realized with a jolt of horror that this wicked face was the last thing Sheila saw before she died.

Before I could shake myself from my shock, he threw Asher in with a laugh. I screamed and jumped in after him. The red mists caressed me as I reached for Asher, and the wind whipped sound around us so intensely I could barely hear his scream. But as we descended, I caught hold of his robe. Then I yanked him to me, hugging him as he clung to me and hid his face in my chest. I closed my eyes and tried to remember what I needed to remember. We could escape this. The Hurricane wasn't a prison; we could leave at any time if we just remembered who we were.

"Cover your ears, Asher, and think of Light! Think of the Big Man!"

With a whimper, he had the presence of mind to listen to me. I held him tighter, wishing I could cover my own ears against the tortured screams and the whispers in the Darkness.

"You've lost . . ."

". . . it's not enough."

"You can't save them . . ."

". . .you're broken."

Then the most distinct voice boomed, *"You failed me . . . You are selfish, sacrificing your friends as you try to make something of yourself . . . I will not stand for you; I will not help you . . . You are dead to me . . ."*

I was back here again, and this time I'd never escape. I deserved it. A child who depended on me was captured because of me. I deserved torture. I deserved it forever.

chapter 29
EVERYTHING IS BROKEN

I couldn't bear the thought of giving in. I couldn't give up! But even being near the Hurricane, you start to feel tainted and alone, like you can never belong with normal people again. Scrunching my face up in pain and determination, I tried to shake the taint from my mind and imagined us back at my house. It was harder than it should have been. My mind was sludge, and my soul felt broken. My brain had a really stupid thought of Dorothy clicking her heels and saying, "There's no place like home!" Before I could chide myself for thinking of something so stupid at a time like this, we were back in my family room.

I'd done it. I'd actually gotten us back. I'd escaped the freaking Hurricane!

Asher refused to let go of me. I wasn't sure what he heard or saw in those few minutes he'd been in the Hurricane, but it was more than any kid should ever be subjected to. I was glad he'd at least covered his ears. His arms were so snug around my neck that he'd have been cutting off my air supply if I were in my body. My body that we were currently kneeling next to. A few angels screamed when they saw it, thinking I'd died, but I could sort that out later.

"Asher," I said gently. "It's okay. We escaped. You're safe. You're gonna be all right. I've got you."

He squeezed me tighter.

I sighed sadly. "You should go back to The Resting Place. I've gotta go, buddy."

He pulled back suddenly. "Go where?" he demanded.

My heart leapt at hearing his voice. He could talk. He wasn't a wanderer again. He was all right.

"I'm not dead," I explained. "I'm just like this temporarily. I can do that sometimes."

His mouth fell open. "What?"

I rubbed my forehead. "Yeah, I can leave my body sometimes to fight demons."

Asher's mouth opened wider. "Are you kidding me? Like Danny Phantom? Did you just *go ghost?*"

"Uh, I don't know what you're talking about." I did know what he was talking about. I used to be obsessed with that show as a kid, and had a weird cartoon crush on Danny's sister, but that was beside the point.

Asher started bouncing around as he threw questions at me faster than I could answer. "Someone told me you used to be an office boy, so I thought you were lame. But you're a superhero! Did you see yourself?" His weird enthusiasm continued spewing from his mouth. "First, you were like BAM, BAM! Then you were like SWISH, SWISH! Then you were like, 'Behold my Light, fart faces!' What was that sword you made? Was it made of Light *and* Darkness? Are you gonna teach us to do that too?" He started singing the Danny

Phantom theme song and pantomimed fighting demons. So, clearly, he was okay.

Before I could respond, I was jerked sideways and dumped back into my body.

Immediately, I felt the tremendous, achy weight of a mortal body. I sat up groggily, suppressing a groan, and the angels cowering around the table shrieked.

"But you were dead!" Mrs. Tempest shrieked.

I clutched my head and smiled reassuringly. "Not dead. Just a temporary coma. Sometimes Hermes lets me leave my body to help." Though not anymore . . . My stomach dropped at the realization that I'd just used up my last chance. I would never do that again. I would never hug my mom again, or join my friends in a fight, or hold Sandra's hand. It was all gone until I, myself, died. And if I got what I wanted, that wouldn't be for a very long time.

Before I had time to truly mope about it, the defenders came to check in with me. The demons were gone, and the angels were gathering my students in The Resting Place, where they could get a head count in a safer location. I nodded in a daze, praying everyone was safe. A lot of the stragglers wanted reassurance from me, and I did my best to encourage them and move them along.

Once everyone was gone, I leaned against the back of the couch and slid to my butt. There was so much to take in.

Then I remembered Sheila. I jumped to my feet again, cursing my pounding head. Had Ted captured her? I'd heard her scream, and then she was gone.

"Sheila!" I yelled.

I jumped when I saw a hand, shrouded in Darkness, slowly rise beyond the countertop.

Stumbling over my feet, I hurried around the counter and found Sheila crouched with her legs pressed to her chest and her head in her knees. She slowly lowered her hand and clutched her legs again.

I knelt in front of her. "Are you okay?"

She didn't answer at first. Then she lifted her head. "I screwed up," she said in a rough, angry voice that belied her horrified face. "I saw *him* and panicked. I'm sorry. I'm pathetic." She grimaced in anger, glaring at the floor.

"It's okay," I said. "We all freeze sometimes."

She rolled her eyes and released her legs, letting them stretch out in front of her. "You should probably check on your little girlfriend hiding in the hall closet."

I started. "What? Kiki went home."

"She came back right when you started class. She forgot her phone. Then, like a little creeper, she stuck around to watch you. When the demons came, she hid in the closet and hasn't come out yet."

I jumped to my feet, and black spots overtook my vision. I felt myself sinking and gripped the edge of the counter until the weakness passed. I felt the back of my head and found a huge goose egg. Ow. I hoped I didn't have a concussion. Ignoring the pounding in my head and the black spots in my vision, I hurried to the hall closet and stopped myself before I threw it open.

"Um, Kiki? Are you in there?"

No one answered.

"Can I come in?"

She still didn't respond.

I slowly opened it and turned on the Light. Kiki looked just like Sheila had a few moments ago, but she was pointing an umbrella at me like a weapon.

I sighed and knelt, pushing the umbrella downward. "You weren't supposed to be here."

She gasped. "What the hell was that, David? I've never felt so much Darkness in my life."

I sighed again and leaned against the wall. "We were attacked by demons. That doesn't normally happen."

"Normally? So sometimes it does? How often do demons come after you?"

"Uh, kind of a lot recently? I've unintentionally made myself a target. But I have a bodyguard. She just kind of lost it today. She's not normally like that."

Kiki shook her head and stood up. "No, I'm not doing this." I braced myself against the wall as I struggled to stand, but she brushed past me.

Groaning, I hurried after her as she ran to the front door. "Wait! Hold on!"

She spun around. "I don't know what kind of demonic shit you've gotten yourself into, David, but I'm not interested." She leaned in. "You know, I didn't say anything, but I could sense when we did that little mole test that that Sandra girl was an ex of yours. Tell me—how did she die? Was it before or after she became involved with all this crap?"

I sighed and rubbed my face. "It was after. But that's not why she died. That was a car accident." Then I paused. The first time she was supposed to die, that *was* because of Malum. He would have killed her if I hadn't jumped in front of that bullet and saved her. And that *was* my fault because Malum was trying to get to me. Kiki was right, the women in my life weren't safe.

"What?" Kiki demanded, seeing the look on my face.

"She did almost die once when a demon came after her… because of me."

Kiki pushed me. "What is wrong with you? Why would you endanger her like that? And me? You used me without telling me how unsafe it is just to be around you."

"I tried to warn you," I said weakly. "I told you it would be dangerous."

She snorted. "Dangerous is riding on the back of some hot guys' motorcycle, or skinny dipping in restricted waters." I raised my eyebrow at that, but she ignored me. She pointed toward my living room, where the attack had happened. "That wasn't dangerous, that was *evil!*"

I nodded, too deflated to contradict her. She was right. I was too dangerous to be around, and I'd selfishly endangered her just because I liked her.

Her face softened. "I'm sorry, David. I like you a lot. You're really sweet and adorable in the cutest way. And I love fake studying with you. But you're a complete lunatic if you think I want to stay with you after all *that.*"

I felt my whole body slump with that emotional punch. Kiki hesitated, then hugged me tightly. Before I had time to hug her back, she was gone.

• • •

Mom showed up right before my Level Two class arrived and freaked out, along with all of my students when I explained what had happened. I didn't want to tell them, but they deserved to know the danger they were getting themselves into. Mom tried to convince me to cancel class, but this attack made it even more apparent that this was too important to cancel.

Mom ended up taking over for me. I was a useless, achy mess, and my head was killing me. I couldn't even see straight. I just sat on my dad's recliner, staring into space as Mom tried her best to instruct demon hunter recruits on how to make Darkness even though she, herself, had never done it. Eventually, Sheila took pity on her and took over the rest of class. That was weirdly surprising. I wasn't sure how I felt about a demon teaching my students, but I didn't have the presence of mind to protest, and they assumed she was just a volunteer. I probably should have been concerned about the fact that they didn't realize her Light was fake. I thought I'd taught them better than that.

There was another thing on my mind that hurt so much I wanted to curl up into a ball and disappear. During class, a defender appeared to share the "casualty report" with me after taking a headcount of my students who'd returned to The Resting Place. One of them hadn't returned. It was Leo. Brave Leo, always there with a comeback, ready to defend those who were being picked on or questioned. He'd been right next to me, and he was snatched right beneath my nose.

The defender sharing this information was very pragmatic about it. She said it was a miracle more hadn't been taken since I was the only trained fighter against a horde of demons. But I could have done more, and I knew this was my fault.

The noise hadn't woken anyone living in the house, so they were all still safely in their beds. Dad had invested in a pair of earplugs long ago, and I assumed Preston was asleep or listening to music to tune me out like I'd advised him to do.

Once class was over, I slowly trudged up the stairs, feeling this awful combination of panic and depression. I simultaneously wanted to scream and hide under a blanket for the rest of my life. Leo was taken, Kiki was gone, and I'd just used up my last opportunity to leave my body. I was just a regular old mortal for the rest of my life. Stuck, with no direction or purpose. I was annoyed with myself for being so emotional. Wasn't this what I wanted? I'd told Hermes that I wanted to live a nice, long life like a *normal* person. But the permanence of it terrified me, and I was furious with myself for being upset by something as stupid as that when there were more important things to beat myself up over. Leo. Kiki. Gone. My fault.

When I got to my room, I flopped on my bed face-first and didn't move, frozen in my internal turmoil. It all came back to the same question: why was I *here*? The Big Man told me he'd place me where he needed me, but if I was needed here, why was I failing so miserably? My purpose was as hazy as ever. Why send me back to a life just to fail? What purpose could that serve? Maybe it really was a punishment. All I knew was that the finality of officially being just a mortal was terrifying, and the fact that I was no longer a part of my team was just as depressing as everything else that had happened tonight.

Angels were dropping left and right. I remembered Ted's face with a shudder. Was that really Ted, or just someone disguised as him? Whoever it was, there was pure evil in his eyes. How could we go on like this?

Kiki was right. I was crazy to ever think I could fight this evil.

I despised myself for still wishing she were here.

HER

I didn't think Malum would take me with him. I thought I'd just release him on The Resting Place, let him cause destruction and upheaval, and then I'd just leave and never come back. Obviously, that's not what happened. No one saw me there, but he took me with him when he disappeared, right to the edge of the Hurricane. He held me there, suspended by the neck, and I'd never felt fear like that in my life. I'd never heard of the Hurricane. Nowadays, all angels know of its infamous horror, but things were different back then. There were demon guards that shouted at Malum about "unauthorized Hurricane punishment." Apparently, demons had rules about that. Of course Malum doesn't follow rules. He simply removes those in his way. The guards joined me at the bottom of the Hurricane, and there I suffered for what felt like an eternity. I saw HIS face as he beat me and killed me, then moved on to hurting our babies. Real and imagined horrors became my entire existence, and I was no longer a person, but a ball of horror and agony. Until Malum offered me a way out.

I didn't plan for any of this to happen . . .

PART THREE

chapter 30
THE INTERVENTION

I woke up to three figures leaning over me, one of them shining a phone flashlight in my eye. I flinched and cringed away. That sudden movement set my head pounding, and everything ached.

"Might be a concussion," a voice said quietly.

I groaned and sat up. Dad, Grandpa, and Preston hovered around me, looking concerned and nervous.

I tried to wipe the sleep from my face. "What are you guys doing in here?" I found my glasses and shoved them on my face, but the world still seemed blurry.

"Grandpa told us you were hurt," Dad said. He was sitting next to me on my bed.

"How would you know that?" I asked Grandpa. He stood next to Dad.

"Your mom told me," he said. "Said there was an attack, and you hit your head pretty bad. She had to go but said we should check on you."

I looked questioningly at Preston.

He shrugged. "I heard them run up the stairs and followed

them in. Just wanted to make sure you were okay."

"Here," Dad shoved a couple of Tylenols into my hand and a glass of water. "It will help with the headache."

"Uh, thanks." I gulped them down and looked around at everyone. Why was everyone being so nice to me?

"So, what happened?" Preston asked.

"Wait," Grandpa said, forestalling my answer. "Is that *thing* supposed to be in here? She says she's your bodyguard, but I know a demon when I see one. Even if she does have strange Light cuffs around her wrists."

I looked up to see Sheila leaning against my door frame, rolling her eyes at being called a "thing."

"Uh, yeah, she's serving time by guarding me. It's a long story." I rubbed my head and winced at the pain and dizziness.

"So, are you gonna tell us what happened?" Preston prompted again.

I eyed him suspiciously. "The explanation involves a lot of things you wouldn't believe."

He shrugged. "Who cares what I think?"

This was weird. My dad, my grandpa, and my boss were crowded around my bed, looking at me like they were waiting for story time in the middle of the night. This was normally the part where I'd say I didn't want to talk about it, or it was something I wasn't allowed to share. But they all seemed so attentive, and it felt weirdly good to know someone was listening to me. So, I told them about what had happened.

Grandpa had no problem believing it, Dad didn't like it, and Preston kept a surprising poker face. Without prompting, they all decided to leave me to sleep. As he walked out the door, Preston ordered me to stay home from work, and I didn't protest. I thought I'd ditch school too. My head was killing me, and I didn't want to see Kiki anyway.

I woke up at 11 AM to my phone buzzing repeatedly. I groaned and flopped around for it until my hand felt the buzzing rectangle. It was Elena calling me. She cut me off before I could even greet her.

"She dumped you?" she demanded.

I sighed and fell back against my pillow. "Who told you?"

"Dad. What a prissy little—"

"Hey! There's no need for that. Kiki had her reasons. And they're good ones."

"I still think she's being a child about this. You don't run away at the first sign of trouble. That's what relationships are! Just a bunch of trouble!"

I rubbed my forehead and sighed. "Elena, if she was your sister and I was the guy she broke up with, you would be one hundred percent on her side."

Elena paused. "Okay, maybe. Demon attacks are kind of . . . like the biggest red flag in the universe. But you're my brother, and I know you, and she doesn't know what she's missing!"

"You kicked me out for the same reason she dumped me," I pointed out.

"Oh, come on! I didn't cut you out of my life. I just didn't want you to bring danger into my house with my kids there.

And I was right to be cautious, okay? I heard you say to that ghost in the shed that you knew they were after you."

I sat up slowly and leaned against my headboard. "I'm sorry, are you agreeing with me now?"

"No, Kiki is an idiot, and you're a freaking catch, and if she can't see that, she doesn't deserve you."

I smiled. She was wrong, but as my sister, she was supposed to say these things, and I appreciated her saying them. "Thanks."

"Want me to come to you for No Kid Lunch today? Bring you food while you recover from your concussion?"

Was it Thursday already? When had that happened? "Um, that's okay."

"No, really," she said urgently. "My intern is driving me up the freaking wall. Please give me an excuse to get out of here."

"Fine. You pick the food and order for me because my brain doesn't work, and I don't want to think. I'll pay you back."

I hung up and went back to sleep.

When I woke up again, I remembered all the things I had to be depressed about. I wished Kiki were here. I always felt better around her. She didn't even have to try; she just had to be her weirdo self, and suddenly life wasn't so bad. But I'd lost her. I'm not sure what I expected in the long run—I hadn't really thought that far. In the moment, it was just nice to have a companion who understood my connection with the other side. I was never going to find that with someone else. I was never going to find another Kiki.

It hurt to think about Leo. What horrors was he facing right at that moment? I didn't want to imagine it, but I couldn't stop fixating on it. He didn't deserve that. He deserved to be rescued immediately, but I couldn't do a single thing about it anymore because I was fully mortal now. I had to depend on other angels to save him. And because they didn't love him like I did, they would wait so they could make a plan for an organized jailbreak. So, he would have to suffer while he waited for rescue, just like Mom and Jake had. I still remembered their faces after I rescued them. Jake was completely dead inside, and Mom was almost there. She was so weak and hopeless. I shuddered just thinking about it.

We were losing this war. Things were only getting worse, and what was I supposed to do about it? I felt suddenly angry for being included in the demon hunters. How could *I* fix this? Also, why was it up to *me* to fix this anyway? No one told me it was my job, so why couldn't I just leave it in the hands of others? Back when I'd first become mortal, my mom had told me that my job now was to live. But how could I live when my focus was always on the other side? No other mortals were risking their lives for angels. And this back and forth was tearing me in two.

By the time Elena showed up, I'd at least brushed my teeth but didn't feel like changing out of my sweatpants.

Elena came through the garage and found me flopped on the couch in the family room without a shirt on. She stood in front of me and wrinkled her nose. "You look gross."

"Thanks," I mumbled into the pillow.

"I brought Jessica."

I sat up too fast and clutched my head, groaning. Ow. Once I had the dizziness somewhat under control, I looked up to see Jessica happily setting the table with nice plates to eat our crap fast food burgers on. Okay?

"Hey, Jessica," I said, as I got to my feet and yanked on my T-shirt.

She waved cheerily. "How's your head? Elena said demons attacked you."

I glared at Elena incredulously. What was this weird openness of everyone sharing my business, especially about the weirdest, most dangerous parts of my life? Elena shrugged as she slurped through her straw and handed me a milkshake.

Jessica, noting my expression, said, "Ah, you don't know. Of course. There's a group chat."

I raised my eyebrows. "What?"

"Jessica!" Elena scolded, swatting her arm. "You're not supposed to tell him that!"

She held her hands up with a smile, not looking apologetic at all. She reached into the fast food bag and set everyone's burgers and fries neatly on the plates.

"Group chat?" I prompted, taking my usual chair to the left of the head. Wait, they'd set out four plates. What was that about?

Jessica shrugged as she took her place across from me. "A family group chat you're not a part of. We talk about you."

"There's a family group chat I'm not a part of? Who's all on it?" I demanded.

Elena sighed. "Just me, Sam, Dad, Charlie, and Jessica."

"That's literally all of you!"

She ignored me and walked around the corner toward Grandpa's room. I heard her knock on his door. What the heck was going on? Grandpa followed Elena out, chatting amiably like they'd already met. When had that happened?

Grandpa sat next to me and joined us without a word, taking one of the unclaimed milkshakes from the to-go container. I looked around at all three of them. "Am I missing something?"

"Yes," Elena said. "We had a family meeting this morning while you were sleeping. Everyone was there, including Grandpa. Well, we were all there on FaceTime, anyway. Even your boss jumped in when Dad invited him to join."

My brain was more broken than I'd thought. "What?"

"We all agree that it's time for an intervention," Elena said matter-of-factly. "No one else could come today, but they share our concerns and trust the three of us to express them." Then she, I kid you not, pulled out an easel with a giant notepad. The first page said, *David's Intervention.*

My head was reeling. "What the heck?"

Before I had a chance to get another word in, Grandpa chimed in. "We're concerned about you, son. This demon hunter business has taken over your life and is likely to end your life if you don't take a step back."

"Like fifty steps back," Elena said. "Like, quit, cold turkey." Before I could say anything, she flipped her notepad to the next page, outlining her argument.

At this point, Jessica stood up and pointed to the first item.

"First off, David, you are alive. Living people should not get involved with the problems of the deceased. Leave them to their own devices as their problems are their own."

"But—"

"It's not your turn yet, boy," Grandpa interrupted. "I know very well that you can't just shut them all out. It's a very fine line to walk—believe me, I know. But you have to find a balance, and you need to set boundaries. Talking to them, fine. Helping them occasionally with a simple task, fine. Fighting for them, now that's crossing the line."

"We're not saying you need to stop being a medium," Jessica added. "You can't. It's the demon hunter stuff we're concerned about."

"But—"

"Second point," Elena said. "Other areas of your life are suffering because you are not fully engaged with your life." She flipped the page and showed a chart of my actual grades. What the heck?

"How did you—"

"Dad saw your grades open on your laptop last week," Elena said. "Snapped a picture when you weren't looking."

My face heated. "That is such a violation of privacy."

"You're also not hanging out with your family as much, and Preston said you've been late to work a lot," Jessica added.

"I was late last week because I was helping Elena!" I protested.

"With a ghost problem," she agreed, "which I'm pretty sure wouldn't have been a problem if you hadn't made yourself such a target for demons."

I rubbed the side of my face. "You guys don't even know what you're talking about."

"And Grandpa tells us you're teaching these late-night classes to angels?" Elena said.

"Living humans need sleep," Jessica said. "Your angel friends may not understand that, but as fellow mortals, we can confirm its necessity."

Elena flipped to a page with a bunch of dots.

"What is that?" I asked.

"How many dead people do you think there are?" Elena asked.

"Uh, of which variety?"

"Let's go with angels," Jessica said.

"No idea. Hundreds of thousands? Maybe a million? The Resting Place is like the size of a really big city. They move on at a pretty steady rate, so it's not as many people as you'd think. But right now it's less than it usually is because fewer people are becoming angels when they die, and angels keep getting captured. So, it's probably more like ten to fifty thousand, maybe. But I don't know, I could be really off."

"Would you say the number of angels today is more or less than the number of dots on this paper?" Elena asked.

I rolled my eyes. "More, obviously."

She took a red marker and circled one dot in the bottom right corner. "This is you. One dot. They have no business putting all these dead people responsibilities on you when they have all these other dots to choose from. There is no way none of the other dots can't do what they're making you do. Even if they're swamped, they can spread the wealth."

I sighed and leaned back in my chair.

The next page said "dating" at the top. Oh brother . . .

"David, would you say you're interested in women?" Jessica asked.

I groaned at the ceiling, leaning my head back on my chair. "Do we have to do this right now? I literally just got dumped!"

"Case in point," Elena said. "The demon hunting is screwing with your love life. I mean, both girlfriends you've had got too close to this demon hunting crap and they both ended up leaving you—"

"Sandra didn't leave me; she *died*, and it had nothing to do with demons!" I said sharply. "Leave her out of this!"

There was a tense and awkward silence caused by my shift in tone. I glared at them, daring them to poke the bear.

Jessica hesitantly asked, "Would you like to settle down someday, David?"

"If I live that long," I muttered down at the table.

Elena threw a marker at me. "THAT! That is what we're talking about! That is the problem!"

"What?" I demanded, with my hands up. "I was never told if this was a temporary—"

"All life is temporary, son," Grandpa interrupted. "No one knows when they're going to die. Any one of us in this room could die tomorrow. The fact that you don't know how long you will live isn't unique. What is wrong is the way that you keep thinking about dying."

"I don't think about dying," I said with a grimace. "I just

have a different situation—"

Elena threw another marker at me. "Shut up. You're here. You're alive. You're mortal. Whatever your past, you are the same as the rest of us. The same! But you're living like you're already half dead. This needs to end."

She sat down and started eating her cheeseburger.

"I like her," Sheila said.

I turned around to glare at her as she leaned against the wall. "Whose side are you even on?"

She shrugged.

I sighed and looked back at the living people. "What, so you think I should just not help my desperate friends that are dropping like flies?"

"Jessica," Elena said with her mouth full, "give her the Charlie speech for me."

Jessica nodded. "Charlie is a military man. Is he fighting right now?"

"No," I said slowly.

"Why not?"

"He's not deployed at the moment."

Jessica nodded. "Is it possible he has friends whose lives are in danger right now?"

"Yes."

"And does he fly across the world to save them?"

"No . . ."

"Right, because it's not his responsibility to save his comrades when he's off duty. Charlie knows that they knew what they signed up for, and their lives are in their own hands."

I sighed. "Okay, I see where you're going with this."

Grandpa leaned forward. "You're too young to be thinking of death, son. You should be running around crazy, forgetting you're not immortal."

I laughed. "I know better than anyone that I'm not. I was seventeen when I died."

"But you're alive *now*," Jessica said. "Now is what we're talking about, David. You need to live your life while you're living. You can't do that if you always have one foot out the door."

I sighed and took a bite of my cheeseburger. Their points were valid. I was just one mortal, and it wasn't my responsibility to protect the dead. I might let people down if I stepped aside, but I thought of all those dots on Elena's notepad. They could always find another dot to fill my place. There were thousands to choose from, so losing one me shouldn't break the entire system. And I was stretched too thin. It wasn't that I had more responsibilities than others, but having those responsibilities span across both sides of the veil was taxing in a way not a lot of people could understand. Sandra felt it when she was alive, and she wasn't nearly as involved with angels as I was.

I took a sip of my milkshake and frowned. "Your points are noted, and I will consider them."

The weird secret messenger came again that night, to Grandpa's annoyance. He conveyed the message after dinner: "I would have pulled him out if you hadn't." I had no idea what it meant, but I was so done with these mind games.

chapter 31
I CHILL OUT

I thought a lot about their words. I hated to admit it, but they made sense. I couldn't change the fact that I was a medium, nor could I change the fact that I was a target for demons, but I didn't have to go looking for trouble by getting more involved than I had to be. I didn't have to be a demon hunter. No one told me why I was made alive, and demon hunting was something Hermes told me I could do, not that it was something I *had* to do. I thought that was the only way I had value—by proving I could be useful and helping my friends. But as Sandra had told me a while back, maybe my value wasn't tied to the things I did. And honestly, with all this extra pressure I'd had on myself, I was feeling less and less like myself. Maybe I didn't have to know what my specific purpose was. Maybe I could just live my life like everyone else.

It didn't take long for Raj to come check on me after what had happened the night before. I'd fallen asleep on my couch and woke up to him sitting in my dad's recliner, frowning at the news. There had been another bombing from the secret terrorist organization that we were sure was run by demons. Reflexively, I kept trying to think of how we could infiltrate them, and wanted to get Raj's thoughts on our next steps. Then, I remembered what I'd just decided. If I was done with the demon hunters, I needed to stop trying to insert myself into their problems. True, these problems weren't just for angels—mortals were absolutely being affected—but I needed to figure out my life before I could even begin to try to make a difference in the world.

I couldn't help feeling bad for Raj. He looked so exhausted, and he was all on his own, guiding a group of angels that were slowly crumbling apart. I felt honored when he started treating me like a partner of sorts, and I was glad to lift his burden of leadership. But it wasn't my place, and I had already decided that I was done.

"That was not what I was watching," I said.

Raj startled and mentally turned off the TV. "Hey, kid. I heard about what happened. You okay?"

"Yeah, I'm fine. But we lost a kid . . ." I sat up slowly to avoid jostling my head too much. It didn't hurt too badly. This was nothing compared to the stuff Sheila put me through when she was trying to kill me, and technically, the concussion was my fault. I should have lain down before leaving my body.

"I'm sorry, David. I know how much that hurts."

I nodded and avoided looking at him.

"Do you want to talk about it?"

"Not right now. Are you just here to say hi, or was there something you wanted to tell me?"

He cleared his throat. "I did want to check on you, but I also have an update. Now that we know who we can trust on our team, I was thinking we could have a meeting here today or tomorrow with everyone—"

I held my hand up. "Raj, I'm gonna stop you right there."

He blinked and looked at me in surprise. "Something wrong?"

I bit my lip, trying to decide how to say this in a way that didn't sound as selfish as it was. But there was no positive way to spin this. Even if stepping away was the right thing to do—and I wasn't sure if it was—I was doing it for myself.

"What's up, kid?"

I sighed and forced myself to look at him. "I'm done, Raj. No more."

His eyebrows came together. "No more what?"

"Demon hunting. I can't do this anymore. It's like I'm trying to be alive and dead at the same time, and it's too much. I know I can't stop being a medium, and I'm sure demons will still attack me, but that doesn't mean I have to go running into the thick of things every time something bad happens. And my classes are better taught by someone else, someone who can actually demonstrate the concepts I'm teaching and who can protect them when something goes wrong." I shook my head. "I mean, it was my fault we were attacked in the first place, and if there's another fight, I'm more useless than ever. That was my last chance to leave my body. And if I quit teaching, I may as well quit demon hunting altogether. I can't join you anymore. And . . . I don't think I even want to. I just want to be alive. Or at least, I *want to* want to be alive. It's just hard to want it when I'm around you guys all the time."

I groaned and leaned my head in my hand, feeling guilt completely wash over me. "I'm sorry, Raj. I wish I was strong enough to handle this, but I'm not."

Raj processed in silence for a moment, then he smiled sadly. "Good for you, kid."

"Good for me?" I asked incredulously.

"For being brave enough to say something."

"I'm sorry," I said honestly. "I don't want to let you down, but—"

"You've never let me down, David, and you never will. You've gone above and beyond so often, and it's taken its toll. Shame on me for putting so much pressure on you."

I frowned uncomfortably. "You didn't put pressure on me. I did. And you guys have ten times more pressure—"

"It's not the same," Raj said. "Yes, it's been hard for us, but we have advantages you don't. As you've correctly pointed out, we've been expecting you to do an angel's job as a mortal. That's not fair."

The guilt felt like it was suffocating me. This was wrong, wasn't it? I was being selfish, but I couldn't find it in me to change my mind. "I'm so sorry, but I'm just so done. I've been burned, chased, trapped, and attacked, and I lose every woman I get close to. The more I fight back, the more the demons just keep coming after me and the people I care about. What if I lose a family member next? I can't risk that, and I can't handle the dread of what will happen because of my involvement with the demon hunters. How the heck am I supposed to actually live a life with all this going on? I can't do both. Once I'm an angel, I'm all yours, but until I die again, I'm done." I stared down at my hands.

Raj tried very hard to hide how disappointed he was, but I could see it. "You don't need to worry about us—we can take care of ourselves. As much as I knew you'd make an amazing teacher, I mainly gave you that job because you wanted to be involved so badly. I thought I was giving you what you wanted. But I should have known that it was keeping you on the team as a mortal that was making you so unhappy. We just love you, David," he said with a smile. "Please don't ever think I'm disappointed. I'm very impressed with you for setting boundaries and taking care of yourself."

I sighed. "You can still come by every now and then. Just because I'm not demon hunting doesn't mean I shun all demon hunters. You guys are still my friends. I'm just going to concern myself more with mortal problems now, since that's what I am."

"I'm proud of you, David," Raj said. "More people could stand to learn from your example in stepping away when necessary." He got up and frowned. "I wish I could shake your hand."

"And I wish I could ignore your handshake and hug you instead," I said with a smile.

"I'll still be checking in with you now and then to see how you're doing. And we can still have our sessions if you still want that."

"Oh, yeah," I said quickly. "I mean, I don't think I'm ready to quit therapy yet."

He nodded. "I'll see you around." Then he disappeared.

As much as I'd been dreading that conversation, I felt relieved.

I felt surprisingly refreshed when I went back to work the next day. I didn't have to worry about an angel popping in to inform me of something awful that had happened, or dropping another responsibility on my lap. I chatted with Jorge and Liam about inconsequential things and agreed to go bowling with them that weekend. I even noticed more of the dead around me, weirdly enough. I had a nice little conversation in the bathroom with Tala's grandpa. And I almost got an acknowledgment from a wanderer hanging out in the hallway. A part of me wished Jake would show up so we could just hang out like we used to before all this mess. I also missed Kiki. I kept thinking about her in my downtime, so I tried my best to keep busy.

I struck up a conversation with Sheila when I was bored at the ticket counter during a slow part of the day. She'd just returned from changing all the high score names on the motorcycle game to inappropriate words. I didn't say anything because . . . well, it was kind of funny.

"Nosy question," I said, "but those old people your daughters live with—are they your parents or his parents?" I avoided saying Ted's name as I knew that was a trigger for her.

"Not sure how that's any of your business," she muttered.

I shrugged. "Just making conversation."

I thought she might not answer. Then she sighed. "They're

his mom and stepdad."

"Does that bother you?" I asked curiously. "That the kids are with his parents?"

She shook her head. "I never had a problem with them. It's not their fault their son turned into a monster. Well, I'm sure his *dad* had a hand in that, but he was long dead before I came around."

"Did you meet his dad when you got to The Resting Place?"

She laughed loudly and disdainfully. "Oh, he's not in The Resting Place, David. That man went straight to Hell. He's been in the Hurricane longer than I've been dead."

"Was he thrown in for disobeying Malum like you were?"

This comparison bothered her, but not enough to stop talking. I was surprised by how much she was revealing. Following me around 24/7 must have been even more boring than I imagined.

"No, he wasn't thrown in," she said with a sardonic eyebrow raise. "He was recruited. He was so good at abuse in his mortal life, they trained him as a torture demon. He's in the Hurricane not to be tortured, but to torture those who get thrown in. Which is a crazy rare situation. Usually, only *natives* can stand the Hurricane. Only the worst *monsters* get promoted to that job."

My mouth popped open in genuine shock. "Are you telling me you threw Ted into the Hurricane, knowing that his abusive demon father was in there and is probably torturing him right now?" Unless Ted was the mole, in which case he wasn't down there any longer. But what if Ted wasn't the mole and that was just someone else wearing his face?

Sheila looked down and pursed her lips. "To be honest, I didn't think about that."

I blinked, and my eyebrows went up. That sounded like a concession that what she'd done was a little harsher than she intended.

"Would you do it again?" I asked softly. "Knowing his dad's in there?"

"I don't know," she seemed to say to herself. Then, remembering herself, she stuck her chin out defiantly. "Of course I'd do it again. He destroyed everything!"

I frowned. Fascinating. Was there remorse in there? Or just a lingering of her old self? The part of her that had once loved him.

A text from Jessica distracted me.

Jessica: Hey, David! I was wondering if you would help me with something??

Me: Sure! What's up?

Jessica: I want to throw a baby shower for Elena, well more of a diaper drive, since she still has a lot of baby stuff, and I was wondering if you'd like to help?? Sam won't do it, and I doubt your dad has a lot of experience in that area. I know you don't either, but I was hoping to get some ideas from your mom and thought maybe you could ask her what she did last time? I'm assuming she was the one that threw Elena's other baby showers.

Me: Uh, yeah! I can ask her when I see her again. But I was actually there for Elena's other baby showers and I remember most of what they did that Elena liked. And all the stuff she vetoed.

Jessica: Really?? Can we meet up and discuss sometime?

Me: Sure!

Preston walked by with a clipboard in his hands, frowning as he jotted something down. Not even bothering to glance up at me, he snapped his fingers in my direction. "No texting."

"Busted," Sheila snickered.

Chagrined, I shoved my phone away.

Sandra was waiting for me outside Chuck E. Cheese after work. Her smile when she saw me quickly made way for a grimace. Without a word, she pulled a gun out and pointed it at someone behind me. Oh, Sheila! I hadn't had a chance to tell Sandra about the arrangement yet.

I hurriedly put myself in front of Sheila and held my arms up, "Hang on, it's not—"

Sandra had already pulled the trigger, though. The irony was not lost on me. Not too long ago, I stood in front of a real bullet to save Sandra's life. Luckily, demon killer bullets couldn't really hurt me. Then again, real bullets shouldn't have hurt me when I was an angel, so maybe I should have been more concerned.

Everything seemed to move in slow motion. Sandra's gun disintegrated as her hands came to her mouth in horror. The bullet of Light and Darkness entered my chest, and it stung with strange, conflicting emotions, overloading me from the inside.

I sneezed. "Well, that felt weird."

Sandra sighed in relief. "David, don't do that! And move out of the way so I can take the she-devil back to prison!"

"She's allowed to be here. She's my new bodyguard." I cringed, anticipating Sandra's reaction.

"What?" she demanded.

"She's still in angel custody," I said, gesturing toward Sheila's manacles. "The second she steps out of line, Hermes will yank her back to The Resting Place. It's a mutually beneficial arrangement. She gets to leave prison, and I don't have to impose on any angels to protect me."

Sandra blinked and shook her head. "I'm sorry, but that's the stupidest idea I've ever heard."

"There aren't enough angels to guard me, and Sheila was doing nothing but staring at walls. It works."

Sandra stared at me like I was nuts. "David, you're smart enough to know this is a bad idea."

I shrugged. "I am a bad idea, what do you expect?"

She rolled her eyes as I started toward my car. A family walking toward the restaurant had paused to view my apparently hallucinated conversation. I smiled awkwardly, and they hurried away, shielding their children with their bodies.

Once in the car, Sandra joined me in the passenger seat while Sheila tagged along in the back.

"So what's up?" I asked Sandra.

She glared at Sheila, but then shook her head and sighed. "I just wanted to see how it's going."

"Raj talked to you?"

"Yeah, he did."

"Are you judging me for stepping away?" I tried to sound light and joking, but I don't think I succeeded.

"What? No, I think it's great! You forget I used to be in your position. I mean, I wasn't a demon hunter, and my life wasn't constantly in peril, but I was an honorary rescuer. That put a lot of pressure on me and really complicated my life. And if you remember, when you first started talking to me, I told you I didn't want to be involved in your demon-hunting business."

I frowned, "I forgot about that."

"Look," she said, "angels have a hard time remembering what it's like to be mortal. And mediums are so rare, once they discover us, they get so excited about utilizing our abilities, they forget that we—you—are still alive. So good for you for setting boundaries. You don't have to do something just because an angel asked you to do it. They aren't always right, you know. Angels aren't perfect just because they're dead."

Sheila clapped obnoxiously. "Say it louder for the people in the back."

Sandra ignored her. "The point is, we are dead, and dead people are our domain. You just need to live while you're alive."

"What original words, Bon Jovi," Sheila said, "you should write a song about that."

"Oh, shut up!" Sandra muttered, casting an annoyed look backward. "Does she have to be here? Can I just stuff her in the trunk?"

Suddenly, my car started blasting the song "It's My Life," by Jon Bon Jovi. Sheila belted along in the back seat, dramatically and obnoxiously pounding her fist in the air when it got to the words Sandra had inadvertently quoted. Sandra covered her ears, and I hurriedly turned the music down.

I cast a look back at Sheila in exasperation. "What is this side of you?"

Sheila met my eyes in the rearview mirror and raised her eyebrows. "What side?"

"Like, kind of annoying?"

"I'm a woman of many layers," she said mysteriously.

"Like an ogre," Sandra muttered.

The two of them bickered the entire drive back to my house, and I didn't know what to do about it, so I mostly tuned them out. But I was glad Sandra had come by. I felt validated in my decision.

It wasn't until I was getting ready for bed that I made the connection to what Hermes had told me the last time I saw him face-to-face. He told me that I would have the opportunity to live a nice, long life, and that was dependent on a choice. This was the choice, wasn't it? Step away from the demon hunters and live the rest of my life like a (mostly) normal mortal, or continue demon hunting and die young again. The life option sounded a lot more appealing.

I just wished I'd come to this realization before I screwed things up with Kiki. My room felt so empty without her. We'd ignored each other at school when we saw each other, and that was rough. It was funny because I could acknowledge that we weren't necessarily going to get married or anything, and it wasn't like I was in love with her—yet—but her absence still made me sad. I didn't realize how much comfort she provided by just being there. The way she distracted me from my problems with her goofy, off-putting ways. I hadn't noticed how much I'd come to depend on her.

A knock at my door interrupted my depressing train of thought.

Sheila peeked through the door, then looked back at me. "It's the old guy."

Grandpa barged in, his hand resting on the doorknob. "I'm tired of being your messenger, so I'll make this quick. The blue lady came back and said, 'You are the trap.' Yes, that's all she said. No, I don't know what it means. Goodnight."

chapter 32
DEMON CONFESSIONS

I was woken up that night to the sound of rough breathing near my ear. I let out a breathless scream and nearly rolled out of bed.

"What's happening?" I gaped as I sat up and clutched my blanket tighter.

The lights flickered, and my bed started to shake. In the flickering light, I saw a dark form at the foot of my bed. It didn't move, it just stood there, radiating Darkness.

"Uh, Sheila?" I whispered.

A whip of Darkness came out of nowhere and wrapped around the form, which swore and started struggling. I hurried and flipped my lamp back on once the lights stopped flickering. The form was yanked along the whip until Sheila had her hand around its throat. I still couldn't see the demon's face as its entire body was one solid black mass. Sheila grinned.

"Let's see, who have we here?" she said darkly. I shivered. She looked and sounded like the Sheila from last year, who was dead set on ending me. Then she put her arms behind the demon's head and slowly pulled them toward her face. She was about to do her evil kiss of Darkness. I wanted to stop her, but I couldn't stop watching. It was like witnessing a tornado forming or a fire burning. I was hypnotized by the horror, but also morbidly fascinated.

"Are you afraid?" she whispered in their ear. The scariest part about her was that she didn't have to disguise her face or voice to look like some kind of freakish zombie demon like the others. She was terrifying all on her own, and she knew it. She didn't need any intimidation techniques other than her own presence.

The demon shivered and struggled as Sheila kissed it and fed them Darkness until it started overflowing and filling the space around them. Slowly, the demon stopped struggling until the mask of Darkness fled from their face, revealing a tiny woman. Her eyes were glazed over, paralyzed with fear. Sheila pulled away and roughly threw the demon out of my room.

It was quiet for several moments.

Trying to steady my breathing, I said, "That was terrifying."

"That's kind of the point," Sheila said.

"I feel like an attack like that hasn't happened in a while. Why do you think that is?"

She grinned wickedly, and suddenly it made sense.

"They're scared of you."

"Oh, they're definitely scared of me," she smirked. "For all they know, I'm still working for Malum. Word has gotten around that I've claimed you as my victim. It seems this idiot missed the memo."

I hadn't noticed before now how infrequently I'd been attacked recently, or how feeble their attempts had been. All they did was intimidate me, but other than that one on the highway, none of them came close to hurting me. And none of them tried to possess me. In fact, I didn't know of any demons who had tried to possess me other than Sheila herself, nor had I seen a demon possess anyone else before.

"Hey, how come no one has tried to possess me?" I asked. "You're the only demon that I've ever seen do that."

"That's because it's gross," Sheila muttered. "It's also illegal. And you don't get to choose how long you get stuck."

I blinked. "Okay, all of those statements need some explanation."

She rolled her eyes and leaned forward on her knees. "Why am I always explaining crap to you?"

I shrugged. "You're the one that keeps answering my questions. I think you enjoy being a know-it-all, even though it puts a damper on your mystery. So go ahead and answer this one, because we both know you want to."

She rolled her eyes and sighed, relenting. "Possession is gross because it's super intimate. Do you want to snuggle up to some random lady you have no attraction to? If I told you to go have sex with some stranger on the street, would that appeal to you?"

I shook my head.

"Well, possessing is even more intimate than that. And it's illegal because it goes against demonic law. Yes, demons have laws. Not a lot of demons follow them—and they aren't great at enforcing the laws down there—but there is a chance you could get caught and punished."

"Why?" I asked. "Why do they even care what you do? I mean, aren't demons supposed to just . . . hurt people?"

She sighed in exasperation.

"What? I'm curious."

"Yeah, that's what makes it annoying!" She sighed again and sat up. "Before Malum took over, the Demonic Council was in charge, and according to them, our job was to provide mortals with choices. Angels provide mortals with good choices, and demons provide mortals with bad choices. I mean, what is a choice if you don't have both sides, right? But certain types of torment take *away* choices, which goes against our purpose. Stuff like killing and possession don't provide mortals with choices—they remove them. So that stuff isn't allowed. And throwing people in the Hurricane is definitely *not* allowed. Only the council can do that as punishment for only the worst scum of the earth. This is why Malum is so shocking even to demons. He shatters all of our rules."

I blinked as I thought about that. It gave a different perspective on demons. Providing people with choices? Helping them exercise their free will? That didn't sound much different than what angels did. I mean, a demon's focus was on the bad, but still. They were just as interested in people being their own agents as angels were. Interesting . . .

"And what did you mean about getting stuck in mortal bodies?" I asked.

She frowned and considered before answering. "Demons

can't escape human bodies once they possess them. Living bodies are kind of . . . sticky. Leaving a body would be like you trying to pull your own spirit out. You can't do it. The only way they can be removed is if an angel—or, I guess, another demon—pulls them out."

"So why do it at all if you're just going to get stuck?"

She rolled her eyes. "Weren't you listening? Most don't. But the few that do would probably love to get stuck in a mortal body. They have access to so much more pleasure. The demons that do it just plan to live it up while they can until an angel comes around and exorcises them."

I frowned. "What about that time Malum possessed that kid at Sandra's school? You know, during the shooting? How did he get out of that body? There weren't any angels around to exorcise him."

"That kid died, David."

"Oh . . ."

I hadn't realized that. Did Malum kill him? Or did he die of a heart attack from being possessed? Or did Malum force him to put the gun to his head and kill himself? I shivered, feeling awful for that poor kid. I wondered where he was now. I would be very surprised if he wasn't a wanderer, haunting the school. I made a mental note to ask Sandra about him sometime. She was good at knowing what was going on with people. She'd know.

Sheila leaned back in her chair. "Enough questions. Go to sleep, you're getting bags under your eyes."

I felt like there was something I was missing about what she had said. A question I had meant to ask was just at the tip of my tongue. But she was right, and I was tired. It shouldn't have been so easy to fall asleep with a demon in my room, but I genuinely felt safe with her there.

chapter 33
DINNER DRAMA

Elena, nosy and pushy as ever, set up a family dinner with Grandpa behind Dad's back. This infuriated Dad, but when it came time to meet everyone at the restaurant, he didn't refuse to go. I was without a bodyguard for the next hour, since Sheila was on leave to visit her kids, but I wasn't worried. Like Sheila said, Demons weren't so keen to come after me anymore since they thought Sheila had staked her claim on my soul.

We were all getting ready to leave when Preston came down the stairs and started digging through the fridge, still wearing his pajamas from the night before. He'd taken a sick day, which I was surprised to learn he hadn't done since getting the job. Despite being a terrible manager most of the time, he was strangely worried about leaving the place in someone else's hands. He insisted he felt fine, but didn't want to scare off customers with his runny nose or spread it to anyone else.

He glanced at the three of us leaving and raised his eyebrows, shocked that we would all go somewhere together with such hostility between Dad and Grandpa. I suddenly felt guilty leaving him alone. I was about to go hang out with my whole family, and the last interaction he'd had with his family was getting ridiculed and slapped in the face in front of his coworkers.

Dad seemed to be thinking the same thing. "Hey, kid, wanna come get some dinner with us?"

Preston hesitated. "Uh, that's okay. I'm not hungry."

"You're literally looking through the fridge," I pointed out. "Just come. You won't be intruding."

He still hesitated.

Grandpa clapped twice and said, "Get your shoes on, boy. You're coming with us!" Preston jumped and hurried to comply. I felt a little disturbed to see him scramble to obey a demand when he'd been so reluctant to accept kindness.

He wasn't even dressed for the day, but he followed us into the car in his white T-shirt and pajama pants while he shoved his feet into the sneakers he'd left by the front door. This was going to be awkward. I'd complained to my family about him on multiple occasions. I texted Elena and Sam a quick warning that he was coming and that they weren't to glare daggers at him. Sam responded with, "Who's Preston?" and Elena responded with, "WTF??????" I quickly shut off the screen and hid it under my leg so Preston wouldn't see.

Weird that Elena still didn't like him. Didn't they say Preston was a part of their family meeting? It must have been Dad who incorporated Preston into that conversation.

After an awkwardly silent drive with Grandpa's radio station of choice (Willie Nelson, which he sang along with the entire time), we pulled into The Cheesecake Factory parking lot. Preston, clearly feeling awkward, followed behind us as we walked inside. I slowed down to walk with him.

"You okay?" I asked.

"I'm in my pajamas," he muttered.

"You're fine," I said, "No one will care."

"This is a family thing. I shouldn't be here."

As we squeezed into the foyer, I said, "My family's really chill. They won't mind."

Dad made his way to the front of the crowd and explained we had a reservation for ten and a baby, then asked if we could have one more seat. We made our way through the rows of booths to the three tables they'd pushed together for our large party. Elena was already there, dealing with an argument between Ginny and Rocco about whether snakes had a butt hole, while Charlie mopped up spilled orange juice and grinned. Their family was my favorite chaos.

"Hey, kiddos!" Dad said.

"Grandpa!" Ginny squealed. She squeezed out of her seat and ran over to hug his legs. Rocco followed her, but then paused when he saw *my* grandpa looking down at him. He hurried away and ran to hide in Elena's arms. Ginny waved timidly, and Grandpa smiled.

"What about me?" I said with my arms out. She jumped into them and squeezed me to death. Seriously, Ginny hugs are the best in the world. I smiled and carried her back to her seat, Preston awkwardly hanging back.

"This is my friend Preston," I said by way of introduction.

Charlie smiled and shook his hand, and Elena avoided

saying anything to him by telling her children to say hello. We settled in just as Sam and Jessica joined us with Little David and Baby Gloria. I ended up next to Grandpa, who took the head of the table, and Preston sat next to me. Dad ended up on the other end because he "wanted to sit by the baby," but we all knew he was avoiding Grandpa.

Preston just watched everyone curiously as we settled in.

"Do you have any nieces or nephews?" I asked him.

He shook his head.

Once we had all ordered, Grandpa cleared his throat and said, "Well, I've been wanting to get together with all of you because, as you may have noticed, I've been absent most of your lives. That was wrong, and I'll admit that. We don't need to get into the details, but I was stubborn and unfair, and it wasn't right to stay away like that. But I'm getting older, and while I may not have much time left, I'd like to spend the rest of my life fixing those bridges I've burned. I hoped that—"

A high-pitched scream interrupted him. I knocked over my water and looked around, trying to find where it was coming from.

"What?" Preston asked.

I looked around and saw that no one else had noticed. No one except Grandpa. We made eye contact and turned toward the screaming teenage girl, following a teenage boy as he stormed out of the kitchen.

She was dead. He was not.

"Don't do it, Matty! Please! Come back!" she screamed.

I tensed and got up to follow, but Grandpa took my arm. "It can wait, son. We're having dinner with family, and I'm in the middle of—"

"PLEASE! MATT, NO!" the angel screamed. "SOMEONE HELP, PLEASE!"

Grandpa frowned and released my arm. "Okay, that sounds serious. Maybe go check it out. Come back and get me if you need help."

I nodded, then ran after the two teenagers as the boy shoved his way out the door and the girl floated through it. I jogged after them to the far side of the parking lot.

"Hey!" I shouted.

The boy ignored me, but the angel spun around.

"What's wrong?" I asked, hurrying up to her.

"You can see me?" she gasped.

"Yes. What's going on?"

"You have to stop my brother! He's going to kill himself!"

My eyes widened, and I sprinted after the boy. I shouted after him, but he ignored me.

He reached his car before I did, and my stomach dropped when he got the keys in the ignition. If he drove off, there was nothing I could do. It wasn't like I had my dad's keys with me. I could call 911, but he could have already done something before they got to him. Cursing to myself, I ran at the car, which was still parked, flinching at the headlights and trying to ignore the mounting panic inside me. Headlights were triggering, and this was not a good moment for me to flip out. As I ran, I saw a different pair of headlights. Felt pain. Saw the ominous lump that turned out to be Sandra's body. I shook my head and forced myself to run toward the car.

When I reached it, I threw my hands on the hood, both to prevent him from driving away and to steady myself. Cold sweat coated my temples. Oh, this was not fun, this was very not fun.

"Stop!" I said hoarsely.

He rolled down his window. "Get out of the way!"

"No," I said. "I can't let you do this. Please get out of the car."

"Who even are you?"

"Don't tell him you can see me," the girl said. "It will just depress him more."

"I'm just some random guy," I said, "but I know what you're going to do, and you can't do it."

"I can do whatever the hell I want! Now move or I'll run you over and two people will die today!"

"I'm sorry, but I'm not moving." I felt like I was going to faint. I forced myself to take deep breaths, but I had no idea what to do next. What if he really did run me over? I started hyperventilating, imagining it happening all over again.

Preston, whom I hadn't even realized followed me out, calmly walked past me with a phone to his ear. "Yeah, I'm gonna give him the phone now." He walked toward the passenger door, and just before he reached for it, I saw the girl next to me make a flicking motion with her hand, and the lock clicked. Preston invited himself in, sat in the passenger seat, and held the phone out to the kid without a word.

The kid, taken off guard, actually took the phone. After shouting at whoever was on the other line, he suddenly started sobbing about how he couldn't do it anymore. I looked questioningly at Preston through the windshield, and he mouthed, "Nine-eight-eight."

"What?" That number meant nothing to me.

"Suicide hotline," the girl said quietly.

"Oh." I hadn't even thought of that.

While the kid sobbed into the phone and Preston kept his eye on him, I pulled out my phone. "Hey, do you guys have a mom or dad nearby?"

The angel nodded eagerly and gave me the number to dial. I didn't dare move from in front of the car until a very concerned father sped into the parking lot, parked his truck crookedly, and pounded on the kid's window until he opened the door. Once the door was open, the man yanked the kid into a bone-crushing hug while a woman hurried from the passenger side of the truck and threw her arms around both of them.

I breathed out a sigh of relief and let my head drop. That had been so close. If we'd been just a minute too late, this kid might have succeeded. It was a heavy realization.

"Is there anything else we can do?" I finally asked the girl.

She shook her head as Preston left the kid's car to come stand next to me. "No, my parents will take care of him. Thank you so much. Both of you." She left us to go stand near her family, smiling in relief.

I gripped Preston's shoulder and shook it a little. "Dude, you just saved someone's life."

He walked away from me, sank down onto the sidewalk curb, and let out a breath. It was overwhelming to realize that a life had almost ended. I sat down next to him. "Seriously, man, that was amazing."

He shook his head. "I just . . . It's not a good place to be. I couldn't just do nothing." He looked over at me. "Also, I wouldn't have even had the chance to get to him if you hadn't stopped him from driving off. Um, are you okay? You look sick."

I took a deep breath. "I will be. As soon as my heart stops beating out of my chest. Headlights are kinda triggering."

I put my head in my hands and took slow, deep breaths.

After a pause, Preston said, "That girl . . . your girlfriend that died in the accident. Do you see her sometimes?"

I sat up and nodded.

"Does that make it any easier?"

I shrugged. "Yeah. I mean, it doesn't change the fact that we can't be together anymore, but I like that I can see her now. I didn't get to at first. I couldn't see dead people until like a month after she'd died."

He nodded. "Thought so. You haven't always talked to people who weren't there. And back when it happened, the loss seemed a lot, I don't know, heavier?"

"Yeah." We sat there awkwardly for a moment before Preston stood and held out his hand to help me up. We walked back into the awkward Grandpa dinner feeling strangely like we were kind of, maybe, sort of friends.

Maybe I really could do good without being a demon hunter.

HER

Obviously, demons aren't great people. They range from trouble-makers to terrorists. But the more time I spent with them, the more I realized that they had legitimate reasons for their hate. Reasons like my own. And The Resting Place was not what it professed to be. It was not a place of righteous angels. It was a place of liars and murderers and cheaters. They covered up their sins with the Light that the Big Man gave them, but underneath it all, their souls were rotten, maggot-filled demons. I was no better, but I didn't claim to be. That's what made me different.

The way I saw it, angels pretend they aren't wicked, while demons just embrace it.

chapter 34
DEATH MAKES AN APPEARANCE

I was starting to feel kind of normal. I mean, homework sucked, and there were days when work was exhausting, but these were normal problems. Nothing I'd need to talk to a dead shrink about. With my nights free of demon hunter classes, I started going out a little more. I made friends at school and even hung out with some work friends now and then. No dates, though. I still wasn't quite over Kiki. She'd texted me a few times since breaking up with me, asking if we could talk. I ignored her. It was immature and childish, but I didn't want to talk to her, and if it was important enough, she could come talk to me after class instead of hiding behind her phone.

Preston started being a kind of cool boss and doing fun stuff like Second Saturday Smashdown, in which every second Saturday after closing, all the employees would have fifteen minutes to play as many games as we wanted and try to earn the most tickets. The prize was the privilege of choosing our assigned duties the following week. I'm not sure if that was technically allowed, but we all loved it. I also had an embarrassing breakthrough with the rat costume. Raj convinced me to face my fear of going near the suit, and I actually got through an entire twenty minutes of wearing it without freaking out. Everyone cheered for me. It was super humiliating, but weirdly touching that they cared.

I wasn't stupid enough to believe that this high would last forever. Everyone knows that life is full of highs and lows. But they were *my* highs and lows, and I was going to savor them. Stepping away from demon hunting was hard, and I still felt guilty about it, but I felt more alive than I had been before.

I felt like a total schmuck, though, when Asher came to my room a couple of days after I quit to demand why I wasn't teaching them anymore.

"Uh, well, you guys are best taught by an actual angel," I said.

"But you finally got kind of cool! I liked you better!"

"Who's teaching you now?" I asked out of curiosity.

"Sandra. Duh."

Ah, that did make sense. Demon hunter and former teacher and all.

"But Sandra's a great teacher," I said in her defense.

Asher rolled his eyes. "Well, yeah, she's way better than you, but I liked *you*." He shuffled his feet in embarrassment.

I smiled, feeling way too gratified that this kid liked me. I opened my laptop and said, "You busy right now?"

He shrugged. "Not really."

So we watched Danny Phantom together on my laptop and acted out all the fight scenes.

• • •

Elena's baby shower was at Dad's place since he had the biggest living room. It was a typical baby shower with just a bunch of ladies, so I planned to stick to the background and just sort of hang out in the kitchen, even though I helped plan everything. I had no desire to be in there when they started discussing things like breast pumps and stuff. I shuddered at some of the disturbing things I'd heard about childbirth and all the weird stuff that happened afterward that no one talks about. What is up with women's bodies being so beautiful and yet capable of such horrors?

Jessica met me in the kitchen about a half hour before the shower with a piece of tape in her hair and a broken vase in her hands.

"People are already showing up!" she exclaimed. "I'm not done setting up!"

"It's fine," I said, "I'll go grab the food."

She checked her watch and swore. "You should have left ten minutes ago! Get out of here! Go!"

"Sheesh," I muttered as I scurried away from her. I almost ran into a woman who had just walked through the front door, chatting with Elena. "Oh, I pooped during all my births," she said.

I gagged and ran to my car, grateful for a chance to escape. I had the simple job of picking up food from Elena's favorite taco joint, which I was happy to do to get away from Jessica's frazzled energy. Of course it wasn't ready yet, even though we'd ordered it ahead of time, so I sat in a worn-down booth with yellow foam showing through as I waited. Mariachi music played in the background, reminding me of Tata Ramon. I smiled, looking at their sombrero wall and all the colorful paintings, crosses, and flowers in bright oranges, yellows, reds, and blues. Sheila lounged against the wall across from me, frowning at the tiny TV in the corner behind me. I turned around to see what *novela* she was watching, but it was just the news. Then I noticed that everyone in the restaurant had turned to watch it. Every single person.

"Turn that up, please," a customer asked the cashier without looking away from the screen. Before she could find the remote, a woman got up on a chair and turned up the volume on the TV. It was showing an unrecognizable location that had been completely destroyed. Buildings were nothing but rubble, and everything was coated in gray dust. A female news anchor's voice spoke over the disturbing images.

". . . tens of thousands dead in this devastating bombing in Tanta, Egypt, one of the most densely populated cities in the world. Rumors are circulating about the involvement of the secret terrorist organization called *Death*—"

The screen suddenly switched from the images of the aftermath to a male news anchor sitting behind a desk, failing to look composed. He cleared his throat and adjusted his chair. "We have breaking news. A video featuring a message from the leader of the terrorist organization known as *Death* has been leaked all around the world, recorded in multiple languages. This video may be disturbing."

The screen switched to a dark basement and a man sitting

on a chair. He wore tattered robes, and his face was covered by a hood. The man twitched as though there were bugs all over him, and his gravelly voice was strained as he spoke to the camera.

"We are Death. We aim to kill as many as we can. We do not care for race, religion, or nationality. No one is safe. No one can hide. We will come for you, for death is inevitable!"

My heart leaped into my throat, and I cringed away from the screen. In a whisper to Sheila, I asked, "Do you think that guy's possessed?"

She didn't answer, so I tore my eyes from the screen to look at her face. She scowled and nodded. I turned back, worried I'd missed something important.

"—and you cannot kill us, for we are already dead! We are the demons you fear, AND OUR LEADER, THE SON OF EVIL HIMSELF, WILL HAVE YOUR SOUL!"

The video blacked out, and the image shifted back to the terrified news anchor, staring with his mouth open. Eventually, he cleared his throat and said, "Investigations on the origins of this video are underway. We are awaiting further response from the president regarding national security, though an emergency special session of the General Assembly of the United Nations is confirmed to take place within the next 24 hours. We will return to Barbara with further reports from Tanta."

"Um, order for David?" squealed the cashier.

I jumped. With shaking hands, I paid with Dad's credit card—he'd insisted—and grabbed the bag of food. I was so shaken that I stumbled into a table and spilled all the salsa containers sitting at the top of my to-go bag. Everyone around me flinched at the sound, then went back to staring at the screen as I hurriedly cleaned up my mess and booked it out the door.

Before I got to my car, Sheila held out her hand. "Hang on, someone's in there."

My heart pounded as she filled her hands with Darkness and then flew in the passenger window. A second later, she came out of the car looking annoyed. "It's just Aussie Captain America."

I let out a relieved sigh. "Wouldn't that just be Captain Australia?"

"Whatever. Your car's clear." Then she settled herself into the backseat.

I was glad for the warning because Jake sitting there silently in the passenger seat would have scared the crap out of me. After I got the food into the backseat and started the car, I turned to Jake. "What's up?"

He just shook his head and sighed.

Uh oh, silent Jake. This wasn't good.

"Uh, did something happen?" I prodded.

He turned toward me, looking almost as haunted as he had after the Hurricane. "You haven't seen it?"

"The video of Malum's demon Death organization threatening to just straight up kill everyone? Yeah, I just saw it."

He shook his head again and looked ahead. Finally, he said, "I was just hanging with the fam while they had brekkie when the news came on. I was packing my dacks when I saw it."

"Meaning . . . what, you're scared?"

He turned toward me incredulously. "What, you're not?"

"Oh no, I'm terrified," I reassured him. "This is bad. I mean, it's been bad, but it's getting worse. The fact that they're openly telling people they're demons is a whole new level of disturbing."

I still felt my heart pounding in my chest, but most of me was hardcore repressing my terror. Would it come back to bite me later? Maybe. But I genuinely could not process it at the moment. The concept of Malum openly trying to destroy the world was too big to grasp, and my mind refused to fully think about it.

And a guilty part of me thought, *Let the angels take care of it.*

"I don't know what we're gonna do." Jake groaned into his hands and then let them slowly slide off his face. "How do we fight this?"

I took a deep breath. "I don't know, man. But it has to work out. The Big Man won't let—"

"The Big Man lets awful things happen all over the world every day!" he blurted. "People are killed, tortured, raped, kidnapped, and attacked every day. *And he lets it happen.* I don't understand! If he lets those things happen, what's to stop him from letting all of us be captured by demons and the world destroyed? I don't get it!"

He slammed his fist on the dashboard, then looked annoyed that it just went straight through.

I glanced back at Sheila, who scowled down at the floor. Was this how her demonic journey started? Anger at the Big

Man? What would it take for Jake to become like her? Turning back to Jake, I said, "Look, man, there's a reason for everything. Even bad stuff. I don't understand it, I really don't, but if he's letting it happen, then there's gotta be a reason."

Jake frowned down at his lap. "What if the reason all of this is happening is because we've failed and we don't deserve to be saved?"

I had no answer to that. I, myself, was a big, fat failure.

"And if the Big Man is so powerful," Jake continued, "Why doesn't he just go capture Malum himself?"

That was a question I'd tried very hard not to think about, because the more I thought about it, the more confused, hurt, and angry I got. Eventually, I just sighed and said, "I don't know, man. Maybe you should talk to him about it."

"And say what? Why don't you fix this mess yourself?" He laughed humorlessly.

I shrugged. "Why not? If it's a genuine question, it's not like he's gonna get mad at you for asking. He wants us to understand."

I waited in silence while he thought, and eventually he nodded. "You're prolly right." He sighed and looked over at me. "Sorry for being so narky, I'm just . . . freakin' out."

"I've freaked out to you about way smaller stuff."

"Like what to wear on a date?" He looked down at his lap with a sad smile. "I miss those days."

"Oh yeah, the simple times when I was an anonymous front desk worker and you were out there kicking butt."

He chuckled and looked back at Sheila. "Hey, did you

know you were his first date? Like, ever?"

Sheila raised an eyebrow. "I'm not surprised. That was probably the worst kiss of my existence."

My face heated. "You know, it wasn't great for me either!"

Jake laughed so hard I was sure he'd have peed if he were alive.

Sheila grinned and leaned forward. "Remember when you said I was 'beautiful in a terrible way'? Like the ocean? It was probably the stupidest thing anyone had ever said to me."

She and Jake played Let's Poke Fun at David the entire drive back to my Dad's house. It was humiliating, but I couldn't help smiling a little, grateful for the distraction from what was happening in the world. The laughs were forced, but we all needed to let off some steam, and if making fun of me was the easiest way to do so, I was happy to take one for the team. Heaven knew what disasters would befall us, and we needed to cling to these moments of peace while we still had them.

The baby shower went smoothly, despite what was all over the news. Turns out humans have a superpower to tune out unpleasant things when it's inconvenient for them.

I helped Elena and Charlie load all their goodies into her car afterward and got to work cleaning up the living room and kitchen. I'm not sure how people at parties are constantly forgetting where they set their drinks. How hard is it to remember which one is yours when you wrote your name on the cup? And most of the drinks were half-full. Not gonna lie, I may have sampled someone's cucumber water out of curiosity. I mean, it would have gone to waste otherwise.

I'd just come back inside from taking the trash out when I found Raj in the kitchen.

"Hey," I said. "How's it going?"

"We need you, David."

I blinked and took a step back. "What?"

Suddenly, that feeling of dread I'd been repressing was back in full force.

He paused, looking grim. "We need you. I'm not asking you to rejoin the demon hunters, but we're having a meeting tonight, and I just . . . feel like you need to be there. I promise I wouldn't ask this unless it was important. Will you please come?"

I took in his grave expression and found myself nodding.

He nodded back. "Good. How soon are you available?"

"Other than homework, my only plans today are over. I'm free whenever. Wanna meet in my room when you're all ready?"

"That would be good." He took a deep breath and just stood there for a while.

"Are you scared?" I asked quietly.

Raj looked up at me and gave me a brief smile. "Terrified."

A year ago, that admission would have made me uncomfortable and worried. But I'd learned since then that Raj was just a person. He had flaws and feelings just like anyone else. And he was allowed to be scared. I also knew that without the option of fear, there was no faith. We had to feel the terror before we could reject it.

"It's gonna be okay," I said quietly. "It seems impossible right now, but somehow, someday, this will all be over."

Raj smiled. "I admire your faith." Then he disappeared.

I knew I'd said I was done with demon hunting, but he said he needed me, and I couldn't just say no. He wasn't asking me to rejoin the team; he just wanted me there for one meeting. I could do one more meeting for my friends, especially with the world in crisis.

Just one more and then I'd be done.

chapter 35
THE ANSWER TO MY QUESTION

The meeting took place at 8:00 that night. Raj arrived first, followed by Jake, Natalie, Sandra, Bill, and Daisy. Each took their place along the outer walls while I sat in my usual spot on the bed, against the headboard. Then Frederick surprised us all by appearing. Raj didn't look shocked, so I assumed they'd spoken prior.

Normally, this would be the part where Raj and Ying Yue would have to yell for everyone to quiet down and quit messing around. But almost half our team was gone, including Ying Yue, and it looked like demons were probably going to end the world, so no one was laughing or joking. No one was even asking Frederick where he'd been. Maybe none of them knew he'd gone missing. The mole had used Frederick's face many times since his capture.

"Light test. Everyone. Now," Raj demanded.

They all threw a ball of Light at him, and then he did the same. Then he made each of us share something with him that only he would know about, and he did the same. They each checked the closets and hallways for demons, and Raj asked Sheila to keep an eye out for them during the meeting. Finally, with an air of relief, he called us all to order.

"I've called you together because we need to change our tactics," Raj said. "Things are only getting worse, and it's time to go on the offensive. Each task force is meeting together as we speak to brainstorm ideas we haven't yet explored. We will each create a plan, and then the task force leaders will present our plans to each other in a larger meeting that will take place tomorrow. Moustafa and Wolff will evaluate each plan before they choose our next steps.

"They are asking for plans to end this. We aren't just gathering information anymore; we are capturing Malum once and for all. I have a few thoughts, but I would like to open up the floor to all of you first."

The room was silent before Frederick stepped forward. "I have a plan to work against Malum, but I don't believe it will be an end solution. More of a stalling tactic to buy us more time and allies, so perhaps it is not worth exploring in this meeting."

Raj held his hand out. "Let's hear it."

Frederick cleared his throat and addressed the team. "As you may or may not know, I've been deep undercover with this secret organization called Death. It is led by Malum and run by his followers. As they revealed in their recent recording, their goal is to kill, indiscriminately, as many mortals as possible. There is no set number or time limit that Malum has given them. They are starting small with these bombings, but those are mostly to inspire terror. He will soon be turning toward biological and nuclear warfare. He plans to have his slaves possess mortals in powerful positions that have access to these devastating weapons.

"Since most of his followers do not serve him by choice, I believe we can greatly reduce the number of his followers by breaking their bonds to Malum in a manner similar to Mrs. Hanson." Everyone was confused until he gestured toward Sheila. Hanson? Oh, was that Ted's last name? Sheila *Hanson*? Yeah, that name was all wrong for her. It sounded like a woman who baked pies and carried around a pink Stanley Cup.

"It's Ms. De la Cruz," Sheila said coolly. "Death parted us when he *killed* me."

"My apologies," Frederick said, bowing his head. He turned back to the group. "As the manacles of Light break Ms. De la Cruz from her connection to Malum, I believe we can set other demons free from Malum's grasp by offering them a similar escape. Angels can use their Light to replicate these manacles and set these demons free. They may not ally with us, but they at least could not be controlled by Malum. The logistics will need further planning, but that is the basic idea."

I felt a tiny spark of hope in me. It was so great to have Frederick back. Despite all he'd done, I still looked up to him.

Raj nodded. "That's a very promising idea, Frederick. I'll run it up the flagpole." He turned back to the group. "Other ideas before I share my thoughts?" No one answered, but Raj didn't let that bother him. Instead, he spread his hand like a professor emphasizing his point. "Let's review our problem."

"Malum's gonna destroy the world," Daisy said.

"And how do we stop him?" Raj asked.

"We need to capture him," Natalie said, "and put him back in prison."

"What is preventing us from doing that?" Raj asked.

"We can't track him down," Sandra said. "And even if we could, we can't hold him. He just paralyzes everyone with fear and disappears before anyone can capture him."

Raj snapped and pointed at her. "Right. So, in clear, concise language, someone sum up what we need to do."

Bill cleared his throat. "We need a way to track him down and hold him captive so he can't escape."

The conversation seemed to fade away as something Sheila had told me came to mind. A way to trap a demon. One that terrified me out of my wits and was all the more awful because it *fit*. It made sense. Suddenly, everything made sense in the worst way possible. Even the hint that was passed along to me through my grandpa.

You are the trap.

The world seemed to swirl around me, and I caught hold of my nightstand before I could fall off the bed.

"David?" I heard Raj say, as though far away.

Sandra reached out to me. "Hey, what's wrong?"

I flinched away from her, not realizing she'd been so close to me. I had no idea what expression was on my face, but her eyebrows came up in the middle when I met her gaze. "What's wrong, David?"

I shook my head and noted all the eyes in the room staring at me.

"Nope!" I slid off my bed so fast I knocked into the lamp. I didn't even pause to catch it as it fell from the nightstand. Without a word, I ran out the door.

My heart pounded as I flew down the sidewalk. I wasn't even paying attention to where I was going; I just had to get away right now. Away from them, away from the situation, away from *me*. This could not be it. No way. I would *not* do that. I would *not!* No one in their right mind would even think of that!

Nightmare images of Malum filled my mind. I remembered the way he held me by the neck and fed me images of pain and horror. Of the nightmares he sent me. The things I saw and heard in the Hurricane. The images swirled around my consciousness like a tornado destroying all in its path. The reanimated corpses of my family members. Sandra broken on the street, cursing me for killing her, that voice from the Hurricane telling me I was lost forever. And the deep, evil laughter overlayed all of it, the laughter that seemed more like a force of nature than a person, more Darkness than human. The Evil One who lived in the Hurricane, just waiting to destroy me from the inside out.

The images continued swirling in my mind until I reached the neighborhood park. I caught myself on a park bench and leaned over on my hands as I stopped to catch my breath. There may have been kids playing on the playground, but if there were, I didn't see or hear them. I was in a state of unreality and denial. Nothing felt real. And yet the thing I'd been denying weighed on me like an elephant sitting on my chest. I shakily sat down on the bench and hid my head in my arms. Part of me was glad no one on my team had followed me, as I couldn't handle the questions. Another part of me was a little hurt that no one cared enough to come and check.

When I finally looked up, I realized why. Hermes stood before me in all his glory. He might have told the gang to stay behind so he could have this little chat with me in private. My heart sank. He wouldn't appear unless this was it. He floated a foot off the ground, a glowing, glorious angel, and his face was as grim as death.

I winced and looked away. "Hermes . . . I can't do this."

"Do what?" he asked quietly. "Speak it."

I shook my head, not wanting to confront the thought. "I can't."

"You can. Speak your mind."

I shook my head and covered my face with my hands. Why was this so horrifying? Was I just being a coward? No, anyone in this situation would be terrified. Right? This was just . . . not okay.

I looked up and prayed with all my heart. *Do I have to do this?*

No answer came. What did that mean? Did he not hear me? Did he not care? Or maybe . . . maybe he was aware that deep down I already knew.

I hated how right it felt. Hated everything. I growled and pounded the bench with my fist. Then I kicked an abandoned soccer ball across the park. Then I knocked over the trash can. Well, I tried to, but it was bolted to the ground, so I kicked it instead. Then I yelled at the sky. I heard a couple of children run away screaming, but I didn't care.

"Are you finished?" Hermes asked.

"No!" I yelled. "What was the point of all this, Hermes? Why did I have to be given all this hope just to have it snatched away?"

I took an old soda can from a picnic table and threw it.

"No one is snatching anything away from you, David. You have a choice in this."

I groaned with my hands in my hair. "It's not much of a choice if the only other option is for tons of people to die. You know I can't just let that happen."

"People die every day, David. You know that it's not the end."

I held my hands up. "What are you doing? Reverse psychology? I know you want me to do this."

"This is a choice that must be made by someone who offers it, without being forced. It will be incredibly difficult, and if you are not fully committed, there is no way to succeed. It would be better for you to refuse than to fail because you were having second thoughts."

I covered my forehead with my hand and shook my head. I couldn't refuse. I knew that I had to do this. Not because anyone was making me, but because I needed all of this to end. Malum's reign of terror had destroyed enough people as it was. If I had the power to end it, I couldn't just walk away. That wasn't the kind of person I was, nor was it the kind of person I wanted to be. I wished it was.

Finally, completely deflated, I fell back onto the bench

next to Hermes.

I took a long, shaky breath and blew it out slowly.

Evading the actual atrocity, I turned to Hermes and asked a related question. "I know I've used up my three chances to leave my body, but I need one more. I promise it will be the last one if you let me."

Hermes nodded gravely. "Granted."

I blinked in surprise. "Just like that? You made it sound so serious that I could only use my gift three times. You also said you wouldn't talk to me again."

Hermes let out a breath. "David. I didn't lie to you, but I did not tell you everything. You weren't ready for it. The whole truth was that you could only use your gift three times . . . and have that long life that I told you could be yours. This is that choice, my friend. If you go forward with this plan of yours . . . well, I believe you've already reached that conclusion."

I nodded slowly.

"Then, permission granted."

"So, if I go through with my idea, will it work?"

"I cannot tell you the future. Do you feel that this is the right thing to do?"

I closed my eyes and sighed, wishing that I didn't. "Yes."

"Then you must make your choice and move forward with faith. Good will always come from doing what is right, even if it is won through sorrow and pain."

"Great!" I laughed hysterically. "Because this plan will include a lot of both. And I'm not even talking about the dying part." Suddenly, my laughter turned to crying. I quickly wiped my tears and sucked it back up. Now was not the time to lose it.

Hermes knelt down in front of me. "You are not alone. You have never been alone. Hold to that. You are the one who will hold the light to lead us through this darkness. So hold firm to your convictions, and do what must be done."

"Will it be fast?" I asked quietly.

He was slow to answer, which I took as a bad sign. "I told you that I cannot tell you the future. But fast or not, it will end, David. Remember that. Pain is not forever."

"Okay," I whispered.

He stood abruptly. "I must go now. God be with you."

And he disappeared.

I ran my hands through my hair and sat back. Sighing, I leaned my head against the back of the bench and closed my eyes. I needed to make sure I could accept the consequences. If it were possible, and I went through with this, everything I had ever wanted would be gone. I'd have to give all of it up. All the things I'd finally allowed myself to imagine would be mine would be snatched away once again.

There was a time when all I wanted was to go back to The Resting Place. Now I wasn't in such a rush to return. There were things I wanted to do. And I was terrified of the pain and horror of what I'd be putting myself through if I were to go through with my plan.

But this wasn't about me. I mentally wadded up all my plans and imaginings for my future and threw them away. I'd wanted to make a difference, and this was my chance. It was suddenly clear that this was why I was here.

chapter 36
THE TERRIBLE, AWFUL, NO-GOOD PLAN

"You okay, kid?" Raj asked when I finally made my way back to my room.

I ignored his question. I didn't have time for emotions right now. "Could a cage of Light trap a mortal?" I asked.

Everyone looked at each other, either confused at the abrupt subject change or unsure how to answer. I saw my mom unexpectedly standing next to Sandra.

"What are you doing here?" I asked.

"I don't know, I just felt like you needed me." She wrung her hands together.

I looked down, blinking the moisture from my eyes, and blew air out of my mouth.

"What's going on?" Sandra demanded.

I ignored the question and repeated myself. "Could a cage of Light trap a mortal?"

"Defo not," Jake said.

"No," Raj agreed. "Mortals aren't physically affected by Light and Darkness. They may feel the effects emotionally, mentally, or spiritually, but they can't feel it with their physical senses."

"What if a demon were possessing someone's body?" I asked. "Would the Light affect that demon the same way it normally would?"

I looked at Sheila standing with her arms folded in the corner of the room.

"Why are you looking at me?"

"Obviously, because you're the only person here who has ever possessed someone. So? Do you think it would work the same?"

She shrugged. "I don't know. Probably. I mean, exorcising a demon hurts for the mortal just as much as it does for the demon, right? So there's some connection between what they feel and experience."

I frowned and nodded.

Natalie folded her arms. "Are you going to tell us why you ran away like a little boy?"

I ignored her. Sheila was probably right, but we had to test it. Hating it, I turned to Sheila and said, "Let's try it. Possess me and we'll see if a cage of Light would trap me inside too."

"No," Sheila said, grimacing. "I don't want to."

Sandra gave her a dry look. "You've possessed both of us."

"Yeah, and I didn't much enjoy it," she snapped. "Imagine some big fat guy wrapping their arms around you from behind and not letting go. And then their body just . . . melds with yours." She shivered and shook out her arms. "It's like that level of disgusting, unwanted intimacy."

I sighed. "Look, I don't want to do this either, but I need to know if it would work before I share my idea. We've got like fifty angels here that can pull you out once we're done."

Raj opened his mouth questioningly, and I shook my head. His questions could wait.

"Wait, what if she *can* get through the cage?" Jake asked. "What if she runs off in David's body?"

"I think the eight of us could outrun her in David's body," Daisy said dryly. "David's not that fast."

"I've got these on, you idiots," Sheila grumbled, holding up her manacles. "I can't do anything to hurt David, or Hermes will yank me away. And I doubt he'd allow me to possess you, anyway."

"He will," I said grimly. "He knows what I'm testing."

"And why does it have to be me who does this? You're all dead. You all have the power to do this."

The angels all looked scandalized. "Possessing a human goes against *everything* in our contract," Bill said.

"You angels and your stupid contracts!" Sheila growled.

"Also, we're trying to test if a demon in a mortal's body would be trapped," I pointed out. "An angel wouldn't be trapped by Light, and you're the only demon here."

"Fine!" She shook out her arms and legs and shuffled from foot to foot, like someone psyching herself up for a race. Then she flew at me and sank into my skin. I was suddenly so filled with Darkness that it made me itch and cough. I got twitchy all over from both of us trying to move my muscles at the same time.

"Let's get this over with," Sheila said with my mouth.

Jake, who apparently did this all the time, created a cage of Light around me in about five seconds. Though this was less of a cage and more of a dome of Light, like a force field.

It was hard with both of us trying to control my body, but eventually we made it to the edge of the dome of Light. I stretched my hand to stick it through and yanked it back when it burned me. We tried to walk through it, but immediately jumped back and cried out. I tried to take it at a running start, but it threw me back on my butt while I sat there panting. Because of Sheila and her reaction to the Light, we were both stuck.

"Well, that answers that question," I said quietly.

"Somebody get me out of here!" Sheila yelled. "I hate being David."

"Hey," I grumbled.

Jake dropped his dome of Light, and then Frederick reached inside me to pull Sheila out. It hurt just as much as before. I fell to the ground and screamed as her spirit was ripped free from my body. When she was finally out, I was panting and sweating.

I gulped and shakily stood up. "It worked."

Everyone nervously looked around at each other. I couldn't tell if they thought I was losing my mind or if they were starting to see where my plan was leading.

A knock at the door made all of us jump. "Hey, you okay in there?" It was Preston. He must have heard me shout.

"Uh, I just stubbed my toe, but I'm fine!"

We all waited in silence until his footsteps faded away and his door shut.

"What's this about, David?" Raj asked quietly, for the first time not so thrilled with one of my plans.

I wasn't a huge fan of it either. So I came out with it as quickly and bluntly as possible before I had the chance to back out. Even then, just saying it made me wince.

"We're going to trap Malum inside my body."

There was a long silence as everyone tried to make sense of what I'd just said. I took the opportunity to explain. "Look, the main issue from the beginning is that we can't pin him down. The minute angels get close to capturing him, he disappears or paralyzes everyone with fear. So this is how we trap him. As Sheila explained to me not that long ago, Demons can't leave a body on their own once they're in it. If he possesses me, he'll be stuck. At least temporarily. Then, if someone drops a cage of Light on us, Malum will finally be captured."

Everyone looked at me like I was nuts and started throwing questions at me too fast for me to answer.

"Why would he even want to possess you?"

"What's to stop him from paralyzing the angels that exorcise him?"

"What if he takes control and runs off with your body?"

"What if he hurts you?"

"How will you—"

"GUYS!" I shouted.

Everyone fell silent.

"I will explain if you will just be quiet and listen for a second. I promise I've thought this through. If you have questions, hold on to them until I've had the chance to tell you my plan."

Raj looked like he wanted very badly to interrupt, but he

pursed his lips shut. I looked around to make sure that everyone was listening.

"All right, so the first question was how we'd convince him to possess me. We're going to put him in a position where that will seem like it's his only option. I'm sure Malum knows about my ability to leave my body. I'll challenge him to a fight—angel against demon. The winner gets to capture the other. I know I'm just me, but I'm sure he'd jump at any opportunity to capture me. From the beginning, I've been the wild card, and I think that scares him."

"How would fighting him out of your body trap him in your body?" Jake asked.

"Because eventually he's going to realize that the only way to truly capture me will be to kill me; otherwise, I can just escape by going back into my body, and he doesn't know that I'm limited in how many times I can do that. Before I challenge him, I'm gonna drive out to the middle of nowhere, where there's nothing around to kill me with. No knives, no sharp corners, no tree branches. Nothing. Then he'll realize that the only way he can hurt me is by possessing me and making me hurt myself."

"How does that help capture him?" Natalie asked. "Any angels that tried to exorcise him would become paralyzed by him. Even Frederick and William froze."

"True, but you aren't going to exorcise him. Once he's possessed my body, you guys will come down with a Light cage and trap us both inside. He'll be physically trapped in my body, so he can't just poof away when you spring the cage on him. He won't be able to make me run, because the Light cage will trap us both there, just like it did with me and Sheila."

"But you'd be trapped in there with him!" Sandra exclaimed.

"And what about getting Malum to The Resting Place prison?" Daisy asked. "We can't take him there in your body. Living people can't get in."

"We would have to exorcise him through the cage," Bill said.

"No," I said quickly. "That's too risky. Once he's out of me, there's nothing to stop him from grabbing one of you and incapacitating you. Who knows, maybe he'd even trick you into letting him out. Once he's in the cage, nobody gets near Malum. There's really only one way around it, and I'm almost positive Malum will take care of it for me. If not . . ." I took a shaky breath, "I'll do it."

"Do what?" Daisy asked.

Sheila gasped and stared at me with wide, unblinking eyes.

"What?" Sandra demanded. I tried to answer, but the look in her eyes, like she truly cared about me, made me too emotional to respond.

"Demons can't leave living bodies on their own," Sheila said. "But there is one last-ditch escape. It's the same for mortals."

"Death," Raj said quietly. "Demons can't possess the dead."

"Your big plan is to let him kill you?" Jake demanded.

"What if he doesn't kill you?" Sheila asked. "What if he stays in your body purely out of spite, just to trap you?"

"Then I'll do it," I said shakily. "I'll have a hidden gun on me or a pill or something—I don't know, I'm not an expert on suicide—anyway, I'll do it once we're trapped in the cage."

"David," Raj said, a tortured look on his face. I continued before he could say anything else.

"You'll just have to make sure we're trapped before either of us can go through with it. That way, at least he'll already be in his cage. Hopefully, after I die, I'll be able to slip through the cage since I'm not a demon, and then whoever is controlling the cage can take Malum to The Resting Place while still trapped inside. That way, no one has to get near him. "

"No!" Mom, looking like she was about to throw a *chancla* at me, marched up to me and tried to poke me in the chest. "You are not throwing your life away! I thought you were past this death wish stage! I thought you were enjoying your life again!"

"I don't have a death wish!" I yelled, too high-strung to contain myself. "I don't want to die! I want to keep living. I want to get a degree. I want to get married and have a family. I want to grow old and have grandkids. I want to earn a bunch of wrinkles and scars and make a billion mistakes. I want to cry and laugh and pray in ways that only mortals can. I don't want this. I hate this plan, but I also know that it's our only shot.

"When I was first turned mortal, I suggested using me as bait. It was always the right plan, it just wasn't the right time yet. Now it is, and it sucks because it's an actual sacrifice now. I don't want my life to end. But I'm lucky enough to know what's waiting for me on the other side, and eventually I'll be okay."

"David," Raj said quietly. "As brave and thought-out as your plan is, there's one big problem you haven't addressed. You've already used up all three chances to leave your body, so this fight between you and Malum can't happen."

"I just talked to Hermes," I said heavily. "The three chances thing was only if I wanted to keep on living. He knew that if I used the gift a fourth time, I would die."

After a long silence, Natalie said, "Maybe it doesn't have to be you. Maybe he could possess somebody else."

I looked down and shook my head. "For this plan to work, a mortal has to die, and we can't ask that of anyone else. I know lately I've been trying to live a normal life, like my second chance at life was just for me. It wasn't. This was the Big Man's plan all along. He needed a guardian angel who understood what was at stake to sacrifice their mortal body. That's what I'm here for."

It was quiet for a long time.

"I hate to burst your bubble," Sheila said, "but whatever terms you set with Malum, he won't follow them. If you want him to meet you in the middle of nowhere with no backup, he'll do the opposite. I've told you, he's a coward underneath it all, and there's no way he's going to face you alone."

Raj rubbed his face. He looked miserable. "Kid, I never thought I'd say this, but I agree with Sheila. Your plan is bold, but it's got about fifty holes in it."

"Well, I'm just one me, and I never claimed to be a mastermind. We'll plan what we can together, then you're going to present our ideas to Wolff and Moustafa so they can make it better. There's no way out of this, Raj. I've made up my mind."

The room was silent while everyone looked at me like I was standing on my grave.

I rolled my eyes and took a seat on my armchair. "Well? Let's get planning."

HER

I thought things couldn't get any worse, but Malum's leash was a lot looser back then. Malum wanted destruction, but he didn't have a specific nemesis he was trying to destroy. Most of the time, I was free to do what I wanted. I just had to be at his beck and call. It was terrible serving him, but I was at least able to go about my business most of the time. I visited my daughters, tempted mortals, and sat around stewing in my anger.

Then David came along.

When we first met, I thought he was stupid, and I obviously saw through his pathetic bad-boy act. I knew from the beginning that he wanted something from me, which made him untrustworthy. The thing is—I would never admit this to anyone—but I had a soft spot for his gullible genuineness. Even if he was a liar, he was always himself. And his stupid smile reminded me of how I felt with *him* before it all fell apart. When we were teenagers, he would giggle stupidly and then rub the back of his neck in embarrassment. David did the same thing. I didn't fall for David. I just liked the way I felt when I was with him. And if I was doomed to

Hell for all eternity, I figured I deserved a little bit of fun where I could find it. A little bit of hope. A little bit of light. I knew it was stupid and foolish, but I wanted something good. And being with him felt good.

And then he took me to a beach and called me beautiful in the most awkward and dorky way possible. And I cracked. I'd had my guard up with him, and I still didn't trust him, but at that moment I wanted to trust him. Even stranger, I wanted to protect him. He'd convinced me he was a demon, but I knew he wasn't evil. And I knew that if I introduced him to Malum the way he wanted me to, Malum would eat him alive.

chapter 37
IMPENDING DOOM

It was strange going from choosing to live my own life to deciding to lay it down. Like this phase of doing what I wanted with my life had just been a dream. I was in a state of numbness by the time the meeting was over. I didn't even notice that almost everyone had left until Daisy came to stand right in front of me. Raj was also lingering behind, likely to check on me, but he went to wait in the hall. Even Sheila left the room. Had Daisy asked to talk with me in private? I couldn't remember.

I blinked and pulled myself out of my slump. "Daisy? What's up?"

She looked even more serious than she usually did.

"I know you're going through something right now and need to process, or whatever—"

"It's fine, just say what you want to say. I'd love a distraction."

She paused as she frowned down at her feet. Then she looked up at me. "I want you to do something for me before you die."

I blinked. "Sure. Of course. I'm guessing this is a medium thing?"

She took a breath. "Tell my parents where my body is. They never found it, and even though it will hurt them to know for sure that I'm dead, they deserve closure."

I blinked and pulled back. Tears stung my eyes. *Oh Daisy* . . . Something truly terrible had happened to her, and I never knew. Based on what she'd just said, not even her parents knew exactly what had happened except that she'd gone missing. I couldn't imagine that pain.

"Hey, snap out of it!" she grumbled. "Don't you start crying on me. This is why I never told anyone."

I forced myself to sit back up, but I was too emotionally high-strung to fix my face. "You don't want people to have empathy for what you and your family have suffered?"

She sighed. "Empathy is fine, but I've already done my crying, and I'd much rather move on. I'm happier on this side anyway."

"Regardless, I'm so sorry, Daisy. We don't have to talk about it, but I hope you've been talking to someone about it. You don't just get over things like that just because you died."

She looked at me like I was stupid. "Dude, that's what the Big Man is for. I already know that. We're pals."

I nodded and forced a smile. Then I sighed. "So what do I tell your parents? Do you want me to call them or go in person?"

"Neither. My dad will probably threaten to shoot you once you start blabbing nonsense about seeing dead people. And they don't use the phone much, seeing as they're both deaf."

"Oh, right. So what do you want me to do?"

"Just submit an anonymous tip to the police. They can't exactly dismiss a tip about a body found. And I'll go down to the station myself and . . . persuade them to investigate if they drag their feet about it."

I had a feeling her version of persuasion was less to do with angel whispers and more to do with haunting, but I figured she was owed a little angry haunting after what she'd been through.

"Is there any evidence I should lead them to? Did the . . . murderer get caught?" I kept having to clear my throat. I was having a really hard time keeping it together.

"Oh, he's already rotting in prison," Daisy said darkly. "He was arrested the next month for a different murder."

I nodded, comforted that at least he wasn't still on the loose. "Okay. I'll do it. Is there anything else you want me to do?"

She looked at me with an uncharacteristic sadness and vulnerability. "I don't think you can."

"What? I'll do it! What is it?"

She sighed. "I want you to stop looking at me that way. Like a victim."

I tried to fix my face, but I couldn't. Just imagining this child in pain, someone that I'd grown to love, was ripping my heart in two.

She sighed again. "You know, that's why I've never told anyone but the Big Man. I knew people would never be able to look at me the same way again."

"Look, you just dropped a bombshell on me. Eventually,

I will be able to look at you without tearing up, but let me have my feelings, all right? Wouldn't you be more concerned about someone who didn't cry at the murder of a child?"

She rolled her eyes. "Fine. Have your feelings. You should feel bad about what happened. Just know that I'm fine now, and you don't need to feel bad for me. I've already had the happy ending. The Resting Place is infinitely better than any place on earth. I'm safe and I'm happy and I have a purpose. It's you living people you should feel bad for. Mortality blows."

I chuckled and nodded. "Yeah, it really does."

Her arms twitched upward, and I smiled, realizing she'd wanted to hug me. She hurriedly folded her arms behind her back to hide her impulse.

"I saw that, and I'm holding you to that hug," I said. "I might need one soon."

She smiled sadly, and then together we called her local police station, very vaguely telling them there was a rumor of a body buried in the location Daisy told me. Through Daisy, I gave them as much information as I could, then I hung up. I was worried they would somehow be able to trace me if they wanted to and make me a suspect in this crime. There were things I needed to do before I died, and I didn't have time to go to jail.

I knew Raj wanted to talk to me, but after Daisy left, I took some NyQuil and flopped on my bed, wanting nothing more than to forget everything just for a couple of hours. I wasn't ready to fully process this hell I was about to put myself through.

• • •

I had no dreams. When I woke up, I couldn't remember—or maybe I was trying not to remember—exactly what I'd agreed to do the day before. But I knew it was awful. I could feel the dread pressing down on me, threatening to smother me. I tried to fall back asleep, but I couldn't, and I rolled over, trying to fight the memories from coming back. They came anyway.

I was going to die. I hadn't even fully processed how distraught I was going to be saying goodbye to my family again, and that wasn't even the worst part. The worst part was that I was going to give myself over to Malum. Not for him to paralyze me with fear, or even to throw me in the Hurricane, but to possess my very body. That creature would be inside my body. He would be completely inescapable. I wanted to scream and cry and go back to sleep forever. I was envious of my first death. I didn't see that coming. The pain didn't even last that long. Yeah, it was a shock, but I would take that shock over this dread.

I ignored my alarm. What was the point of going to work? What was the point of leaving my bed? What was the point of doing anything? Nothing mattered. I was alone. I was freaking out, and I was alone.

When I turned over and opened my eyes, Raj was there. I didn't even have the energy to be shocked.

"Get up," he said.

I scowled. "What?"

"You're getting up and you're going to work," he said firmly. His face betrayed none of the pity I saw the night before.

"Why?"

"Because you have a job and you're going to be late."

I groaned and threw my arm over my face. "What's even the point? If we go through with this plan, I'm just going to die anyway. What does a job even matter?"

He walked closer to my bed and looked down at me. "Kid, I am not going to let you spend the rest of your life moping in bed. I know you. I know your tendencies when you're depressed, and I'm not going to let you miss out on the rest of your life. Get up. Go to work. It won't take away your worries, but it will help. I promise."

I groaned again and rolled over. "I don't want to."

The lights started to flicker on and off like a strobe light. "I will keep doing this until you get up. I'm serious."

I tried to block out the flashing light with a pillow, but then my alarm went off again. I growled and turned it off, then stumbled over to the light switch to turn it off. I flicked it back on and scowled at Raj.

"You have twenty minutes to shower and get ready." He clapped at me. "Let's go."

I growled and threw a pillow at Raj before grabbing my stupid work polo shirt and some pants from off the floor. I may have slammed the bathroom door a little too loudly.

I had time to contemplate everything while in the shower and as I got ready for the day. Admittedly, Raj was right. We might not even go through with this plan. We still needed the go-ahead from Moustafa and Wolff. And if they did agree, I'd probably hate myself if I spent the last days of my life moping . . . Ugh, just thinking the phrase "last days of my life" made me feel like I wanted to cry and scream again. I slapped myself and glared into the mirror. "Get it together, Garcia!" Then I took a deep breath and hurried back to my room for my phone and keys. Raj was still there.

He smiled as he noted me wearing my work polo and grabbing my keys. I rolled my eyes and stalked out of the room. Then I went back to my room, unable to look him in the eye, and muttered, "Thank you."

He was right. No matter what happened, I had to keep living my life. Until the very last day. Whenever that would be.

"Hey," he said. "Look at me."

I did so, reluctantly.

"This is the part where you need to get your mind off things," he said. "Go about your day. Stay busy. Get distracted. But eventually, you're going to need to feel those feelings. Cry, scream, throw stuff. Do whatever you need to do to get those feelings out, or they're going to fester. Understand?"

I nodded.

"Do you want to be alone when that happens, or will you want company?"

I sighed and looked down. "I don't know. I'll have Hermes call you if I need you."

"Please do."

After a big breath, I looked back up at him, unable to say

all I wanted to say.

He smiled at me like he was proud of me. "We'll talk later. You're gonna be late. Now go be David."

I didn't deserve Raj.

At work, I went through the motions and tried to get my mind off my impending doom. I smiled and joked and got kicked in the shins by a little kid. The weight of my fate hung over me, but I valiantly ignored it. I hate to admit it, but I've gotten the sense that I'm kind of an open book. People know how I'm feeling, even when I try to hide it. But I must have acted my part pretty well, because no one asked me what was wrong or looked at me with worry. No one, except the last person I ever expected to care.

I was pushing the cleaning cart down the hallway when someone grabbed my sleeve and tugged me after him.

"I'm cleaning, Preston!" I tried to wriggle out of his grip, but he didn't let go until he opened his office door and pushed me inside, practically shoving me into a chair.

I lifted my hands. "Dude! What the heck?"

Preston sat at the edge of his messy desk, knocking several things to the floor. He folded his arms and glared at me. "Okay, I've had this nagging feeling all freaking day that I need to check on you, so I'm gonna need you to tell me what's going on."

I glanced behind him to see his mom shrug guiltily.

I sighed. "Looks like our moms have been talking."

Preston raised his eyebrows. "Wait, so I'm right?

Something *is* going on?"

I nodded.

"Something big?"

"You could say that."

He sighed in annoyance. "Are you gonna tell me?"

The weird thing was, it didn't seem weird for him to ask. We were friends now, somehow. It would have been weirder if he hadn't asked.

I looked up at him and considered. Then I looked away and shook my head. "I will tell you eventually, but to be honest, I'm still sort of in denial, and I kinda need to sit with it before I tell anyone."

Shoot, now I was thinking about it. Remorse rushed through me as I realized I'd have to say goodbye to my work family. And heck, was I sad to say goodbye to Preston? He was the weirdest friend I'd ever had. I used to hate him. I thought I was supposed to help him be a less sucky person, but how many times in the past few months had he checked up on me? I was going to miss this stubborn, earnest jerk.

I tried to justify going back on my convictions. Maybe this wasn't necessary. Maybe I could stay and have friends and family and a future. But at what cost? The entire world? Either Malum could destroy the world, or he could just destroy me. Obviously, the latter was the better choice . . . But what about *me*? Why was I chosen for this? Was it just because I had already screwed up so badly that if I failed and Malum dragged me away, it wouldn't be much of a loss? But if I failed, everyone failed, didn't they? If we went through with this plan, it would all depend on me. Somehow, I had to do this, but I didn't know how. How would I resist Malum when no one ever had? I'd done it before for a little bit, but I eventually gave in. He'd proven time and time again that he was stronger than any one angel on their own. Heck, he was stronger than a team of angels together. I wished I'd never had the idea in the first place.

"You won't be alone, David," Norah said quietly. "You don't have to be strong enough. The Big Man is strong enough for you."

I blew air out my lips and blinked, mortified that my eyes were watering.

Preston raised an eyebrow as he studied my face. "That bad, huh?"

"Kind of the worst thing I can think of."

He gave a dry laugh. "You're not dying again, are you?"

I felt my chin start to quiver, and I bit my lip. I looked down, trying to blink the moisture from my eyes.

Preston's eyes widened. "Oh, shit! Dude, are you actually dying?"

I started bawling right then and there. In front of Preston. At work.

Damn him.

I tried to remind myself that this plan wasn't set in stone. But it felt set in stone. It felt like this was always going to happen, and I knew it would. Funny how not that long ago I was depressed that I was *alive* when all my friends were dead. But now I had friends on both sides. As a medium, I could keep in touch with all of them. As a dead person, everything would be one-sided with all the living people. And most of them would never know I'm there. There was a loneliness to that. For the longest time, I felt like an orphan with no mom or dad I could turn to.

What surprised me most was the fact that Preston was so upset when I told him. He didn't want me to die. That was kind of nice. I mean, I didn't want people to feel sad, but if someone's sad when you die, it means that they cared. It's always nice to know someone cared about you.

I wasn't ready to tell anyone else yet. When we finally left his office, all red-eyed and puffy-faced, Joanna froze on her way to the kitchen, gaping at us. "Oh my gosh, did someone die?"

I whimpered a little, then cleared my throat. "I'm moving."

She blinked and raised her eyebrows in surprise. "Wow, I didn't realize your bromance went so deep. When are you leaving?"

I took a breath, schooling my emotions. "I'm not sure. But soon."

"Well, you have to tell us before you go so we can have a going-away party. Piper's gonna kill you if you don't let us have a proper goodbye."

"She won't have to," Preston muttered.

"Dude!" I shoved him, shocked at how morbid he could be.

"What?" Joanna asked.

"Yeah, a party would be nice," I said quickly.

Preston cleared his throat and straightened his shoulders.

"All right, that's enough chatting. Everyone, back to work."

I said, "Aye, aye, captain," and rushed off to clean the bathrooms. I really hoped I wasn't going to spend the rest of my life crying, because this was getting seriously depressing.

chapter 38
GOING OUT OF BUSINESS SALE

I put off telling my family I might be leaving soon. There was no need to upset them before I had to. But among my dead friends, it seemed the plan was a pretty done deal. They kept checking in on me and trying to encourage me, which was sweet, but only reminded me of what I was trying not to think about.

Daisy wasn't the only one who suddenly wanted to take advantage of my medium powers before I died. Grandma came and found me after work a couple of days later. Even though I wasn't sure when I was leaving, Joanna immediately told everyone I was moving, and that Saturday, the team all stuck around after closing to throw me a little going-away party. It was nice, and honestly, I was really happy I got to say goodbye to everyone. It wasn't necessarily my last day—I didn't want to quit until I was sure about the plan—but I was glad I got closure with these people I'd come to love. While I was sad to leave them, I felt lucky to have met them. We mostly just joked and ate pizza, but at one point, Jorge brought out a rat piñata and Liam handed me a bat.

Preston shrugged. "While I'd love to let you set the rat costume on fire as a going-away catharsis, we can't vandalize the company's property."

"So instead you get to beat the crap out of the piñata and pretend you're killing the rat!" Piper grinned.

I did. I beat the crap out of that thing, and we all left with candy.

Preston and I hung out in the parking lot for a while afterwards, leaning against my car and eating our candy. I had just caught a Smartie in my mouth when Grandma showed up, wringing her hands.

I choked on my Smartie and rasped, "Hey, what's up, Grandma?"

Preston curiously glanced in the direction I was looking.

"Hey, Pumpkin!" Grandma said, her smile not quite meeting her eyes. "I need you to do me a favor."

Dad was watching TV when I got home. Well, he had been watching TV, but by that point, his head had lolled back, and he was snoring. I didn't want to wake him, but Grandma was pretty insistent.

I sat on the edge of the couch and said, "Hey, Dad?"

Dad snorted awake and yawned widely. "Hey, how was work?"

"Good," I said. "I, uh, need to talk to you about something."

His eyes flicked to mine, looking nervous and suspicious. Could he sense something was off with me? If not, he didn't say. "What is it?"

"Actually, Grandma wants to talk to you. Would you be up to that?"

Dad's eyebrows went up, and he leaned back. "Grandma? What does she want to talk to me about?" His tone was defensive and on guard. Clearly, his relationship with her wasn't much better than his relationship with Grandpa.

I glanced over my shoulder at Grandma, who had somehow struck up a conversation with Sheila in the hallway. Sheila had her arms folded and responded with annoyed reluctance. I smiled. Grandma was probably trying to convince her to date me again. It seemed that dating a demon would be preferable to being single in her book.

I looked back at Dad. "Well, she didn't exactly say, but she did say she wanted to talk in private where we won't be overheard. Can we, uh, go to your room or something?"

Dad frowned, but he just shrugged and led the way. After following him in, I shut the door behind us. Grandma stood next to me, wringing her hands. Sheila gave us some privacy and waited in the hall.

Dad put his hands on his hips. "Is she in here?"

I nodded my head to the right, where Grandma was standing.

"So? What do you want to talk about?"

Grandma looked down at her hands and whispered, "It was me."

I repeated her words, and Dad frowned in bemusement. "What was you?"

"I was the one who made your father stay away," she

blurted. "I made you think he was the bad guy, but it was me. He might not have been the best father, and he made a lot of mistakes, but I was the one who cut you out of our lives."

It was hard for me to relay her words fast enough to keep up with her. Dad stood there with his mouth open as Grandma plowed on.

"I was hurt, all right? I sacrificed so much to create what I thought was the perfect life for you, and you rejected all of it. The perfect girl, the perfect college, the perfect career—I thought I was looking out for you by setting you up for the best life you could have." Dad started to open his mouth, but Grandma didn't give him the chance. "Those are explanations, not excuses. I was wrong to prevent you from living the life you wanted. I was controlling and manipulative, and it was wrong. When you chose Gloria, I acted like you were choosing her over us. So I told your father that if you left us, then you weren't part of this family anymore."

Grandma sniffed and bit her lip as tears fell from her face and disappeared. Her voice wavered as she continued. "Your father was angry with you, but he was softening to the things you'd said to him. He was willing to try and see things your way, and tried several times to extend an olive branch, but I stopped him. I told him that if he reached out to you, I would leave him. It was you or me. That was the ultimatum I gave him."

By this point, Dad had sat down on his bed in shock, staring at nothing while Grandma plowed on.

Grandma walked up to him, crying and wringing her hands. "He chose wrong, but I was the one who forced him to make that choice. And I convinced him that you wanted nothing to do with us. I ripped up your wedding invitation and threw it away. And every birth announcement or birthday party invitation or Christmas card went straight to the trash."

"I never sent you those things," Dad said hoarsely. "After you didn't come to my wedding, I didn't even try."

"Gloria did," Grandma said with a sad smile. "She tried calling a few times too. I never gave her the chance to speak before I hung up . . ."

Dad hung his head and closed his eyes.

"She called your dad after I passed," Grandma said quietly. "She was very kind, and they had a nice, long conversation. They spoke a few other times over the years, but your dad was too ashamed of his behavior to reach out to you. He couldn't face you. Not after all we'd done." She sat down next to him. "I won't minimize your pain at the neglect we've shown you. No child should have to live their life without the support of their parents. No child should have to feel unloved or unwanted, or even as though they had to earn their love. I should have given my love freely, no matter what you did with your life.

"I don't expect you to forgive me—that's asking too much. But please forgive your father. He only did what he had to do to keep the love of his life from leaving him, and once I was out of the way, it was the shame and guilt that held him back. That accident he got into was a blessing in disguise. Please, don't let this blessing go to waste. Your dad is old, and soon he'll be gone. Please patch things up while you can. I know what it's like to die in your guilt. Please don't let that happen to him."

After Grandma finally finished, I let out a slow breath and just stood there uncomfortably while Dad shook his head and said nothing. Grandma bit her lip and drummed her hands on her thighs.

Personally, I was reeling. My sweet, kindly grandma was kind of a monster. I had no idea she had that side to her. One thing was apparent to me, though, and that was that she had changed. I mean, the fact that she supported me having a relationship with literally anyone was proof that she no longer had the strict biases she once had. The grandma I knew would be thrilled for my dad to be with my mom—she just loved love so much. I wondered what that growing experience had been like for her. Had she spoken to my mom since she died? Had they patched things up? People were all so complicated, and that doesn't change when you're dead.

Finally, Dad let out a breath and quietly said, "I'll think about it."

Grandma nodded and stood, accepting that this was probably as far as Dad was able to go at this time. Grandma came up to me and tried to pat my arm. "Thank you, Pumpkin. Sorry you had to hear all that."

"Anytime," I said quietly.

After Grandma left, I wondered if I should say something to Dad, but he seemed like he needed some time alone.

After all the drama, I went straight to my room and flopped on my bed, completely drained.

Sheila sat in the chair in the corner. "I don't understand what you're so upset about. Your dad will forgive her. He's like you, and people like you suck at holding grudges."

"I'm not upset about that," I mumbled.

"You can't tell me you're still moping about the plan that isn't even a plan yet."

I turned over and glared at her. "I'm gonna die, you heartless demon!"

She shrugged. "Maybe, you don't know that for sure."

"It's gonna happen," I muttered. "I can feel it."

She rolled her eyes. "Oh, boo-hoo. It's not like you haven't done it before. Once you're dead, you're not gonna care. You'll be flopping around like a happy little angel, singing about how life is so much better now that you're dead."

I sighed. "Yeah. Probably. I just don't look forward to the thing that's gonna kill me."

She pursed her lips and looked down. "Yeah, I don't envy

you there."

I flinched when someone knocked on my door—a dead person, by the sound of the ball bouncing off the wood. My heart felt like it was rapidly filling with lead. "Come in?"

Raj floated through the door looking grim. He did a quick Light test on me and Sheila, then he just stood there in silence.

I felt like everything inside me had deflated. "They approved the plan?"

He nodded. "Three weeks."

"Three weeks?" I gasped.

"They wanted to carry out the plan in two, but I talked them up to three. We need time to solidify all the moving parts of the plan anyway. Sorry I couldn't buy you more time, kid."

I fell back on my bed and stared at the ceiling. "No, thanks for getting me the time you did, Raj. It's three weeks more than I had the first time I died."

He slowly walked over and sat on my bed. "You know, you don't have to go through with it. It's your life. You have the right to decide."

I sat up. "But you think I should do it, right?"

He pursed his lips, struggling with something.

"Maybe you just don't think I can." I flopped on my back.

Raj sighed and shook his head. "No, David, that's not it. The problem is that the task force leader and the real me have very different opinions. The task force leader thinks it's a very clever plan that might be our only hope. The real me wants to protect you from more pain and suffering. That side of me wants to tell you to run away and save yourself."

"And if I don't go through with it?" I asked quietly. "If I do run away and save myself?"

He shrugged. "We find another plan. Or someone else who's able to carry out your plan. There are plenty of other mediums we could contact."

I sighed, shoving my hands through my hair. "Yeah, but then they would have to give up their life. And anyway, it's me that Malum wants. He's not going to possess any random person who tries to goad him into it. And in the meantime, while you're finding someone else, thousands of people could die while Malum continues destroying everything. I can't let that happen. I'm not happy about it, but I am going through with the plan. It's what the Big Man wants me to do."

Raj didn't speak for a while. Then he gave me half a smile. "You're a good man, David."

I sat up and raised my eyebrows. "Man? Not kid?"

"What makes you think men stop being kids?" He quirked an eyebrow. "My dad called me 'beta' until I was old and stooped and using a cane, and he continued to do so after I died. It means 'son' in Hindi. I think I'm always going to be a kid to him. The way your dad will always be a kid to his dad."

"Huh," I said, thinking of how Tata still called his adult children "mijo" and "mija."

"You know, someday you'll mentor some young, insecure angel and he'll look up to you and never know that once upon a time, you were just like him."

I smiled. "I'm sorry, but I don't think anyone will ever not see that I'm a dork who's obviously floundering. I mean, even Asher knows that I'm lame. And Leo . . ."

My face fell as I remembered Leo. Was he still down there? Had anyone rescued him yet? I still couldn't believe that he was captured. It hurt my heart to think about it.

"Remember him and all those that have been hurt," Raj said passionately. "Let their memory fire you up." He seemed to throw his professional mentor hat out the window as he leaned in and whispered, "Then use that energy to kick that monster's ass."

That startled me into laughter. "Will do."

I figured it was time to tell the family now that I knew for sure. I was dreading this conversation, mostly because I didn't know how to hold it together. I kept trying to find my composure and failing. This whole plan rode on my shoulders, and I was starting to seriously doubt I could do it. What if I tripped at the finish line? How could I face him? Malum's power is in dredging up and enhancing all of the trauma you keep inside. The first time he met me, he was disappointed because he didn't have much to work with. My life was pretty boring the first time around. And yet, despite having little to work with, he still completely traumatized me. Since Malum had escaped, I'd had a lot of horrific experiences Malum could draw from. Sandra's death, Sam pushing me away, all the demon attacks, losing Leo, almost failing Asher, and everything I experienced in the Hurricane. His mind torture was going to be a whole lot worse. How could I withstand that? And how could I set all my worries aside to tell my family I was leaving them without completely falling apart in front of them?

I made Elena and Sam come over after they had their kids in bed. Maybe I should have invited Jessica and Charlie, but someone had to stay with the kids, and I kind of just wanted to talk to my immediate family first. I hadn't planned out what to say, but they deserved to know I would be leaving them soon. I wanted to give them a heads-up this time.

Elena showed up in pajamas and a bathrobe, waddling like she was about to pop, and Sam showed up a couple of minutes after, still in his button-up shirt and slacks. They didn't question me when I texted them and said I needed them to come over now. I guess that's such a rare thing for me to do that they knew this was serious.

It was super awkward, and everyone was nervous and confused when I had them all come to the family room. Sam kept nervously checking his phone, and Elena kept adjusting her bun, while her eyes darted around the room. Grandpa frowned at me shrewdly, and Dad's leg wouldn't stop bouncing.

It would have been easier to tell them all over text or something, but this was better. They deserved to hear it from me, in person. Mom showed up, completing the circle, and I smiled at her.

"Take a deep breath," she said. "I'm here for you."

My throat had a huge lump in it, and I tried to swallow it down, but instead of going away, it just made my eyes water. How was I going to get through this? I loved these people so much! How could I leave them?

Elena stopped playing with her hair and glared at me. "Dude, what's going on? Why did you have us all come over here?"

I looked around at my family, trying to figure out what to say. I took a deep breath as Mom had suggested and forced myself to speak. "I'm going to have to leave again. Permanently. I'm really sorry, but I have to go."

It was silent for a solid five seconds while they tried to make sense of what I'd just said. Then, they all spoke at once, throwing questions and protests at me too fast to even respond to. Eventually, I held my hands up and shushed them loudly enough that they paused to look at me.

"Look, I don't think I can really explain it. I just wanted to give you a heads up so you're not blindsided again. I can't tell you how guilty I felt when I left the first time with no warning at all."

"It wasn't your fault!" Elena shouted. "They can't take you again. You deserved this second chance!"

"Everyone dies at some point," I said softly. "It never seems fair, but it has to happen."

"They?" Dad stood up suddenly. "Who's they? Who's making you leave? Is someone trying to kill you? We'll call the cops. We'll protect you!"

I sighed heavily. "Nobody's making me do this. It's my choice this time. And, I'm sorry, but it's going to look really bad . . ." My voice cracked. "Like, really, really bad."

"Your choice?" Sam stood up, pointing at me accusingly. "So you're choosing to leave us? Look, I finally came to terms with the fact that you didn't mean to abandon us the first time, but it kinda sounds like that's what you're trying to do now. You can't leave us, David. We still need you."

My heart felt like it would explode with all the conflicting emotions. The fact that he thought I would abandon them felt like a punch in the gut, but the way he thought he needed me made me feel wanted.

I sighed. "I'm sorry. I can't explain. Even if I could, I wouldn't want to. It's too much."

"Try," Dad said quietly. "Tell us everything. We can handle it."

How could I tell them everything? So much of it had to do with the other side, and a lot of it would be too disturbing to share. I was struggling to process it all myself.

YOU CAN TELL THEM.

Should I, though? Would it make it any easier?

"Honey," Mom said gently. "They'd rather know you sacrificed yourself than believe you took your own life. Trust me, it will be more painful if you don't tell them."

And so I told them, starting from the beginning. Some of it they already knew, but they didn't seem to mind the repeat. Oddly, it was Dad asking all the questions, while Elena silently wiped her eyes, and Sam stared at me, white-faced. Grandpa's poker face gave nothing away, and since he was so close to Grandma, I was sure a lot of this conversation was old news to him.

I told them about the good as well as the bad. My friends on the other side and my job at the front desk with Nana Maria and Grandma Gertie, the way I loved The Resting

Place, and how peaceful it felt to let go of all your earthly worries. I told them about my first encounter with Malum and how I blamed myself for freezing. I told them about seeing Mom for the first time after she died. I told them about joining the demon hunters and all the crazy shenanigans I'd gotten myself into. It was kind of an exciting story to tell. I was surprised by that. It was nice to realize that I'd done so much and come so far since that day Malum ruined everything.

Then I told them about my plan to capture Malum, sparing all the gory details. Unfortunately, Dad kept asking me questions, so I had to get more specific than I wanted to. When I reached the end of my story, we all sat silently, staring at one another, unsure of what to say. Dad's giant wall clock ticked quietly in the background, interrupted only by quiet sniffles.

"Of course you had to go and be the hero of the day," Sam muttered.

"I don't want you to go," Elena said in a thick voice. Her shoulders shook as tears streamed down her face.

I opened my mouth to try to say something brave and comfort her, but all that came out was, "I don't want to go either."

I didn't. I didn't want to give up my life. I didn't want to surrender myself to Malum. I didn't want any of this, and I was scared out of my mind.

"It's all right, baby," Mom said softly. "You don't have to hold back your feelings just because you don't want to hurt them. It's you who has to go through with this. Let them be there for you."

"Are you okay?" Sam asked quietly.

I closed my eyes and pinched the bridge of my nose. "Not really."

"You don't have to do this, David," Dad said.

I shook my head and blinked. "I do have to do this. Not because anyone's making me, but because of who I am. If I can do something about this, I have to do it. I'm just . . . scared."

"Is there anything we can do for you?" he asked quietly.

"No. I mean, I don't know. I don't know what I need. I just can't help feeling that I'm going to fail, somehow. I always fail."

"How have you failed, David?" Grandpa asked.

"So many ways! I let Malum escape, for one—"

"No, that was Sheila," he interrupted. "You aren't responsible for that."

"I refused to let Sandra die and got turned mortal for screwing that up."

"You were supposed to become mortal," Elena said. "We got to have you back, and we needed you. And this whole stupid plan wouldn't work in the first place if you weren't mortal. So that wasn't a screw up either."

"I failed to save all my students when demons attacked my class."

"It was you against like thirty demons, stupid," Sam said. "And do you blame your task force leader every time one of your team goes missing? You did all that you could, and more than most."

"Okay, fine. Whatever. I just… I'm scared he'll get the better of me. He always does, in the end. I'm not supposed to say this, because it sounds like I don't have faith, or whatever, but I don't want to do this."

I tried to breathe deeply to force myself to keep it together, but my defenses snapped when Elena said, "I don't want you to do this either, David, but if anyone can, it's you."

I shook my head and turned away. They couldn't see me like this. But I couldn't fight this terrible feeling that it *wasn't* going to be okay. I was going to fail. He was evil incarnate, and I was just a guy. I couldn't do this. But I had to! Those two overwhelming ideas warred within me, and I felt like I was going to explode.

My dad slowly walked over and wrapped his arms around me and squeezed me so tight, it was like he was trying to fuse all my broken parts back together. Sam and Elena joined in on the hug. They didn't say anything, and they didn't need to. The hug said it all. All this time, I thought I was here to be their guardian angel, but I was starting to realize that I was the one who needed them.

I felt like I was crying with them at my own funeral. Except this time, there would be no funeral. I wasn't even sure what would be left of my body.

I pulled away and wiped my face, though it did no good. Tears continued to flow. We ended up in an emotional tangle on the floor, a circle of people refusing to let go of each other.

"I want you to know, I will always be here. Okay?" I said in a thick voice. Elena whimpered, and Dad sniffed. Sam wiped his face, and Grandpa just paced in the background.

"Even when you can't see me. I won't really be gone. Talk to me whenever you want, even if you're not sure if I'm there. Just because I'm dead doesn't mean I'm not still a part of this family. I'll be here, watching over you with Mom and Nana Maria and Grandma Gertie. We'll protect you, and we'll be there whenever you need us. And one day, hopefully not for a long time, you'll join us and we'll all be together again. And it will be okay. Somehow it will all be okay."

"We know, David. And you'll be okay too," Grandpa said, finally breaking his silence. He put his hand on my head and smoothed back my hair like I was a kid. "You're gonna be happy on the other side. All angels are."

I don't remember the rest of what we said or did. We hugged and laughed and cried, and there may have even been some pancakes involved. We sat and talked all night, until the sky outside the windows slowly faded from black to dusky gray. It was an incredibly surreal experience, and for a moment, time seemed to stop, and the life outside this room didn't seem real. Even though we were all mourning, I felt strangely safe and whole. This shared experience bound us together like no other experience had before.

I knew I'd burdened all of them with my problems, but I can't deny that I felt a little lighter afterward. I didn't have to bear this alone. And I decided that for the next three weeks, I would spend every possible moment of my time with my family. I would quit school and work, and I would spend the rest of my life with the ones I loved.

I felt blessed to realize that there were so many people in my life who loved me.

• • •

I spoke to Charlie the next day. Of course he was upset. We didn't see as much of each other as we used to, but he was one of my best friends. But unlike the rest of my family, he accepted what I would have to do with a grim understanding. He was a soldier—he understood sacrifice. He also agreed to a couple of risky and disturbing favors that only he could be trusted with.

By that point, I'd done all I could do. The demon hunters and defenders had their own part to play, but my preparation was finished. All I had left to do was live the best I could for three more weeks. And then it was time for me to face my Goliath.

HIM

I don't think anyone realized how young I was when I joined the demon hunters. I was still fresh from dying. I'd been around long enough to be trained as an usher, but I was still learning the ropes. I don't know how I got onto the demon-hunting task force. Sheer luck and determination? I just knew I had to do something. I was the reason we were in this mess. I couldn't make up for what I'd done, but if I was going to deserve the forgiveness the Big Man offered, I had to at least try.

And what a shocking surprise when I realized that a boy on my task force was assigned to a demon that just happened to be my wife. While he sat there blaming himself for letting Malum go, the real perpetrator was the one he thought he was dating, and her murdering husband sat right across from him every week. Like a coward, I said nothing.

chapter 40
HIT STUFF

The next week was a blur to me. I wasn't going to school or work, since there wasn't any point, and I wanted to spend as much time as possible with the people I loved. Unfortunately, those people all had jobs and lives that they couldn't just put on hold for three weeks to hang out with me. They all agreed to take that last week off, and we would all have a sort of family vacation at home together, but until then, I was mostly on my own. So I brought food to a different family member each day and had lunch with them—including the kids—and then ate dinner at a different house each day. I always ended up sleeping over because we stayed up so late talking.

I wasn't sure what I was supposed to be doing in the time between. I spent a lot of time doing projects around the house. I painted Elena's living room since she and Charlie never had time for it, and I replaced the light fixture in Sam's master bathroom since he kept forgetting to do it. I knew these were nice things to do, but I felt like I was doing it wrong. What is one supposed to do when they have three weeks to live? Go skydiving? Travel? Check off their bucket list? I wasn't interested in anything but being home.

I felt restless. Like time was moving too slowly and too quickly at the same time, and I just wanted to *do* something. I felt like I should be devastated that I was dying or terrified of facing Malum, but during most of the waiting period, I just felt numb. By the end of the first week, I was starting to panic that I'd already wasted what precious time I had left. I only had two more weeks to live! What was I supposed to do with myself?

The Monday of that second week, I was starting to genuinely flip out. What was I doing? Why was I doing this? Who was I to face the Prince of Darkness? What if I failed? How could I *not* fail? He was going to kill me and then take me captive, I just knew it. And how could I willingly leave my family again? What if I missed the birth of Elena's baby? She was due any day now, but what if she was late? I'd never get to meet my niece in person. And what if all of this was for nothing because I screwed everything up? What if this entire plan was a bust because I failed again? What if the mole discovered the plan and leaked it to Malum? What if I got run over by a bus tomorrow and died before I could fulfill my purpose?

Sheila was on another break from guarding me to go visit her daughters, so that didn't help my sense of vulnerability and restlessness.

A knock shook me from my panic-induced pacing. I frowned at my bedroom door. It was a living person, because they didn't use the ball on the string, but it was still during the day when everyone was working. Unless it was Grandpa.

"Yeah?" I asked.

"It's Sam."

I blinked in surprise and hurried over to open the door. He was standing there in workout clothes with his hands in his pockets.

"Get your shoes and your wallet," was all he said before he headed back downstairs.

"What?"

He didn't answer, so I slid my wallet into my pocket, grabbed my shoes, and ran after him. I followed him out the front door to his truck parked in the driveway. "Uh, are we going somewhere?"

He unlocked the truck. "Obviously."

"Okay, but where?"

He looked up from his phone to grin at me. "You'll see."

Then he got in the car and just waited for me to follow. Well, what the heck? I wasn't doing anything else with my life. I buckled in and finished tying my shoes while Sam clicked through his Spotify shuffle.

"So you're not gonna tell me where we're going?" I asked.

"We're gonna go smash stuff."

"I'm sorry?"

He sighed. "I'm not good with feelings, okay? But I'm sure you're feeling a lot of stuff, and I'm feeling a lot of stuff, and sometimes breaking things is a good release. So we're going to a rage room and we're going to break stuff."

I smiled. "I've always wanted to go to one of those." After a beat, I asked, "Are you cool to do this? Like physically? You know, with your Multiple Sclerosis?" We'd never actually talked about it, but I heard things from Jessica. Sometimes his balance was off, or his eyesight would get really bad in one eye. Most of the time, he was just really tired and achy.

He rolled his eyes. "Would I be doing this if I didn't feel up to it?"

I shrugged. "You might."

"Well, this is a good week for me, so I'm fine."

We didn't talk much on the drive. Sam isn't much of a talker, but it wasn't as awkward as I would have thought. We sang along to songs we grew up with and made bets on who could break the largest thing in the room with the fewest hits. I never got to hang out with my brother much in either of my lives, so it was a pretty novel experience.

When we got there, the lady at the front desk told us the cost per person, and I looked at Sam.

He raised an eyebrow at me. "You're paying, dead guy."

"Fair enough," I said. I had no reason to save money.

After paying, the lady gave us the safety spiel and handed us jumpsuits. I got distracted putting mine on when I realized the TV in the corner was replaying the Death threat to the entire world. I froze with my arm partially through the hole, suddenly reminding me of what I was up against, filling me once again with terror. Sam caught my expression and abruptly reached up and turned off the TV. I nodded a thanks and finished zipping up my jumpsuit.

After suiting up, we entered our rage room. There were various electronics throughout the room. Old computers, printers, and TVs. There were beer bottles lined up against one of the walls and a clip hanging from the ceiling where we could hang things to swing at. The wall adjacent to the beer bottles had a few weapons of choice. Sam hefted the sledgehammer, and I eyed the bat.

Before I could hit something, Sam cleared his throat. He twisted the hammer in his hands and blew air out of his mouth. "Okay, wait, I just want to say something first."

Oh boy.

He sighed and looked down. "I'm glad we got to have you back for the time we did. I'm really pissed that you're leaving us again, and part of me blames you for that because this was your choice. But I understand it, and I just want you to know, I think what you're doing is really brave. I know I'd never be able to do that, but instead of being jealous and angry at you for always being a better person than me, I'm freaking proud of you." He looked up at me. "I'm proud of you, man. You're kind of my hero." His face turned playfully threatening, and he pointed the sledgehammer at me. "If you tell anyone I said that, I will shove this down your throat. But seriously, I love you and I'll always love you, even when you're gone. I wanted to say that."

Before Sam showed up, I had been doing just fine at hiding my emotions, going about my day with fake smiles and reassurances that I was just dandy, but now all the feelings I'd been trying to ignore flooded to the surface, and I felt like I was going to explode. I groaned and turned away from Sam. "Dang it, now I'm freaking out again! Sorry, I mean, I love you too. And I'll always be near, but . . . ugh, I can't do this right now!" I clutched my hair and started pacing.

"Dude." Sam tapped me on the shoulder with the bat, then swung it around to extend the handle toward me. "Hit stuff."

I swung my bat at the dinosaur of a computer in the corner.

"What was that weak-ass hit?" Sam yelled. "Grandpa could do better than that! Are you upset?"

"Yes!"

"Then hit stuff!"

I swung the bat harder, cracking the computer screen.

Sam yelled and threw a beer bottle. "Are you angry?"

"Yes!"

"Hit stuff!"

I swung even harder, and the crack widened.

Sam took a swing at a TV in the corner and yelled, "Are you scared?"

"YES!"

"HIT STUFF!"

I swung my hardest, and the screen of the computer burst into a hundred shards of glass. Something cracked inside of me, like a dam had broken, and a crazed grin spread across my face. Adrenaline kicked in, and the two of us demolished that room. All my anger, fear, and heartache were flung across the room with every hit, throw, and kick. We yelled and screamed like we were going to war, and for a second, I let myself be upset about all I was giving up and all I was about to face. My situation sucked, and I let every breakable surface in the room know it.

After our time was up, Sam and I looked around at our

handiwork. It looked like a tornado had stormed through the room. I grinned at Sam and hugged him. Then he pulled out his phone and took a selfie of us surrounded by all the destruction. It was a good picture. Our helmet hair stuck out at weird angles, and we each looked ridiculously exhilarated. We looked like brothers. I was so glad I got to share that moment with him before I died.

After Daisy and Grandma, I assumed other angels would be lining up to take advantage of my strange gift before I was gone. What I didn't expect was Sheila.

I was in my dad's office, printing out the picture of me and Sam to frame for him, when Sheila awkwardly came and sat on the desk next to me. She didn't say anything; she just sat there, looking down.

"You have a favor too?" I guessed.

She remained silent, and instead of asking her, I just waited. If she wanted me to do something for her, I at least expected her to ask.

"My girls," she said quietly. "I want to talk to them."

I blinked. "What, like, through me?"

She rolled her eyes. "Obviously."

I set down the photo paper I'd been loading into the printer. I opened my mouth to say something, but decided to wait to see if she'd elaborate. She eventually gave in.

"They've been without a mom for most of their lives," she said quietly. "I just want them to know I'm around. And that I never meant to abandon them, but I made the only choice

I could to keep them safe."

I had about a billion questions, but I sensed that now was not the time for an interrogation. "Okay," I said softly. I sat next to her and asked, "What are their names?"

She took a moment to respond before quietly saying, "Ellie and Fae."

"They sound like little fairies," I said with a grin.

"We named them after our grandmothers," she said, nervously picking at her nails. "My mom's mom was named Elenor, and his mom's mom was Fae."

"I like that," I said. "And they still live with his parents?"

She nodded.

Then I frowned, noticing an awkward wrench in this plan. "What if the girls ask about *him*?"

She looked like I had just slapped her.

"I just mean, they're probably gonna ask about him. You know, because he's their dad. They're gonna wanna know where he is."

She stared at me and shook her head.

I bit my lip, trying to force myself not to push it. But I was the go-between here, and I knew this was a situation that was going to come up.

She continued to stare at me, and like an idiot, I started rambling. "I just mean, they're going to wonder about their dad, and it's kind of thanks to you he's not around anymore."

I immediately cringed. That was not the right thing to say right then.

She closed her eyes and let out a frustrated sigh. "No, David, it's the other way around. It's thanks to *him* that *I'm* not around."

"I know, I'm sorry," I said quickly. "That was insensitive. I was just wondering how you'll explain about Ted. I mean, you know they're going to ask."

She held her hands up. "Will you stop obsessing over that? For all we know, *he's* the mole."

"If he is, it's likely because Malum enslaved him after you threw him into the pit. Because before that, he was doing all he could to help us bring him down."

I didn't know what was making me say all this. Angering Sheila is never a great idea. The problem was, she was no longer a scary demon to me; she was just a person. And knowing she was just a person, just like everybody else, it was unfair that she felt that she could just do whatever she wanted without consequences. I knew there had been consequences to her actions—her enslavement to Malum being one of them—but at that moment, I was just annoyed with her for being so casually callous about torture. Also, I was just coming off my smash room high, so I was feeling a little daring and reckless.

Sheila blinked at me and clenched her jaw. "Is there something you want to say to me, David?"

This would have been the smart place to say, "Nope! Just kidding! And might I say, you look lovely today!"

Like an idiot, I let her have it. "You know, it's interesting how you can't forgive him for what he did to you, and yet, after you've already had your revenge—on him, as well as the entire world—you still can't let it go. I'm not saying he shouldn't be held accountable for what he did to you. I'm on your side—the way he hurt you wasn't okay, and I don't blame you for feeling traumatized and furious. If I were you, I'd want vengeance too. He was in the wrong, no matter what mental condition he was dealing with.

"But can't you see that you're being a hypocrite here? From what I understand about the situation, he hurt you because he didn't deal with his crap and get himself help before tragedy struck. And I notice that you're doing the same thing. Instead of getting help for yourself and trying to get your own crap together, you lash out, traumatizing others, just spreading the pain around. How does that help anyone?"

I knew once the words were out that I'd gone way too far. I was expecting the printer to start shooting papers out and the lights to explode. I was sure the fan was about to start spinning so fast that it would fall from the ceiling.

What actually happened was that Sheila started crying. My eyes widened in surprise, and I froze. She clenched her teeth and furiously wiped her face. "Really? Even you. The one person who actually . . ." She shook her head and covered her face with her hand. She didn't speak for a long time, but when she did, her voice was low and tired, and somehow even more intense because of that.

"No. Just no," she said, glaring at the floor. "You don't even know what you're talking about. You died at seventeen, and while that sucks, it also means that you know nothing about life. You've never had to support yourself or a family. You've never even been in a relationship long enough for things to get hard. And you'll never know what it's like to be a woman in this world." She looked up to meet my gaze.

"You'll never be talked down to for the simple fact that you have two X chromosomes, mocked for being overly emotional when you finally do stand your ground, and getting your ass slapped by strangers that think they deserve a piece of you. You'll never have to fear that, despite how strong you are as a person and how powerful you are as a woman, someday some *man* will overpower you and you'll end up in a ditch somewhere, where no one can find you. And you'll never understand what it's like to have daughters that you can do nothing to protect or prepare for this evil, sexist, rotten world." She wiped away bitter tears. "And now you're sitting there, condemning me for what I've done, and you know nothing about loss or heartbreak or pain—"

"That's not true," I said quickly.

Her eyes flashed, and she glared at me until I shut my mouth. "I know I'm the bad guy in your eyes, but if you get off your high horse for a second, you'll realize that I didn't know all of this would happen, okay? I didn't know Malum would try to destroy the world, and I sure as hell didn't intend to help him do it. I was angry and hurt because *HE* got into The Resting Place despite what he'd done to me, and yeah, I lashed out, because it wasn't *fair!* He deserved to be punished, not welcomed in just like everybody else. It was like what he did to me didn't even matter." Her voice got thick, and her eyes filled with more tears. "But everything I've done since then has been forced on me by Malum and *wasn't my choice.*

"And every time I've gone against his demands to help you, I was punished for it. I was punished for saving your life and for helping you save your mom from the Hurricane. I was punished every time I purposefully pulled my punches when he commanded me to utterly destroy you. Do you have any idea how much I've suffered because of you specifically? And look at what I'm doing for you now!" She held her wrists out to show me her manacles. "Do you have any idea how much this hurts? I'm in constant agony, and you don't even care!"

"Sheila, I'm sorry," I said quietly. "I was out of line."

She looked up and lifted her hands helplessly. "Why can't anyone see that I'm the victim here? I was *murdered* and tortured over and over. None of this is my fault!"

I pursed my lips, trying to restrain myself from saying what I was thinking.

"What?" Sheila demanded, noticing my expression. She clenched her jaw. "Just say it."

"Malum didn't force you to kick Ted into the Hurricane. He wasn't even there. That was completely your choice."

She rolled her eyes and growled in exasperation. "Oh my gosh, give it a rest! He hasn't even been down there that long. I've been down there multiple times, for way longer than he's been in, and nobody gave a shit!"

"I did," I said quietly.

She shook her head smiled bitterly. "No, you didn't. You cared about doing what's right, but you didn't care about *me*. You just knew that if you left a broken woman down there, pleading for help, your soul would be tarnished. It wasn't about me; it was about you. Don't think I don't know how angels think. It's always about becoming better and holier, not actual people. You act like rule breakers are the scum of the earth, and you never once try to understand that maybe people have reasons for what they do. And yet when *you* break a rule, it's okay. You lie and hurt and spread Darkness, but it's all right because you do it in the name of good. And then you dare to call *me* a hypocrite?"

Feeling defensive and strangely ashamed, I stammered. "I . . . you're wrong. We're trying to make the world better, not just ourselves. I mean, some of us suck at it, but we're trying—"

"Oh, shut up," she muttered bitterly. "I'm done with this." She stood abruptly. "Screw you. Screw all of this."

The next moment she disappeared, leaving a silence that felt deafening.

She didn't break or destroy things; she didn't hurt me in any way. And yet, I would have preferred it if she had. This wounded, vulnerable rage was so much worse. Feelings of anger and guilt warred within me as I leaned against the wall and slid to the floor.

Sheila never did come back. I asked Hermes what had happened, and he told me that he'd returned her to her prison cell. She refused to guard me again. Angels would pop in to check on me now and then, but from now on, I was on my own. Oddly enough, the protection of Sheila's reputation extended until the day I faced Malum. Not a single demon came after me because she'd so thoroughly scared them all off.

I tried not to stew on what had happened. I didn't want to

spend the rest of my life feeling guilty about something I could do nothing to change, but I felt awful about what I'd said. What possessed me to say those things? I mean, a part of me still felt like I was right, but that didn't mean I *was*. And that was beside the point. Who cared if I was right? It wasn't up to me to tell her how to grieve or process her trauma. And now, because of that stupid argument I started, Sheila would never get to talk to her daughters like she'd been longing to since she'd died. Why couldn't I have just kept my stupid mouth shut?

chapter 41
KIKI OUT OF CONTEXT

I was going to have dinner and spend the night at Elena's that night, but as I was packing some clothes into a backpack, there was another knock on the door. My room had become a very popular place lately.

Curious, I hurried over to the door and opened it to find someone completely unexpected.

Kiki, looking very Kiki in baggy overalls with her hair in pigtails. She smiled nervously at me, for once not showing all her teeth. I was weirdly angry at how cute she was.

My mouth fell open. "Uh . . ."

"You haven't been to class in over a week," she accused. "And you're one of those little nerds that sits in the front row and checks his grades like other dudes check the football score."

"So?" I asked.

"So, something's wrong," she said impatiently.

I rolled my eyes. "Why do you care?"

It was rude, I know, but there was a lot going on already without my ex showing up in my bedroom out of nowhere, reminding me of how much her breakup stung. As much as it sucked to be rejected, I'd been grateful that at least I wouldn't have to say goodbye to her. We had already cut ties, and she was one less person I'd have to worry about. But now she was confronting me about it, and now I'd have to have the conversation.

Kiki visibly deflated, her shoulders slumping and her eyes dropping to the floor. "I'm sorry, this was stupid," she said.

She turned to leave.

I caught hold of her arm. "Wait. I'm sorry, that was rude. Just tell me why you're here."

She spun around and yanked her arm out of my hand. "I just wanted to check on you, you jerk! What's wrong with you? You ignored all my texts after we broke up, and when you showed up to class, you ran away every time I tried to come talk to you. And now you're not coming to class! Either you really hate me, or something's wrong. And if you hate me that much, fine! I'm fine with giving you space if you need it. But I just wanted you to know that just because I don't want to *be* with you doesn't mean I don't still care about you."

Other than our breakup, I'd never heard her get through an entire sentence without cracking some kind of joke. The fact that she was completely serious felt like someone had dumped a bucket of water on my head. I was ashamed to realize that I'd never fully treated Kiki like a person with feelings as deep and complex as mine. Just because she knew how to laugh and acted like a psycho didn't mean she didn't still hurt and cry and mourn. I rubbed my face, realizing for the second time that day what a terrible, ignorant jerk I was.

I sighed. There was no avoiding this conversation now that she was here, and she deserved the closure. "Let's go for a walk."

We took a walk around the neighborhood, and I told her the whole story. How many times had I recited my story lately? The more I shared it, the more unbelievable it sounded, and the more it seemed like something that was happening to someone else. Kiki was quiet, which freaked me out. She just listened. When had she become a good listener? Or had I never given her the chance to listen to me? I suppose I had always treated our relationship as something casual. She was someone to relax and have a good time with, but I'd never really confided in her. That seemed weirdly selfish now, like I was using her to forget all my worries, never giving us the chance to form a real connection. Had she wanted more? I never gave her the chance to open up to me either. Was it because I knew I didn't like her in that way? Or because I was too scared to get hurt again? I mean, the last girl I loved went and died on me.

We walked around the entire neighborhood, and I reached the end of my story just as we made it back to my house, standing in my bedroom doorway where this conversation had started.

Kiki stared at me with an unreadable expression. Then she shoved me into my room and shut the door.

"I have two hugs to give," she said, off-putting as usual.

"What?"

"This one's for you." Softly and tenderly, she put her arms around my neck. She held me close, breathing softly. "I'm sorry this is happening to you," she said quietly. "It's not fair you have to leave again so soon, and you are so brave."

This took me by surprise. I didn't know she had this much tenderness inside her. I breathed in and out, trying to appreciate the comfort of her touch.

Before I could fully sink into the hug, she pulled away and then shoved me onto my bed. She sat next to me, and her sad face broke my heart.

"This hug is for me."

She little spooned this hug, putting her arms around my waist instead of my neck so she could lay her head on my chest. She squeezed me tightly. "You're a jerk," she sniffled.

"For dying?" I asked.

"For being all stupid and cute and funny and making me like you!" she said into my chest. "And yeah for dying! Back when I just broke up with you, I could just write you off as a crazy demon weirdo and move on. But there was still a chance I could come back to you if I wanted. But now that you're dying, I'm always going to wonder what could have been and feel all bad for you for being an annoying little tragic hero!"

I chuckled humorlessly. "Well, then you're a jerk too, for being one more person I care about that I have to say goodbye to. This sucks and I hate it."

She pulled away suddenly, wiping her face. "Let's do something crazy!"

I blinked. "What?"

"Bucket list, stupid! What's something crazy you wanna do

before you go?"

I sighed and shook my head. "I don't really have a bucket list. I just want to hang out with my family."

She shoved me. "Screw that! Come on! Anything!"

"What's on yours?" I stalled.

She started tossing out ideas like throwing knives. "Single-handedly dig out and open the Nickelodeon Time Capsule. Interrupt a high school play with an impromptu performance of 'Parkour!' Meet someone named Tito. Make out with Peter Dinklage."

I raised an eyebrow. "You have a very strange bucket list."

"Stop stalling!"

I blew air through my lips and thought about it. I hadn't indulged in anything really fun in a long time, so it took me a minute.

"I haven't been on a roller coaster since I was ten . . ."

She yanked me to my feet and dragged me out the door before I could protest.

By the time we got to the nearest amusement park, there were only three hours left until it closed, so we made the most of it. We ran around like crazed children, giggling and snapping pictures, and eating a disgusting amount of cotton candy. We rode all of the rides and then went back to my favorite ride twice more. It was the one that went straight up and down. Kiki just watched the third time and laughed when she could hear me screaming from the very top. It was honestly one of the most fun nights of my life. I was exhilarated and crazed.

I couldn't remember the last time I'd allowed myself to truly let go. Anytime Kiki sensed me getting sad again, she kissed me and yanked me off to the next ride.

When we got back to the house, Dad was waiting up. He looked about to yell at me for not telling anyone where I'd gone, but something about the way we looked gave him pause. Maybe it was the grin on my face, and he thought I was due a little fun. He just raised his eyebrows and went back to watching his game.

Kiki came back to my room with me, and we stayed up almost the entire night talking about everything and nothing. I felt a pang of misery as I realized that even if we hadn't stayed together romantically, Kiki was the kind of person who could have quickly become one of my best friends. The kind of friend you may not see often but always comes back to you.

It wasn't the same way I felt for Sandra. Sandra had burrowed deep into my heart. Kiki was someone I could let go of if I had to, but that didn't mean it didn't hurt. I'd never taken the time to evaluate how I really felt about Kiki, because I never actually believed I would live long enough for it to develop into something real. I didn't think I could keep her. But I was starting to realize that I did love her. I wasn't exactly in love with her, but I cared for her, and I wanted to be with her. I wanted to keep her.

We fell asleep in the wee hours of the morning, my arm around her waist, and her face in my neck. I had melancholy dreams as my subconscious recognized that this was the first and last time I'd ever have a woman in my bed.

• • •

She left early the next morning. We hugged at the front door for a long time. I gave her one last goodbye kiss and then brushed her hair back and cupped her face in my hands.

"I'll miss you, Kiki Li," I whispered. We hadn't dated for more than a couple of months, and I wasn't even sure if this was the kind of relationship that would have lasted anyway. But it might have. Just because I wasn't in love with her now didn't mean I couldn't eventually fall for her. For all I knew, we might have ended up together and had the weirdest kids in the universe. But it wasn't meant to be.

She wrapped her arms around my waist and hid her face in my chest. I hugged her back and kissed the top of her head. Part of me still wished she'd never come. This goodbye was so much harder than just disappearing from her life. But she deserved a goodbye. She deserved closure. And, honestly, so did I.

"For what it's worth," I said quietly, "I don't think our relationship was a waste of time just because we didn't end up together. I think you were just what I needed. You gave me hope and reminded me how to laugh when I was confused and scared. Thank you for that. Thank you for being you."

She just continued clinging to me.

Remembering that she could sense dead people, I asked, "Do you want me to visit you when I'm gone?"

She nodded in my chest and then looked up at me and tried to smile. "I'll know it's you because you'll give off really awkward vibes." Her smile lasted maybe a second before a tortured grimace took over her face. Then she released me, wiping her face as she hurried to her car and drove away.

I blew air out through my lips and looked up at the sky. That was . . . a lot. With a deep breath, I walked back into the house and leaned against the front door.

Preston was in the kitchen eating cereal. "Was that Kiki?"

I nodded.

"Did you guys just say goodbye?"

"Yep." I pushed off from the door and flopped onto the couch, throwing my arm over my face. I don't think I realized just how much I was going to miss Kiki until I said goodbye. I knew I'd never meet anyone else like her. And she'd seriously just given me one of the best days of my life.

I removed my arm when I heard Preston walk up. He stuck his head over the back of the couch, grinning. "Did you guys . . . you know? I mean, she was here all night . . ."

I shrugged. "Maybe we just stayed up all night talking."

His face fell. "Seriously?"

"Maybe. Maybe not. Either way, it's none of your business."

"I'd tell you," he muttered.

"I'm sure you would, Preston, but I'm not you."

He sighed in annoyance and went back to eating his cereal. "I guess I wouldn't want you to be."

Just then, Dad skidded into the room in his socks. "The baby! She had the baby!" He dropped his shoes on the floor and started stuffing his feet into them.

I rolled off the couch. "What?"

"Elena went into labor last night and didn't tell anyone!" Dad grinned. "There's a new grandbaby! Come on, let's go!"

Suddenly, everything I'd been sad about melted away. A big, foolish grin spread across my face as I raced up the stairs to grab my shoes. I shoved my feet into them at the bottom of the stairs and ran back into the kitchen. "You wanna come?"

Preston smiled and shook his head. "No thanks. Tell her congrats!"

I whooped and ran out to Dad's car, which was already waiting by the side of the road.

chapter 42
BABY HOPE

Elena looked like she'd just had the workout of a lifetime, but there was a smile on her face when Dad and I peeked into her hospital room. Charlie was holding their baby girl, looking tiny in his massive arms. Rocco and Ginny were uncharacteristically solemn as they snuggled up to either side of their exhausted mother.

"Congratulations!" I grinned.

Ginny scooted off the bed to hug me, and I lifted her to kiss her cheeks. "You have a sister, Ginny!" I danced her around the room until her somber face smiled, and Rocco came to join us. Dad walked up and kissed Elena on the forehead, smiling from ear to ear, and looked down at the baby girl in Charlie's arms. Charlie looked happier than I'd ever seen him.

I passed Rocco to Dad and gently hugged Elena. "What's her name?"

"Well," she said, "we decided to let you name her."

I stepped back, stunned. "Me?"

"Yes," she said with certainty. "You."

I had a moment of utter panic. I couldn't name a baby. I'd never even thought of baby names before. And this baby wasn't even mine.

Charlie came up to me and held her out to me. "Go on. Hold her and then tell us what you think." There was an almost pleading look in his eyes, like this was a little piece of me I could leave behind for them after I was gone.

Overwhelmed, I took her in my arms and held her close, looking down at her tiny little face with her perfect little nose and her sleeping mouth open in a tiny O. She had a few wisps of brown hair peeking through her hospital beanie. Looking down at her little face, all my worries and heartache of the past few weeks seemed to melt away, replaced by that burning feeling that gives us strength in even the darkest times in our lives.

"Would it be too cliché to name her Hope?" I whispered.

I could acknowledge that it was the go-to baby name in books and movies when there's a baby born at the end, but I couldn't think of anything more appropriate.

I looked up to see Charlie and Elena share a look. "I love it," Elena said.

"Hello, Hope," I said, looking back down, "Nice to meet you."

Her mouth twitched upward in her sleep, and I kissed her forehead. They let me hold her for a long time, and when she finally opened her eyes, the two of us just stared at one another, this indescribable connection making it impossible for either of us to look away. I loved her so much. She was part of my family and, therefore, part of me. There was already a special piece of my heart sectioned off just for her.

Charlie murmured something to Elena, and when I glanced up at them, I had the sudden and unexpected realization that I'd never have this moment from Charlie's perspective. I would never be a dad.

As I held her close, I allowed myself just a moment to let down all the careful walls protecting my heart. Against all instinct, I indulged myself, and I pretended just for a moment that she was mine. I pretended that I'd be the one she called "dada" and the one she'd run up to and hug when she got off the school bus. I pretended that I'd be the one to put Band-Aids on her scraped knees and kiss them better. The one to dance her around the house just to hear her laugh. The one to teach her to stand up for herself and correct anyone who didn't treat her as anything other than the most incredible person in the world. For that one glorious moment, I let myself pretend.

And then, with a heavy sigh, I let that dream die. It wasn't something I was meant to have, and I was hardly the first person to never be a dad. I could still love Hope without her being mine, especially because even if I were her father, she still wouldn't have been "mine." The only one we truly belong to is God. Mortals tend to get hung up on labels and defining the kind of love they feel toward someone, be it a friendly love, romantic love, or fatherly love. In the end, the label doesn't matter, just the love.

But before I gave her back to Elena, I whispered in Hope's ear. "I will watch over you all your life, and when we meet again, I'll give you the biggest hug."

I decided to stay at Elena's house for the rest of the time I had left. No one questioned it. They seemed to sense that Hope was just what I needed in those last days of my life. Elena and Charlie, wanting to do anything they could to make me happy, let me take care of her as much as possible. I changed her diapers and rocked her to sleep. Unless she was nursing or sleeping, I was holding her. She helped me carry on when I wanted to fall into despair. My sweet Hope. I was so grateful I got to meet her.

Three days after Hope was born, Grandpa called.

"Your mystery messenger came back," he said. "She said it has to be tonight. Malum and his terrorists are planning another attack in two days, but if you take him out now, you might prevent it."

I froze. Tonight? I was supposed to have another week! Just one more week with my family. Was that too much to ask? And who was this messenger, anyway? Were they actually on my side? They had to be, right? They gave me the idea for the plan and were always giving me cryptic reassurances. But what if it wasn't someone on our side? What if it was a trap?

"Did you hear?" Grandpa asked when I didn't respond.

I cleared my throat and looked down at Hope, who I was rocking in her bedroom. My eyes watered looking down at her sleeping face. I didn't want to give her up. I didn't want to give anyone up!

Hermes?

IT'S TIME, DAVID.

I sighed deeply. I couldn't complain about my time being cut short. I got two beautiful weeks of goodbye, and that's so much more than I had before. It wasn't enough, but it would never be enough, and there was no use crying about it. I would be grateful, because at the end of the day, I was lucky to have so many wonderful people to love. I smiled down at Hope again, trying to memorize this moment.

"David?"

"Yeah," I said hoarsely. "Yeah, I heard. Thanks. Uh . . . I guess this is goodbye."

Grandpa didn't respond for a while. "You aren't coming to your dad's before you go?"

"No, I don't think so," I said quietly. "I've already done my goodbyes with everyone. Don't tell anyone I'm leaving tonight. They'll know soon enough."

Grandpa took a while to respond again. "Good luck, son." Then he hung up. He didn't say he loved me, but I was okay with that. It wasn't something Grandpa said to anyone, but it didn't mean it wasn't true.

I set Hope in her crib and took a deep breath.

Alright, Hermes. Contact the defenders and demon hunters. I'm ready.

chapter 43
NOPE

The only person I told when I left was Charlie because he was necessary for the plan. I didn't want to start some kind of murder investigation when my remains were found, so Charlie agreed to take care of my body when I was gone. He was the only one I knew who could handle it. I trusted he'd do it in a way that would remove any obvious trace of either of us being there.

I told him after he tucked the kids in that we had to do it tonight. He nodded and went back to his bedroom to lie to Elena about going to the store. She'd know it was a lie soon. He would be gone for hours, and I would never come back.

"I'm using a friend's truck," he said once he'd emerged from their room. "I'll meet you outside in fifteen minutes."

Then he left, and I just stood there in the kitchen by myself, too shocked to believe this was happening. Finally, I blinked, squared my shoulders, and headed to the front door.

I didn't see Ginny in the darkness until we almost collided. She stood there in the partial light from the streetlights outside, holding a blanket in one hand.

"Ginny, what are you doing up?" I whispered.

"Where are you going?" she asked me, rubbing sleep from her eyes.

I didn't know how to answer that. There are probably a hundred things I could have said, but at the time, all I could think of was the truth. When I'd first come back to mortality, she'd asked me where I'd been, and in her child-like mind, she'd believed the truth with no problem. People in movies come back to life all the time—why wouldn't her weird uncle? So, in as simple terms as possible, I told her the truth.

I knelt in front of her. "I have to go away, Ginny. I came back to life for a while, but I have to go back now."

Ginny blinked and stared at me. Then she said, "Mama likes a Christmas movie like that. An angel comes and helps a church guy and his wife for a little bit, but then he has to leave in the end. Is it like that?"

I smiled, impressed at the quick connection she'd made. "It's just like that; except you'll still be able to remember me."

"I don't want you to go, Uncle David." Her chin started to quiver.

I pulled her into a crushing hug, and she squeezed me as tightly as her little arms could allow. I was going to miss these Ginny hugs. She was always so aware of when others were hurting and knew just how to fix it. When we were done hugging, I wiped her eyes and smiled at her. She was such an amazing girl, and I couldn't wait to watch her grow up. Eventually, I scooped her up and took her back to her room to tuck her in. I knelt down next to her bed. "I won't really be gone, you know," I whispered. "I'll still be around; you just won't be able to see me."

"If I talk to you, will you hear me?" she asked.

"Of course. You can talk to me all you want. I'd love that."

"Okay," she said, and her eyes began to droop.

I put my hand on her forehead and smoothed her hair back. "Love you, Ginny." Then I kissed her forehead and walked over to Rocco's room to do the same.

And then I left.

Charlie was waiting for me in a truck across the street. I got in without a word and buckled myself in.

Charlie pulled something small from his pocket and handed it to me. "Bite down on it when it's time."

I wondered by what shady means he'd obtained it but didn't question him. I zipped it up in the pocket of my joggers to keep it safe. He handed me another pill as a backup, which I placed in my front T-shirt pocket. That place was less secure, but it was closer at hand and more easily accessible.

"Are there any weapons in this truck?" I asked.

"Why?"

"If demons find us, they could use them against us."

"I've emptied the truck of anything harmful. The most dangerous things here are in your pockets."

I nodded in relief.

We drove for two hours to my dad's cabin, and Charlie barely spoke. It was weird seeing this side of him. Charlie was a peculiar combination of nerdy jock, always joking and giving people crap, and then chatting up librarians about the latest best sellers. I was sad I couldn't see much of the real Charlie in these last hours together, but his ability to compartmentalize and put his personal feelings on hold for later was what made him so good at his job, so I wasn't complaining.

My heart started pounding once he pulled into the driveway. This was it; it was happening. I just stared out the window, unable to move until I noticed Charlie looking at me with that emotionless face. I could almost feel him warring between wanting to comfort me as a friend and giving me a mental slap on the face to galvanize me into action. I cleared my throat and forced my shaking hand to push the door open. I stumbled as I got out of the truck and led Charlie up the gravel path to the front door. Hands still shaking, I took the key from the lock box under the porch and unlocked the door. I showed Charlie around in a daze, then stopped in the kitchen and forced myself to look out the window to the place where this all would happen.

There was a huge clearing in the forest about three miles north of the cabin, with nothing around but grass and a few tiny shrubs. Nothing around that Malum could use to harm me. The only way he could hurt me would be with my own hands and the things hidden in my pockets. I just needed to hide that information from him until the time was right, or all of this would be for nothing.

"You need a minute?" Charlie asked.

I shook my head. The longer I waited, the longer I would have to talk myself out of this. I took a deep breath, still staring out the window. "I'm going now. Just, uh, don't come down for me until you're sure I'm dead . . . and even then, I'd wait a few hours just in case I failed and he's still lingering around."

Mechanically, I walked to the front door and put my hand on the doorknob. Before I could force myself to open the door, Charlie put his hand on my shoulder and turned me to face him. I saw both Charlies on his face. The hardened soldier who could kill without hesitation, and one of my best friends.

"You can do this, David," he said quietly. "If you were brave enough to make this choice, you're brave enough to follow through. Just focus on your goal. You've got this. I admire the hell out of you, and I'm so lucky to have known you."

He pulled me into a quick hug, opened the door, and gently shoved me forward, somehow knowing that I needed a little push. I barely heard what he'd said; I was in a daze. It was almost like my spirit had already left, because I could barely feel my body, like I was watching this all from a third-person standpoint.

I walked through the long grass into the darkness alone, wondering if this had all been a huge mistake. I had to believe I could do this but still didn't know how. I believed everything would somehow be all right in the end, but it was Malum I was afraid of. Regardless of the outcome, this was going to hurt. I kept clenching my fists and breathing deeply, but my heart would not stop racing.

I'd been hiking down the hill for almost five minutes before I noticed someone walking beside me. Strangely, I wasn't startled. Everything around me felt like a hazy dream.

"Sandra?" I whispered.

She didn't say anything. She didn't even look at me. She just walked with me, silently, somehow knowing that was all I needed. Too soon, we reached my destination, standing in an empty field in the middle of the night. We stood in silence for a long moment, neither of us wanting to end the momentary reprieve from my dark, lonely task.

"I didn't want you to be alone," she said quietly.

I looked away, refusing to get emotional. I had to hold it together now more than ever.

"I appreciate that," I said tonelessly. "But you have to leave now."

She was quiet for so long that I made myself look at her. She silently held my gaze, and for the first time . . . she felt like a ghost to me. Then her eyes flicked up nervously, and I could tell Hermes was talking to her, commanding her to let me die the way I failed to do when Malum targeted her.

I sighed and squeezed my eyes shut. "You need to go now. Please. I'll break if he hurts you, and I can't break. Please leave. I'll meet you on the other side when it's over."

She continued to stare at me, then she approached me, kissed my forehead, and disappeared.

I hadn't realized how much Light she was shining until she was gone. The darkness of the night felt oppressive, and the stars looked so cold. A breeze stirred the grass, and I shivered, hugging myself. I'd never felt so alone.

I closed my eyes, took a deep breath, and lay down, forcing myself to focus. No more reminiscing. No more feeling sorry for myself. The sooner I got this over with, the better.

All right, Hermes. One more time. Let's do this.

And I floated out of my body. I took a moment to enjoy how much lighter I felt. My physical exhaustion, hunger, and weight evaporated. Soon, I would be this free forever. I had to remember that being dead wasn't all that bad. Soon, all of this would be over, and I'd be back in The Resting Place like I'd longed to be since I'd revived. Maybe I couldn't be with my living family in the same way, but I had my mom and grandmas on the other side, along with my whole team. And Jake. And Sandra. I could touch her again. After all the time that had passed, my hand still felt empty without hers in it.

I glanced back at the cabin, barely visible on a hill in the distance. That was where Charlie would be waiting. I hoped he'd at least wait a few hours before checking on me with his binoculars. I didn't want him to see this.

Because this was it. It was time to provoke the living embodiment of nightmares.

Taking a deep breath, I shouted, "Malum! I'm here, all alone! You want me? Come get me! One-on-one; no backup. This is the only chance you'll get, so I hope you're not too scared to fight me without your little army." I repeated the words in my mind, doing my best to telepathically send my message straight to Malum.

As Sheila had pointed out, there was no way to force Malum to come alone. But I was hoping he wanted me badly enough to avoid pushing me too far or frightening me off. He also had his ego to protect. Refusing my one-on-one offer would show everyone he was afraid of me. We weren't stupid enough to hang this all on hope, though. The defenders and demon hunters had plans to keep his other demons busy in case he called for them. They hadn't shared those plans with me, since Malum was about to have direct access to my brain. I just hoped I'd given them enough time to do what they needed to do.

The owl hooted again, and I floated there above my body for what felt like ten minutes. I kept looking around for any sign of him. Darkness, mist, even his human form. Nothing at all.

Like some kind of idiot, I'd forgotten to look down.

Something tickled my foot, and I flinched. The grass beneath me slowly lengthened into black, waving tendrils seeming to span almost an acre around me. All at once, the rustling in the trees stopped, and the crickets silenced. One by one, the stars went out. And then a ghostly laugh pierced the silence, sending a shiver down my spine. I spun around, looking for him, squinting through the black fog, as my heart raced.

"Mine!" The voice echoed through the night.

"Mine!" It repeated behind me. I jumped and spun around.

"Mine!" This time, it was nothing but a whisper in the wind.

"Show yourself!" I demanded. "Or are you too afraid? You've been losing support lately, haven't you? It's because of me. They know I'm more powerful. The only way to win them back is to prove to everyone that you are more powerful than me. So, fight me!"

These were all lies, of course. He was losing support

because Frederick had been capturing his followers and putting manacles of Light around their wrists to break their connection to Malum. And I wasn't delusional enough to believe I was more powerful than Malum. But he didn't know that. He was afraid of me because he didn't understand me. For all he knew, I was just as strong as him and had been stealing all his followers.

And maybe I was stronger. Not even the Hurricane was able to penetrate my Light when I shone as brightly as I could. Light is always stronger than Darkness, especially the kind of Light from an archangel. But fighting him at full strength wasn't the plan. He had to think he had the upper hand, or he would disappear. His greatest weakness was also his greatest strength. His cowardice was what made him so slippery and impossible to catch. So, I resolved not to fight back. My job was to be the sitting duck and to allow him to do what he wanted with me.

The swaying tendrils of Darkness swirled around me, creating a vortex, rotating faster and faster until I was wrapped in a cocoon of Darkness. Reflexively, I created Light in my hands and pushed the Darkness away when it got too close. It pulled away from me, but continued to expand around me, blocking out the moon and stars. Not even my Light was bright enough to see by. It was complete sensory deprivation. Then a hand reached out and grabbed my ankle. I pulled away, but a claw grasped my wrist. A rope fell around my neck and tightened like a noose. Bugs seemed to drop into my hair.

I convulsed and cried out. A spider snaked up my spine. I

shivered and squirmed, trying to free myself of all the arms and claws and ropes tethering me in place. One of the bugs dropped down the neck of my robe. Another felt like it was burrowing into my face. Then a hand squeezed my neck from behind, and a voice screamed in my ear.

I'd been here before. Malum, with his hand around my neck, feeding me fears and lies. As if from far away, I heard Sandra screaming, saw Little David in the arms of Demons, felt Sam with his hands around my throat, and then baby Hope, her choking cry as she gasped for air.

FOCUS, DAVID! GIVE HIM THE IMAGE YOU WANT HIM TO SEE!

It wasn't hard. I'd been dreading this moment for weeks. I simply let down my defenses and thought of Malum possessing my body. Inside my body, inside my mind, controlling it. Controlling *me*. In my brain, more closely and intimately than ever before. Hurting me with my own hands, throwing me against the ground, strangling me, and screaming. I didn't have to fake my dread; it was all-consuming, and Malum only intensified it.

No, No! I change my mind! I don't want this!

Suddenly, I was back in my body. I coughed on dirt and jumped to my feet, swaying from vertigo. Then I saw Malum with his strangely forgettable face and body cloaked in Darkness. His arm still outstretched where my neck had been, he slowly turned toward me and tilted his head. With a deep chuckle, he glided toward me, and I bolted.

I was no longer acting. Like the coward I'd always been, I was genuinely afraid. I suppose that was what made me perfect for this plan. I didn't have to act like a wimpy little coward; I already was one.

I ran through the grass faster than I'd ever run in my life. I tripped over an uneven patch of grass and scraped my palms as I fell, but I was up in the next second, not even sparing a second to look back. While fleeing, I at least had the presence of mind to run away from the cabin. I didn't want to lead Malum toward—

No, no, don't think about that—he'll read your mind!

Why hadn't he caught up to me? Was he just toying with me? Letting me run before catching up? Playing with his food?

I looked back, and he wasn't there. But when I turned back around, he was right in front of me, grinning with his dead-looking face and Darkness oozing from his eyes and mouth. I screamed and stumbled back, falling to the ground. While in my body, I couldn't feel his Darkness physically, the way I could as an angel. But mentally and emotionally, it filled me with terror.

"No!" I whispered, barely able to speak.

His grin fell, and he closed his eyes. "Yes. Yes, I will do this. It is the only way to capture you. Kill you, then take you."

And then he disappeared. I spun around in a panic, adrenaline zinging through my body. Where had he gone? The grass swayed around me, but the night was deathly silent. All I could hear was my own gasping breaths.

And then I screamed in agony.

chapter 44
CAN WE SKIP THIS PART?

I had never felt so much Darkness in my entire existence. Not even when I was in the Hurricane. Everything in the Hurricane is external. The Darkness is all around you, but it isn't *inside* you. And if a person tried hard enough, they could escape the Hurricane. You can't exactly escape your own body. I'd been possessed twice by Sheila, a girl I believed to be filled with Darkness, but she had nothing on Malum. He had so much Darkness inside that he couldn't even contain it all. It was always leaking out of him. It was a parasite that had grown too large for its vessel. And suddenly, I was the vessel. I felt the fear, pain, and torment of the thousands of souls Malum had tortured. He was like a collector, gathering Darkness from every source he could find and then *keeping* it. Making it his own. How did he stand it? It was too much!

I could hear him breathing inside my mind. Breathing, fuming, laughing. This was hilarious to him. He shook out my limbs and cackled with my mouth. It had been a while since he'd experienced a mortal body. He yelled into the night sky with my head tilted back. Testing out my strength, he began running, jumping, rolling on the ground, reveling in this power over me. Then he slammed my head into the dirt as hard as he could. I groaned and laughed and then literally ate the dirt. I slammed my head into the ground again, my head screaming in pain. As blood started to trickle down my forehead, I caught it in my hand and drank that as well, screaming and laughing and rolling around.

No, that wasn't me. That was Malum! Not me, not me!

The worst part was that I knew he was just warming up. Just testing out my capabilities. He hadn't even begun to truly hurt me yet. In a brief moment of clarity, I remembered that I was supposed to be doing something, but I couldn't follow through until they dropped the cage of Light on us.

"So many places to break," Malum whispered with my mouth. "How shall we do it? How shall we die?"

I could hear his thoughts as he noticed with dismay that there was nothing around here to kill me with. No knives, no sharp objects, no tree branches. I hadn't even brought my glasses with me. There was nothing around us but grass and shrubs for at least a three-mile radius.

"We'll just have to make this interesting, shall we?" he hissed.

How long was I supposed to wait for someone to come and drop the cage around us? They were supposed to be ready to trap us the moment Malum possessed me. I tried not to think about it, tried to hide my plans from him, but when I read his train of thought and what he was planning to do to me, panic set in.

Hermes! Where are they with the Light cage? I've got him!

I couldn't hide that thought from Malum. He was in my head more intimately than anyone ever had been. He dug through my brain, experiencing my emotions, reliving my experiences, discovering my plans. This was a trap, and now he knew it. He made me scream at the air, and then the real torture began.

He proceeded to torment me from within my mind, beat me with my own hands, and strangle me with my clothes. I'm not arrogant enough to claim to have suffered the most traumatic thing a person could ever experience, but it's got to be up there. Had I known the horror I was walking into, I don't know if I would have done it. I was terrified going into it, but not nearly enough.

And through it all, I was alone. No one came for me, and Hermes never answered me. They'd abandoned me. Even the Big Man had abandoned me. It was like when I'd saved Sandra and got shot, and no one came for me to take me home.

I drifted in and out of consciousness, disassociating from my own body, waiting, waiting to die.

Wait, I had a way to do that, didn't I? *There was that little pill in my pocket.*

Malum, catching the direction of my thoughts, grinned. He knew at that moment that he wasn't supposed to know about the pill. Even as he'd dug through my brain, I'd devoutly refused to think about it because I couldn't let him kill me until he was captured.

Well, now he knew.

I tried with all my might to fight my arms as they dug into

my pockets. My body was shaking from all the conflicting signals. He managed to unzip my pocket and took hold of the pill, but I yelled in defiance and threw it away.

"Enough!" I yelled, and Light flared in my hands.

I yelped. There was actual Light in my hands!

What? I was mortal! How was I doing this? That shouldn't be possible! Unfortunately, with Malum inside my body, I was having the same reaction to the Light as he did. My hands burned like they were on fire! I released the Light, disturbed by what was happening.

Hermes! Where are they with the cage?

HOLD ON, DAVID. WE'RE HAVING DIFFICULTIES. DO NOT SPEAK TO ME IN THIS MANNER; MALUM CAN HEAR ALL OF THIS.

He certainly could. He was so angry, he made me knee myself in the face. I didn't even know my body was capable of that. It loosened one of my teeth, but I didn't have time to moan about it because the next moment he forced me to my hands and knees. We combed frantically through the grass, but the pill had disappeared. Good thing he didn't know about the one in my shirt pocket.

He grinned.

Shit.

Wanting to distract him, I made my hands light up again. Then I made the Light spread inch by inch across our entire body. The two of us ran around screaming like someone on fire. I couldn't hold it for long. This fight between us was impossible. Neither of us could hurt the other one without feeling it ourselves.

I had a momentary lapse in concentration, and Malum took over once more, searching for my shirt. It had fallen somewhere in the grass when he'd taken it off and tried to strangle me with it earlier.

"Stop."

We froze at the sound of the voice. I almost toppled over as we stood. Despite the adrenaline, I was starting to feel my injuries. I couldn't remember how I'd sprained my ankle or broken my fingers. There was a huge gash on my arm, and I was pretty sure some of my ribs were either cracked or broken. These were only a few of the injuries I was becoming aware of, but I knew there were more. My entire body felt black and blue.

Slowly, we turned around to find the source of the voice.

My heart lifted. "Will—"

"Silence, fool!" William said, his face as hard as stone. He radiated so much Darkness that it was hard to see him through it. His face creased in hatred as he stepped closer.

"Remove me from this body," Malum demanded. "Where are the reinforcements?"

I wanted to cry as the realization hit me that William was the mole.

William, the strong and silent rock of the group. He was often overshadowed by Frederick, just because he wasn't as showy, but his quiet strength always inspired me. A calming presence and a voice of reason.

I couldn't stop thinking of that moment when he'd visited me in the hospital with Ying Yue and Daisy after the fire. "You're one of us, and we need you," he'd said. He was so sincere, so concerned. His presence was Light itself.

Now he stared at me like he wanted nothing more than to kill me slowly. He took a deep breath, struggling to contain himself. He spoke in a flat voice, but I could see his hatred simmering beneath the surface. "The reinforcements are coming, master, but they were held up by the Demonic Council, who unified with the angels at the last moment. It won't be long before our side breaks through. Most of the angels have been captured, and the remaining fighters are making their last stand. Soon, they will be no more."

I didn't think my hope could sink any further. All was lost! My friends were being captured one by one, and no one was coming to save me. I could feel Malum's pleasure as his heart lifted in savage glee.

"You will be rewarded," Malam said impatiently, "but first you must remove me from this disgusting sack of meat."

"You promised, master . . ." William said in a dangerously quiet voice.

I could almost hear Malum's mind working. He had promised William he could torture me himself while Malum held me captive. He didn't intend to keep that promise, but at the moment, he was at William's mercy. Allowing William to have a go at me would make it appear like he was doing William's bidding. And yet, there was nothing he could do to fight him, so he had to act like this was his idea to keep the upper hand.

"Yes," Malum breathed eventually. "Show your master how you've grown in your Dark abilities."

William stepped close enough to touch me, glaring at me

with pure loathing. Then he shot a beam of Darkness into my chest that was so strong, I staggered. Darkness isn't physical, and yet his was so powerful I fell to my knees in despair. He formed a rope of Darkness that he slowly wrapped around my neck and squeezed. It didn't strangle me like a physical rope would have, but it burned like fire from the depths of the Hurricane. How could he do this? How could he make Darkness so intense it could be physically felt by mortals? I thought of Sheila, and how good she was at being a demon, automatically jumping to second-in-command under Malum's regime. Were fallen angels better at Darkness than even demons? How? Why?

"You . . ." William whispered, shaking in rage. He leaned into my face as he pulled the rope tight around my neck. "You pathetic coward! You *worm!*"

"William, please—"

"Shut up! I have lost everything because of you! My integrity, my mind, my *soul!* I was an archangel, and now I am a demonic slave! I have endured torture and watched others tortured before my eyes. I've inflicted it myself! I am everything I once despised, and it is all because of you! You are the author of all our pain, and yet, you're nothing but a coward, always running, always hiding. How have you caused so much evil? You have single-handedly destroyed everything!"

He's right, Malum cackled. *You are a curse upon this earth. You belong with me. All of this is your fault. You deserve this!*

"I'm sorry," I choked.

"You are not nearly sorry enough, but you will be soon.

You will be captured and never escape again. You will suffer all that you deserve."

A shock of Darkness electrified me through the rope around my neck, and Malum giggled inside my mind, reveling in my pain. Darkness radiated from my body, and I couldn't tell if it belonged to William or Malum. It pressed down on me from all sides, locking me in place. I couldn't move, couldn't breathe, I couldn't even think. My mind flashed back to being trapped in that burning closet. Except this time, it was Darkness, not smoke, sapping all my strength. Like a caged animal, the only panicked thought I had was for escape.

"I want you to listen carefully," William whispered in a calmer, deadlier voice, leaning in close. "You will lose tonight. In fact, you have already lost. There is nobody left in the cosmos who cares enough about you to come to your aid. You are alone, and you will *always* be alone. And the worst part is that you will not be defeated by hordes of angels or demons, but a single mortal boy."

What?

William laughed, and I felt a strange stab of fear from Malum that froze us in place as thoroughly as the time I'd first met him. Before either of us had the chance to react, a cage of Light slammed down around us, sealing us in on all sides. Like Jake's cage, it had no bars—just solid, translucent walls.

"NO!" Malum screamed. He ran at the walls, but they just threw us back, burning us so badly I felt like my skin should be blistered and bleeding. He continued to run at the walls and screech like a wild animal.

I was vaguely aware of William on the other side yelling, "Now, David! Get out of there now!"

Remembering the pill, I finally spotted my shirt in the grass. Part of it stuck out beneath a wall of Light, and I knew I could pull the rest through if I just took hold of the corner. Before I could lunge for it, Malum punched me with my fist. It seemed now that he was captured, he wasn't so keen to allow me to use that pill. The longer he prevented me from leaving my body, the greater the chance he'd somehow find a way out of this.

He clawed my face and neck until my hands came back bloody. He pulled hair out of my head in chunks. He bit my arm so hard, my loosened tooth came out. Then he punched my injured ribs until I fell to my knees, wheezing. He tried to force me to my feet, but I collapsed and vomited. Cackling, he broke my fingers against the ground, and I whimpered pitifully, losing the willpower to fight.

"David!" William shouted. "Come on, lad! You're right at the end!"

There was a pop in my arm, and I screamed. I couldn't fight him. He was too strong. Tears streamed down my face. I wasn't strong enough. I couldn't do it!

This was it. I was never going to get free. I was never going to win this battle. How had I ever thought it was possible? I was nothing. I was no one. And Malum was more powerful than us all. I'd failed.

Oh God, I'm so sorry! I failed!

Something whizzed past me, just an inch from my face, snapping me out of my lament. Was that a bullet?

"STEADY!" William called.

I didn't even stop to wonder who was shooting at me. My first instinct was to crouch down and clutch my arms around my legs. Not to hide from the shooter, but to hold myself still and make myself an easier target. Standing would have given Malum too many free limbs to manipulate. And so, while he fought me and screamed within my head, I used my last bit of willpower to burst with Light. Malum shrieked, incapacitated, as I locked one broken arm around the other, clenching my teeth so hard something cracked, and—

THE SNIPER

"Hit. Target down."

I let out a slow breath, careful not to move my rifle. The mound in the grass lay still, but I had to make sure that monster wasn't faking. "Confirm the target is down."

My spotter waited a full minute before replying. "Confirmed. No movement."

I let my head fall and forced myself to breathe in and out. "You good?"

Head still down, I gave a thumbs up. Later, I'd think about it later. I pulled away from my rifle while my spotter stood and stretched his cramped muscles. He'd been hiding under a tarp in the truck bed for two hours, along with all our gear.

David said not to bring weapons, but I never believed that the pill would be enough. I didn't doubt his courage, but willpower crumples under torture, especially for those not trained to resist it. And how could he take the pill without control of his limbs? He needed a backup plan. One he didn't know about, so the demon couldn't pick it out of his head. That was where I came in.

I never told David I was a sniper.

chapter 45
TRAPPED

The release was the most glorious thing I'd ever felt.

I exhaled and closed my eyes, relishing the relief of leaving behind my broken body. Exhaustion left me. Pain left me. The weight of all my troubles left me. I was free! I looked through the Light walls, seeing glowing angelic figures appearing all around us. A hand reached toward me, and a voice urged me to grab hold quickly.

I lifted my arm, but Malum took hold of my neck and shoved my head down to stare at my dead body. "LOOK AT IT!" he screamed. "LOOK!" I tried to look away, but his grip was too strong. I was forced to look at the body he'd mutilated beyond repair. My corpse was broken in so many wrong angles and oozed blood into the dirt. It was me, but there was no one inside. Though I was free of that body, I flinched, remembering the excruciating pain it had gone through. I was reminded of the way Sandra's body looked when she died. Except that a car had done that to her, while my own hands had wrought this destruction. I could see the evidence in my own bloody fingernails. I'd have vomited at the sight if I still could. I squeezed my eyes shut, trying to avoid looking at it, but Malum pried my eyes open with his fingers. "Look at it!" I struggled feebly to pull out of his grip, but I was weaker than I'd ever been. My own dead eyes stared up at me, a look of horror frozen on my bloody, broken face.

Malum put his mouth right next to my ear, and I could almost feel his breath, even though I knew that without a body, he didn't breathe. "You are mine now!" he whispered. "No one loves you enough to come in here and save you. They're ashamed of you. You pathetic weakling! All you're good for is dying! That's why they picked you!"

I was just so tired of fighting! I had already given all I could possibly give, and my will crumpled beneath his.

I found myself trapped in a nightmare of the past half hour—fighting Malum, getting possessed, torturing myself, getting shot. Then other visions filled my head. Charlie disgusted and traumatized at what he'd just watched, Elena crying as she woke up in the night and realized I'd left her, Sam throwing something through a window in anger, Mom reliving her Hurricane fears as she watched me being tortured and unable to help me, Jake sinking deeper into the Hurricane and his screams gradually falling away as he sank back into his wandering state . . . These visions and nightmares felt real. Either I was watching reality, or Malum had switched tactics. Instead of zombie Hurricane horror dreams, he felt something closer to the truth would hurt the most. And it did. All this suffering because I tried to play the hero and ended up tripping right at the finish line.

It all replayed over and over in more gruesome detail each

time, and in the background was Malum's laughter and continuous repetition of the words, *"You will never be free!"* I was too overcome to even try to make Light. Even if I'd thought of it, I had no Light left in me. He had me, and it didn't matter that I'd gotten him in the cage. He still won, because I was his prisoner.

"You gave yourself for your angels, but I still beat you! You are my consolation prize, and you will never be free . . . You are mine forever . . . There is no escape! You are *mine!*"

More images filled my head, and I felt as though I'd explode. I twitched and shrieked, panic finally breaking through my frozen horror.

"Someone! Help! GET ME OUT OF HERE! *HELP ME!*"

But I was trapped. The original nightmare of the Hurricane returned. Malum transformed himself, committing the worst blasphemy I would ever witness. Big Man floated before me and refused to take my outstretched hand, no matter how much I howled and pleaded.

"You pathetic coward . . . You weakling . . . You gave up, and now you are corrupted . . . Tainted . . . The Son of Evil is inside you, and there is no cleansing you of the Darkness... I want no part with you . . . You belong to him now . . ."

I was trapped in a hurricane once again, but there was no one to pull me out this time.

I don't know when it happened—time had ceased to mean anything—but eventually I gave up. Everything. Time.

Purpose. Feeling. I gave it all away and floated in a gray nothingness. Time was forever and never. I no longer felt or thought. I no longer knew who I was. I was nothing, and nothing existed but the gray void where I floated.

If I'd ever had a name, it was lost to me.

I was no more.

PART FOUR

HER

I kept thinking of *him*.

Alone in my prison cell, a memory kept returning to my mind and refused to let me go.

He never spoke about his father. But one night after we moved in together, he had a nightmare and said some chilling things in his sleep. He screamed when I tried to touch him. It took a while to calm him down enough to realize he was awake.

Before I lost my nerve, I whispered, "Who hurt you?"

He didn't answer for a long time, so I lifted my head.

His forehead was pinched, and his eyes were closed. Then, finally, he whispered, "My father."

That was the most I ever got out of him, but I deduced from the things he would say in his sleep that he'd been horribly abused. I started having nightmares about it myself. I saw him as a little boy, crying for help while someone hurt him, and every time I tried to save him, he was always farther and farther away.

And ever since David pointed out that I'd handed that little boy over to the man that twisted him up—the father that was so evil he'd been recruited as a torture demon in the

Hurricane—I couldn't stop thinking about it. Those old nightmares returned, and I could not shut them out.

Imprisoned for abandoning David, I had a front-row seat when Malum was captured. The prison guards brought him back to his cell, newly reinforced with soundproof walls so weak-minded angels like me wouldn't be tempted to let him out again. What they didn't know was that as they were in the process of detaining that foul monster, one of their other prisoners simply slipped through the bars of her cell.

How did I do it? There's only one way. Once the guards were distracted, I took a deep breath and stepped right through the Light, the way no demon ever could.

I shuddered and gritted my teeth, but it wasn't nearly as excruciating as I'd imagined. I'd already decided I'd walk through fire if I had to.

Someone needed to be rescued.

chapter 46
DRIFTING

I heard faint voices through the void, but I had no sense of time. I didn't know if the voices were talking to each other, or if I was only catching pieces of conversations over hours, days, or weeks.

"David!"

"How long has he been in there?"

"Can't someone go in and get him?"

"I hate seeing him this way."

"Can you blame him?"

"It's not fair!"

"My boy!"

"Please come back to us."

I heard voices, but their words meant nothing. When I did find myself thinking about what they said, I instinctively shied away, deeper into my cocoon of nothing. I barely even noticed the Darkness trapped in there with me, the blackness in my cloud of gray. It couldn't reach me in my apathetic state, so it didn't worry me. Nothing worried me. Nothing except being pulled from the void.

• • •

At some point, there came a voice that I heard loud and clear, even inside my gray nothingness. It gently nudged, poked, and prodded at my defenses, until it finally broke through.

"David," the voice said. "It's time to go."

No!

I squeezed my eyes shut and covered my ears. I was vaguely aware that this had happened before; this voice had prodded at me often since I'd entered the nothingness, and each time I'd shut it out. I knew that if I listened to this voice, I'd start to remember, and that was unacceptable. I hated that he'd just said my name. I didn't want to be David. David was traumatized and in pain, and I wanted nothing more than to get as far away from him as possible.

That's not my name, that's not my name, I have no name, I'm nothing, no one . . . nothing . . . no one . . . nothing . . .

"Take my hand, David."

I squeezed my eyes shut and shook my head, forcing myself not to come back to the surface of reality. But it was hard. I tried not to look, but I saw him melt through the walls of the cell and silence the Darkness with a look. The Darkness shivered in the corner and remained dead where it was.

There was some recollection in the back of my mind, but I fought it. I knew that I knew who this was, but I refused to acknowledge it. I repeated my mantra.

Nothing . . . no one . . . nothing . . . no one . . .

He approached me and put his hand on my cheek. "Look

at me."

This had also happened before. I don't know how many times, but I hid in the gray nothingness each time. I was too scared to leave it.

"Enough is enough, my son. I know you, though you pretend not to know me. You don't want this. Let go of your Darkness and look at me."

I tried to deny him, but I couldn't. I was too weak. Trembling, I looked up at him and broke, dissolving into horrified sobs as it all rushed back to me. I didn't want to remember it, but I did. I was tortured and possessed by the Prince of Darkness. I mutilated my own body and was shot in the head. I was trapped in a cage with my tormentor and my own brutalized corpse. Malum had whispered Darkness in my ear until the pain and horror were too much, and I— unable to bear it anymore—became a wanderer. It was just too much to take in all at once, and I longed to return to the safety of the void I'd taken refuge in. While horrified sobs wracked my body, the Big Man held me close and cried with me.

My sense of time was off, but I think he stayed in there with me for a long time. Trapped with Darkness in the cage of Light, and even though I wanted to go home more than anything else—unsure exactly what home was anymore—I couldn't imagine leaving. I belonged in this cage. If I left, who knew what awaited me? At least the pain was familiar.

Eventually, I fell into a quiet numbness. "I'm sorry," I whispered against his chest. "I'm sorry I failed. I tried, but it was too much for me. I broke. I was too weak."

His voice was calm and low. "You did not fail, David. You captured the Darkness. You just lost yourself inside of it."

"I'm sorry, I didn't mean to," I said, as images of all that had happened continued to play before my eyes. Those words I'd heard kept echoing in my head. *You are tainted now. I do not want you. You failed me. Let the Darkness have you.* "Please forgive me! Please don't cast me out!"

He put his hand on the back of my head. "I do not cast out my children. They are the ones who leave me."

"I'm sorry, I didn't mean to!" I was too ashamed to face him, but I clung on even tighter. I wished I'd stayed in the gray void of nothingness. I hated everything. I hated myself. I wanted to disappear.

He put his hands on my shoulders and pulled back enough to look at me. Then he placed his hands on my cheeks. "You have suffered, my son. There is no shame in suffering. I know this more than anyone, and I do not love you any less for showing weakness. I've never asked you to be perfect. I only ask that you trust me."

I pulled back and couldn't keep the accusatory tone from my voice. "Why did you let him take me? Why did you leave me here with him? I thought you would be with me, but I couldn't feel you at all."

"I was with you, David. I am always with you. But you are unable to feel me when you are filled with fear. Fear is the blindfold that hides me from you."

I sniffed and wiped my nose. "I didn't mean to give up, I just couldn't do it anymore."

He was silent, and an even greater shame came over me.

"You mean . . . I could have escaped if I'd had more faith? It really was my fault? I knew it. I'm worse than a failure, I'm a quitter and a coward!"

I sank down to the floor and covered my face.

The Big Man sat with me until I was strong enough to lift my head and face him. I was ready for a reprimand, but he cupped my cheek in his warm, weathered hand and looked intently into my eyes. His face was pained, but softer and kinder than any face I'd ever seen before. "I love you, and I will never stop loving you. You have done as I asked, and you have done it well. You faced death and Darkness and held on until your task was complete. You stumbled in the end, but I've caught you. No more fear, my son. Let it go."

Let it go? How could I let it go? The Darkness and fear were inside me. It tainted me. I was ruined.

In a sterner voice, he said, "This is not you, David. Let it go."

If this wasn't me, then what was? All I could remember was the Darkness. But there must have been Light at some point. I had a vague memory of warmth. How I suddenly craved it now . . .

I took a shaky breath and nodded. He stood and helped me to my feet.

"Good. Now, it is time for you to vanquish the Darkness." He turned me around to face the churning cloud in the corner of the cell.

I backed up. "W-what? No! What do you mean?"

The Big Man squeezed my shoulders. "I've held him temporarily at bay, but I am going to release my hold. Then *you* will vanquish the Darkness."

I tensed in sheer panic. "But I can't! He's stronger! He beat me!"

The Big Man leaned in to whisper in my ear. "Do you believe I can vanquish the Darkness?"

"Yeah."

"And who does your Light come from?"

"You . . ."

He said nothing, waiting for me to take the leap.

I felt something stir within me. An ember waiting to be stoked. He was right. This wasn't me, and it was time I lived up to the person he knew I was.

I closed my eyes and took a deep breath. Then I squared my shoulders and nodded.

The shrunken Darkness swelled and howled, like living smoke on a stormy wind. It came at me, and I knew I had to do something now, before Malum could get in my head again. I closed my eyes, feeling the Big Man's hand on my back. Then I opened them and shone with all I had. More than I had. Light pierced the Darkness like a blazing sunrise, filling up the whole world. The Darkness screamed and smoked, breaking apart into tar-like animalistic shapes, reaching, clawing, oozing around the cage and climbing up the walls, trying and failing to escape the Light. Surprised at myself, I reached out and touched a bat-like creature as it flew at me, dripping Darkness and baring its fangs. My hand was almost too bright for me to look at, and as I made contact with the creature, it dissolved into smoke. Something with tusks charged me, and it also dissolved when I touched it.

The Darkness, now all around me, changed tactics. After sending a few soldiers to test my abilities, it now knew it would have to give everything or be destroyed. Claws and hooves drummed the floor. Wings and wind flapped around me. With shrieks, growls, moans, and cackles, the creatures of Darkness flew at me all at once. A ghost of my old fears pulsed inside me, but I banished it with thoughts of the Big Man. Closing my eyes, I reached my arms out and pushed my Light in all directions, piercing each creature with arrows of Light. When I opened my eyes, all that was left was wisps of smoke and a cowering man in the corner.

I released the blazing Light and let out a long, slow breath. When I'd collected myself, I looked around to confirm that none of the Darkness had been left behind. Only Light remained, along with a quivering man with no aura. Surprised at my own boldness, I approached the figure on the floor. He shrieked and cringed away from me, curling up in the fetal position. I frowned, realizing with embarrassment that I probably looked just like that when the Big Man first approached me. Turns out Malum, without his Darkness, wasn't any stronger than me at my weakest. I got a nice, long look at his face before he covered it with his arms. He had the same features—mousy, colorless hair, ambiguous eyes and skin, unremarkable in every way—but the lack of character felt less sinister now and more . . . boring? Lame? Could the Son of Evil really be described as lame?

With morbid curiosity, I stepped closer. He flinched, whimpering and cringing deeper into his little corner.

I raised an eyebrow. He was really just a man. Just a sad,

pathetic man. Also, I don't know why, but he kind of looked like a Steve, which immediately removed all sense of fear. The guy was no more intimidating than the dude from Blue's Clues. How had I been so afraid of this? Had he always been *this* beneath the Darkness? Just this whimpering, pitiful wretch?

The Big Man looked down at Malum with sorrow and anger. Then he looked back at me and whispered, "It's time for you to go now. You don't belong here, and there are things you need to do."

HIM

No more.

No more.

No more.

I repeated that prayer over and over in my head until it was all I could think.

No more.

No more.

No more.

I wished I could lose myself as other angels do. Become a wanderer and drift. But he wouldn't let me. He knew just the words to snap me out of it. The words that hurt like jabbing a knife into my gut over and over, shocking me from the void I longed to sink into. He impressed on me images that would horrify me the most. Because he knew me. He knew what hurt. He made me what I am!

No more.

No more.

No more.

Too horrified to wander . . . Too agonized to drift . . . *Someone just let me die!*

No more.

No more.

No more.

A light shone above me. A trick. A lie! I hid my face in my arms. *Stop mocking me! Stop it! Stop it!*

No more.

No more.

No more.

"Leave him alone, you son of a bitch!" There was a flash of light and a scream. I curled up tighter, hiding my face. Someone approached me and I trembled in fear.

"Ted?" the voice whispered.

I gasped and hid my face further in my knees. It couldn't be her. Not her! This was a trick! A lie just to torment me! Not fair! Not fair!

"Hey, look at me. I'm not going to hurt you. I'm going to get you out of here, okay? The nightmare's over. It's time to move on."

No! Hide! Hide away! It can't be!

She touched me, and I flinched. Unable to fight it anymore, I slowly looked up. She was bigger than I remembered. Or was I smaller? I looked down at my little arms and hands. I was just a child. I looked back up at her with trepidation. She held her arms out, and the child in me couldn't resist. I needed love. I needed protection. I needed someone. Anyone. But I wanted *her.* I threw myself at her and wrapped my arms around her neck. The screams of tortured souls in the Hurricane echoed around us, but she was safe, and she was warm.

She scooped me up like a child and said, "Come on. Let's get you out of here."

I didn't stop to ask her how she'd do it. I didn't look to see where my father had gone. I simply clung to her and hid my face in her shoulder. Home. She was home. In the deepest pits of Hell, I was home.

chapter 47
HOMECOMING

Strangely, the thought of leaving the cell was terrifying. The angels out there were so full of Light, and even though I was glowing again, I knew there was still Darkness inside of me. A kind of Darkness that none of them had felt before. Malum had been inside of me, not just my head, but my body too. He *was* me. I felt tainted. Stained. There was no way that someone like me could fit in again with angels. I was broken, and they were whole.

The Big Man shook his head. "They are not whole. The fact that they are still here and have not moved on to the next place means that they still have more to learn. Just like you."

I knew in my heart of hearts that what he said was true, but a part of me still couldn't believe it. I covered my face and groaned into my hands. Why did everything have to be so difficult? Why couldn't I just snap out of this? The Big Man was here. He helped me defeat Malum. He'd personally come to save me from my prison, and here I was wasting time having another breakdown.

"David."

All he did was say my name, but it resonated in me like a gong strike. I blinked, took a breath, and looked up at him.

"Do you trust me?" he asked.

I took a breath and nodded.

"Then take my hand. We'll walk out together."

It took every ounce of bravery in my incorporeal body, but the minute I took his hand, the fear vanished. I was safe. Nothing could hurt me now. I was ready to go back home. The old me rushed back, and suddenly I felt guilty and worried about everyone I knew and loved, living and dead. What was my family going through now? Had Charlie found my body? Where was my mom? Was she worried sick about me? Where was Sandra? Would things change between us now that we were both dead? What about my team? Would we even be a team anymore now that Malum was captured? Wow, we'd captured Malum. It was over!

The Big Man pulled me from the cage, past sentinel angels guarding the demon we left behind, then through a familiar hallway with conference rooms on either side. Up ahead, I could see the wide-open lobby and the front desk. I'd never been to the prisons in The Resting Place, but I'd always known where they were. This was the hallway Malum had come down when he escaped and attacked me and Grandma when all this mess began.

The lobby was bustling with activity, and the old me stirred inside, feeling the need to jump behind the counter and help organize the piles of paperwork.

"Are you ready?" the Big Man asked, still holding my hand.

I snapped out of my thoughts and nodded. Then I turned and looked up at him. "Thank you for coming back for me. Thank you for not giving up on me, even when I'd given up on myself. I'm sorry I cracked in the end. I'm afraid that I don't deserve any of this."

He put a hand on my shoulder. "Enough of that. That feeling of unattainable forgiveness is not coming from me. I already forgave you. It's you who must work on forgiving yourself. Let it go, David. You've suffered in order to save your brothers and sisters, and I accept your sacrifice. Now the Darkness is behind you, and I've washed it away. It's time to move on." Then he turned me to face a horde of familiar faces that had caught sight of me and started yelling my name. "Go to them. Then, when you're ready, come see me in my office for your interview. You can tell me about your idea then."

"What idea?"

His eyes twinkled, and he disappeared in a burst of Light.

A body barreled into me, and started sobbing, shoving my hair back, and kissing my face. "My boy, my boy! My poor baby! Have you come back to us? I love you so much! You're safe now. You don't have to hide away anymore. You're safe. I've got you."

I closed my eyes and hugged my mom. I wasn't sure how she still smelled like garden dirt and lemon bars, but she did. It was a blessing to still be able to see her when I was alive, but this was so much better. I felt safe again for the first time in what felt like forever. I buried my face deeper into her shoulder. "Sorry for worrying you. I love you, Mom."

She pulled back and put her hands on my cheeks, wiping tears I hadn't noticed I'd shed. "Are you going to be okay?"

I smiled. "I'm okay, Mom."

"David!"

Now another woman was squeezing the death out of me, and I pulled away so I could look at the face I loved the most. "Sandra!" I felt like I was floating. Probably because I was, but that was beside the point. I could touch her now! I hugged her again and smiled with my eyes closed and whispered, "I missed you so much!" She pulled away to look at me with a look of concern, and I squeezed her hands—my favorite hands in the whole world. I felt a familiar urge to kiss her, but time had passed, and things had changed. I couldn't just assume she still felt the same way. I couldn't read her face, but her eyes were shining in a way that drew me near. I opened my mouth to say something, but Raj interrupted, grabbing my shoulder.

Unable to maintain his professional distance, he put his arm around me, pulled my face to his chest, and roughly kissed the top of my head. My eyes widened in surprise, and I chuckled. Jake shoved Raj away to give me a hug and was soon interrupted by my grandmothers sandwiching me between them. Everyone wanted a piece of me, hugging me, shaking my hand, patting my back, and tousling my hair. I barely knew who was touching me.

"All right, all right, give the poor bloke some space!" Jake said eventually, pushing everyone away from me like a police officer holding back a crowd. I breathed a sigh of relief as I was saved from the mountain of angels threatening to smother me.

I looked at my team, still hovering around me in a daze of awe and awkwardness. This second family of mine took up space in the middle of headquarters beneath the famous crystal chandelier. Curious onlookers queued up to turn in reports and paperwork, stealing glances at us, but I only had eyes for my team.

Raj, Ying Yue, Frederick, William, Bill, Daisy, Natalie, Jake, Sandra, Mom, even Grandma Gertie and Nana Maria had shoved their way in. Ted was still absent, but I chose to put that worry on hold for the moment.

"So . . . that was fun," I said lamely, rubbing the back of my neck and looking down at my feet. I tried not to feel ashamed of what I had become and how they had seen me when I was a wanderer. Had they watched when Malam attacked and overtook me in that cage?

Raj put his hand on my shoulder, "I can't believe we let you go through with it. We shouldn't have. The way he tortured you . . . I should have stopped you."

"It was the right thing to do," I said firmly. "It's not your fault I cracked in the end."

"Anyone would have! Most people wouldn't have lasted long enough to get him in the cage!"

"Yeah, sorry I was a no-show, mate," Jake said, sympathy making his whole face scrunch up. I knew that out of all my friends, he understood me the most. He'd been in the Hurricane long enough to become a wanderer himself. "We were trying to capture all the demons that were coming to Malum's rescue, but there were so many of them. I was kicking butt, but then I got thrown in the Hurricane, and that's why I wasn't there to drop the cage on you. But I got myself out this time." He grinned with pride.

"Good on ya, mate," I said with a grin.

"Frederick ratted out all the hidden *Death* demons and helped free a lot of the slaves with Light manacles," he explained. "Some of them joined our side, but a lot of them still wanted to join Malum. We would have lost, but then Ying Yue showed up, leading a group of demons that wanted to take him down. Turned out she'd also escaped the Hurricane and had been undercover working with their demon judge this whole time. When Fake Frederick—a.k.a. William—said Eurydice was no longer working with us, it was just misdirection."

"About this whole mole business . . ." I narrowed my eyes at William. "What the heck, man? Was that really you from the beginning? When you impersonated Raj, I about peed my pants."

He bowed his head. "My apologies. I needed to maintain my connection to Malum, so I was unable to create Light, or that connection would be broken. That meeting with Rajesh was my way of sharing with you important information without blowing my cover. You were too shrewd to believe my disguise, however, so I resorted to demonstrating the false Light myself, hoping you would pass along the information. After that, I resorted to passing messages through your grandfather. I couldn't risk you discovering my identity by some small slip on my part."

"Oh, you were the blue lady!" I said. "Wait, so this whole

plan was your idea? You were the one who told me that I was the trap."

"That was mostly Frederick's idea," William said. "I was simply the messenger."

"You guys were working together behind the scenes?" I asked Frederick.

He nodded. "This was why we did not wish you to discover the identity of the mole. Our covers would have both been blown."

For a moment, everyone seemed to have run out of words. We all just stood there, looking around at each other, hardly able to believe that we'd actually done it. It was surreal to be back here, where it all started, and no longer worried about the end of the world. I still felt like I should be panicking, like letting my guard down was dangerous, but I tried to smother that feeling. Hopefully, with time, I'd be able to really relax again. The Resting Place is supposed to be a restful place, after all.

"So, are we done with the demon hunters now?" I asked, looking to Ying Yue.

"The demon hunters were created to capture Malum," Ying Yue said. "He is captured, so we have disassembled. It's time to return to our regularly scheduled duties and put this all behind us."

That weirdly made me sad. This entire journey had been a complete nightmare, but I loved our team, and I was going to miss working so closely with them. But I decided to be happy even as our dynamic shifted. They would all still be around. Well, all except Ted… and the student I failed—

"I told you it was him! I told you!"

I felt a smile spreading across my face before I fully registered the voice. I went on my tiptoes to try and look around Jake's head, before I remembered I could simply float a little higher. Asher was dragging Leo behind him as he ran across the room. "See! He's back! He's back!"

"Asher!" I grinned as he threw his arms around me. With my free hand, I gripped Leo's shoulder. "I'm so glad you're okay! I was so worried about you!"

"Eh, I'm fine." Leo pulled away and gestured at Asher. "This kid's a menace."

Asher pulled away and bounced from foot to foot. "I saved him! From the freaking Hurricane! I made myself invisible and snuck into a defender meeting when they were planning the last jailbreak, and then I went with them, and nobody knew!"

"Asher!" Sandra scolded. "That is so dangerous!"

"What, you didn't know about this?" I asked.

Sandra's mouth was still open. "No!"

"Wait, so what happened?" I asked.

Leo shook his head. "I was going all lame and wanderer-y, and then suddenly Asher was there, shining like the sun and screaming, 'Eat my Light, fart faces!' Then he grabbed me and pulled me out. I was saved by a little kid while I just floated there, staring at nothing." He grimaced at the ground, embarrassed by his weakness.

"Kid," I said, my hand still on Leo's shoulder. "Three of the people here have been wanderers. I literally just came out of it. It's nothing to be ashamed of; sometimes it's okay to need to be rescued."

"As long as I'm the one doing it!" Asher yelled, spinning and kicking invisible foes. "I'm gonna be a defender *and* a rescuer, and then I can save Oliver, and we can kick demon butts together!"

"Cool the jets, mate," Jake chuckled. "I'll put in a good word for ya, but ya gotta learn how to listen first."

"What about the rest of the angels in the Hurricane?" I asked the group.

"The angels that had been unjustly imprisoned have been released," Ying Yue said. "Honorable Judge Eurydice has made sure of that and is now monitoring the Hurricane much more closely than before. As the newly appointed angel-demon liaison, I will continue to communicate with her so we can improve angelic and demonic relations. But yes, to answer your question, most angels are now free."

"Most?"

She pursed her lips. "Somehow, Ted has gone missing. We're sure he's down there somewhere, but no one can find him."

My heart sank.

"Also," Jake said. He leaned in close and whispered, "Your little demon friend escaped. We're trying to keep it quiet for now, but no one knows how she got out or where she went."

I frowned. "That's concerning."

Jake bit his lip in worry. "Think she'll pull another mad stunt like the one that started all this?"

I shrugged and shook my head. I wanted to believe Sheila had changed, but I had no idea.

Suddenly, Mom was beside me. "Hey, um, after you've had your interview, you might want to go visit the family. They don't know what happened to you, and they're worried sick."

I swore, thinking of Elena, whom I'd promised to visit as soon as I crossed over.

"Yeah," I told my mom. "I'll go do my interview now. Um, I don't have to do a tour again, do I? Get a new assignment?"

"Yes." I jumped as Hermes popped into existence next to me. His kindly middle-aged face smiled down at me. "Come with me for your tour and assignment. I promise to make it quick." Then he held out his hand. "Welcome home, David." I ignored his hand and threw my arms around him.

HER

We appeared just outside The Resting Place, and Ted clung to me more tightly than I thought imaginable. His face was buried in my shoulder, and he wouldn't move a muscle. We sank to the ground, his arms still clinging to me. He looked like the man I knew by now, no longer the child I'd found in the Hurricane. But I would never be able to forget that face. I'd always known that was inside of him, but seeing it firsthand broke me.

"You can let go now," I said quietly.

He pulled away quickly. "Sorry! Sorry, I shouldn't . . . touch you." He wiped his eyes and turned away.

"What, you're still dangerous?" I demanded.

"No, not anymore. It was a problem with my mortal body. Like a chemical imbalance or something. And brain damage from . . . stuff. I was just sorry for touching you without asking. After what I did to you."

I sat there feeling like four sides of me were at war. I wanted to hide from him, then slap him, then hug him, then throw him back into the Hurricane. My mind replayed jumbled memories of him kissing me, hitting me, dancing with the twins, and screaming at me. He'd only hurt me once, but that memory shouted so much louder than the rest.

He turned toward me, unable to meet my gaze. His voice shook as he spoke. "Nothing I can say will take back what I did or make it better. But I am so sorry for what I did to you, Sheila. I can't express how much I hate myself for hurting you. I was messed up, but it was still my fault. I should have gotten help. And I never should have married or lived with anyone in that condition. I—"

"Shut up!" I groaned. "I'm the one that asked you to marry me. I'm the one that convinced you to move in with me, and I'd known you long enough to know what I was getting myself into. What you did was horrific, and it's haunted me since I died, but can you stop with that stupid 'I shouldn't have endangered you' argument? Because that part was me. I hate you for what you did to me, and what you almost did to the twins, but I think we're pretty much even now, so just... enough."

Weirdly enough, I meant it. Years and years of rage, and I was finally just done.

He looked at me with his sad brown eyes. His bottom lip quivered pathetically. "You think we're even? I know I hurt you, and I know it was unforgivable, but how could you do what you did to me? How could you throw me in there?"

"It was payback," I grumbled.

"It's not the same! I never meant to hurt you, and once it was over, you went to The Resting Place. You were safe and at peace. You sent me to Hell!"

I cringed, knowing what he was going to say.

"My dad was down there! He tortured me! It was like when

I was a kid, but a hundred times worse! How could you do that to me? He's the one that messed me up!"

He clenched his hair and started rocking back and forth, and I remembered all of those times when he woke up from nightmares like this.

"I'm . . . sorry," I whispered. "I'm sorry, Ted. I went too far." I wasn't ready to forgive him for what he'd done to me, but I was done trying to punish him.

I sighed and stood up, needing some space. I ran my hand through my hair and took a deep breath before turning around. "Come on, get up." I held out my hand to him. He took it, and I pulled away before I could do something stupid again, like hug him. "You need to go see the Big Man. You need help, and I . . . well, I don't know where to go, but I can't go back there."

My situation hit me then, and I don't know if I'd ever felt lonelier. I'd destroyed everything, and with my rage cooled, I had nothing left. Nothing. I wasn't an angel, but I was done being a demon. What did that make me?

Ted looked at me with those big eyes, all earnest and genuine. His stupid hair fluffed up at the front. I looked down and stepped away, ashamed and uncomfortable.

"Sheila-girl, do you see yourself?" I could hear the smile in his voice as he said it.

Sheila-girl? I'd forgotten about that stupid pet name. Why did it make my eyes water?

He slowly took my hand and held it up to my eyes. I was glowing with Light. Of course I was. That was how I escaped my prison cell, but that didn't erase the Darkness inside. I hid my hand behind my back and backed away. "I'm not an angel. I almost destroyed the entire world! Don't try to act like I can just come back from this."

"Sheila," he whispered. "Forget about being worthy. Do you want to come back?"

I didn't respond. I just stood there frozen, trying to prevent myself from burying my face in his chest and wrapping my arms around him, which was absolutely ludicrous. I hated this man! But I'd spent so long being terrified of the monster inside him, I'd forgotten what the real Ted was like. I hated how much I suddenly missed him.

He cupped my cheek with his hand. Gently, so gently, giving me all the power to pull away if I wanted. I sank into it. For the first time, I didn't have to fear what his hands would do.

"Sheila," he whispered. "Please look at me."

I opened my eyes, and unbidden tears fell down my cheeks. I felt so stupidly fragile and vulnerable, and I hated that, but I also didn't want to pull away. When was the last time someone had touched me like this?

"I know you think it's impossible," he said intently, looking right through me, "but do you want to come home?"

I nodded, so tired of lying to myself.

He smiled that stupid smile, and I couldn't help feeling a sense of home. "Well, lucky for you, I'm an usher now, and I know of a safe place I can take you where you can go to wait until you're ready to face him again." He held his hand out. "Can I take you there?"

I bit my lip and turned around, staring sightlessly around

me as I reflected on all the bridges I'd burned. There was nothing left for me out there. Nothing but my children. And they deserved to be watched over by someone filled with Light.

I turned back to Ted, waiting patiently for my answer.

With nothing left to lose, I followed that stupid, foolish hope inside me and took his hand.

chapter 48
THE SAFE HOUSE

Hermes actually gave me a tour. I couldn't tell if it was a joke or if he was that much of a stickler about rules and procedures. The people we passed were kind of weird to me. Those I'd met before smiled too widely and waved too awkwardly to feel genuine. Others stared at me or whispered things to their friends when I passed. I felt my face flush.

What had they all seen and heard about me? Was everyone in The Resting Place there when they brought in Malum with me in tow? What had I looked like? Was I crying, screaming, or staring creepily into space? Wanderers are really off-putting, and I hated that others had likely been creeped out by my own blank stare. I shuddered again. Some of those memories were too painful to think about, while others were foggy and dream-like. I had a feeling therapy was going to be brutal for the next while as we "unpacked" it all. I shook my head and tried to focus on Hermes again. Later. I could deal with that later.

"And this is the front desk," Hermes said unnecessarily.

I blinked out of my thoughts. "Huh? Oh, right."

"This is where you will work again as one of your assigned duties."

I raised an eyebrow. "One of them?"

He smiled like some of the other people we'd passed. What was it? Pity? Disgust? Embarrassment?

"I think you've proven yourself more than capable of an additional job, don't you?"

Oh? Maybe it wasn't embarrassment. Maybe he was . . . impressed? Huh.

"Uh, yeah, I'll take another job," I said quickly, remembering how boring front desk duty got when it was all I had to do.

"As your second assignment, you will be a rescuer. This over here is where the rescuers meet."

He showed me their conference room for meetings and introduced me to my supervisor, who was a guy named DeAndre I'd seen around before. I was excited! As someone who had been on both sides of rescuing, it was a job that really meant something to me.

And then it was time for my interview with the Big Man.

Hermes walked me to his office, then patted my back and left me to it. I knocked on the door, and when he called for me to come in, I floated through. I got a silly little thrill from that. I could float through doors again! I was above the laws of physics!

This time, when I entered the office, I saw something I'd never seen before. There were still a chair and a bench, the white walls looking insubstantial and yet solid at the same time. But now there was another door on the other side of the room. A white door, seeming to stand on its own. It didn't have a doorknob. Shaking my questions from my mind, I knelt before him until he told me to stand. Then I hugged him and sighed, feeling the warmth of his Light. All was right in the world when he hugged me back.

"Please take a seat," he said, gesturing to the bench, then added with a smile, "It doesn't matter which side you sit on."

I grinned at his throwback to our first meeting, where I was so flustered I couldn't even decide where to sit. This time, I plopped myself right down in the middle.

"Hi," I said, unable to keep the smile off my face.

"Hello, David. Welcome back."

"What's that?" I asked, pointing at the door across the room.

"That is a door," he said obviously.

"Yeah, I can see that," I said, grinning. "But what's it for? Where does it go?"

His expression became very sober and peaceful all at once. "That is the door to the next place."

My jaw dropped. "The next—wait, why wasn't it there last time?"

"The door was always there," he said. "You simply couldn't see it because you weren't ready. Now you are. You've reached that point along your journey where you've become worthy of going through the door if you so choose. This often happens when one becomes an archangel."

My eyes widened. "Are you telling me I could move on to the next place?"

He nodded. "If that is what you wish."

I blinked. "Wait, you said this happens when one becomes an archangel? So, all the other archangels out there could move on if they want, but they choose not to? Why?"

"That is their business, not yours. Now, what is it you wish to do, David? Do you wish to move on?"

I thought about what that meant. If the upgrade was anything like the difference between mortality and The Resting Place, then the next place had to be pure bliss and joy. And I could almost sense something on the other side. I couldn't tell what it was, but it felt like it was calling me home.

Home.

I could go home! My real home! A feeling of homesickness for something I couldn't even remember rushed through me. I didn't realize I'd left the bench until I was floating closer and closer to the door. I started to remember things I'd forgotten. It was vague and fuzzy, but the closer I got to the door, the clearer it became. I needed to go through that door, or I would forget again, and I didn't want to forget.

Home. Home. *Home!*

I reached out my hand to push the door open.

And then I remembered why I'd come here. My idea. The idea he knew I'd have. I thought of my loved ones I'd be leaving behind. Could I really move on from them? On my own? There was a reason most people waited for the majority of their family to die before moving on.

My hand dropped, and my hopes plummeted.

"I don't think I'm ready," I said quietly.

"There is more you would like to do." It was a statement, not a question. He already knew what I wanted to talk about.

I nodded, and he gestured for me to return to my seat.

I took one last longing look at the door before drifting back to my bench. It would be okay. Someday, I would go through that door and find my real Heaven. As for now, I still had some work to do.

"What do you want to talk about, David?"

This idea had been stewing in my mind throughout Hermes' guided tour. I was only half listening most of the time, because I'd been busy making plans. I'd just gotten back here, and already I was making plans for the future.

"I had this idea," I said, looking down at my feet, a little embarrassed for some reason. I was doing that thing again, where I jump headfirst into a plan that's way too big for me to handle. What if I failed? What if he agreed it was too much for me?

"Then there is no reason to doubt yourself," he said. "There is nothing that cannot be accomplished with my help. We are a team, you and I. If it is good, and if I approve, then it will be done."

I nodded and continued. "So, I was thinking of a way to help those of us still in The Resting Place. I mean, I'm not saying there is anything wrong with it. It's perfect. Obviously. I mean, you made it, so it's perfect."

He shook his head slowly. "Except for me, nothing on this side of that door is perfect. My Resting Place is run by imperfect angels who are still in progress. It is good, but it is not perfect. So, tell me, what is your idea for improvement?"

I shifted forward on the bench, unable to hide my earnestness. "Maybe angels would be able to move on sooner if they dealt with their own internal demons, rather than just focusing on others. I mean, I agree that dedicating our time to service is important and super rewarding. But people are more capable of taking care of others if they know how to take care of themselves. I think it's important to remember that the point of all of this isn't just to help everyone else grow and progress and ignore ourselves. It's about helping each other. It's about us. It's about the 'we'. And 'we' includes 'me' too.

"Also, I think people need to know that it's okay to feel sad that they died. It's okay to feel unfinished. It's okay to have regrets. The Resting Place shouldn't be about smothering all negative feelings but learning how to process them and growing stronger because of it."

I looked down at my hands and smiled. "I think I finally figured out what I want to do with my life. I want to help people who feel the way I did and still do sometimes. I want to have a space where we can talk about it so we can work things out together. I mean, I can't help thinking that if Sheila and Ted had sorted through all their issues when they got here, none of this mess with Malum would have even happened. Not that I'm blaming anyone, but a lot of people experience trauma when they die, and that doesn't just go away without your help and some serious work.

"Anyway, this is what I want to do. And I was going to ask permission, but it feels right, so I'm just going to tell you that I'm doing it and ask for your blessing."

And so, I told him my plan to create what I would call the "safe house", which would be a place for people to talk about their issues. People who died too young. People who experienced trauma. People who left family behind. People who were left behind by family that moved on to the next place without them. I just wanted to help people sort through their issues in a healthier way than I did, having a nervous breakdown ten years after dying. I doubted I was the only one who struggled to come to terms with my death, and I doubted I was the only one to just keep pretending I was fine when I wasn't.

"Anyway," I said at the end, "I wondered if you could help me? I know this is something bigger than I can accomplish alone."

He grinned broader than I'd ever seen, clearly pleased by something I'd said. "Well done. I would love to help. What would you like me to do?"

That threw me for a minute. He was asking me how he could help me? Didn't he know best? Was this a test?

"Um," I said. "I honestly don't know. I'm gonna need help with everything. But I guess the first part would be finding others who would be interested and have experience in this area? I'm sure Raj could help. Also, we'll need somewhere to meet. We could meet in some of the conference rooms at headquarters, but I feel like it would be better if we had our own separate building. Is that possible? I'm not sure how construction works on this side."

A piece of paper appeared in his hands, and he handed it to me. "These are names of people who will help you."

"Seriously?" I blinked and sat back. "Wow, that was easy."

"I won't give you all the answers at once—it would be a

disservice to you and would deprive you of the lessons you learn when you work and struggle—but I will always be here to help. Remember that."

I nodded and looked down at the list:

Yetta Cazacu (architect)

DeAndre Richards (psychologist)

Lisa Lennox (therapist)

Baako Al-Katib (manager)

I recognized DeAndre from the rescuers, but I didn't know anyone else. I felt my heart plummet a little. Raj's name wasn't on the list. Why not? This was right up his alley. This was his thing! Why wouldn't he want to help me? Was he sick of me and the way I was always depending on him?

"Speak your concern," the Big Man said.

I looked up at him. "I notice Raj's name isn't on here."

"It is not."

"Why not?"

Someone knocked on the door.

"There he is now," the Big Man said. "Go speak with him. He will be visiting with me afterward, so this is goodbye for the present. I hope you will come back to speak with me again soon, David. Please don't wait too long."

Feeling an inexplicable sense of foreboding, I nodded and floated through the door. Raj was, indeed, waiting there. He looked oddly emotional.

"Hey, kid, we need to talk."

"What's going on?" I asked.

He paused and looked down, blinking rapidly. He couldn't meet my eyes. And was he trying not to cry?

My heart filled with dread. I'd never seen Raj look this way. I'd seen him angry and sorrowful, but this was something else. Almost guilty, like he knew what he was about to say would hurt me, personally. It almost reminded me of how he looked when my mom had been captured. My stomach dropped. Had someone else been captured? Was Malum free? Was it Sheila? Did she hurt someone?

"What's wrong?" I demanded.

"I'm moving on," he said quietly.

I froze. That was the last thing I'd expected him to say. I felt like the rug had just been pulled out from beneath my feet. Then I remembered that the Big Man said Raj was going to see him after me.

"What, like, *right now?*" I asked in a high, panicked voice. He couldn't leave me! I still needed him!

He nodded.

I took a second to try to control my face and force myself not to beg him to stay. "Congratulations," I said numbly. "I'm so happy for you."

He raised an eyebrow. "Yeah, you sound happy."

I just shook my head. I was speechless. How could this happen? Everything was supposed to click into place now. We'd captured Malum, and I was back in The Resting Place. Everything was supposed to go back to normal now. I was supposed to heal and move on, not rip open new wounds.

"I'm sorry, Raj. I know I should be happy for you, I just don't know what I'm going to do without you."

"You don't need me anymore, kid."

I gaped at him. "Are you kidding me? Did you not see

what just happened? You were the one who told me I needed help, and that was after I'd been in the Hurricane for like five seconds. But I mean . . . he was literally *inside* me, and . . ." I shuddered and squeezed my eyes shut.

Don't think about it! Don't think about it!

I fought the urge to let the gray nothingness pull me under again. It was so tempting.

"Breathe," Raj reminded me.

"I'm dead, I don't need to breathe," I muttered.

"It still helps."

I took a deep breath.

"Look at me, kid." He waited until I reluctantly opened my eyes. "I didn't say you don't need help. We all do. You just don't need me. You've learned all I can teach you."

"Then who?" I asked.

"Come on, you're smarter than that. Who understands you better than anyone, and is constantly urging you to come talk to him? You're an angel again, David. You can just walk into his office now and talk to him face-to-face."

I looked over at the Big Man's door. "Oh." I took a moment to breathe again and let it all sink in. "Why now?"

"It's just my time." Raj looked past me, unable to meet my eyes. "I've been staring at that door for twenty years now, and I'm ready to be with my family again. I was going to leave a while ago, but I felt like I was needed, and then Malum was released. I'd planned to leave once Malum was captured, but I was waiting for you to come back to yourself. I couldn't bear to leave you while you were still trapped in that cell." He forced himself to look at me. "I want you to know, I didn't abandon you, David. I visited you all the time. I talked to you for hours, but I doubt you remember, if you even heard me. Only the Big Man could help you in the end."

I forced myself not to think back on that time in the cell and focus on what he was telling me. He'd wanted to move on, but he'd stayed because he was worried about me. What if I'd been a wanderer for years, like the ones in Sandra's apartment? Would he have still waited? Would I have wanted him to? I looked down, feeling like a great big burden. "I'm sorry for holding you back."

"Hey," Raj said sharply. "Look at me."

I slowly forced myself to meet his gaze.

"Don't apologize for suffering."

I nodded, pursing my lips and trying to hold it together.

"Why would I say that?" Raj challenged. "Tell me."

I took a deep breath. "Because I did the right thing. And it was traumatizing. And I'm allowed to have a hard time with it."

He smiled and hugged me. "You've grown so much."

"Why does it feel like you're dying?" I asked, glad our hug was hiding my face.

I felt him sigh. "Because, like death, this is a hard goodbye. It's hard for me too, kid."

I took a deep breath and did my best to put on a brave face. This was a monumental moment for Raj, and I knew I shouldn't ruin it with my pathetic neediness, even though this was tearing me up inside. When he pulled away, I tried to smile. "I'm happy for you, Raj. Good for you."

He smiled wanly, knowing I was lying through my teeth.

"This Safe House idea of yours is incredible, by the way. Seriously incredible. I am so proud of you."

"I haven't even told you about that yet!"

"The Big Man told me. I was worrying about you while you were in that cell, and he reassured me that you were going to be okay in the end and would go on to do amazing things. And you will, kid. I know you will. Just by being yourself, you make other people better, and I admire that about you." He took a deep breath and let it out slowly, looking down as he tried to hold it together. "After all this time, I think that you were my unfinished business. I'm so grateful I got to stick around and see you grow." He smiled at me, his eyes twinkling with pride.

"Thanks for all you've done for me," I said quietly.

"We'll see each other again someday." He put his hands on my shoulders. "No more putting yourself down, all right? No more second-guessing yourself. If something feels right, you stick to your guns and proudly be the David we all know and love. Promise me."

I nodded, unable to speak.

"I love you, kid. Like you're one of my own."

And then he went to talk to the Big Man before walking through *the* door and leaving me behind.

I stood there staring at nothing, unable to process what had just happened.

Raj was the one who saw me when no one else had. When I told my family and friends I was going to try out as a demon hunter, they all laughed at me. He didn't. And he was always pushing me because, somehow, he saw my potential. He always supported my ideas and was there for me when I was at my lowest. When something awful happened, I always knew I could go to Raj. I couldn't imagine The Resting Place without him.

I wasn't sure what to do, so I went to my room at Dad's house and lay on my bed, annoyed at the stupid angel tears I couldn't hold back anymore.

HIM

We paused before the door, and I turned to Sheila.

"This is The Waiting Room," I said, reciting the usual script given to ushers. "You are here by choice, and you can leave at any time, but there is only one way out. While you are here, you will suffer for what you've done wrong in your life. Or . . . afterlife," I added. "No one will harm you—the torture will be in your own mind. Each day, the Big Man will come to your door and ask if you're ready to come with him. He can and will take away your suffering when you are ready to accept it. Now you must decide: do you choose to enter in? Or will you wander on your own?"

Sheila looked at me with a timidity I'd rarely seen in her. She had always been such a firecracker, but right now, she was vulnerable and scared. I understood. It was that fear of hoping that held her back. Broken hope is the worst kind of pain. I offered her an encouraging smile and waited for her to consent.

"Is it safe? Is it real?" she whispered.

"Sheila-girl," I said with a sad smile, "this is how I got into The Resting Place."

Comprehension lit her eyes, and she blinked, understanding. This made more sense to her. She thought I'd never suffered or paid for what I'd done. She thought I never cared. And I could see her mind working. If this place could handle a murderer like me, maybe the Big Man could handle her too.

She looked at me with that fierce determination that made her face come alive again, and I smiled. There she was.

I opened the door and recited, "Enter into your suffering, and emerge when you are ready to accept his help."

Before she disappeared through the door, I caught hold of her hand. She spun around and pulled away, angry that I would delay her from the decision it took so much courage for her to make. I held my hands up and backed away. But before I shut the door, I whispered, "You don't have to suffer, you know. He's not going to punish you; he'll heal you. Don't stay in there as long as I did, okay?"

Her brave, determined eyes were the last I saw of her.

SAM SR.

With a heavy breath, I pushed open the door to David's old room. He'd been gone for almost three weeks, but somehow it still smelled like him. He'd cleaned before he left. The bed was made, and there were vacuum lines on the carpet. I went to the dresser just to look at and touch his clothes. I don't know why—I guess I hoped that holding something he'd touched would make him feel closer. Dad still hadn't heard from him, and my heart clenched every time I thought about all that could have gone wrong when my David went out to save the day. I missed him so much it hurt, and I wished Gloria were here to help me through losing him again. But she was gone too.

Following some strange instinct, I closed the door and sat on his bed.

I looked over at the side of the bed where he usually slept. Maybe it was my imagination, but I felt like maybe he was nearby. Maybe. I wasn't like Dad as much as I wished I was, and I couldn't imagine why David wouldn't have visited him first before coming to his old room to be alone. But I chose to pretend on the off chance that maybe he could hear me.

"I don't know where you are, David, but I just want to tell you that I love you. And also, even though this is hard, and even if you're hurting right now, I know you're going to be okay. The family will too. I'm not sure I believe that time heals all wounds, but it softens them enough for us to eventually realize that it was still worth it. When we love people, we open ourselves up to the pain of losing them, but I still believe that the pain is worth the love. It really is. And even when we lose someone, there are always more around us that we still get to keep with us. Focus on those around you, and remember that those who leave aren't gone forever. That's what I'm telling myself at least . . . But I believe it's true. You're going to be okay, son. I know it."

I looked down and shook my head, feeling foolish. What was this, a pep talk to myself? Everything I'd said applied to me and my situation, but I wasn't sure how that could have helped David. Maybe he felt lonely sometimes, being invisible to us. I'm sure I would.

I sighed and slapped my thighs before standing up. "Give your mom a hug for me. And when you get the chance, come see your grandpa so we can have an actual chat. I want to hear what you've been up to."

Before leaving, I glanced back at the spot where I imagined David to be and smiled. "Love you, son."

chapter 49
BACK IN THE SADDLE

How had he known? He didn't even know I was there, but he said exactly what I needed to hear. I just stared at him, slack-jawed the entire time. After Raj left, I felt like I'd lost two dads in one day. But I hadn't. Somehow, my dad was still dad-ing me from the other side.

I got up and took a breath. It was time to stop moping and visit the rest of the family. I wasn't the only one struggling here.

I went to Elena's house first. I probably should have started with Grandpa so he could call everyone and tell them that he'd seen me, but I wanted my first experience with each family member to be personal. I wanted to remember what it was like to love them behind the scenes. Eventually, I'd appear to Grandpa, and maybe we'd have a family gathering, and I could tell them all that had happened. For now, though, one at a time.

Elena was lying on the couch, looking exhausted and depressed, with a sleeping baby on her chest. The kids were at school, the house was a disaster, and a single tear slid down

Elena's cheek as she stared at nothing. Her hair was in a crazy knot on her head, and the bags under her eyes looked big enough to hold the weight of the entire world. Her arm that wasn't holding Hope in place was dangling off the side of the couch, clutching her phone like she was waiting for a call that would never come.

"Someone's having a bad day," I said quietly.

She obviously couldn't hear me, but I knelt down next to her anyway.

"Hey, Elena, I know you're exhausted, but I'm here if you wanna talk."

She didn't respond, which made me sad, even though I knew this was how it would be. She was right there, but she felt a million miles away.

"Where's Charlie? Didn't he get paternity leave? He must be at the store or something."

As an experiment, I threw a ball of Light at her. The corner of her mouth barely twitched, then drooped down again, looking more depressed than before.

"Okay, I know I can't make you happy. That's not fair. You're entitled to your feelings. But if it helps at all, I'm here now. Sorry I was gone for so long. Not that I'm assuming all of this is because of me. Obviously, you're exhausted because you have a newborn and all the stress and lack of sleep that come with that. And maybe you're missing Mom too. Anyway, I'm here . . . not that that means much."

I was feeling extremely useless. I was out of practice as a guardian angel. How did I use to help family members when they didn't know I was around? I honestly couldn't remember.

I leaned in closer to get a better look at Hope. She was awake and just lying there looking around. I smiled and said her name, and then her lips puckered as she cooed. I swear she was looking right at me. Babies are weird like that. Sometimes they see things they shouldn't.

"Hi, sweet girl," I said with a grin. "How've you been?"

She wiggled and grunted, still looking at me, and I laughed, feeling supremely special.

Elena closed her eyes and sighed.

All right. It was time to resort to my little cheat. I went to the cabinet in the kitchen where I'd hidden my little contraption before I died. After focusing on what was hidden behind the door, a bell started to ring.

Elena did nothing at first, then I heard her sit up slowly. "What is that?"

I continued ringing the bell until she cautiously came into the kitchen, looking around for the sound. "I swear the next toy someone gives the kids that makes stupid sounds and never shuts up, I am going to throw it out the window!"

"Over here!" I called.

Eventually, Elena located the cabinet and threw it open. Then she frowned. Shifting Hope to hold her with one arm, she pulled out the plaque I'd hidden there. It was a wooden board with four bells attached to it. Above each bell was a name and a picture of someone who had died. At the top of the plaque was this inscription: "Someone you love is saying hi!"

Elena blinked, and her eyes watered. "What the heck?"

I made the David bell ring, and Elena dropped the plaque.

"Careful," I griped. "I spent hours on that."

Slowly, she picked it up again and set it on the kitchen table, shoving the mess to the side. A sippy cup and a bowl of old cereal fell to the ground, but she didn't even notice. I made the David bell ring again.

"What the heck?" she repeated in a thick voice.

"It's not that difficult to understand," I muttered, ringing the bell again.

"David Gabriel Garcia!" she shouted. "Shut up! You did not do this! Is it really you?"

I made the bell ring again, and she sank to the floor, sobbing with a baby in one arm and the plaque in the other. Then Hope started crying because she felt left out, I guess.

"Gosh," I muttered, kneeling next to her. "Sorry, I thought it would be nice to know when we're around. I didn't mean to make you flip out."

"I'm hormonal and sad!" she sobbed. "I can't help it!"

I chuckled. It almost felt like she was answering me. We had a nice little chat there on the kitchen floor. She couldn't hear me, of course, but every so often she'd ask if I was still there, and I would ring the bell again to reassure her that I was.

Next, I visited Sam. He was slumped at his desk at work, his head resting on his hand while he scrolled through emails. He also looked exhausted and sad. His light brown hair was disheveled like he'd been running his hands through it. There were about three energy drinks on his desk, all empty and knocked over.

"Hey, Sam."

He blinked and sighed, slumping further into his hand.

"I'm not sure what to do with you," I said honestly. "I think if I sent you a sign, you'd just get scared. I never got the impression you were a fan of ghosts."

Sam sat up and tried to slap himself awake. Was he not sleeping?

"Maybe you could take a little break?" I suggested. "Wanna go for a walk?"

Sam frowned, checking his watch.

"*Come on,*" I whispered. "*Let's go for a walk.*"

Surprisingly, he listened. We walked until we got to a park across the street from his office building and sat on a bench. I had a one-sided chat with him while he just stared straight ahead. He didn't give any indication that he heard me, but I stayed there next to him until he decided to go back in. He stood, looked up at the sky, and closed his eyes.

"If you're out there, David, I hate you for leaving us again… We were supposed to have another week with you. I had all this stuff planned, and then you just left without warning. That wasn't okay. But I guess I forgive you… I don't know if I believe in an afterlife, but if you are still around, I hope you're happy and that you're doing better than the rest of us."

"Love you too, Sam," I whispered.

• • •

The day was coming to an end, and there were so many others I could have chosen to visit. Preston, Tata Ramon, who I hadn't seen since I came back to life, my nieces and nephews, and Kiki, eventually. But I knew there was someone who deserved a visit today more than the others. I'd been putting it off because I knew it would be uncomfortable for both of us. I may not have been a wanderer anymore, but there were definitely some things I was still repressing that I didn't want to acknowledge.

With a deep breath, I closed my eyes and appeared in Charlie's car.

There was no music on, and he looked . . . weathered. He had bags under his bloodshot eyes, and his jaw was clenched. It was the face of someone exhausted, who couldn't afford to rest. His shoulders drooped, but he gripped the steering wheel so tightly that his knuckles were white.

"You okay?" I asked stupidly.

I shook my head. Of course he wasn't okay. I didn't want to act like I was important enough that my loss would devastate him, but he was family and one of my best friends. And he was there to see all of *that*. I knew what it felt like to experience it, but I had to acknowledge that it would have been horrifying to watch. And, while no one had yet confirmed it to me, I was pretty sure that he was the one who shot me. It was the best thing anyone could have done for me, and yet . . . it felt strange to sit next to the man who had killed me. That part would be worse for him, though. Being the one that pulled the trigger on his friend.

I squeezed my eyes shut, trying to block out the memories

of that night. This was part of why I didn't want to see Charlie. Being near him made me face it all again. But he needed to know that I didn't blame him, and I was starting to realize that maybe I needed to talk about it with the one living person who understood what I went through.

I blew out a breath and shook my head. "Screw it. You deserve more than just a little sign. We need to actually talk." That meant involving Grandpa.

I had been putting off seeing him as well. He actually knew what a wanderer was, and I was ashamed to admit what I'd become. Would he see me as a weakling or a coward?

Then I remembered what Raj said about not putting myself down and sticking to my guns. And the way the Big Man wasn't mad at me for tripping at the finish line—he just wanted to help me. And the way I'd told Leo that it was okay to need to be rescued sometimes. Taking a breath, I banished those thoughts and forced myself to be brave.

I leaned closer and told Charlie to go to my dad's house

Charlie frowned but made no move to change his course.

"Charlie! Go to David's dad's house, go to David's dad's house, go to David's dad's house."

"That doesn't make sense," he muttered.

I hounded him until eventually he shook his head and sighed in exasperation. "I'm going crazy . . . This is stupid." He made an illegal U-turn and headed toward my dad's neighborhood. When we got there, he stared at the front door for a while before ringing the doorbell. What was he afraid of? Did he think he'd have to confess to my family what he did? Did he think they'd blame him? Did he blame himself?

Neither my dad's nor Preston's cars were in the driveway, so Grandpa was the one to answer the door. He frowned at Charlie, then his eyes widened as we made eye contact. *"David?"*

Charlie cleared his throat. "No, I'm Charlie, remember?"

Grandpa shook his head and pointed. "It's David. He's standing right behind you."

Charlie flinched and looked around in trepidation, probably wondering if I'd come back to haunt him.

"I actually came here to talk about him," Charlie muttered, still looking fearfully around for a sign of me.

Grandpa didn't take his eyes off me as he responded. "It looks like David might want to talk as well."

"Hey, Grandpa," I said with a half-smile. "Care to translate?"

He nodded and wordlessly led us to the living room, where we awkwardly settled in.

"Where've you been?" Grandpa demanded.

I rubbed my neck uncomfortably. "I, uh, well, we did it. Malum's captured. But it was kind of awful, and I sort of went wanderer for a while . . ." I looked away in shame. "After we caught him and I died, he caught hold of me and kept torturing me, and I just sort of gave up, eventually."

Charlie's hands clenched into fists on his knees. "What did he say?"

Grandpa relayed my words, and Charlie scowled. "What's a wanderer?"

Grandpa sighed, looking at me with an embarrassing amount of compassion. "There's a state the dead can enter when they've experienced trauma. They become wandering spirits with no sense of self. They don't talk, and they barely think. They turn off all their emotions and just sort of float. It's like they're there, but no one's home. But everything they hide from is still in there, deep down. It's just hard to pull them out of it. Many stay that way for years."

Charlie's face screwed up. That night, when all of this happened, he was a rock because he had to be. The soldier with an iron will. But here he was just Charlie, and Charlie had a very soft heart.

I faced him and told Grandpa to translate for me. "I don't blame you for anything. You saved me that day, Charlie, and I just wanted to thank you. I'm sorry about what you had to see and do that night. It wasn't fair for you to have to do that, but I really am so grateful. You put me out of my misery, and I can't thank you enough."

Charlie, still scowling at the ground, wiped his eyes. "According to what you just said, you weren't put out of your misery. You've been suffering."

"The longer I was alive and possessed in that cage, the greater the chance that something could go wrong, and he'd escape again, and everything we'd done would have been for nothing. Once I was dead, it was easy for the angels to transfer him to his prison. Yeah, I went with him, but at least he was captured. And I got out eventually. I'm okay now, Charlie. I'm doing better, and I'm taken care of. We're all going to be okay."

He sniffed and nodded, wiping his eyes.

I wished I could have hugged the poor guy, and eventually

made Grandpa do it for me. It was quite a long hug, and I could tell Grandpa was uncomfortable with the waterworks, but he bore it. Grandpa was the oldest medium I knew, and he knew how to set his needs aside for those who needed his help.

Someday, Charlie and I would get back to joking and teasing, but today was about airing out all the guilt and shame between us. Those feelings didn't come from the Big Man, and it was time to let them go. Or at least begin the process of letting them go.

We didn't say much after that. I think we both needed time to let it all sink in. But as Charlie left, he saluted me, honoring me like a soldier he respected. Somehow, he didn't think I was a weakling. He thought I was brave. I smiled and saluted him back.

chapter 50
LIFE GOES ON

Sandra found me on a bench in The Resting Place, after I'd visited everyone. Not long after the Charlie conversation, Grandpa put together an impromptu family dinner so that I could personally tell them all that I was all right. I wasn't totally in the mood for more drama and crying, but they deserved to know. And I ended up being a lot happier afterwards. With all the grandkids over, the house was crazy. Kids laughing and screaming, pots clanging in the kitchen, and a constant barrage of questions for me. It wasn't as sad as I thought it would be. It was actually kind of amazing. I wasn't used to being acknowledged while invisible. My dad even pulled Preston into it, and he was the one person who didn't treat me differently now that I was dead. Which was weird, because he had always been twitchy about ghosts. I guess a David ghost didn't count as scary.

Despite the joy of being with my family, I was emotionally exhausted, and a big part of me was still hurting over Raj leaving. I just had so much I wished I could talk to him about, but I tried to remember what my dad had said about the price of love and decided it was all worth it. I was still broken over what I'd been through, and hurting over what I'd lost, but I found myself genuinely feeling like I was going to be okay. I wasn't there yet, but I would be. I would smile and laugh and love again. I knew that my life wasn't over just because I was dead.

I assumed Raj had already said his goodbyes to the team, because Sandra didn't ask me why I was sad. She just sat next to me and hesitantly reached out her hand with a hopeful, questioning look. Wanting nothing more, I took it with a smile and covered her fingers with my own. Eventually, I looked at her in the same questioning way before putting my arm around her. She melted into me, laying her head on my shoulder, like the time apart meant nothing. I closed my eyes and just basked in her closeness, remembering all the times we'd sat like this on her couch. It felt so right, I couldn't believe I'd gone so long without her.

"I still love you, Sandra," I said quietly. It might not have been the right time to say it, but I couldn't help myself. "Maybe you've moved on. Maybe you found someone else. Maybe you're happy being by yourself. Whatever way you find happiness, I support you. But I never stopped loving you, and I'll always want to be with you."

Sandra sat up and frowned, studying my face. "David. Not to be a killjoy, but you just broke up with Kiki, and I'm not looking to be anyone's rebound. I'm sorry if I'm sending mixed signals. I just . . . wanted to be near you. I've missed you."

I chuckled. "Sandra, you are not my rebound, you're my

initial shot." She raised an eyebrow, and I sighed. "Look . . . I cared for Kiki, but I was never actually over you. It was always you I wanted. Always."

She blinked and tilted her head, searching my eyes, waiting to see if I'd take it back. Then she smiled and touched my face. "Are you sure?" I nodded, and she drew me into a kiss. It was bittersweet and tender—a mix of all the pain and uncertainty we'd been through with the unbelievable relief and joy that somehow we'd ended up here. Together.

After she pulled away, I leaned my forehead against hers. "Does that mean you love me too?"

"What do you think?" she asked.

"I think I need to hear you say it."

She pulled back and put her hands on my cheeks. Her beautiful eyes were shining, and I swear her Light was brighter than before. "I love you, David Garcia. I loved you back when you were a clumsy, depressed mortal having nightmares and running into walls, and I have never stopped loving you. I've been waiting for you. And I know that you're this big hero and all, but I don't care what others think about you or what you've done. I love you because you're *you*. Dorky, incredible, big-hearted you. Does that answer your question?"

I nodded and couldn't help the huge grin that spread across my face as she snuggled back under my arm.

"You were waiting for me, huh?" I asked after a pause. "I must be pretty special."

"Don't push it."

"I'm just saying, I basically saved the world. It's about time a Hufflepuff got some credit."

She snorted against my chest. "You're such a nerd."

I smiled and closed my eyes in contentment. There was so much that was still broken, but this thing I had with Sandra was not one of them.

So, life went on after death. Eventually, we got the Safe House up and ready, and Jake and I started attending a group session for former wanderers. The Darkness still crept into my thoughts at times, but I was healing, and I knew that I wasn't alone. Eventually, I'd start leading the group for those who died young, and once I was qualified, I might start meeting with angels one-on-one. But that was for the future, and I had nothing but time.

I visited my family often, and sometimes they actually talked to me. Whenever I visited, I rang the David bell on the plaque I'd left in each house, and even my nieces and nephews started responding, shouting things like, "Hi, David! Guess what? I lost a tooth!" I'd ring it twice when I left, so they knew to say goodbye. Easily one of the best ideas I've ever had.

Ted returned to The Resting Place, followed—unexpectedly—by a glowing Sheila. She immediately Darkness punched me, hugged me, and stormed out, flipping off the gawking onlookers. So, at least she was still Sheila. Ted hurried after her, red with embarrassment, but smiling.

Others passed through The Resting Place over the years—learning, growing, and moving on in their own time. Frederick and William gave up their contest to see who could last the longest in The Resting Place and decided to move on together. Not long after that, my grandfathers joined us, and I finally got a great big garlic-scented hug from Tata Ramon. I was glad for my family that no one else had died, but I looked forward to the day when we'd all be here together.

As for me, I wasn't leaving anytime soon. There was too much I still wanted to do. I wasn't finished with this world yet, and that thought was weirdly hopeful. I thought back to that field when Raj forced me to confront why I joined the demon hunters. When a younger, less fulfilled David had a nervous breakdown because he died before he accomplished anything. That David had so much to learn.

I've decided that "Dead" is a stupid word. My body might be dead, but *I'm* not. I'm growing all the time. And the only way to truly fail at the afterlife is to stop growing. Maybe that was me, once upon a time, but not anymore.

It's funny, but even though I'm dead, I feel like I'm finally doing something with my life.

The End

Extended Epilogue

(If you want more. . .)

On the day of my youngest niece's seventh birthday, the family was playing soccer at the neighborhood park. Rocco, who was now some kind of twelve-year-old prodigy, was demolishing his cousins. Little David—now ten—was giggling like an idiot, eight-year-old Gloria was screaming in frustration, and I'd never seen the now teenage Ginny look so focused on a task as when challenged to defeat her brother. Eventually the adults, who had begun by shouting on the sidelines, joined in on the game. Jessica and Dad with Rocco, and Sam with Gloria, Ginny, and David. They soon added to the giggling and yelling.

Birthday presents were stacked up on a picnic table, and "Happy Birthday!" balloons were tied to the seats, but the birthday girl was noticeably absent. After a quick scan of the park, I found her sitting on a swing all alone, staring down at her toes. I floated down to the empty swing next to her.

"Hey, David," she said.

"Why aren't you playing with your cousins?" I asked.

Hope shrugged and dragged her feet back and forth as she swung, creating two long trenches in the sand. A loose balloon floated away from the picnic table, and the two of us stared as it floated away. It shrank to the size of a pinprick as the blue sky swallowed it up.

"What's it like up there?" she asked quietly.

"Well, seeing as I'm not an astronaut, I've never actually been to space."

She smirked and raised an eyebrow, looking remarkably like Elena.

I chuckled. "I know what you meant. Unfortunately, I can't really tell you."

"Is it better than here?" she asked, looking back down at her feet.

"What's wrong?"

"Nothing!"

I frowned and floated in front of her, so she'd have no choice but to stop swinging or go right through me. "What happened?"

She dug her heels into the sand, stopping herself before she collided with me. "I said it was nothing. Why don't you go prank my mom or something?"

I shrugged. "Fine. I'll go."

As soon as I started to disappear, she said, "Wait!"

I paused and waited.

Her lip trembled, and all the feelings she kept cooped up inside spilled out. "It's my birthday, and my daddy isn't here, and I just want him to come back home because I miss him so much. He's always gone on my birthday. And Little David and Gloria were just whispering about how my dad's been gone for a really long time and how he's probably dead, and I know he isn't because Mom would have told me, but I'm still so worried. It's just not fair. And right now, everyone's over there playing soccer, even the grown-ups, and no one even cares that I don't like soccer and it's my birthday and we should have done hide-and-seek like I wanted to. And mom's not back with the cake yet, so I just have to sit here by myself on my birthday while everyone else has fun."

I sat on the swing next to her. "That's a lot of stuff."

She nodded.

"I'll play hide-and-seek with you."

She rolled her eyes. "You can't play that with just two people. Plus, you're a ghost, so you could cheat and hide inside a tree or something."

"I would never cheat."

She gave me a look.

I grinned. "Okay, maybe a little. But you cheat in games all the time."

"With your help!"

I chuckled, and we both fell silent while out on the field, Rocco kicked the ball so hard it knocked David over with an *oof*.

"Your daddy's fine," I said. "I always check on him before I come to visit you. You know I'd tell you right away if something happened." I refrained from telling her about the phone conversation I overheard where he and Elena discussed this possibly being his last deployment. I had a feeling Charlie would be home soon, but I didn't want to give hope before it was certain. And it wasn't my news to tell.

She didn't speak for a while, but her chin started to tremble. "If my daddy died, would he visit me like you do?"

I sighed and said, "Close your eyes for me and imagine I'm hugging you, please." I waited until she closed her eyes and wrapped her arms around herself. "Your dad would absolutely come to visit you all the time, and he'd watch over you just like me and Nana Gloria do. And you'd be so lucky that you would get to see him still. Most people don't have that gift. I'm sorry that you miss your dad and that he can't be here for your birthday. It's hard to be away from people you love. But try to enjoy all these people that are still with you right now. They love you, even if they don't always show it."

She opened her eyes and stopped hugging herself. She dug her toe into the sand as she said, "I'm glad that I at least get to have you here. I know it sounds dumb . . . but sometimes you feel like another dad to me."

My eyes watered, and I had to take a breath to compose myself. "You have no idea what that means to me."

She made a face. "Are you gonna cry if I tell you I love you?"

I gave her a watery grin. "I love you too, sweetheart."

The familiar sound of rubber tires on asphalt distracted us, and Hope sprang to her feet, yelling, "Mom's back with cake!"

I watched as she rushed up to Elena and yelled for everyone to come to the table for cake and presents. I joined in with the singing, even though only the birthday girl could hear.

I had to leave after a while for front desk duty, but I returned that night to tell Hope bedtime stories, as had become our custom. Eventually, she fell asleep, and Sandra appeared next to me.

"Oh, she's sleeping," she whispered. "I'm sad I didn't make it to the party! That stupid meeting went way too long. How's our girl?"

Our girl. I loved how she said that. Sandra was a huge part of Hope's life, teaching her all about how to navigate the world with the ability to see the dead. And the two of them loved to gang up on me and make fun of me. It was one of their favorite games.

"Our girl is great, because she's amazing and incredible and perfect."

Sandra chuckled. "You are quite smitten, my love."

"Yes. Yes, I am."

She kissed my cheek and hugged my arm. A calming quiet settled over us as we watched Hope sleep. Her lips puckered slightly each time she breathed out as though she was blowing bubbles in her dreams, reminding me of when she was a baby. I loved every little thing about her. Her round little nose, her tangled hair, even her ears. Who would have thought ears could be cute? I'd never loved anyone the way I loved her. It wasn't that I loved her more than my other nieces and nephews—each and every one of them held a special place in my heart—I just had more of a connection to Hope. She was just a little more mine than the others. We were woven into each other's stories in our own special way. Sandra leaned her head on my shoulder, and a profound sense of peace washed over me.

"What are you thinking?" Sandra whispered.

I closed my eyes. "I'm thinking this feels an awful lot like what I thought I'd given up."

She pulled back and touched my face. I hadn't done it on purpose, but my face had changed over the years. She traced the crow's feet around my eyes and the smile lines around my mouth. She ran her hands through my hair that she'd styled herself, and the subtle stubble I kept just because she liked it. She smiled in a way that I couldn't interpret.

"What?" I asked finally.

"You grew up, David," she whispered. "You went and grew up."

For a kid who died at seventeen, I'd assumed that "growing up" was off the table. Yet somehow I had. I smiled and kissed Sandra for the billionth time.

My path had never gone the way I wanted or expected. Every bend in the road took me farther away from what I had planned, always leading to more pain and suffering. But that path brought me here. It wasn't the happy ending I once dreamed of, but I was happier than I ever imagined I could be. So often I questioned where all this was leading, but God had a plan all along. And that plan was still unfolding.

"I love you," I whispered.

I didn't know who I was talking to. The Big Man, Sandra,

Hope, my entire family . . . It hardly mattered. I was filled with and surrounded by love.

I wasn't sure what came after The Resting Place, but I was pretty sure that this was Heaven.

The END End

Acknowledgements

This was the hardest book I've ever written. I'm not quite sure why. I had the end in mind from the beginning of the trilogy, but David's journey was a lot heavier than I anticipated. I think I knew it would require me to tap into some very personal things inside of myself, so there were sections I put off writing for a very long time. As you can see, I did eventually get through it. David's story is finished, and regardless of how it's received, I am proud of it. This is the story that I needed to tell.

While every story begins as the author's baby, it doesn't remain theirs for long. That is what separates writers from authors. There are some amazing writers out there who still haven't overcome the hurdle of sharing their work and asking for help. It's an incredibly difficult step, so I don't blame anyone for not taking it. But once that terrifying step is taken, once a writer opens themself up to criticism and judgement on something so near and dear to their heart, the book becomes so much more than just theirs. It evolves into something so much more than it could ever have been on its own. Therefore, I have some big "thank-yous" to share, in no particular order.

Family is everything to me, and this book would not exist without my family. Both because of the support they've shown me as an author, and the love they've shown me as a person. Mom, Dad, John, Alex, Aimee, Sydnie, Jax, and Lily, you inspire me every day. You are my people forever and always, and I am the most me when around you. I would not be me, and this book would be without you.

In addition to my family, I am also incredibly grateful for the support and feedback of some really awesome people. Rebecca, my love, thank you for hyping up my books when I can't do so myself. I know you would do so even if the books were utter crap, and I genuinely appreciate that. Ian, thanks for making me uncomfortable by fangirling over my books in front of me. It's actually really amazing to know that my words meant something to someone. Jared, thanks for the helpful feedback and suggestions. Thank you for continuing to share your thoughts despite the pushback I often respond with. You've made my books better. Lyndsey, who has been an editor, supporter, and friend since *The Aurella Trilogy*, thank you for your continuous support. You're amazing! Karen, my alpha reader, you were the first to finish my very first draft. It was really crappy back then, so thank you for sticking with it, despite the mistakes. The book has changed quite a bit since then, and you were instrumental in helping me see which parts were working and which parts were not. Thanks for helping me make it better!

And, of course, thank you to my readers. You are few and far between, but I hope that some of my words have impacted you in some way. If nothing else, I hope this story gave you hope.

About the Author

Anni Sezate is a Yale University graduate with an MA in literature (pronounced LIT-chruh-chu) and lives with her high school sweetheart, Henry Cavill, and their four beautiful children in the English countryside.

Just kidding, she's a piano teacher that lives alone with her cat. She would like to point out that while she and Henry never worked out, she does have a super cool family, loves her beautiful Arizona desert, and has an awesome life full of books, plants, and children. So there ☺

**Check out bonus content
and keep in touch!**

AnniSezate.com
IG: @Anni_Sezate